Wartime on Sanctuary Lane

KIRSTY DOUGAL

PENGUIN BOOKS

PENGUIN BOOKS

UK | USA | Canada | Ireland | Australia
India | New Zealand | South Africa

Penguin Books is part of the Penguin Random House group of companies
whose addresses can be found at global.penguinrandomhouse.com.

First published 2024
002

Copyright © Kirsten Hesketh, 2024

The moral right of the author has been asserted

Set in 12.5/14.75pt Garamond MT Std
Typeset by Jouve (UK), Milton Keynes
Printed and bound in Great Britain by Clays Ltd, Elcograf S.p.A.

The authorized representative in the EEA is Penguin Random House Ireland,
Morrison Chambers, 32 Nassau Street, Dublin D02 YH68

A CIP catalogue record for this book is available from the British Library

ISBN: 978-1-405-95866-0

www.greenpenguin.co.uk

Dear Reader

I hope you enjoy this first book in the Sanctuary Lane series. I've loved researching and writing it – and I'm so excited to share the adventures of Ruby and her friends and family with you all.

I am fascinated by the idea of ordinary people living through extraordinary times and, for me, there is nothing more extraordinary than World War I. Whilst the 'war to end all wars' was obviously horrific in very many ways, it was also a time of great social and economic change; new horizons opened, and women in particular were given opportunities that they could previously only have dreamed of. Throw patriarchy and class division into the mix and there is no more exciting time to write about. I've set the story in the East End as, in many ways, the working class had both the most to gain and the most to lose from the war, and I've tried to reflect that in Ruby's story.

My paternal grandfather, Joseph 'George' Biggs, served in France as a teenager. He never talked about his experiences but, at the end his life, he was apparently right back in those trenches, hiding from the shells. That haunted me and taught me, more than anything, what the young men in the Great War endured and how it must never, ever be forgotten. On the other hand, my maternal grandmother, Maria Wildermuth, was brought up in the East End of London and was a teenager during the First World War. Her tales of hardship and loss and her general stoicism and 'make do and mend' attitude helped to inspire this story, as did her German surname and heritage and the challenges and difficulties that that presented.

Ruby, her family, and friends – both two- and four-legged – and her animal hospital are all fictional, but the descriptions of the East End, the munitions factory and the wider events in World War I are as accurate as I could make them. The Brunner Mond factory really existed and was destroyed in an explosion in early 1917; its main role was to purify TNT – although information on whether it also assembled the shells and their detonators is more ambiguous. And, it seems, women really did have to 'drop skirts' at some of these factories! The Zeppelin raids are real, although I have tweaked the date of one. And, most importantly, the animals really were suffering; most of the vets were at the front, and poor people couldn't afford their services anyway. As such, there are several examples of small animal hospitals and clinics being founded in the East End around this time, chief amongst which being the People's Dispensary for Sick Animals, which was founded a year or two later than this story is set – and which, of course, still exists today.

I thoroughly enjoyed developing the characters in this book and their journeys against the backdrop of such a turbulent part of our history. I hope you grow to love them as much as I do and that you will come back to discover what happens to them and the animal hospital as the war progresses.

Kirsty x

Prologue

1905

Ruby crouched in the bushes, heart thumping.

She was well hidden here, the only way through the dense foliage a small gap on the river side. The others would take ages to find her. She settled on to the damp earth, spreading her skirts, surveying her hiding place. The leaves were still trembling from the morning's rain. There was a little spider eyeing her from the tatters of its web; she must have broken the delicate threads as she crawled in. Sorry, little spider.

Oh, no.

What was that?

Running footsteps. Closer now. Ruby held her breath. Too soon . . . far too soon.

'Found you!'

Darn. It was her older brother, Harry. How on earth had he found her so quickly? He was twelve and usually too old for hide and seek and he didn't know the park nearly as well as she did. But here he was, crawling in and settling the leaves a-rustle again. He grinned at her, merry brown eyes a-sparkle, a leaf atop his dark, curly hair.

'Careful,' whispered Ruby, shuffling up and pointing at the spider. It was dangling from the end of a new thread, its work destroyed for the second time in as many minutes.

Harry shrugged. 'It's only a spider,' he mouthed back, sitting down beside her. 'And stop talking. The others are coming.'

The two children sat silently as the footsteps outside their hiding place grew ever closer. But these footsteps were too heavy and slow to belong to any of the children they were playing with. And, heavens, what was that *noise*? High-pitched screams; plaintive, desperate . . .

A man came into view, striding towards the river. He was tall and thickset, his cap pulled down low over his face. There was a large brown sack over his shoulder, moving with a life of its own. And from its depths came the most heart-tugging cries. They sounded exactly like their younger brother Charlie as a baby had done . . .

'It's babies,' she hissed to Harry. 'There are *babies* in that bag.'

Harry's eyes met hers, round and wide in horror.

They watched as the man crossed the grass, vaulted the low stone wall and disappeared. Ruby was out of the bushes in a trice, blinking in the light, brushing down her dress. Harry appeared beside her.

'Found you!' shouted one of their playmates from somewhere behind them.

'Shhh!' hissed Ruby and Harry, without turning around.

As one, they ran to the wall just in time to see the man wade out over the mudflats and splash up to his knees in the gunmetal water. Then, without ceremony, he swung the bag off his shoulder and in a wide arc into the Thames. There was a loud splash before the bag billowed across the surface and slowly began to sink. The cries grew in volume but the man didn't turn around. He waded back through the water and across the mud further down-stream, over towards the Brunner Mond factory. If he saw the children, now crouched behind the wall, he didn't acknowledge them.

Ruby waited until the man had disappeared round the bend. Then she climbed over the wall – just as the other children skidded to halt beside her. Hitching up her skirts, she set out across the mud. It oozed over her boots, sticky and unforgiving, slowing her down.

'Ruby,' yelled one. '*Don't.*'

'You'll drown!' shouted another.

'You'll get your dress all wet and muddy,' added Harry in a quieter voice.

Ruby ignored them all. She ploughed on, keeping her eyes on the exact spot in the water where the bag was dis-appearing. And here was Harry, appearing without ceremony by her side. Together they splashed into the water, slipping and sliding on the stones and in the mud. The water was icy cold, tugging at Ruby's dress, weighing her down . . .

Hurry.

Must hurry.

'Here. It was here,' panted Ruby.

She reached into the water, fingers straining for the coarse material. It was much heavier than it had looked. Harry helped her lug it clear of the water and together they struggled back to the bank. Then, with shaking fin-gers, they untied the thick canvas knot.

The bag contained kittens – two black, one ginger, one tabby.

'It's not babies,' said Harry dismissively. 'It's just cats.'

Ruby didn't answer. The kittens were still and quiet and, for a horrible, heart-searing moment, she feared that she had been too late. Then, to her exquisite relief, three of the little bodies began to wriggle and mew. Only the tabby – the smallest and presumably the runt of the litter – didn't stir.

Ruby crouched down beside them all, not sure whether to laugh or cry. Who cared if they were cats and not babies? They had feelings. They would have known what was about to happen.

And they would have been terrified.

She scooped up the three living kittens, trying to dry them with her dress, whilst hastily formulating a plan. They would bury the poor runt with dignity right here on the foreshore and she would carry the rest to a stray cat she knew had recently given birth near the Brunner Mond factory.

It was all she could do.

'Ruby. Your dress!'

Ruby glanced down at herself. Her pleated cotton Sunday-best with its pretty purple flowers was covered in thick brown river sludge.

And they all knew what that meant.

'I'm proud of you, Ruby.'

Ruby blinked. That made no sense at all. Her father was about to *beat* her. He'd just beaten Harry and now it was her turn to bend over the arm of the parlour chair.

Ruby's father followed her gaze to the strap in his hand. 'Necessary, I'm afraid, for ruining your Sunday clothes,' he said. 'But trying to rescue those kittens? That were spirited.'

Really?

Now didn't seem to be the time to ask her father how she should have attempted the very brave rescue *without* getting her clothes all wet and muddy. Should she have taken her dress and apron off? Gone into the river in her drawers? It was almost funny . . .

Except it wasn't.

Her father indicated her forwards and Ruby duly assumed the position.

She heard the strap whistle down and, a second later, a line of fire exploded across her bottom. Five more – and an extra one if she cried out. How on earth could she stand it? She bit her lip. Harry hadn't made a sound when it was his turn – and she wouldn't either.

Besides, the sting of the strap was worth it.

Worth it because she had managed to save three of the kittens who, hopefully, would live to fight another day.

And worth it because she now knew, once and for all, that even a working-class girl from the East End of London could make a difference if she followed her convictions and instincts.

That was something she would never, ever let herself forget.

Hampstead, London
March 1916

The back doorbell rang just as Ruby started to lay the dining room table.

More deliveries.

She smoothed down her wavy, honey hair as best she could and nipped down the stairs to the back entrance of the mansion block. Elsie from Number 8 was already there, leaning against the doorjamb, watching Mrs Henderson's flowers being unloaded in the pouring rain. Elsie *always* seemed to be there – regardless of whether she was expecting a delivery – waiting to make eyes at the delivery boys. Ruby nearly laughed out loud when she saw that this particular delivery 'boy' was actually a girl.

'*Another* soirée?' asked Elsie, as Ruby signed for the order.

Ruby understood the implication all too well. With the country at war, parties and soirées were unpatriotic. Extravagance was unpatriotic. Everyone knew that. There were posters all over London encouraging people to cut back and to do their bit. But regardless of what Ruby personally thought about the matter – and actually she had given it a great deal of thought – it wouldn't do to speak ill of Mr and Mrs Henderson. Elsie wasn't the most discreet of people and Ruby didn't want anything getting back to them.

Not until she had decided what she was going to do.

So, she just said, 'You can't eat flowers,' smiled politely at Elsie and headed back upstairs with her armfuls of sweet peas and roses.

The preparations for that evening were in full swing.

War or no war, the Hendersons were hosting a dinner party for some of Mr Henderson's business associates. Ruby quite liked soirées – they were a welcome break from the everyday – but, goodness, they didn't half add to the workload. Unlike many households, the Hendersons still had a cook, and, even more luckily, Mrs Henderson had called Agnes in today. Agnes usually only came in on a Monday to help with the washing and to do the windows, but she was already in the scullery making a start on the spuds while Cook wrestled with the leg of lamb. But even with Cook and Agnes sorting the food, there was still a great deal to do and Mrs Henderson would make her feelings abundantly clear if Ruby fell behind on her own allotted list of tasks. There was no time to waste, so she quickly but carefully carried the Chinese vases into the kitchen to make a start on the flowers.

'I'd be quite looking forward to tonight if "he" weren't coming,' she commented to Cook as she filled each vase with water.

'He', of course, was Sir Emrys. Most of Mr Henderson's clients weren't too bad; dreadfully dreary and impossibly la-di-da, of course, but they kept their hands to themselves. Sir Emrys was different. Horribly different. Just about every time Ruby proffered him a serving

8

platter, he would run one leisurely hand up her leg; up and up until it was almost cupping her bottom. And Ruby just had to stand there, holding the blasted dish steady and with a pleasant smile on her face. Every time it happened, she marvelled that Mr and Mrs Henderson didn't say anything. That Sir Emrys' *wife* didn't say anything. Surely, they all knew. Surely, if nothing else, Ruby's flaming cheeks always gave the game away . . .

Cook, inserting garlic and rosemary slivers into the leg of lamb, straightened up and tucked a few stray wisps of sandy hair back under her cap. 'If I had a penny for every time I've heard you say that,' she said, not unsympathetically. 'You're twenty-one years old and you've got to learn to stand up to these people. Otherwise, Sir-Bleeding-Emrys ain't got no reason to stop grabbing your arse, has he?'

'How am I supposed to do that?' wailed Ruby, as she started to snip the bottom leaves off the roses. 'Scream blue murder? Slap him? Oh, it's perfectly fine for you and Agnes to laugh – there ain't no one trying to pinch *your* bottoms in here.'

'I'd like to see them try,' muttered Cook with a grin. 'I'd have their guts for garters before you could say Jack Robinson.'

Ruby smothered a smile. She didn't doubt that Cook would be as good as her word. Cook rarely had anything nice to say about Mr or Mrs Henderson – or anyone from the upper classes, for that matter – and her manner towards them was habitually just short of surly. Ruby had a sneaking feeling that Mrs Henderson was a little bit afraid of her, as were they all; Cook was hot-headed, quick-tempered, and certainly didn't suffer fools gladly. But, despite all that – and despite the fact that the two were a generation apart – Ruby was very fond of Cook. She was certainly the closest Ruby had to a friend at the Hendersons' and their sense of loyalty and camaraderie had only grown since the war had started and thrown everything up into the air.

'At least you'll get to meet Clara Williams,' said Agnes, poking her freckled face in from the scullery. 'I reckon it'll be worth getting your arse pinched black and blue just to hear her sing.'

'Almost,' agreed Ruby, fanning the roses out prettily in their vases.

Her dread of the imminent arrival of the repulsive Sir Emrys *was* slightly offset by the evening's guest of honour. Clara Williams was not only a second cousin of Mrs Henderson but she was also a famous singer. Mrs Williams had sung for King George, and King Edward before him, and even for Queen Victoria. Ruby's mother loved Clara Williams; she had once seen her at a concert to raise money for the soldiers at the People's Palace and hadn't stopped going on about it for months. And now Ruby was going to meet her! She had already polished Mrs Williams' cutlery until she could see her dark-blonde hair under its snowy cap reflected back in each piece . . .

'A word please, Ruby,' said Cook, once Agnes had retreated and Ruby had nearly finished arranging the sweet peas in amongst the roses.

'One tick,' said Ruby, picking up a vase. Cook was bound to want to give her more advice on handling 'him', but Ruby knew she'd never have the audacity to carry any of it through. 'I'd better get these flowers in position before Mrs H gets back from her walk.'

She took the first vase, manhandled it into the drawing room and carried the second one into the dining room overlooking Hampstead Heath.

'Not done in here yet, Ruby?'

It was Mrs Henderson, long, thin face radiating disapproval. She was clutching armfuls of ivy, her terrier Boniface at her heels. A trail of leaves and muddy pawprints followed in her wake.

Ruby bobbed a little curtsey. 'Nearly finished, Ma'am,' she replied.

She would, she reflected, be a lot more 'nearly finished' if she now didn't have to sweep and mop the floor all over again. Why oh why hadn't Mrs Henderson taken both the ivy and Boniface straight to the kitchen? It would have been the sensible and the considerate thing to do, but Mrs Henderson had never shown herself to be overly endowed with either quality. Not that it was Boniface's fault, of course. Ruby adored the terrier and she knew the feeling was mutual. Boniface was, even now, looking at her with his head on one side and Ruby fancied that he was trying his best to apologise for the extra work.

Still, with the table all laid up, the dining room really did look beautiful. Like the drawing room, it looked directly over the ponds and meadows of Hampstead Heath and it was hard to remember that they were only a few miles from the centre of London. Aside from their wonderful, open views – dull and misty as they might be on this dreary day – both rooms were papered in the modern ivories and creams. With electric lights throughout the house, there was no need to mask the soot stains as they had to in the East End. Everything looked fresh and clean because everything *was* fresh and clean.

Even Mrs Henderson seemed charmed by it all.

'Even if we have to cut back on food nowadays, at least Jerry can't stop us using our best china and silver,' she said, running her finger over one of the side plates.

Ruby found it hard to suppress her smile. Oyster soufflé, lamb with anchovies and several other courses might be Mrs Henderson's idea of cutting back – but most of London couldn't contemplate such a meal regardless of whether they were trying to be patriotic. She had overheard Cook saying the lamb had cost ten shillings! *Ten shillings!* Back in the day, Ma had to run her entire household – rent and all – on about a pound a week.

'I've picked some ivy from the Heath to make the flowers go further,' Mrs Henderson was saying. 'I wanted to order more but the florists were out of stock. You'll need to redo those vases. Come along. Spit spot!'

By the time the guests were gathered in the drawing room after dinner at ten o'clock that evening, Ruby was exhausted. Proper right-through-to-your-bones exhausted. Too exhausted to appreciate Clara Williams seated at the piano and singing 'It's a Long Way to Tipperary' and 'When Tommy Comes Marching Home'. Too exhausted to be concerned that the gentlemen were saying Britain had merely been marking time in the war and that efforts needed to be stepped up. Too exhausted even to be relieved that an unusually subdued Sir Emrys had kept his hands to himself all evening.

Thank goodness Agnes was doing the washing-up.

Ruby started circling the room with a pot of coffee and a jug of cream. Two of the wives were perched on the turquoise sofa together, deep in conversation. They didn't look up as Ruby approached.

'I hear Cook is off,' one was saying. 'No notice, of course. Off to join the *police*, of all things.'

Ruby concentrated very hard on not splashing the coffee. It didn't have to mean *Cook*.

'Fanny's devastated,' the other woman replied. 'But it might be a blessing in disguise. Those oyster soufflés *were* very heavy.'

Ruby's arm shook involuntarily as she finished pouring the coffee. Mrs Henderson's first name was Fanny and the soufflés had looked uncharacteristically on the stodgy side tonight . . .

Shocked, *stunned*, Ruby hurried out of the room, not much caring what it looked like to the guests. Cooks were leaving households all over London, of course – Ruby knew that. They were off to 'do their bit', enticed by new opportunities and larger wage packets . . .

But she simply hadn't reckoned on Cook joining their ranks that evening. Her only ally; upping and offing and leaving her in the lurch!

One thing was for certain; the police would be lucky to have Cook.

A glance at Cook's face and Ruby saw that it was true.

'I tried to tell you earlier,' said Cook, filling up the coffee pot. 'To be honest, I only found out today that I'd been accepted.'

'I know you did,' said Ruby. 'And then we both got swept up in all the preparations. But – oh, Cook. I will really miss you. And who's going to do the cooking now?'

Cook gave an elaborate shrug. 'Buggered if I know,' she said. 'It's a topsy-turvy world out there nowadays and I'll not lie; they'll find it hard enough to replace me. I reckon Mrs H will have *you* knocking up a roux before the month's up.'

Ruby had an uncontrollable urge to laugh. She put her sleeve over her mouth to drown her giggles.

Her?

Do the cooking?

Cook was taking off her apron. 'By the way, love, young Agnes has got a terrible headache and I've sent her off home. I've left the worst of the dishes soaking and I'll be in at midday tomorrow, but until then, I'm afraid it's all down to you.'

The urge to laugh disappeared and suddenly Ruby was on the verge of tears. She was tired. So very tired. And the washing-up would take *hours*.

And then the kitchen door burst open.

'There you are,' Mrs Henderson hissed at Ruby. 'I knew I'd find you malingering in here. Sir Emrys is asking for more coffee. Now!'

Ruby picked up the coffee pot. 'Yes, Ma'am,' she said.

'And when you're tidying up, don't you dare touch any of the leftover lamb,' Mrs Henderson called after her retreating back. 'That's *all* for Boniface.'

Ruby slunk back into the drawing room.

Clara was still at the piano, leading a rousing rendition

14

of 'Keep the Home Fires Burning'. Voices rose and fell and twisted around each other and suddenly Ruby wanted to cry for quite a different reason. She wanted to cry for the whole mad world and especially for her brother Harry who had recently been conscripted into the 47th (London) Division and who might never come home – no matter how brightly the home fires burned.

Ruby tiptoed around the room, offering coffee, topping up cups. As she bent over to fill up Sir Emrys' cup, she suddenly felt his meaty hand on her thigh. It paused and then leisurely moved higher until it was resting right on her bottom.

Impotent rage surged through Ruby. What could she do? A girl like her didn't have choices. She was a nobody, a dogsbody, unfit even to eat the leftover meat.

But then she heard Cook's voice in her ear and another thought – nothing more than an impulse, really – surged through her.

She *did* have choices.

The choices might have repercussions – but that didn't mean that she didn't have them.

Calmly, almost casually, she straightened up and looked Sir Emrys in the eye. Then, giving him a wide smile, she poured scalding coffee straight into his lap.

She would hand in her notice in the morning.

It hadn't been an impulsive decision, Ruby reflected, as she tossed and turned into the small hours.

Not really.

It was true that she hadn't planned to leave service that day ... or even that week. And she certainly hadn't planned to throw coffee over Sir Emrys that evening in a bid to precipitate the whole thing. But she had, more or less, decided that she was going to go home. Back to the East End where the need was greatest and she would be best able to 'do her bit'. She'd just been waiting for the right opportunity.

The seed had been planted a couple of weeks ago when Ruby had last gone home. Her brother Harry was leaving to start his army training in Buckinghamshire and Ruby had wanted to say goodbye to him in person. To be honest, she hadn't really thought this day would ever come. Pa had been dead these four years – killed in an accident at the docks where he and Harry had both worked – but Ruby knew he would never have countenanced any of them getting directly involved in the war. Pa had always been adamant the working classes should stick together – regardless of whether a person happened to have been born English, Russian or even German – and his words had stuck. And, so, when the war had started almost two years ago, Harry had carried on working at the docks and

Ruby had continued her job in service, both determined to keep their heads down until the whole damn thing was over.

But now everything had changed.

Harry still hadn't chosen to join the army . . . but the army had finally come for him.

Earlier that year, Lord Derby had introduced the Military Service Act with compulsory conscription for all single men over eighteen. And whilst there seemed to be an endless list of exemptions, none of them had applied to Harry – and off he had gone.

Ready, if not willing, to do his duty to King and Country.

Poor Pa would be turning in his grave!

And, whilst all that had been going on, a new munitions factory had opened a stone's throw from Sanctuary Lane. Ma had said they were desperate for female workers to replace the men who had gone to the various fronts. Women and girls to manufacture the very weapons that would help get Harry and the others back home as quickly and as safely as possible.

As soon as she heard about it, Ruby knew that she had to sign up to work there. Pa would have hated it, of course. Ruby still missed her father; he had been a harsh disciplinarian – like many fathers in Silvertown – but he had also been funny and kind and wise and Ruby had always known, without a doubt, that she was loved. But now it was time to help her mother. Harry had gone away but hopefully having her daughter home would take away some of the sting. Her younger brother Charlie was still at home, of course, but, at only fourteen, he was still a child. Besides, not only would Ruby be 'doing her bit' for the war effort but, by all accounts, the money was a huge increase on what she was currently earning; 35 shillings a week if some of the rumours were to be believed! It might even be enough to allow Ma to stop doing shifts at the laundry around the corner – and wouldn't that be a fine thing? Ma had been looking very old and tired when Ruby had last seen her.

But, on the downside, the munitions factory would, no doubt, be full of girls from school. Ruby had *hated* school. Oh, she had enjoyed the lessons well enough – the reading and writing and sums had come easily to her and she had always been top of the class – but she had never quite managed to fit in. Not properly. She had never known the right thing to say; she hadn't been interested in films and film stars and she couldn't have given two figs about ribbons and skirt lengths. Worse still, she hadn't even been able to *feign* an interest and so she had spent most of the time on the outside looking in. When school finished, she had left for her job in Hampstead – Ma's cousin had known Cook's sister who knew the Hendersons were looking for a housemaid – with a curious mixture of relief and regret. To be fair, she hadn't been much good at making friends in Hampstead either – far preferring to take Boniface for long walks across the Heath or visit the horses in the stables than indulge in tittle-tattle with the maids from the other apartments.

Either way, it was now time to go home.

She had certainly burned her bridges with Mr and Mrs Henderson. Ruby could hardly believe she had deliberately spilt coffee over one of their most important clients. Sir Emrys had gone puce in the face and, with his wife clucking impotently behind him, had disappeared down the corridor to the bathroom, shouting incoherently and clutching his nether regions. Ruby hadn't seen what had happened next because Mrs Henderson had forcibly removed the empty coffee pot from her hands and frogmarched her back to the kitchen. Ruby had fully expected to be dumped unceremoniously out on the street – fired without a reference – but instead Mrs Henderson had hissed that she was not to show her face again, that she was not to go to bed until the kitchen was spotless and that they would have 'words' the next day. No doubt Mrs Henderson didn't want to be lumbered with the washing-up and would fire Ruby first thing in the morning.

Ruby had been tempted to just leave there and then. But it was too late for the Tube to be running and she didn't have the money to fork out for a taxi all the way back to the East End. There was no choice but to stay the night. Then she had been tempted to collapse into bed and to hell with the washing-up. She could hardly be fired twice! But something – pride? guilt? inability to leave a job half finished? – had stopped her. Instead, she spent a couple of hours doggedly working through the tottering piles of plates and cutlery and glassware, emptying the ashtrays, mopping the floors – until everything was ship-shape and Bristol fashion. Only then did she allow herself to creep upstairs to her little room in the attic and slip under the cosy eiderdown.

What a night!

If only Cook and Agnes had been there to witness her moment of glory.

*

Ruby got up as normal at five o'clock and, for want of anything better to do, started her daily routine. She didn't want to just disappear – where was the honour in that? – and nor could she very well just barge into Mr and Mrs Henderson's elegant bedroom and announce that she was off. In an ideal world, she would wait to say her goodbyes to Cook, but that was probably wishful thinking. By the time Mrs Henderson was ready to 'have words', Ruby had already cleaned the kitchen range, sifting the cinders that had been too hot to handle the night before and polishing the stove with a leather. She had lit the fire, filled the kettle and put it on to boil and was just laying out the breakfast cloth when Mrs Henderson swept into the dining room and sat down at the head of the table. She gestured for Ruby to stand in front of her and then folded her hands into a steeple, her face grave. Ruby had a vision of Mrs Henderson pulling on a black cap to pronounce sentence and had to stifle a wholly inappropriate giggle.

'Well, that was a pretty rum show last night,' Mrs Henderson started without preamble.

Ruby found herself unable to look her employer in the eye. 'Yes, Ma'am, but didn't you see Sir Emrys? He . . .'

'Sir Emrys is your elder and better and also happens to be a very important client of Mr Henderson,' interrupted Mrs Henderson. 'There is absolutely no excuse for how you behaved . . .' She broke off and slammed her hand down on the table. 'Damn it, girl. Look at me when I'm talking!'

Ruby ventured a glance.

It wasn't an altogether comfortable experience.

'I'm sorry, Ma'am,' she tried again. 'And, in fact . . .'

'Enough!' snapped Mrs Henderson. 'I don't want to hear another word.'

Ruby shut her mouth mid-sentence.

This was it.

She was about to be fired.

Mrs Henderson inhaled slowly. 'I'm sure yesterday was nothing more than an unfortunate accident,' she said firmly.

'Ma'am?' Ruby's word came out almost as a squawk. Whatever she had imagined Mrs Henderson might say, it hadn't been . . . *that*! Of course it hadn't been an accident. Sir Emrys had had his hand fully on her bottom and . . .

'Those coffee pots are very heavy and difficult to manhandle when they're full,' Mrs Henderson went on. 'I said as much to Sir Emrys and he was happy to accept the explanation. If it happens again, there will be severe repercussions, but for now I am happy to consider the matter closed.'

Ruby paused. It seemed that she was about to be reprieved. But she didn't *want* to be reprieved. And Sir Emrys didn't deserve to get off scot-free. Mrs Henderson really should be 'having words' with him!

'No, Ma'am,' she said. 'I spilt coffee on Sir Emrys on purpose because he put his hand on my . . . er . . . derrière.'

There was a pause. Ruby could have sworn she saw Mrs Henderson's lips twitch.

'I shall pretend that I didn't hear that,' said Mrs Henderson. 'What an absurd thing to say! I expect Sir Emrys was reaching for his whisky or for the ashtray and that he brushed against you by accident.'

'*No*, Ma'am,' Ruby insisted. 'Sir Emrys deliberately put his hand there. He's always doing things like that – brushing me bosom, squeezing me arse – and most times I just put up with it. But yesterday I'd just found out that Cook were off and I'd had enough.'

There was nothing like being honest.

'Ah, yes. Cook,' said Mrs Henderson, latching on to the new subject with evident relief. 'Most inconveniently, Cook has seen fit to leave us. Maybe for the best as one or two things have gone missing over the past few months and my money was always on her. But, before she goes, I would like you to make it your business to learn a repertoire of straightforward recipes so that you can be responsible for our lunch and supper from now on. It's a good opportunity for you and, if your work is satisfactory, we might consider giving you a pay rise at Christmas.'

Finally, Mrs Henderson's strange behaviour began to make some sort of sense.

In any other circumstances, Ruby would already have been given her marching orders. But Cook had given her notice and the Hendersons couldn't afford to lose both their servants in one fell swoop. With the war on, and new opportunities appearing for women every day, goodness knew when Mrs Henderson would be able to replace them.

But, then again, Ruby had already made up her mind to leave.

And as for that rubbish about Cook pilfering items, Ruby didn't believe a word of it. Mrs Henderson was just trying to save face and keep the upper hand.

'No,' she said firmly.

'No?' Mrs Henderson's eyebrows shot up in surprise.

'If you ain't going to fire me, I'm handing me notice in anyway.'

Mrs Henderson looked visibly shocked. 'Come now, Ruby,' she said. 'Don't be too hasty. Maybe we can review your salary in October.'

'No,' Ruby repeated. 'I'm right exhausted as it is. If I do your cooking as well as everything else, I'd hardly get to bed at all. Besides,' she added, as Mrs Henderson opened her mouth to speak, 'I'd already made up me mind. I'm going back to the East End to do me bit for the war and, for your information, I'll be paid a ruddy lot more for it, too. And I won't have to put up with the likes of Sir Bloody Emrys sticking his hands where they've no bloody right to be.'

Twenty minutes later, Ruby had packed her meagre possessions into her battered suitcase and was ready to go. Mrs Henderson had twice tried to dissuade her from leaving but, finding Ruby resolute, had finally retreated to her bedroom in defeat. How Ruby wished Cook had been a fly on the wall to hear her finally stand up for herself!

In the meantime, should she tell Ma she was on her way home?

She didn't want to give her mother a heart attack by turning up out of the blue. The trouble was, how to get word to her? The post was down to four times daily nowadays, so it was extremely unlikely a letter would make it home before she did. And even in the unlikely event that Mrs Henderson let her use the telephone — well, who would she call? Nobody she knew in the East End had a telephone at home. She could always splash out on a telegram, of course – but who in their right mind would do that in the middle of a war? The telegraph girls and boys weren't nicknamed the 'Angels of Death' for nothing and it simply wouldn't be fair on Ma.

No, she would just have to arrive home unannounced.

Ruby picked up her case and suddenly Boniface was at her heels, pushing his wet little nose into her hands. Ruby dropped to her knees and buried her head in the terrier's warm fur, kissing him over and over. He was a marvellous dog and the truth of the matter was that she would miss him far more than she would the Hendersons.

There was no one else to wave her off, so she walked slowly down the rear steps and opened the back door. The sky was grey with clouds scudding past at quite a clip, but all at once she felt an overriding sense of lightness.

Whatever came next, however difficult it might be, she was free.

'Oi! Where are you off to?'

It was Elsie, leaning against the back door and lighting a ciggie.

Ruby smiled at her. 'No more soirées for me,' she said. 'I'm being patriotic and I'm going home. Say goodbye to Cook for me, will you?'

3

It was a mere ten miles from Hampstead to Silvertown in the East End of London, but it might as well have been another planet.

Teeming Silvertown – with its docks, its factories, its oppressive red-brick tenements and terraced houses – was always something of a shock after leafy, genteel Hampstead. Today, as Ruby alighted at Silvertown Station and began the fifteen-minute walk home to Sanctuary Lane, the contrast seemed even sharper. From the little groups of ragged urchins to the haggard-looking women corralling toddlers, everyone looked pinched, miserable and thinner than ever. Sharp eyes watched Ruby from every doorway and from the entrances to the closes. She knew that Mr and Mrs Henderson would dismiss them all as beggars, prostitutes and robbers, but Ruby just saw desperate people in an environment of filth, smoke and destitution, and realised just how cocooned she had been in service for the last five years.

Under leaden skies, she walked quickly down the high street. Somehow, the war seemed so much closer here. From the female conductress on the bus sweeping past to the many shuttered shops – '*Closed for the Duration*' – everything served as a reminder that most young men of working age had now enlisted. Hampstead hadn't been immune to any of this, of course, but – because the population was older — it had felt far less pronounced. Here in Silvertown, there were more recruitment posters — *Join the Army and See the World* — more drunk soldiers back on leave, more poverty . . . more of *everything*.

But Ruby could only see the animals.

Everywhere she looked there were dogs and cats walking on three legs or dragging broken or injured limbs. Some looked blind with mange, others were scavenging in the gutters, ribs and shoulders protruding. Many of those would be strays, of course, but even in the yards there were painfully thin goats and rabbits huddled in corners and emaciated ponies and donkeys in little more than broken-down sheds. Ruby knew that these animals belonged to people who depended on them for their livelihoods, their security, or their health and that they simply couldn't afford to look after them any more.

What the war had done to them all was terrible.

And here, right in front of her, was a dog tied to a lamppost outside a shop. A black and white mongrel with similar features to Boniface and the same beseechingly melting brown eyes. But there the similarity ended. This little fellow had weeping sores all down one side of his face and you could count every one of his ribs through his matted fur. He gave a little whimper as Ruby bent down to pat his head and her heart turned over. The poor little chap. She thought of Boniface, positively plump through treats and titbits — to say nothing of the leftovers from yesterday's leg of lamb. Out of nowhere, the hymn 'All Things Bright and Beautiful' came to mind and she railed at the injustice. The Lord God might have made them all, but who, exactly, was looking out for the animals of the East End?

And then it started to rain.

Ruby gave the little dog one last pat and trudged on, resisting the urge to turn around as the dog gave a piteous whine. She was powerless to help and, anyway, she had to get home before it started to pour in earnest. The hem of her skirt was already filthy from the stinking mix of animal manure and urine that everyone politely referred to as 'mud' and it would get ten times worse if she got caught in the rain. Maybe she should adopt the new above-the-ankle dresses that Mrs Henderson said were very *à la mode*, although no doubt Ma would have something to say about *that*!

Ruby hurried past the final parade of shops, turned right and . . . there it was.

Sanctuary Lane.

No one really knew why it was called Sanctuary Lane. Maybe there had once been a church or chapel there; a holy place – long disappeared – which had offered safety from pursuit. Or perhaps people escaping persecution from Europe had arrived at the nearby docks and sought refuge here. There was a multitude of possible reasons and no one knew – or cared – which one was right. It was just a name – just as the neighbouring streets were called Victory Lane and Waterloo Terrace and no one knew why they had been given those names, either.

Like many of the residential roads in Silvertown, Sanctuary Lane was flanked by terraces of red-bricked, two-storey houses, each with a very small backyard and opening straight out on to the street. It was a long road, starting right in the centre of town – indeed, strictly speaking, Muller's the haberdashery and Fisher's the bakery were actually on Sanctuary Lane itself – and then heading straight down towards the river. At the bottom of the street, bearing down on them all, was a large, imposing red-brick factory.

Home!

For a second, Ruby just stood and stared down the street, her heart quickening with excitement. Silly really; she might have lived in Hampstead for nigh on five years, but it was hardly as if she never came home. Still, Sanctuary Lane was where she belonged. It was imprinted on her heart and soul in a way that Hampstead – for all its green, hilly splendour – could never be. On a whim, she delayed her homecoming to nip into Fisher's to buy cakes. They were eye-wateringly expensive but, at the very least, they might help cushion the shock of her arrival . . .

And then finally Ruby was running down Sanctuary Lane to Number 139. The skies completely opened – of course they did – so she sprinted the final stretch with her suitcase over her head. Number 139's step and door knocker gleamed, even in the murky light. The door was on the latch and Ruby smiled as she pushed it open. Never mind that there was a war on; hell would have to freeze over before the front door was locked.

Ruby dumped her case unceremoniously and ran down the short passage to the kitchen. She pushed open the door and there were Ma and her sister, Aunt Maggie, drinking tea at the oilskinned table, thinner and paler even in the past couple of weeks. Both women got to their feet – their mouths round O's of surprise – and then Ma was in front of her, hands on hips, and . . .

'What on earth are you doing here, Ruby?' she demanded. 'Have you got an unexpected day off or summat?'

'No,' said Ruby. 'I've left! I ain't ever going back there again.' Suddenly, the reality of what she had done hit her and she wasn't sure if she was laughing or crying.

Ma took Ruby by the shoulders and looked deep into her eyes. 'Are you in trouble?' she asked. 'Lordy me, you're in trouble, ain't you?'

Ruby bit her lip to stop herself from smiling. Of course she wasn't in trouble. There wasn't anyone she could have got in trouble with in Hampstead – even had she been so inclined. It wasn't as if she'd been living in a great country pile with butlers and valets and footmen coming out of the woodwork. Mind you, Elsie had stepped out with a lad who had worked in the communal gardens one summer and Mrs Henderson's previous maid had married one of the delivery boys way back when. And, of course, if Sir Emrys – or another of his ilk – had chosen to follow Ruby into the scullery or the back stairs – well, who knew what might have happened?

And that wasn't funny at all.

But she just said, 'Don't worry, Ma. I ain't in trouble. Not unless you count leaving without giving notice. I've come home to do me bit for the war in the munitions factory.'

And Ma stepped forward and wrapped Ruby in a bosomy embrace. Ruby, not much given to hugs, resisted the instinct to wriggle free and instead patted Ma awkwardly between her thin, protruding shoulder blades.

'I'm so proud of you,' said Ma.

'I'm not sure Pa would say the same,' said Ruby, with a rueful grin. 'But I hope Harry might be pleased.'

She hadn't particularly missed Harry's presence yet; even on a Sunday, he'd have been down at the Royal Victoria Dock helping unload grain into the silos and warehouses of the various flourmills that lined the river. But now her eye was drawn by the black and white photograph – fancy! – of Harry in uniform on the mantelpiece and her heart gave a little lurch. *Harry wasn't here* and goodness only knew when she would see him again.

'I'll make another brew,' said Aunt Maggie.

Oh, it was lovely to be home.

Lovely to sit in the warm, steamy kitchen and drink cup after cup of warm, sweet tea. Lovely not to be shouted at to 'do this' and 'don't do that' and 'get a shift on' by Cook or Mrs Henderson. She knew Ma and Aunt Maggie weren't above saying all or any of those things, but just for the moment, it was marvellous to be treated as a Very Important Person – almost as if she was a grand lady from Hampstead rather than born and bred in Sanctuary Lane. So, she sat and told her mother and aunt all that had happened at the dinner party, even the bit about Sir Emrys putting his hand on her bottom and her pouring coffee into his lap by way of reply.

'Well, well,' said Ma, shaking her head in wonderment. 'My little Ruby who wouldn't have said boo to a goose as a little girl.'

'So now I'm home,' Ruby finished simply. 'And, like I said, I want to do me bit. I'm going to sign up at the munitions factory as soon as I can. Tomorrow, if possible.'

'You'll be bright yellow before summer's done,' Aunt Maggie said sourly.

Ruby was confused. 'Bright yellow?' she echoed.

'Oh, yes,' said Aunt Maggie with something approaching satisfaction. 'All the girls that work there turn bright yellow from the chemicals. Canary girls – that's what everyone's calling them.'

'But can't they wash it off?' Ruby was nonplussed.

'Wash it off?' Aunt Maggie repeated incredulously. 'My dear, the colour goes right through them. If you cut them open, their hearts, their livers, *everything* will be bright yellow.'

'How can you possibly know that, Maggie?' said Ma with a laugh. 'And not all the girls go yellow, do they? Not even most. Don't go putting Ruby off before she's even applied.'

'I'll tell you how I know,' said Aunt Maggie, sitting forward. 'You know Nellie from the dogfood barrow? Well, I heard her daughter had a baby not two weeks ago and it came out of her bright yellow. Gave Nellie quite a shock, I'm telling you.'

Goodness!

'It don't matter,' said Ruby, staunchly. 'If going yellow is a price I need to pay, so be it. Harry will be putting himself in harm's way every day if he ends up in France so I think I can put up with me skin changing colour.'

'That's the spirit,' said Ma. 'Although you was much safer in Hampstead. I didn't have to worry about you so much there.'

'They're both London, Ma,' said Ruby. 'Only a few miles apart.'

Ma sighed. 'I know,' she said. 'Only Hampstead ain't got the docks and ports and factories and the Hun ain't trying so hard to bomb it to smithereens.'

Ruby was silent.

Goodness; she hadn't thought of it quite like that.

'Yoo-hoo! Only me . . .'

A voice from the kitchen door made all the women turn round. It was Annie-Next-Door who had obviously let herself in through the unlocked scullery door.

'Hello, Annie,' said Ma.

'I saw Ruby out front just before the heavens opened and thought I'd pop round to say hello,' said Annie-Next-Door. 'Only seems a matter of days since her last visit home!'

Ruby pressed her lips together in amusement. She seriously doubted that Annie-Next-Door had come round purely to exchange social pleasantries. In fact, Annie-Next-Door hadn't had much time for Ruby ever since the day Ruby had accidentally barged into her at the Sanctuary Lane Coronation Street Party and sent her prize cake flying. No, Annie-Next-Door had clearly come round in search of gossip she could send speeding up and down the street before anyone could say 'Bob's your uncle.'

'Cuppa, Annie?' said Ma. 'Yes, Ruby's left service and is back to do her bit at the new munitions factory.'

Annie-Next-Door narrowed her bright blue eyes and Ruby knew exactly what she was thinking. Was it really a good idea to let so clumsy a girl loose with all those poisonous chemicals around?

'Already got yourself a job lined up, have you?' Annie-Next-Door asked.

'Not yet.'

Ruby suddenly realised she had absolutely no idea how to set about getting signed up. In fact, she had no idea whether the factory was even hiring, let alone if she fitted the bill. Oh goodness! Maybe she had left Hampstead on nothing more than a fool's errand.

'Not to worry,' Annie-Next-Door was saying. 'I know for a fact they're desperate for more women. In fact, you know Sarah two doors down from me? Well, her sister's daughter – Daisy, I think her name is? – started work there not two weeks ago. She'll know what you need to do.'

Without further ado, the Sanctuary Lane network sprang into life. Within five minutes, Sarah-Three-Doors-Down had been summoned and, fifteen minutes later, her sister Bea-Round-The-Corner together with her niece Daisy – whose skin wasn't yellow at all – turned up. Daisy – who only looked about seventeen – confirmed the munitions factory was still recruiting. And, no, there wasn't a formal recruitment programme; she had just turned up with some friends one morning and had been signed up straight away. Daisy's next shift was at nine o'clock the next morning, so maybe if Ruby showed up at the main gates just before then, Daisy would point her in the right direction . . .

'It's just for the duration,' said Daisy's mum, Bea. 'That's what they keep saying. Just until the war is over.'

Ruby didn't say anything. It was hard to imagine a time after the war. Would everything go back to exactly how it had been in 1914 or would the world have changed forever?

And how long would they all have to wait to find out?

The rest of the afternoon passed in a blur.

At some point, Ruby's younger brother Charlie returned home from mud-larking at the river's edge. Ruby looked at his clothes with a sigh, remembering the day she had received the strap for getting her own dress muddy as a child. There was none of that now, of course; everything had changed since Pa had been killed. Ma just gave an indulgent sigh and instructed Charlie to get changed before supper. And, no, she wasn't interested in what he had brought home from the river's edge, thank you very much; not unless it contained any coins that could be used in March 1916 . . .

Charlie just grunted. He was at that age when he was half-man and half-boy – all gangly limbs, fuzzy chin and features that were too large for his face – but, with his broad face, dark-blond hair and hooded brown eyes, there was no doubt that he was a handsome lad.

'Hello, Charlie,' she said, as he turned to leave the room.

Charlie gave another grunt by way of reply. He was, it seemed, supremely uninterested in Ruby's return – almost treating her reappearance as he might a benign but essentially boring elderly aunt. To be fair, Ruby had never been particularly close to her younger brother – with over seven years in age between them, Charlie had always just been a noisy nuisance rather than a potential friend. She had been closer to Harry, who was less than two years older than her and the mellowest and easiest of companions – but, as Ruby had been living away in service for five years, and Harry wasn't really one for writing letters, she sometimes felt that she didn't really know *him* any more either. Hopefully she would become closer to *both* brothers now that she was back for good.

'Poor Charlie,' said Ma, as Charlie duly disappeared upstairs to get changed.

'Why "poor"?' asked Ruby.

She was genuinely curious. It seemed to her that Charlie wasn't too badly off at all; allowed to come and go as he pleased, no repercussions for getting his clothes filthy . . .

How times had changed.

Ma gave an indulgent sigh. 'Well, he misses his brother, of course,' she said. 'And with your pa gone, who's going to teach him manly things now? He'll need to start shaving before the summer's out.'

'True,' said Ruby. 'But surely half of London – half of his class at school, for that matter – are in the same position? He's hardly unique.'

'And then his friend Joe has just lost his father,' added Ma, as though Ruby hadn't spoken. 'That's shaken Charlie no end, let me tell you.'

'He's been a good pal to Joe and his family though, I'll give him that,' interjected Aunt Maggie.

'He has,' said Ma, with satisfaction. 'He's always there after school, helping Joe and Mrs Tyler with this and that. I'm proud of the lad, I'll say that. Now, enough of this chatter. I need to get the spuds on or none of us will be having no supper tonight.'

That evening, Ruby sat down to her first meal at home in several months. The pork chops, mashed potato, carrots and swede were all delicious but there wasn't much of any of them. Of course, Ma hadn't been expecting Ruby to be eating with them, so everything was having to stretch that bit further, but the portions would hardly have been huge even if she hadn't been there. No wonder everyone looked so thin.

'You're tired, love,' said Ma, as Ruby stifled her third yawn over a tiny portion of dead man's leg. 'Of course you are. All that way from Hampstead. Why don't you get some sleep? Your room's ready for you.'

'Thanks, Ma. I think I *might* turn in.'

'Of course. I hope to heavens we have a quiet night tonight, but if the Zeppelins do come across, you're to go under the table in Aunt Maggie's room. That's unless we judge there's time to get to the Woolwich Tunnel. Understood?'

Ruby hesitated at the doorway.

That sounded very serious.

In Hampstead, they had all become rather blasé about the threat posed by Zeppelins and it had rarely been mentioned in recent weeks. Ruby hadn't worried about them for months. Yes, there had been a couple of coordinated Zeppelin attacks already that year – but they had been miles away, near Hull or Birmingham or Liverpool.

London hadn't been targeted since the previous autumn.

'Do you really think it's likely?' she asked.

Maybe Ma was just going through the motions.

Ma shrugged. 'Best to be prepared,' she said, mildly enough. 'According to Annie, they targeted Dover yesterday. If they're going for the ports . . .'

She trailed off and Ruby swallowed hard, feeling the first prickle of real fear.

Maybe she had been hasty in leaving Hampstead.

'And "Aunt Maggie's room"?' she queried.

Ruby's aunt lived not far away in Whitechapel and Ruby had assumed that she would be returning home after supper as she always used to.

Aunt Maggie pursed her lips and looked slightly smug but didn't otherwise reply.

'Aunt Maggie is sleeping in the parlour for now,' said Ma firmly. 'She has refugees from Belgium in her flat at the moment.'

Ruby just nodded. It wasn't for her to question Ma's decision but it was all rather rum. Aunt Maggie was such a grumpy old stick – and as for sleeping in the parlour! What right did she have to take the largest room in the house and to deprive them all of their living space?

Ruby went upstairs feeling a little miffed. There were three bedrooms at 139 Sanctuary Lane, just as there were in every house in the street. Ma's was at the front of the house, Harry and Charlie's at the back, and there was a further tiny box room where Ruby, as the only daughter, had always slept. It was a nice enough room with no damp and plenty of light and fresh air – but it was *small*. And of course, not only were there no electric lights, but there was no indoor water closet either. Instead, there were oil lamps and either the chamber pot under the bed or the dreaded trudge to the outside privy and the largest spiders in the western world. It all seemed rather like going back in time after her modern little room in Hampstead.

Ruby unpacked her meagre possessions, undressed and slipped into bed. She lay there in the dark and listened to the sounds of the house getting ready for the night. Ma and Aunt Maggie chatting downstairs and clattering from the scullery. Neighbours having a to-do in their backyard. A dog barking, close at hand, and then an answering howl.

Home.

It didn't feel as safe as it used to, and Ruby resisted the temptation to pad to the window and check for Zeppelins sliding silently into view with deadly intent.

Still, it was the start of a new chapter in her life and she needed to face it with courage and fortitude.

4

Ruby knew exactly where the Brunner Mond factory was.

Its tall brick chimney had been a local landmark all her life, standing high above the terraces and docks, dominating and defining the space. It had been visible from her classroom at school and from outside church on Sundays – and you could even just about see it if you stuck your head out of her bedroom window and looked in the right direction. And, of course, Pa and Harry had worked at the docks which were right next door. Whenever Ruby had accompanied Ma there as a child to deliver sandwiches or the like, she had had to tilt her head right back to see the top and it had seemed like the tallest building in the world.

Way back when Queen Victoria had been on the throne, the factory had employed many of the menfolk from the Silvertown terraces and tenements to manufacture all manner of chemicals. Ruby vaguely remembered many of the workers being laid off before the war, when production of caustic soda had been cut – including a couple of neighbours on Sanctuary Lane. It had hardly been a disaster for the town – there were plenty of other places to work nearby and Ruby had grown up with her parents proudly telling her that every household in the country owned at least one item manufactured in Silvertown.

And then, two years into the war, the idle part of the Brunner Mond factory had been commandeered by the

War Office to help address the army's crippling shell shortage. Ruby had read about it in Mr Henderson's newspapers – habitually retrieved from the bin, squirrelled away, and read from cover to cover once she was alone in her bedroom. There had been a huge backlash because the idea was to use some of the factory's spare capacity to purify the explosive TNT, a process apparently much more dangerous than manufacturing the stuff in the first place. Despite the objections, production had started several months ago. At first, the factory had been staffed mainly by men, but ever since compulsory conscription had been introduced, they had been desperate to employ more women.

So, Ruby really knew quite a lot about the Brunner Mond factory. In theory at least. The trouble was that, knowing it all – growing up with it – didn't mean that she knew anything practical that was going to help her on that Monday morning.

Things like where the main entrance was for new recruits.

Or the best way to walk there from Sanctuary Lane.

The site was huge – more like a small town than a factory – and there were a dozen different locations around the perimeter that Ruby could head to. Why oh why hadn't she asked Daisy to be more specific the night before or even suggested that the two of them walk down together?

The weekend's gloom had persisted and it was a chilly morning, the leaden skies threatening snow. So far March had been pretty grim weather-wise and was doing little to raise the nation's spirits. Ruby left home at eight thirty in her second-best navy skirt and white blouse (the only things that were clean) and headed straight for the Brunner Mond chimney. She was halfway down Victory Lane when she noticed the dog that had been tied up outside the shops yesterday, now tethered to a lamppost outside Number 42. Ruby stopped to pat his head and, by way of reply, the dog gave her a great big smelly lick on the back of her hand. Enchanted, she sat down on the pavement and started patting his skinny flanks. The sores on his face looked even worse today, although Ruby noticed that some were beginning to scab over. The poor creature: whatever had happened to him? It didn't look as if he had been in a fight. Could he have been burned? She put both her arms around his scrawny frame and nuzzled her face into his fur and the dog licked her ear over and over again.

'Useless bloody creature!'

Ruby hadn't heard anyone approach. Looking up, she saw a middle-aged woman leaning over and beginning to untie the dog from the lamppost. She was probably not much older than Ma but she had a pinched, prematurely lined face, the skin deeply puckered around her pursed lips.

Ruby stood up. 'He ain't useless!' she said indignantly. 'He's one of God's creatures!'

'God's creatures,' the woman scoffed, beginning to lead the protesting animal inside Number 42. 'Is that what he is? Well, you're welcome to him.' And then, when Ruby put her hand out for the lead, 'Not really, you daft ha'porth. Be away with you. Come on, Mick. Inside.'

And the door to Number 42 shut in Ruby's face.

Ruby dusted her skirts down, thoughts awhirl. For a

moment she had really thought the woman was going to let her take Mick home. How marvellous that would have been and how disappointing that it wasn't so – even though, of course, there was no guarantee that Ma would have even let the little dog through the scullery door. She could hear Mick whimpering inside and she knew – just knew – that he wasn't happy at home. How could he be, tied to a lamppost outside the house like that?

The nearby church clock struck the quarter hour and Ruby started in consternation. Goodness: she had wasted so much time! She now had only fifteen minutes before she was due to meet Daisy and she still had no real idea where she was heading. Heart thumping, she rushed to the end of Victory Lane, hoping to take the alleyway she and Harry had always used when they were going to the river. Damn! It was boarded across and quite impassable.

A girl was running down Waterloo Terrace, hand to hat, cheeks beet-red.

On impulse, Ruby stepped out in front of her. 'Excuse me?' she said.

'Sorry. I'm in a hurry.'

'I can see that! You're not heading to the munitions place, are you? The Brunner Mond factory?'

The girl nodded. 'I am,' she panted. 'And I'm late.' She gave Ruby the ghost of a grin. 'Follow me,' she said.

And off she ran, Ruby in hot pursuit. Down Waterloo Terrace, right then left then right again, zigzagging towards the chimney, until Ruby's lungs were fit to burst. More and more people – many young women – were heading the same way. They were rushing out of front doors and from the entrances to the closes, all moving at a brisk trot, all evidently trying to meet the 9 a.m. deadline. Eventually, the trickle of workers became a steady stream and then a torrent and then finally it became a crush and Ruby had to stop.

The boundary fence stretched as far as the eye could see. It was topped with copious amounts of barbed wire which Ruby was sure hadn't been there before the war. Her sense of apprehension grew as the pack inched towards the perimeter gate. There was no sign of Daisy, but, then again, how on earth was Ruby supposed to spot her in this melee of close to two hundred people? Anyway, chances were that Daisy wasn't looking out for Ruby at all. Maybe she'd never had any intention of doing so and had just offered because it had seemed the right thing to do.

Feeling a little deflated at this thought, Ruby allowed herself to be carried forward with the crowd, waves of chatter breaking over and around her.

'If I'm late again today, Miss Davies will have me guts for garters.'

'Never mind guts for garters; if I'm late today Mrs Lloyd will have me on overtime and I've me sprog to get back for and tea to make for me old man.'

'I wonder who's worse; my Miss Davies or your Mrs Lloyd?'

'Peas of a pod, most like. They get a bit of power and it goes right to their heads.'

'You're right. Phew; we're moving. Good luck to you.'

'And the same to you.'

The crowd kept shuffling forwards. As she got ever closer to the perimeter, Ruby tried to work out the system. There were four women in uniform supervising the gate and distributing blue tickets to the workers. Once in possession of a ticket, you could proceed to a further checkpoint where you presented the ticket to one of several policewomen and thus gained entry to the site. The distribution of cardboard tickets seemed to be completely arbitrary, with people reaching over each other's heads to grab one, and Ruby was hard pressed to see how it all worked.

Suddenly, she was being funnelled forwards. On either side of her, people were being greeted with smiles and salutations and handed tickets before continuing to the barrier. But there was no blue ticket for Ruby. No one bade her a good morning. No one smiled at her. In fact, no one did anything at all. More people streamed past on either side, a couple tutting that she was blocking the entrance . . .

Oh, this was awful.

Awful.

It reminded Ruby of those terrible days at school when she had always been the last to be picked for games. It had happened every single time and the hurt and humiliation had never really gone away.

'Oi, you!'

Goodness.

One of the officials was pointing straight at her.

Ruby endeavoured to stay calm. 'Please could I have a ticket?' she asked politely.

The woman laughed, not unkindly. 'No, you can't have a *pass*,' she said, 'because none of us recognise you. Do you have your papers?'

Ruby shrugged. Papers? What papers?

Oh, this was just going from bad to worse. She was

sorely tempted just to turn on her heel and walk away, all the way back to Sanctuary Lane. In fact, maybe she would just keep going, walk all the way back to Hampstead and cook Mr and Mrs Henderson toad in the hole for their supper.

This had been a ludicrous idea . . .

'Ruby!'

Ruby started and looked around her.

The voice was coming from inside the site, beyond the recognisers and the police. Ruby strained to see who was calling her and then saw Daisy, being waved through by the police and walking over to the perimeter gate.

'What are you doing here, you daft whatnot?' she said, pulling Ruby over to one side. 'I told you to meet me by the main entrance!'

'But this is . . .'

'No, it isn't. It might have been the main entrance for the Brunner Mond once upon a time, but it's the entrance for the shifting sheds now.'

'The shifting sheds?'

'Where you get changed before you go on the factory floor,' said Daisy impatiently. 'But that doesn't matter now. The point is that you'll never get in this way. This entrance is for people who already work here, and the recognisers don't know who you are.'

'Oh, goodness,' muttered Ruby. 'I'm ever so sorry. I just followed someone and . . .'

'. . . didn't think it through,' Daisy finished for her. 'Not to worry. It were just a good thing I came looking for you and that you happened to be at the head of the queue. Let me see if I can get you in this way – otherwise we'll have to go round the houses and then I'll be late for me shift and all.'

She turned away and started rapidly talking to one of the recognisers. Seconds later, Ruby had a blue pass in her hand and Daisy had taken her by the wrist and was ushering her past the policewomen at the second checkpoint.

Thank goodness for that.

And then the two of them were striding briskly through the site, past long, concrete hangars, smaller brick buildings and scrubby patches of grass. Suddenly a loud whistle almost made her jump out of her skin. People started swarming out of the buildings and the whole place became busier than Piccadilly Circus.

'Nine o'clock,' pronounced Daisy. 'I'm officially late reporting for duty.'

'I'm sorry,' panted Ruby, struggling to keep up. 'This place is as big as a town.'

'There are over a thousand people working here,' replied Daisy. 'And that's just the government side of things. It ain't a bad place to work once you know your way around, though. Look, here we are.'

The two girls had arrived at a smart brick building close to the perimeter of the site. It was obviously the reception building and, once again, Ruby felt a little silly for blindly following the first person she'd seen without checking where exactly she'd been going. Daisy opened the door and ushered Ruby inside. A tall, serious-faced young woman wearing spectacles, her mousy hair tied in a messy bun, was standing behind a counter. In front of her, a dozen or so women were sitting, busily filling in forms attached to clipboards.

Daisy led Ruby over to the counter. 'This is Ruby Archer, a potential new recruit,' she said. 'She tried to come in through the shifting shed entrance so, rather than going all the way around, I've accompanied her through the site.'

'Thank you.' The bespectacled woman handed Ruby a clipboard and pen without further comment and gestured towards a chair.

Ruby turned to Daisy. 'Thanks ever so much for helping me,' she said. 'I feel a bit of a chump for getting it so wrong.'

Daisy gave her a conspiratorial smile. 'If you must know, I did the same on my first day!' she whispered. 'Even if you knew this building before, everything's changed nowadays. Good luck – although you don't need it.'

And she was off.

Ruby stood staring after her, reflecting how much more confident the girl seemed when not in the company of her mother and aunt.

'Is there a problem?' asked the lady behind the desk. Her spectacles magnified her grey eyes several times over – it was a little unnerving – and her voice was gratingly la-di-da.

Ruby decided she didn't like her much. She was very like a younger version of Mrs Henderson. Supremely entitled and supremely sure of herself.

'No, Miss.'

'Then if you wouldn't mind filling your form in as quickly as possible, we can all go through for the medicals.'

'Yes, Miss. Sorry, Miss.'

Ruby sat down and did as she was told. Name, age,

address, previous employment . . . it was all quite straight-forward. Hopefully they wouldn't be checking references!

'All finished?' Miss La-Di-Da asked, just as Ruby was signing and dating the form. 'If I could gather them all in. I'm Miss Richardson and I'm one of the personnel managers. Follow me; we'll get you checked over by a doctor and, hopefully, cleared for work.'

Ruby and the others duly followed Miss Richardson across the compound and Ruby took a good look at the other prospective candidates. They were a motley group: a few were Ma's age or even older; the youngest looked barely sixteen. A couple wore clothes that were little more than rags and clearly came from the nearby tenements, whilst others wore smart coats and tailored skirts which immediately marked them as a class above. Ruby felt comfortably in the middle on all counts although she was clearly amongst the youngest. There was one girl – exquisitely pretty, with blonde hair and a heart-shaped face – who Ruby felt sure that she recognised. Yes: it was Elspeth Carson from the year below her at school. She had always come across as a silly, simpering little Miss and, as Elspeth laughed theatrically at something – throwing her head back, hand to her pale, slender throat – Ruby decided that she hadn't much changed.

Miss Richardson led them into another building and upstairs into a room which had been divided into cubicles by curtains. It looked a little like a hospital ward, not unlike the one Pa had lingered in for a few days before he died. Ruby swallowed hard, remembering the terrible day she had been recalled from Hampstead to say her goodbyes, and reminded herself that this was quite different. There were no beds in these cubicles, for one thing, just a couple of chairs and a rickety wooden table.

'Each of you in a cubicle, please,' said Miss Richardson. 'It doesn't matter who goes where. And draw the curtains around you.'

Ruby scuttled into the furthest cubicle, relieved to be on her own for the first time in what seemed like ages. She exhaled a ragged breath and sat down on one of the chairs.

'Drop skirts, please,' Miss Richardson called briskly, her voice right outside Ruby's cubicle.

Ruby started to her feet and stared around in bewilderment.

Drop skirts?

She tweaked open the curtains. Miss Richardson was standing outside with her back to Ruby.

'I beg your pardon, Miss?' Ruby whispered.

Miss Richardson spun on her heels. 'Drop skirts,' she repeated, swishing the curtains to Ruby's cubicle firmly shut. Despite her steady voice and the graceful poise of her head on her slender neck, Ruby noticed that two bright spots of colour had appeared on her cheeks.

Maybe Miss Richardson was finding this almost as awkward as Ruby was.

On the other hand, she wasn't the one being asked to flash her privates!

Oh goodness; there *must* be some misunderstanding. She couldn't imagine any of the other women liking this very much either. Some of them had been elderly and eminently respectable to boot. Ma and Aunt Maggie would never stand for this.

Tentatively, Ruby stuck her head through the curtains. 'Excuse me, Miss Richardson?' she hissed.

'What now?' Miss Richardson made no attempt to hide her impatience.

'I ain't wearing no drawers,' Ruby offered weakly.

Miss Richardson was, Ruby knew, likely to be wearing lace trimmed bloomers. But Ruby – like everyone else from Sanctuary Lane – went as bare as the day she'd been born under her skirt and petticoat. Maybe Miss Richardson wasn't aware of that.

But Miss Richardson simply gave her a tight-lipped smile. 'Good,' she said. 'That will make this all the easier.'

Ruby shut the curtains again and sat down heavily. There might have been indignities aplenty in Hampstead, but nothing like *this* had ever happened. Not for the first time, she wondered if she was making a huge mistake in leaving. In fact, so acute was her humiliation, she was sorely tempted to open the curtains for a third time and to simply stalk out of the room with her head held high. But she had left one job and she very badly needed another.

With clumsy fingers, Ruby unbuttoned her navy skirt and let it drop to the ground along with her petticoat. She picked them both up, placed them carefully over the back of one of the chairs and then just stood there, listening. She could hear footsteps and curtains being opened and the mumble of voices getting louder, but she couldn't work out for the life of her what was going on. Finally, the footsteps stopped in front of her cubicle and the curtains were yanked apart. Miss Richardson's gaze dropped briefly southwards.

'Very good,' she said, with a little nod. 'You can get dressed again.'

So cursory had the inspection been, it hardly seemed worth the effort.

'But . . . ?' started Ruby, reaching for her petticoat.

'Don't want men dodging the column, do we?' said Miss Richardson simply. 'And isn't it best to get that out of the way before we waste Dr Welch's time?'

Ruby had never heard of such a thing.

Were men really disguising themselves as women in order to avoid compulsory conscription? The war was a dreadful, dreadful thing and everyone knew that the working classes were suffering disproportionately, but Harry and all the others had gone off bravely to do their bit. They certainly hadn't pretended to be girls to get out of it.

'Take your top half off so Doctor can give you the once over,' Miss Richardson was saying.

Ruby bobbed a little curtsey – ridiculous since she was practically starkers. 'Yes, Miss,' she said.

And Miss Richardson was gone.

Ruby was almost smiling to herself as she removed her blouse and chemise. After flashing her privates, this was positively tame. And the doctor who finally arrived was so kindly and avuncular that Ruby felt almost at ease. She wasn't particularly bothered about being weighed and measured and being asked to turn this way and that, to open her mouth, to touch her toes, to read letters off a board on the wall. She knew she was strong and healthy. After all, she rarely got so much as a cold.

After much tapping and prodding, Ruby was pronounced fit for service. Her application form was stamped and dated and she was sent to a downstairs office to wait for Miss Richardson.

'I think you were in the last cubicle, dear?' said one of the older women as Ruby sat down and Ruby nodded. 'So, that means there are only eight of us left.'

'Looks like four didn't pass the medical,' added the woman sitting next to her. 'Such a shame . . .'

'Or else the other four were all men,' interrupted Elspeth, pealing with laughter at her own joke. 'Or maybe they just couldn't face the thought of dropping their drawers first thing on a Monday morning.'

Goodness, she was irritating!

Calculating as well. Ruby had to hand it to Elspeth – that was quite a clever way of telling everyone that *she* was grand enough to wear drawers, thank you very much.

And then Miss Richardson joined them, standing at the front of the office like a teacher and clapping her hands together for attention.

'I'm very pleased to let you know that you have all been declared fit for duty and will be working on the main factory floor,' she said. 'There's some paperwork to complete and a few formalities to go through, but then you'll be ready to do your first shift.'

Miss Richardson started walking around the room, distributing densely typewritten documents. 'This is the Official Secrets Act,' she said. 'What you will be doing in this factory is classified information and must not fall into enemy hands. As such, by signing this paper, you are promising not to speak about our work outside the factory. Not to your mother, not to your sweetheart, not to Aunt Ethel – not even if they press you for information.

Idle chatter could cost lives — and that is never more important than here.'

Ruby found that her hand was shaking as she signed the document. Her, little Ruby Archer of Sanctuary Lane, signing the Official Secrets Act! And she didn't mind at all not being able to share what she got up to at work. That would stop Aunt Maggie in her tracks. Her and her gossiping and her thousand and one questions . . .

'Now,' said Miss Richardson. 'Working here is, of course, nothing like as dangerous as what is being asked of the men at the front. But that doesn't mean that it is without its risks. As a military installation, we are, of course, on the front line for enemy fire. We have a comprehensive lookout system, and you will be told where to shelter if the sirens sound. Sometimes that will be on site, and sometimes — if there is time — you will evacuate to the nearby streets. Secondly, you will be handling — or will be near to — materials which are highly explosive and flammable. That means that anything that could cause the slightest spark — matches, jewellery, metal hairpins — is banned from the main factory floor. This rule is treated with the utmost seriousness. You will be searched every time you go into the sheds and any transgressions will be punished with severity. If you disobey the rules — or even if you forget them — you will be prosecuted, and you may well be sent to prison.'

Ruby started with shock. How terrible! She would never knowingly break the rules, but what if she forgot?

'Me shoes have metal in them,' said a short girl with curly dark hair, freckles and an upturned nose.

'Ah. That brings me neatly on to my next point,' said

Miss Richardson with a little smile. 'You will have seen that some workers wear a uniform here. You will be provided with trousers, a tunic and a cap for your hair. You will also be provided with clogs, Dot – so there is no need to buy new. In addition, you will also be given tags which need to be pinned to your clothing at all times. Any other questions?'

'Will we go yellow, Miss?' asked Elspeth.

Trust Elspeth to ask that.

She hadn't changed at all since school.

Still only concerned with the fatuous, the frivolous, the superficial . . .

Miss Richardson gave a little smile. 'If you are directly handling TNT, there is a good chance you will temporarily turn yellow, despite the protective clothing and all the other preventative measures that we take,' she said, matter-of-factly. 'And, if I am being totally honest with you, turning yellow is the least of our problems. It's what's going on *inside* that we should be more concerned about. The powers that be have known for a year that TNT can cause toxic jaundice. It isn't ideal but, as TNT is what goes into shells, it's a risk we choose to take.'

Goodness.

That even shut Elspeth up.

The next stop was the shifting sheds where the new uniforms were being quickly and efficiently distributed.

'Try them on, please,' the woman in charge was shouting out. 'No corsets.'

'No corsets?' repeated Elspeth loudly, wrinkling her pretty nose. 'You mean, not only do we have to wear shapeless tops, but we ain't even allowed to *try* and create a waist underneath?'

'You can if you want,' said Dot dismissively. 'But if there's an explosion, your stays will slice through you like butter. Still, you'll be wearing tags, so at least they'll be able to identify your body.'

Ruby swallowed a smile, despite the sobering words. It sounded like someone else was fast getting the measure of Elspeth.

The 'trying on' started in earnest.

Each woman was given a slim-fitting pair of khaki trousers – Ma and Aunt Maggie would have a *fit* – which were only saved from positive indecency by a matching tunic which came halfway down the thighs. There was also a gathered cloth cap to cover the hair and the promised clogs. As a little girl, Ruby had loved 'dressing up' – the chance to pretend to be someone different, someone *better* – and this felt much the same.

A modern, independent woman well and truly doing her bit to help Harry and all the boys at the front.

'Look at me,' said Elspeth suddenly, mincing down the middle of the changing area for all the world as if it was a Paris catwalk. She paused and peeped coquettishly over one shoulder and then dissolved into a fit of giggles.

Something inside Ruby snapped. Here she was thinking about King and Country and her brother in the army . . . and it was all just a great big joke to Elspeth.

'Oh, for goodness' sake, Elspeth,' she said tetchily. 'This isn't about you.'

Elspeth spun round. 'There ain't nothing wrong with having a bit of a laugh and joke,' she said. 'But what would you know, Ruby Archer? You always was a bit of a killjoy at school. Everyone used to say so.'

There was an embarrassed silence.

Ruby turned away in frustration, in *humiliation*. She had hoped Elspeth hadn't recognised her because she had kept to herself so much at school – but, obviously, no such luck. Suddenly she felt exactly as she had done back then: a clever but boring stick-in-the-mud . . .

'Oh, for heaven's sake,' interrupted Miss Richardson impatiently. 'Do I really have to remind you all that this is a government munitions factory and not an elementary school playground? Buck your ideas up, the pair of you, and stop squabbling. We've a war to win.'

'Sorry, Miss,' mumbled Ruby. She could feel herself colouring with humiliation as all eyes turned her way. That really had been most unfair. How could Miss Richardson tar her and Elspeth with the same brush? Elspeth had been the one being all childish and theatrical and Ruby had merely been trying to stop her.

Gah!

Ruby decided once again that she didn't like Miss Richardson.

No, she didn't like her one bit.

5

The women were silent as they followed Miss Richardson out of the shifting shed and across the compound to one of the huge concrete hangars. Three female police volunteers materialised as they approached and searched them all – even Miss Richardson – taking their time as they carefully patted hair for stray pins and emptied pockets for contraband. It took so long that Ruby couldn't help but wonder how any work got done at all. Finally, though, they all passed muster and Miss Richardson manhandled open a heavy wooden door, ushering them all inside.

Ruby could see a cavernous space, heavy machinery and dozens of workers – mainly women – scurrying around. But she couldn't concentrate on any of it – couldn't even begin to take in what she was seeing – because of the noise.

The *noise*.

It was hard to work out exactly what was causing the racket but, whatever it was, it was absolutely deafening. Ruby couldn't hear herself think, let alone what anyone else might be saying. There was the deep rumble of heavy machinery that echoed through the building and reverberated through Ruby's head. Boom-boom-*boom*. There was the higher clang of metal on metal which set her teeth on edge. And, over the top of it all, were the shrill voices of workers attempting to communicate with each other and making the whole thing ten times as bad.

Ruby felt suddenly helpless and trapped – as claustro-phobic as if she had been locked into a tiny cell – it was all she could do not to clamp her hands over her ears and run straight back out of the door. With some difficulty, she tried to tune into what was going on. It appeared that they were all reporting to a short, stout man with an impres-sively bristly grey moustache, called Mr Briggs. Their role would be to carry bags of powdered chemicals from the railway terminus outside, across the factory floor, to a mas-sive cauldron with an automatic stirrer. Someone else would decant the contents into the cauldron, but if the newcom-ers worked very hard and proved themselves worthy, they too might have the honour of doing this one day. The other thing Ruby surmised was that Mr Briggs didn't think very much of the female workers who had been foisted upon him. It wasn't just the sneer of his thin lips beneath the curving moustache – although that was bad enough – but the disdainful way he said that he hoped the young ladies before him would be able to live up to their responsibilities because there were many – *very* many – who hadn't.

Ruby would show him.

With nervous smiles at each other, the newcomers put on gloves and goggles and joined a small group outside at the blissfully quiet railway terminus. There had obvi-ously just been a delivery of raw materials because there were *hundreds* of small sacks stacked neatly beside the tracks. When she was directed to do so, Ruby picked one up. It was unwieldy and heavy, but, all in all, quite bear-able. She joined the little line of workers, ignoring a couple of likely lads who were making a big show of picking up *two* sacks – goodness knew why *they* hadn't been conscripted – and carried her bag inside, depositing it near the cauldron.

Phew!

Fascinated, she was tempted to watch what happened next, but she didn't have the chance for more than a glance before Mr Briggs pointed at her to head back outside for the next sack.

And the next.

And the next.

It wasn't so bad, after all. Very straightforward. In fact, if it wasn't for the infernal ringing in her ears every time she went into the factory, Ruby would think the whole thing positively civilised.

Her new outfit was liberating, the work was pleasantly repetitive in a manner that allowed her mind to wander and one – the *only* – good thing about the noise was that there was no need – no way – to make polite conversation whilst inside the building. But all the little smiles and nods between the new women as they went about their work made Ruby feel that she was part of the gang. Even Elspeth didn't seem quite so exasperating now that no one could hear her speak!

Another one.

And another.

And another.

After a dozen sacks, Ruby's shoulders were beginning to ache. Her arms were starting to feel a little heavy. And one of her new wooden clogs was starting to rub right at the base of her big toe.

Another one.

And another.

And another.

An hour had gone by and already every sinew in Ruby's shoulders and across her back was protesting – dull ache giving way to screaming pain. Her arms were lead weights, her foot was being slowly pulverised and the tight cap was beginning to give her a thumping headache . . .

How had she ever thought this would be better than dusting the sideboard or sweeping the floor at the Hendersons'? How long ago the morning and starting work now seemed.

Maybe all the smiles and glances from the other girls had really been grimaces.

Suddenly there was another ear-piercing whistle, setting Ruby's teeth even further on edge. All around her, people stopped what they were doing and streamed towards the doors.

'Lunch,' said an older man who was walking with a definite limp. 'Hop to it! Otherwise, all the good seats will be gone.'

Ruby didn't need telling twice. She fairly ran out of the factory and into the compound outside. Oh, the blessed relief of no more sacks and no more noise! It was almost worth having suffered it because it was so marvellous when it went away. Like that time she had had a wobbly tooth and Pa had tied it to a string and tied the string to the door and . . .

Oh!

There was Daisy, scampering across the compound, deep in conversation with a friend. How lovely to see a friendly face.

'Daisy,' she called but Daisy didn't hear her. Ruby set off at a brisk trot in hot pursuit and when she'd narrowed the gap between them, she tried again. This time, both Daisy and her friend turned around.

'So, they let you in?' said Daisy, face creasing into a grin.

'They did! I think they were desperate.'

'I wanted to warn you about the "drop skirts" bit . . .'

'I'd have run a mile, so it's probably best you didn't,' said Ruby with a laugh. 'Might I join you for lunch?'

Daisy smiled. 'Of course,' she said. 'This is Iris, by the way. Follow us!'

The three women had just set off when Daisy suddenly stopped and held up a hand. 'Where is it you're working?' she asked.

Ruby didn't understand. 'The Brunner Mond munitions factory?' she quipped.

'No, silly,' said Daisy, giving her a friendly shove. 'I meant which department?'

'There.' Ruby gestured back to the building she'd just left. 'With the cauldrons.'

'Ah,' said Daisy. 'Then I'm sorry, but you won't be able to join us. You lot on the front line have your own canteen.'

'The front line?' echoed Ruby, confused.

'Working directly with the chemicals. Your canteen is over there, up that grassy bank towards the perimeter fence. Good luck!'

And, with that, Daisy and her friend were gone, swept up in a rush of workers.

Abandoned and overwhelmed, Ruby turned and started trudging towards 'her' canteen.

6

Everything, but everything, was bright yellow.

That was Ruby's first thought as she opened the door and stood surveying the smoky, steamy scene. The tables, the chairs, the counters . . . everything was stained bright canary. Ruby had never seen anything like it. She wasn't entirely sure whether everything had been painted yellow to disguise any staining, or whether the staining had discoloured everything this uniform lemony hue. Either way, it was little wonder the workers who manned the 'front line' were restricted to their own canteen.

Ruby's second thought – or rather her instinct – was to scarper. The place was *packed*. Every table was crammed with a jolly crowd and the room echoed with chatter and laughter. If it wasn't for the fact that Ruby was starving, she really might have turned tail and fled. It was all just too much like the first day of school and she was used to a quiet and civilised household. Not . . . *this*. She would queue up for one of those delicious-looking pasties and, despite the gloomy weather, she would take it outside. Somewhere she could be on her own and start to process the morning . . .

'Yoohoo, Ruby! Over here.'

Ruby narrowed her eyes and scanned the busy tables. It was her fellow 'new girls' waving and beckoning to her from a table over by one of the windows. Somehow, in the time she'd been off on her wild goose chase with

Daisy, they had managed to get served and seated. Half-relieved and half-disappointed to have been spotted, Ruby waved in reply and, when she'd been served, carefully carried her tray over to join the little group. There were no spare seats, but Dot – the short girl with freckles – shuffled up on her chair.

'Sit yourself down,' she said. 'You look as exhausted as I feel.'

'Thank you.' Gratefully, Ruby eased herself down next to Dot and picked up her pasty.

'How do they compare with the ones from Dot's bakery?' asked Elspeth with a laugh, pointing at Ruby's pasty.

'Dot's bakery?' Ruby was confused. Besides, how could she compare anything? She hadn't even taken a bite yet. Goodness, Elspeth was annoying.

'Dot *Fisher*,' said Elspeth, archly.

Oh!

Dot's family must own the bakery at the top of Sanctuary Lane. The bakery had been there for what felt like forever and, now she thought about it, Ruby vaguely recognised Dot as well. She was a couple of years older than Ruby and had very possibly been in Harry's class at their local primary school.

Ruby took a mouthful of her pasty. It was rich and savoury and flaky – delicious!

Meanwhile, she could feel Dot bristling beside her on the chair. 'It ain't a competition,' she said tartly. 'Most of the people who come to the Mothers' Arms can only *dream* of having a luncheon like this.'

'The Mothers' Arms?' asked Ruby, more to avoid having to talk to Elspeth than anything else.

'It's in Bow,' said Dot, perking up. 'It used to be a pub called the Gunmaker's Arms and it's been taken over by the East London Federation of the Suffragettes for the duration. We ain't campaigning at the moment, but we're helping people in need with meals and milk for their babies and things like that. Those are the things that really matter, Elspeth. You should come along and see.'

'If you say so,' muttered Elspeth rudely.

'I think it sounds marvellous,' said Ruby. 'Do they help with animals as well? I were shocked at the number of sick and injured animals when I walked home yesterday – I can tell you. I'd really like to do something to help them.'

'Animals?' scoffed Elspeth. 'We're in the middle of a war, Ruby. Mind you, you always was a bit of an animal-nut. I can still remember you crying over a dead mouse at the edge of the playground . . .'

'It gets easier,' interrupted a flame-haired woman, stopping at their table and obviously interpreting the stony expressions as exhaustion. 'In barely no time, you won't notice that your hands are blistered and you can't hear anything any longer.'

Almost despite themselves, the three women laughed.

'I'm Sarah, one of the Welfare Officers,' the redhead continued. 'Part of my job is to monitor the health of the women working here – so, while I've got a captive audience, what about joining some clubs? We're very keen on sport here to keep everyone in tip-top condition and we're always looking for new blood.'

'What kind of clubs?' asked Dot.

'All sorts. Football is the big one. The main team, the Brunner Babes, is flying high at the moment – we beat the

Woolwich Wanderers for the first time the other week – but there are lots of other options too. We're very keen on keeping you fit and healthy – despite slowly poisoning you with TNT.'

Laughter all round, again.

'No, thank you,' said Dot politely. 'I'm very busy with the suffragettes.'

'Well, *I* think it sounds like fun,' said Elspeth. 'Besides, it will be a good way to meet *friendly* people,' she added pointedly. 'Where do I sign up?'

'All the information is on the noticeboard at the back of the canteen,' said the Welfare Officer. 'Fancy giving it a go, as well?' she added to Ruby.

'No thanks,' said Ruby with an exaggerated shudder.

She had loathed team sports at school, largely because she was so dreadful at them. Oh, she could run fast enough, but all that passing and tackling and remembering who was on whose team . . .

No, she would give the Brunner Babes a miss, thank you very much. Just coming home and joining the munitions factory had been more than enough for now.

It didn't get any easier after the break.

This time, the shrieking muscles and the pulsating feet and the throbbing ears started almost immediately.

She'd get used to it.

She had to.

And, if she didn't – well, she didn't *have* to stay.

At the mid-afternoon break, Ruby took one look around the jolly chattering faces in the canteen and decided that she just couldn't face it. She liked Dot, but Dot was already – for some reason – sitting with Elspeth, and Ruby had had more than enough of *Elspeth* for one day, thank you very much. She could, of course, try to meet some other people, but she found she was simply too tired to make polite chit-chat with a load of strangers and she certainly didn't want anyone trying to rope her into any ludicrous exercise classes.

Even when a hovering Welfare Officer pointed out that she could – *should* – at least get her free mug of milk to help offset whatever horrors the chemicals might be doing to her insides, she didn't change her mind.

It was still cold outside – horribly cold for March – but at least it hadn't started to snow. Ruby skirted the canteen and headed for the patch of grass beyond it. Despite the weather, a little group of three had had the same idea; sitting in a little huddle, they were deep in conversation and ignored Ruby. Ruby headed for an empty space over towards the canteen kitchen door and flopped to the ground with a little sigh of relief. That was better. Even if the ground was decidedly damp and she really should have got her coat from the shifting shed, it was lovely to be off her feet and in the fresh air. She shut her eyes and took a few deep breaths. She could hear pots and pans and all the other noises of a busy kitchen coming through the open canteen door, and somehow it soothed her. It could almost be Cook, banging the frying pan around and berating her or Agnes for some real or imagined transgression. For all its repetition and drudgery, life in Hampstead had been predictable and calm. And quiet.

Oh, this was lovely.

Hang on.

What was that?

Something warm and furry brushing her outstretched hand. Ruby snatched her hand away and snapped her eyes open.

Rats!

It was bound to be rats so close to the canteen kitchen and, whilst Ruby quite liked rats – she liked all creatures – Mrs Henderson had had a fit every time one was even mentioned and had drummed into Ruby just how dirty, pestiferous and liable to spread disease they were.

Only, it wasn't rats.

It was a cat – barely more than a kitten – pushing against her hand. A cat that was jet-black all over save one white paw and . . . a bright yellow nose! Suddenly Ruby found that she was laughing out loud. There was just something so sweet and incongruous about such a tiny, vulnerable creature in the middle of a huge factory compound. Oh, she knew that many people loathed cats – thought them almost as bad as rats – but Ruby didn't care. She reached out and scratched the kitten behind its ears and it responded by rolling on to its back and purring loudly.

'Where have you come from, little thing?' she asked, turning her attention to the kitten's fluffy tummy.

It wasn't hard to work that out. The patch of grass ran right up to the boundary fence and the back alley of the terraced housing beyond. The cat probably lived in one of the houses and must have wriggled through the narrow gap in the metal fencing in search of food. There was a chance it was a stray, of course. Or maybe it was deliberately 'employed' by the canteen kitchen to keep rats and mice at bay. But, at that exact moment, Ruby heard an exasperated voice from the canteen shout 'shoo, vermin!' – so that theory was obviously wrong.

Seconds later, a second cat darted into view – a virtual carbon copy of the first except that this one had a white star on its front rather than a white paw – and Ruby clapped her hands together in delight.

'Two of you,' she exclaimed, stroking the newcomer. 'And you've just got to be twins. I wish I had some food to share with you. I promise I'll bring you something tasty next time I'm here.'

As she spotted Dot and Elspeth chattering together on their way back to report for duty, Ruby stood up and dusted her trousers down with a wry smile.

Despite the noise and the exhaustion, and the fact she now had a damp bottom and was freezing half to death, she was already thinking about next time.

It looked as though she would be staying.

7

Slowly, slowly, Ruby began to get used to it all.

Her muscles still ached, her feet were still cut to shreds and her ears were still ringing – Ruby would never describe the work as exactly *easy* – but gradually it all became a little more bearable. Sometime during her second week, she was 'promoted' from manhandling the raw materials into the factory to carefully transporting the purified product back out to the railway head. Despite her gloves and her goggles and some new rubber over-boots, she knew that this was dangerous work and she couldn't help but feel a little thrill at being trusted with something so important for the war effort.

The front line of the Home Front, the girls would say proudly to each other. For the duration.

Each evening, Ruby arrived home, barely able to put one foot in front of the other. Aunt Maggie would talk darkly about how her skin was becoming tinged with yellow and how Ruby would never find a husband thus disfigured. And Ma would push platefuls of hearty food at Ruby and tell her that she wasn't yellow at all. Then Ma would tell Aunt Maggie that it was a very good thing Ruby was doing and that the money was very useful too, thank you very much. Thirty-three shillings a week to Ruby – and ten of them straight to Ma. And Ruby would tell Ma to take more of her earnings and to give up her laundry job whilst she was at it, but Ma would have none of it. After her contribution to the housekeeping, Ruby's money was hers to put aside. Aunt Maggie would mutter that Ruby *needed* to put it aside because she was heading to be an old maid the way things were going. And then talk would turn to the war and the recent attempted Zeppelin attack on the east of England and to Harry who was never far from any of their minds. They would say a little prayer for his safe return and then laugh because they knew Harry was still safe in Buckinghamshire and, according to his short and sporadic letters, fairly revelling in practising drill even though the food was rum and his pillow beyond redemption. And then Ma would praise Charlie, who always seemed to be out of the house, either helping Mrs Tyler or supporting Joe in his grief. It often meant that he was late for dinner and had to walk home in the pitch dark now that the gaslights had been extinguished. Still, as Ma said, that was what true friendship was all about.

And then, every night, Ruby would sleep the sleep of the dead and wake up, barely refreshed, in time for another twelve-hour shift.

It sounded strange to admit it, even to herself, but it was partly the animals who were getting Ruby through it all.

Every morning and every evening, she would look for Mick as she walked down Victory Lane. The little mongrel was nearly always there, tied to the lamppost outside his house, and Ruby fancied his face pricked up in delight whenever he saw her approaching. Certainly, his tail wagged all the harder as she drew near, until his whole body was wriggling with delight. Ruby would crouch down on the pavement and make a huge fuss of him, rubbing his ears and kissing his disfigured little face, wondering, time and time again, what had happened to him. Every day, she made sure that she had some little morsel to tempt him with – and every day she wished she could take him home with her.

It was the same with the cats. Ruby didn't always take herself off at lunchtime, of course. By this time, Elspeth had – thankfully and predictably – already ingratiated herself into the 'popular' set, but Ruby and Dot often sought out each other's company. Ruby was becoming fond of the feisty, intense baker's daughter with her passionately held views on equality and social justice, and loved putting the world to rights with her. But whilst Ruby largely shared those views, it felt like half the world was already helping with the *human* poor of the East End. Ruby had already told Dot that if she was going to get actively involved in any cause, it would be one to help the animals. So, whenever Dot was busy with Brunner Mond's own suffragette group at lunchtime, Ruby would grab something from the canteen and retreat to 'her' place on the bank by the canteen kitchen. There were, she learned, five cats who considered this grassy knoll to be part of their territory, and every day Ruby was joined by at least two of them. She quickly came to learn their different personalities. From there, it was only a matter of time before she gave them all names. The two (nearly) black cats Ruby dubbed Tess and Jess – although even she kept forgetting which one was which and she wasn't even entirely sure that they were girls. There was a large ginger tom who she named Sir Marmaduke because of his regal air, and a tortoiseshell tabby she called Mr Darcy because he was – initially at least – as aloof and self-contained as the character from *Pride and Prejudice*. (Ruby had borrowed the Jane Austen novel from Mrs Henderson's little library one rainy afternoon off and fairly devoured it.) The little ball of grey fluff she named Fluffy because . . . well, surely anybody would!

Ruby quickly became very fond of them all. She loved the weight of them on her lap, kneading their claws into her trousers until they got themselves quite comfortable, ta very much. She loved their wet, yellow little noses, pushing into her hand for attention and treats. She loved their deep throaty purrs that made everything seem right with the world, and the fact that they didn't show off or make silly comments or demand anything of her at all.

Like Mick, they were all so much easier than people.

But one lunchtime, in her third week at the factory, everything changed.

Ruby emerged from a particularly busy and exhausting shift to find another woman sitting in 'her' exact spot on the bank behind the canteen kitchen. The woman had her back to Ruby and was stroking Sir Marmaduke on his ginger tummy, and Sir Marmaduke, for his part, was stretching luxuriantly. Ruby could practically hear his purr from twenty yards. The little traitor!

Rage jostled with indignation as Ruby's heartbeat ratcheted up a gear. Logically, she knew it wasn't 'her' spot any more than it was anyone else's. Everyone had a right to sit there, and competition for space had clearly increased as March turned to April and the weather improved. And they certainly weren't her cats – even though she felt that they were because no one else usually paid them a blind bit of attention.

She had no right to be cross.

But she was cross.

Furious!

More to the point, where was she going to go and what was she going to do now?

Desultorily, Ruby glanced around her. A large group of both men and women – including a noisy and very flirtatious Elspeth – were kicking a ball around and aiming at a target chalked on the canteen wall. Ruby could think of nothing that she would like to do less, even though a couple of the men were quite handsome and one was definitely shooting sideways glances at her.

All that squealing.

All that *Elspeth*.

Dot was deep in conversation with another girl on the other side of the lawn. Ruby knew she would be welcome to join them, but from the fervent expression on Dot's face and the defeated look on the girl's, Ruby predicted that the poor sap would be reluctantly volunteering at the Mothers' Arms before the week was up.

Ruby needed to find herself somewhere else to sit.

As if she could tell she was being watched, the woman stroking Sir Marmaduke turned around. Oh goodness, it was that dreadful la-di-la Miss Richardson from personnel. The woman who had seen Ruby *down there*. The woman who had most unfairly ticked her off for taking Elspeth to task. Somehow, that made the whole thing ten times worse. Blooming management, thinking they owned the place. Surely they had special areas where they could take their breaks? More to the point, why wasn't someone as grand and disapproving as Miss Richardson absolutely disgusted by the very idea of touching a cat? Fancy seeing her being so kind and tender to them.

Ruby was about to stalk off in high dudgeon when Miss Richardson smiled and suddenly her whole countenance changed. The smile lit up her otherwise grave features, revealing small, even teeth and two unexpected dimples.

'Do sit down if you'd like,' said Miss Richardson. She patted the grass beside her to emphasise her point. 'I've seen you here during your breaks and I don't want to drive you away.'

Ruby wasn't sure what to do. It didn't *sound* like an order, but she could hardly just walk away now. She sat down tentatively and wrapped her arms around her knees.

'Aren't the kitties adorable?' said Miss Richardson, reaching out her hand to Mr Darcy who was slinking over to them. 'This one's a real character. I've been trying to sketch them but I'm afraid my attempts aren't very good.'

'They're ever so sweet, Miss,' said Ruby. 'I know some people say they carry disease, but that's never bothered me.' Oh dear, that had come out all wrong. It had made her sound irresponsible. 'I mean, I don't want to pass on disease or nothing,' she added hastily. 'I always wash me hands after I've touched them.'

'I know exactly what you mean,' said Miss Richardson with a warm smile. 'Anyway, humans transmit diphtheria too, and we don't all shun each other.'

'Exactly, Miss,' said Ruby, thinking how much warmer and friendlier Miss Richardson was when she wasn't on duty. 'Well, I shun a couple of people, to be honest,' she added, with a little giggle. 'But somehow the cats are much easier to talk to than the girls in the canteen.'

She paused, blushing.

Oh, goodness – did that sound strange?

Would Miss Richardson think her an awful chump?

But Miss Richardson just made a little face. 'Not many people want to talk to me, anyway,' she said matter-of-factly. 'The men resent the female supervisors and the women avoid management like the plague.'

Ruby blinked in surprise.

That was an unexpected turn in the conversation. Girls tended to avoid management because it was what was expected of them. 'Not getting ideas above your station' had been drilled into them all ever since they were babies, along with minding their Ps and Qs and respecting their elders and betters. Ruby would no more have dreamed of asking Miss Richardson if she wanted a chat than she would have asked Mrs Henderson if she fancied a ciggie by the backstairs.

One just didn't.

'That must be hard, Miss,' she replied.

Carefully.

Neutrally.

'I wish we could have less of the "Miss" out here,' said Miss Richardson, making another little face. 'My name is Leah.'

'Oh, no, Miss. That wouldn't be right . . .'

Miss Richardson shrugged. 'It just seems so silly when there's a war on and everything has gone mad,' she said. 'And, after all, the cats don't care about that sort of thing, do they?'

Ruby giggled. 'Sir Marmaduke does,' she said, pointing at the ginger tom. 'He's *very* particular about titles.'

'Oh, it's Sir Marmaduke, is it?' said Miss Richardson with a laugh. 'I'll be sure to mind my Ps and Qs around him from now on, then. Although I'll admit I rather had him down as plain old Bertie.'

Ruby let rip with a most unladylike snort of laughter. '*Bertie?*' she echoed. 'That ain't nearly grand enough for him, Miss. He's a proper gentleman, ain't you, Sir Marmaduke?'

But Sir Marmaduke just gave Ruby a disdainful look and twisted around to clean his bottom.

Miss Richardson laughed. 'Such a gentleman!' she said. 'What have you named this one?' she added, reaching out to stroke the tortoiseshell tabby.

'Mr Darcy, Miss,' said Ruby. 'He can be ever so stand-offish sometimes.'

'You've read *Pride and Prejudice*?' said Miss Richardson, and Ruby fancied that she looked a little surprised.

'I have, Miss. I read all sorts when I were in service.'

'Well, good for you,' said Miss Richardson. 'Only don't get me started on that book. I think your Mr Darcy needs to wise up; we're in the middle of a war and things are about to change.'

'What do *you* call him, then, Miss?' asked Ruby, beginning to relax.

Who would have thought that Miss La-Di-Da Richardson with her specs and her severe expression would love cats and have such a marvellous sense of humour to boot?

Life was full of surprises.

'Silas Slink,' said Miss Richardson with a little grin. 'He moves in a slinky way, don't you think? And the two little black ones with the white patches are Tweedledum and Tweedledee.'

'No! They're Tess and Jess,' said Ruby with a giggle.

'And the grey, fluffy one is Fluffy.'

'Yes!' exclaimed Ruby. 'I called him Fluffy too.'

The two women laughed easily together.

Oh, this was fun.

The most fun Ruby had had since joining the munitions factory.

The most fun she'd had in a long, long time.

'What did you do before you started here?' asked Miss Richardson conversationally. 'You mentioned you were in service?'

And so, Ruby told Miss Richardson all about life in Hampstead. As coincidence would have it, Miss Richardson's family home was not far away in St John's Wood and she thought her businessman father might even be a client of Mr Henderson's accountancy firm. How strange all of this was. It should have been an awkward situation, two women of different class thrown together like this. Before the war, she would have been serving Miss Richardson at table, bobbing curtseys and minding what she said. And now look at them, swapping confidences, thick as thieves.

'What about you, Miss?' asked Ruby. 'What did you do before the war?'

'An awful lot of nothing, really,' said Miss Richardson, making a face. 'I wanted to train as a vet after I left school, but my mother was having none of it.'

'Oh.' Personally, Ruby could think of nothing better than being a vet, but it was so out of her league on so many different fronts that she might as well have said she wanted to go to the moon. 'What does your mother want you to do instead?'

'Get married, mainly,' said Miss Richardson. She looked so gloomy that Ruby couldn't help but laugh. 'She was constantly lining up the ghastliest saps for me to choose from.'

Ruby laughed again. She couldn't imagine Ma trying to line *her* up with anyone – sap or otherwise. But then again, as Ruby hadn't lived at home for years, it would have been impossible for Ma to do anything like that, even had she been so inclined.

'Between you and me, I was quite pleased when the war started,' said Miss Richardson. 'Oh, don't look at me like that – it came out all wrong and you know it. I've got people in the army and I've already lost a distant cousin, so I know how beastly it all is. I just mean it gave me the opportunity to leave home and, even though I'm living in a cramped boarding house with half a dozen other managers, I've more freedom than I've ever had before. Mother wants me to go home each weekend, naturally, but I keep telling her that my shifts change all the time and that it's hard to make plans. And you don't know just how marvellous that feels.'

'I can imagine, Miss,' said Ruby. 'I'm quite the opposite really. The war has made me come home but, like you, I have much more freedom here than I ever had in service.'

'Well, then,' said Miss Richardson. 'That's something we have in common. As well as both of us loving animals.'

Ruby smiled.

As Miss Richardson had said, everything was topsy-turvy nowadays.

8

And suddenly, it was the end of the first three weeks.

In the shifting shed on the Friday afternoon, the talk quickly turned from the war – stalemate on the Western front with both sides waiting out the cold weather in a series of trenches – to weekend plans and how they were going to spend their wages.

Elspeth was going to buy material to make a new dress; she had seen just the thing at the market last weekend – purple, sprigged with flowers, ever so elegant. She might even buy a new bonnet too. Some of the girls who lived in the staff accommodation were off to the cinema to see *20,000 Leagues Under the Sea* – if they could hear a damned thing after working in the factory all week. Dot wasn't buying anything – she was volunteering at the milk clinic in Bow over the weekend and would barely have a moment to herself.

'How about you, Ruby?' someone asked.

Ruby hadn't given the subject much thought. She wasn't one for fashion and fripperies and she hadn't really got anyone to go to the cinema with. The cats were all well and good for keeping her company between shifts, but they had their limitations. She would buy tobacco for Harry as she always did – that was all he really asked for – and she might buy some wool from Muller's to knit socks to send to him along with the fruit cake that Ma was baking. But, apart from that . . .

The thought arrived out of nowhere.

Ruby looked round at the women in various stages of undress with a wide smile on her face.

'I'm going to buy a dog,' she said.

As soon as Ruby said the words out loud, she wondered why she hadn't thought of it before.

It was so obvious – so *perfect*.

In fact, she would do it that very afternoon – on the way home.

The other girls were nonplussed.

'A *dog*,' said Elspeth with considerable scorn. 'Why would you *buy* a dog when strays are ten a penny?'

'Strictly speaking, they're not ten a penny,' Dot pointed out. 'They're free.'

'What does your ma think about it?' Elspeth persisted. 'Me ma would have fifty fits if I just brought a dog home.'

Ruby didn't bother answering.

She changed out of her trousers and tunic as quickly as she could and flung on her skirt and blouse.

She was a girl on a mission.

This wasn't any old dog.

This was *Mick*.

Victory Lane was a carbon copy of Sanctuary Lane – the same rows of terraced red-brick houses opening straight on to the street and, at first glance at least, seemingly untouched by the war. Like Sanctuary Lane, it was only subtle clues like cracked windows and broken front steps that served as a reminder that many people could no longer afford to pay for repairs to their homes – or that there were simply too few builders and joiners and glaziers to go around.

But Ruby didn't dwell on any of that as she made her way briskly along the street. Instead, her thoughts quickly went to the fact that Mick wasn't for sale and, furthermore, that his owner had already made it perfectly clear she had no intention of parting with him. But Ruby wasn't going to let a small detail like that stand in her way. 'Where there's a will, there's a way,' Pa had always said, and Mick always looked so sad and lonely. Worse, he looked in pain and his poor face showed little sign of healing.

Ruby had to try and rescue him.

More than that, she had to *succeed*.

Of course, that would only be the first hurdle surmounted. Then she would have to convince Ma and Aunt Maggie . . .

One step at a time . . .

As usual, Mick was tied to the lamppost outside his house. Ruby stopped and gave him some of the lunchtime pasty she had put aside especially for him. Then she stood up and took a deep breath. There was nothing to stop her from simply untying the dog and just walking away with him. Chances were she would get away with it and it would save her an awful lot of money and bother in the process. But Ruby resisted temptation. She walked down Victory Lane twice a day on her way to and from work, and someone would be bound to put two and two together. Besides, she was now an employee of the government munitions factory and she had standards to uphold.

At the very least, she didn't want to get sacked.

Ruby drew herself up to her full height and knocked at the door of Number 42.

The door opened almost immediately and there was Mick's owner, looking characteristically displeased.

'Yes?' she said distractedly.

She clearly didn't recognise Ruby.

Ruby's palms began to sweat and she rubbed them surreptitiously on her skirts.

'I've come about Mick,' she said, with a confidence she was far from feeling.

'Mick?' The woman looked over Ruby's shoulder at the dog still tied to the lamppost. 'Is there some problem?'

'Not at all,' said Ruby briskly. 'Or, at least, I hope not. But I would like to buy him and I've come to discuss terms.'

Terms?

Hark at her.

'*Buy* him?' The woman's eyes swivelled from Mick to focus on Ruby's face and then she let out an incredulous laugh. '*Now* I recognise you,' she said. 'How much are you going to offer me for him, then? A couple of ha'pennies from your pocket money? Go on, be along with you.'

The woman's words stung.

Ruby hated being treated like a silly little girl. She had her wages with her – *proper* money – and she was not going to be dismissed so easily.

'I work at the munitions factory,' she said, with as much dignity as she could muster. 'And I have the means to pay. You don't even like Mick. He's always out here, tied up on his own . . .'

'What's that to you?'

'And his face is getting worse . . .'

'That's none of your business. Now, if you don't mind . . .'

Ruby could sense it all slipping away.

'I'll give you half a crown for him,' she blurted out.

It was the first figure that came to mind and, she suddenly noticed, Number 42 had a cracked windowpane. Chances were that the money would come in very handy.

'Half a crown?' the woman repeated incredulously.

Obviously not enough.

'A crown then.'

The woman paused and then shook her head. 'I can't . . .' she started.

Ruby took a deep breath. 'I'll give you ten shillings,' she said firmly. 'Not a penny more.'

The woman stared at Ruby for a moment. Then she untied Mick from the lamppost and pushed the front door wider.

'I'm Mrs Driscoll,' she said, ushering Ruby inside with a sigh. 'Goodness only knows why you want Mick so much, but you'd better come in.'

Ruby followed Mrs Driscoll down the passage and into the kitchen at the back of the house. The room was warm and steamy, but so gloomy with its brown wallpaper and oilskins that it took Ruby's eyes a while to adjust. There was a girl of about six in a dirty pinafore on the sofa; she was sniffing loudly and there was a slice of turnip bread abandoned on the sofa next to her. A toddler with bright red cheeks was sitting on the floor by the range, one fist stuffed into his mouth. Mick gave the little boy a friendly lick on his face.

Suddenly a large black dog darted from the scullery and leapt, snarling, at Mick. Ruby jumped backwards with a little start. Mick didn't react for a moment – he obviously hadn't heard – but then he cowered against the sofa, ears back against his head. Mrs Driscoll grabbed the black dog by the scruff of its neck and dragged it without ceremony into the scullery, shutting the door firmly behind it.

'*That*'s why I can't leave the two dogs together,' she said, almost to herself. 'That is why Mick is so often outside.'

'Rex doesn't like Mick,' the small girl added dolefully.

So, Mick was often tied to the lamppost outside because there was another dog inside waiting to go for his jugular.

Poor Mick – no wonder he always looked miserable.

'Did Rex do that?' she asked, pointing at Mick's disfigured face.

'No, me ma did,' the small girl said matter-of-factly. 'Before Rex even lived here.'

Ruby laughed. What on earth was the little girl talking about?

'Maude!' Mrs Driscoll reached forward and slapped her daughter sharply on the bare leg. 'Enough!'

Maude dissolved into tears. 'But you did,' she said, rubbing her rapidly reddening thigh. 'You set him on fire!'

Oh dear.

'Was there an accident?' asked Ruby.

'No, she did it on purpose,' said Maude.

Mrs Driscoll dragged Maude to her feet with one hand and delivered a well-aimed smack to her bottom with the other. 'What have I told you about not speaking until you're spoken to?' she said. 'Upstairs with you! And don't let me see your face before tea-time.'

Maude disappeared, snivelling, and Mrs Driscoll turned to Ruby.

'I did do it,' she admitted, hands on hips. 'But it weren't like you think.'

'How then?' Uninvited, Ruby perched on the sofa and wrapped her arms around Mick's neck.

How on earth did one accidentally on purpose set fire to a dog?

Mrs Driscoll took a deep breath. 'A month or so ago, Mick got the canker,' she said. 'His ear were a horrible mess and he were going deaf to boot, and I weren't sure what to do. And then I was at Nellie's Dog Barrow up the market and someone said I should pour petrol into his ear and set fire to it . . .'

'So you did?' Ruby finished for her, hardly believing what she was hearing.

Mrs Driscoll nodded. 'They said that would cure his canker good and proper.'

Rage swirled like a red mist inside Ruby's chest.

'That was a terrible thing to do,' she almost shouted.

'The woman said . . .' Mrs Driscoll started defensively.

'I don't *care* what she said. It were clearly ridiculous. How would you like it if someone poured petrol into *your* ears and set fire to them?'

'I were just trying to make him better. I didn't know what else to do . . .'

'There must be some sort of medicine.'

'*Medicine?*' Suddenly Mrs Driscoll sounded harder. Less on the defensive. There was even a note of sarcasm in her voice. 'I can't afford medicine for me own children, let alone for me dog, and I've already had to pay for a new guard dog now that Mick can't hear very well. Next, you'll be saying I should have summoned a vet. Oh, away with you.'

Mick placed his head on Ruby's knees and looked up at her with beseeching eyes.

'I ain't going without Mick,' Ruby said firmly. 'It's the best thing all round. It's pointless you paying to feed two dogs, and I can offer Mick a happy home whether or not he can hear. I think we agreed ten shillings?'

Mrs Driscoll just looked at Ruby for a second and Ruby found it hard to interpret her expression.

Relief, certainly.

Something approaching disbelief.

Maybe a smidgen of something more.

Regret?

Guilt?

Ruby couldn't be sure.

Then Mrs Driscoll gave an almost imperceptible nod of her head.

'We did,' she said.

Ruby handed Mrs Driscoll the note from her wages. She would be short that week – she would have barely enough to cover her housekeeping to Ma and she wouldn't be able to afford treats at the canteen – but she would manage. Mrs Driscoll put the money on the mantelpiece and then bent down and patted Mick awkwardly – the first time Ruby had ever seen her show any affection to the dog.

'Goodbye, old boy,' she said. 'I'm sorry for the way things worked out.'

And she turned away.

A minute later, Ruby was on her way, leading a pliant Mick on his rope halter down the passageway.

She was doing the right thing.

Wasn't she?

*

86

'And who's this?' asked Ma when Ruby arrived home ten minutes later.

Her tone was calm – indulgent, even – but Ruby knew better than to make assumptions.

'This is Mac,' said Ruby simply, going into the scullery and pouring water into a bowl. She rolled the new name round on her tongue, trying it on for size. Yes. She liked it – it was sufficiently similar to the old one not to confuse the dog, but different enough to signify a fresh start. If, indeed, Mac was allowed to stay. 'I've bought him. He's had a terrible time and he needs a new home.'

'You *bought* him?' Aunt Maggie gave an incredulous cackle which set Ruby's teeth on edge. 'With a face like that, they should have paid you to take him away!'

Ruby resisted the temptation to toss the water into Aunt Maggie's face. Instead, she put the bowl down on the tiled floor and stood back as Mac started drinking very loudly.

Goodness, he was adorable.

'Where did you get him from?' asked Ma, coming and standing in the scullery door. Her face was impassive and Ruby felt the first flicker of foreboding. There really was no way of knowing how this might go.

'A house on Victory Lane,' she replied cautiously.

There was no need to give more details.

'Ah, yes. I've seen him tied outside,' said Ma. She gave a deep sigh. 'But really, Ruby, whatever possessed you? It's simply not on to wander around Silvertown buying animals without so much as a by-your-leave to anyone. You wouldn't have done this if Pa were still alive. And what happened to his face?'

Ruby's heartbeat ratcheted up a gear.

It was all still in the balance . . . and potentially tipping the wrong way.

'He got burned,' she said diplomatically. She didn't want to go into details with Aunt Maggie listening from the room next door.

'At least they didn't try to cover up the sores with boot polish,' Aunt Maggie called out sourly. 'That means the joke's on you because you could see exactly what you were buying.'

Ruby kept her mouth shut.

Starting an argument was hardly going to help her cause.

'It looks like it might be getting infected,' said Ma, patting Mac on the head. 'We'll need to get on top of that, the poor little thing.'

We.

That sounded hopeful.

'I'm going to take him up Nellie's Dog Barrow to see if anyone can give me any advice,' said Ruby.

And, of course partly – *mainly* – to give Nellie a piece of her mind.

Telling people to set fire to their animals, indeed.

Ma ruffled Ruby's hair. 'You've got it all worked out, ain't you?' she said. 'And I expect Mac will do very well as a guard dog. I've heard about coal being stolen from the yards – clothes, too. Desperate times and people is getting very bold.'

Ruby thought about lying – if only by omission.

But she couldn't.

Not to Ma.

'Mac can't hear, Ma,' she hissed, so that Aunt Maggie couldn't hear. 'Or at least he can't hear very well.'

There was a pause and Ruby held her breath. Was Ma going to tell her that Mac couldn't stay? And what would Ruby do if she did? She couldn't let him go.

Not now.

Not ever.

Support came from an unexpected quarter. Charlie, wandering into the scullery from the backyard, took one look at Mac and started laughing. But it was a kind laugh and then the boy knelt down and put both arms around the dog's head.

'Please can we keep him, Ma?' he said, smiling up at his mother. 'Please. I think Harry would be ever so happy to come home and find him here.'

Ma threw her head back and started laughing.

'Look at the two of you ganging up on me,' she said. 'And a lame duck, eh, Ruby? Only you would do something like that. Still, he's welcome here, provided you pay for his food. There's room for all sorts under this roof.'

Ruby reached out and hugged her mother. And then she hugged Charlie, for good measure. She wasn't a big one for embraces, but the occasion seemed to merit it.

Her lovely family.

What on earth would she do without them?

9

Mac settled in as though he had always lived in Sanctuary Lane.

He really was the most wonderful dog, calm and affectionate, and, as she had known she would, Ruby quickly came to love him wholeheartedly. Charlie, too, adored Mac from the start, falling over himself to take him for walks when Ruby couldn't and spending hours constructing him a kennel in the backyard. Ma clucked around Mac like an old mother hen, and more than once Ruby caught her giving him titbits from her plate. Even Aunt Maggie, for all her carping about him being a useless hound, was happy for Mac to sit beside her of an evening, bending forward to scratch him between his ears and talking to him gently under her breath.

Everything was perfectly marvellous.

Meanwhile, as she had promised, Ruby took Mac to confront Nellie the next weekend.

Ruby hadn't been up to the Silvertown market for years. To be honest, she hadn't been to *any* market like it for years: the Hendersons had preferred the exclusivity and refined offerings of department stores and speciality shops. Ruby had occasionally frequented the eclectic Hampstead Market for her own personal needs, but it was much smaller and less bustling than the typical East End equivalent.

Despite the war, nothing had really changed.

The barrows and stalls still spilled along the edge of the pavement and on to the road. The hawkers and stall-holders still shouted out *'lovely juicy oranges'* and *'take a gander at me greens'*, the organ grinder still cranked out 'Knees Up Mother Brown' and the carts still clattered across the cobbles, scattering shoppers in their wake.

And the *people*.

Thronging the street, gossiping in little groups, queuing three abreast outside the bakery and making it impossible to walk in a straight line.

It was all just as Ruby remembered it. Except, that was, for Schmidt's the barber's where Pa used to get a shave for a special occasion. Instead of the thriving little business that Ruby recalled, there was now just a shuttered shop with wooden boards across the windows and *'Huns Out'* dabbed crudely on the white brickwork. Ruby had heard, of course, about the attacks on German businesses in London, but it was still a shock seeing the results up close. Mr Schmidt had oozed charm and bonhomie – and he'd also had a glass jar full of bullseyes for any visiting children – and it was sad that he had obviously been hounded out of town. Ruby wasn't sure how she felt about Germans continuing to trade in London, but she did know that Mr Schmidt had always seemed like one of their own and it somehow felt like the residents of Silvertown were turning in on themselves and on each other.

Soberly, Ruby continued pushing through the crowds. She had never been to Nellie's Dog Food Barrow before, but Ma had told her roughly where it was. In any case, both the stench and the attendant cloud of flies were more than enough to announce its presence from thirty yards. Ruby wove around a couple of old donkeys and a skinny dog scavenging in the gutter and joined the little throng of customers surrounding the cart. It was piled high with grisly-looking offcuts of meat fresh from the abattoir, but it was cheap – especially, apparently, if you went for the pieces with knobs on them.

Ruby didn't expect that Mac would mind those very much.

She stood and waited her turn. Only, she wasn't exactly sure when that would be. There didn't seem to be much of a system, just people pressing in from all sides and randomly shouting out their orders to the two women who were bagging up as fast as they could.

'What on earth's happened to your little chap's face?' the older of the two serving women suddenly barked at her.

Ruby started in shock. It rather sounded like the woman – Nellie, presumably – was accusing *her* of being responsible for poor Mac's injury. And in front of all these people, to boot.

How *dare* she?

'I shouldn't have thought that *you* of all people would have to ask that!' Ruby shot back, the words out before she could stop them.

Curious faces craned in her direction, but Ruby didn't care. Nellie deserved it, after all.

Nellie paused, one huge meaty bone held aloft like a weapon. 'I ain't no idea what you're talking about,' she rasped. 'But don't you go using that tone with me, missy.'

Ruby could feel herself growing hot with embarrassment but she was determined to stand her ground.

'You told Mrs Driscoll to pour petrol into Mac's ears and then set fire to it to cure his canker.'

92

'I never did.'

'She told me!'

Nellie sighed. She replaced the bone she was holding on to the cart and came out from behind the barrow. Then she took Ruby's arm and drew her to one side. The crowd shifted and turned back to the cart, uninterested.

'It weren't me,' said Nellie. 'I'd never suggest something that daft. But folks do tend to swap remedies here, for sure. I've had to dissuade people from that one before.'

There was something about Nellie's tone that sounded genuine, and Ruby's anger began to evaporate. Now she thought about it, she wasn't sure whether Mrs Driscoll had actually said that the suggestion to pour petrol into Mac's ears had come from Nellie herself. On reflection, Mrs Driscoll might have – and probably *had* – said that a fellow customer waiting at the barrow had suggested she do so . . .

Ruby had probably walked all the way up to the market on a fool's errand.

'Well, it's dreadful, whoever said it,' she said crossly. 'Mac could have been killed. Whoever suggested it should be reported. Put in prison. Hung!'

'Come now,' said Nellie, giving Ruby's arm a little squeeze with her filthy fingers. 'What good would that do? And what choice do people have, for that matter?'

'There must be somewhere people can take their sick or injured animals,' said Ruby.

'There ain't,' said Nellie flatly.

'What about a vet?' asked Ruby. Mrs Henderson, she remembered, had once summoned a veterinary practitioner when Boniface had been poorly.

Nellie laughed, not unkindly, showing several missing teeth. 'Vets cost an arm and a leg,' she said. 'Most folk round here would have more chance of getting King George to look at their animals. Anyway, even if you could afford one, most of them is out at the front looking after the horses.'

'What about charities?' Ruby persisted. She simply couldn't believe there was *nowhere* an animal owner could get help.

Nellie shrugged. 'There's the odd animal nut feeding the cats under the arches,' she said. 'And there's a vicar doing a sterling job keeping the strays down with a lethal chamber on the high street. But that's your lot around here. Now, let's have a look at your boy. I'm not claiming to be an expert but I've seen one or two dogs in me time.'

She knelt and took Mac's face in her hand, peering at the puckered, yellowing skin. 'Definitely infected,' she said. 'But I reckon the old boy's fighting it off on his own.'

'That's good,' said Ruby, in relief.

'Vinegar for scalds, next time,' said Nellie. 'Takes the pain right away.'

'I hope there ain't a next time.'

'True enough,' said Nellie. 'It's reinfection you need to keep an eye out for now. I've got a salve I can sell you if you'd like. Just in case.'

Ruby swallowed a smile. Somehow, she would have put money on the wily old woman having a variety of dubious 'remedies' she sold on to desperate customers.

'How much?' she asked.

'To you, because I like you – and I like your dog – two bob . . .'

'. . . And to everyone else, a shilling,' Ruby finished for her with a smile.

It was something that Pa used to say and it had always made her laugh. And now Nellie was laughing too.

'You've got your head screwed on, you have,' she said. 'Very well, a bob to you. It's packed full of good things. Mr Smith at the chemist made it up for me.'

'I can't even afford that after buying Mac,' said Ruby, patting the little dog on the head. 'But I will take two pounds of bones with knobs on when it's my turn and I'll know where you are now if I do need the salve.'

'It's your turn when I say it's your turn, said Nellie. 'And your turn is now.'

Ruby smiled.

Somehow, she had guessed that that was how the system worked.

Fingers crossed she never needed the salve.

10

Meanwhile life at the munitions factory went on.

Ruby had now been working there for a month and whilst she was still exhausted at the end of each shift, her arms no longer felt that they were being pulled out of their sockets and her shoulders no longer screamed with quite the same desperation. Even the noise, whilst still overwhelming, was no longer quite so torturous. And meanwhile, no matter how difficult a shift might be and no matter how isolated she might feel from some of the other girls, 'her' cats were waiting for her every breaktime and every lunchtime. Ruby could just be herself with them, and that made everything both bearable and possible. As the weather warmed up, the grass became punctuated with early daisies, their simple, cheerful little faces boosting Ruby's spirits. She would often pluck a few, threading their stems together into a chain and slipping it on to her wrist before fussing over whichever cats happened to be around.

Sometimes Ruby's visits to the bank coincided with Miss Richardson's. The conversation between the two of them always flowed freely and they chatted about everything from animals to the war to social justice. Sometimes Dot would join them too. But whether she had had human company or she had been on her own with the cats, Ruby always returned to the factory floor calmer as a result.

*

'I know a vet,' said Miss Richardson, a few days later, when Ruby was telling her about the visit to Nellie's. 'He's based not far from here, as well. Hackney or somewhere like that.'

Ruby laughed. 'It feels like you know everyone, Miss,' she said.

Miss Richardson smiled. 'Not everyone,' she said. 'But I do know a vet, so they can't *all* be at the front.'

'Ah, but does he treat small animals?' asked Ruby.

'Reluctantly,' admitted Miss Richardson. 'He's one of the saps my mother's trying to marry me off to,' she added. 'She forced me to sit next to him at dinner the other weekend and he rubbed me up the wrong way by saying small fluffies were beneath his salt. I gave him a piece of my mind at that, I can tell you.'

'Why isn't he at the front?' asked Ruby.

'Flat feet, apparently.'

'Very convenient.'

It was strange how many well-to-do people had somehow managed to avoid the sign-up. It didn't seem to be a luxury afforded to the poor of the East End.

'Very,' agreed Miss Richardson. 'Anyway, he looked at one of our dogs the other month – as a favour – and I overheard Daddy moaning about the cost. Your Nellie wasn't lying when she said vets cost an arm and a leg.'

The amount she mentioned made Ruby's eyes water.

'Do you think he knows how many animals are suffering in the East End?' Ruby asked, reaching out to stroke Sir Marmaduke. 'Animals like Mac who end up being maimed because people can't afford to treat them properly?'

97

Miss Richardson shrugged. 'Probably not,' she said. 'He probably never has any call to come here.'

'But if we showed him,' said Ruby, perking up. 'If he knew what things were like here, do you think he might help then?'

Miss Richardson shook her head. 'I shouldn't think so for a minute,' she said. 'The trouble is that the people around here can't afford to pay him. The best bet is probably a charity.'

'Like the East London Federation of the Suffragettes?' said Ruby. 'Oh, look – there's Dot. Let's ask her.'

She waved vigorously and Dot smiled and raised her hand in reply. Picking her way through the little groups of people enjoying the midday warmth, she came over to join them.

'Hello, Ruby. Hello, Miss,' she greeted them. 'Ooh, it's nice to be out in the fresh air. What are you two talking about so seriously?'

Sitting down, she shut her eyes and raised her face to the sun in pleasure.

'The poor animals of Silvertown,' said Ruby. 'Sorry, not much of a cheer-up.'

'To be honest, not much is a cheer-up nowadays, is it?' said Dot, opening her eyes and reaching for her sandwiches. 'The papers have started talking about the build-up to a new offensive and this war just seems to be going on and on and on, don't it? And ever since you mentioned the suffering animals, Ruby, I've started seeing them everywhere I go. There's a cat with some kind of disease which hangs around the bakery stores – I think it comes from one of the houses round the back.

It looks in so much pain and I wish we could do something to help.'

'That's exactly what we was talking about,' said Ruby excitedly. 'The vets ain't interested, but we was wondering about a charity. Like your ELFS. They do clinics for mothers and babies; they could easily have some for animals too.'

'They could,' said Dot, somewhat doubtfully. 'I've never heard them mention animals but that don't mean . . .'

'Would you ask them?' Ruby interrupted.

'Ruby,' cautioned Miss Richardson. 'I'm not sure it's ELFS' remit and that's quite a large favour to ask of your friend.'

'Oh, I don't mind asking,' Dot said cheerfully. 'Sylvia Pankhurst – she's the one in charge at ELFS – is ever so nice and approachable and she's always asking us if we've got any ideas. Besides, I'm in a good mood today. Johnnie, the young chap who delivers the flour – ever so handsome, he is – well, he's enlisting and he's only gone and asked me to write to him. So I don't mind who I ask what today! I'd even ask Mr Briggs if he fancied a twirl round the floor on the Saturday night dance – pardon me impertinence, Miss!'

The three women laughed easily together and Ruby looked round at her colleagues with pleasure. Dot's freckled and usually intense little face was screwed up with pleasure and Miss Richardson's usually solemn grey eyes were dancing with merriment behind her thick glasses. Ruby wouldn't call them close friends – not quite yet – but wouldn't it be wonderful if the three of them *could* put something in motion to help the animals of Silvertown?

'Shall we meet here tomorrow lunchtime to find out what Sylvia Pankhurst says?' she ventured.

Miss Richardson made a face. 'I've got meetings tomorrow lunchtime,' she said regretfully.

'And I've got a suffragette meeting here and all,' added Dot. 'But I promise I'll let you know what Miss Pankhurst says, Ruby – just as soon as I can.'

'Wonderful,' said Ruby. 'And, in the meantime, I'll keep the cats company for you.'

But the next day, the cats weren't there.

The morning hadn't started well. Dot had arrived at Ruby's house before their shift started; one look at her face and it was clear she had been given short shrift the night before.

'Miss Pankhurst weren't rude, as such,' Dot explained, as the two young women walked to the factory together. 'But she made it very clear that this weren't something ELFS would do – especially during a war. And the worst thing was that some of the other women tittered at the very idea. I'm sorry, Ruby; *I* think it's a great idea, but it ain't something we can do on our own, is it?'

And that, it seemed, was that.

Disappointed and frustrated – although she knew that she really had no right to be – Ruby momentarily lost concentration during the morning shift. As luck would have it, she banged the sack she was picking up against Elspeth who was characteristically dramatic about it all. The incident did not go unnoticed by Mr Briggs, who proceeded to tear a strip off Ruby in front of everyone. Thanks to her inattention, she had injured another worker. The factory floor was a dangerous place and there was no room for silly girls who couldn't keep their mind on what they were supposed to be doing. He'd got his eye on Ruby now, good and proper, and if there was one more slip-up – *one more* – she would be given her marching orders and no two ways about it. Ruby had stammered out her apologies and spent the rest of the shift biting back her tears. She just wanted to be on the grass, hugging the cats to her, feeling their solid, non-judgemental weight on her lap . . .

But there was not a single cat on the bank behind the canteen kitchen that lunchtime.

Ruby looked around in bewilderment. Not every cat was in attendance every time she went outside, of course. They came and went as they pleased, and part of the fun was seeing which ones chose to show up on a particular day. But it was unheard of not to see a single cat – especially on a warm and sunny afternoon like today.

Confused, she walked closer to the kitchen door. Maybe one of the kitchen hands had just thrown a whole heap of fish heads into the outside bins and the cats were trying to help themselves to a right royal feast. But there was nothing. The kitchen door was closed, the bins were all lined up neatly and everything was clean and tidy.

What on earth was going on?

Ruby quickly checked the scrubby bushes that dotted the site, but drew a blank there too. Then, concern rising, she wandered over to the perimeter fence, looking for clues. The fence was tall – a good ten feet – and the metal posts were close together: far too close for a human to navigate, but it would be easy enough for a skinny cat to squeeze through. On the other side of the fence was the back alley which linked the yards of the terraced houses bordering the site. The gates to the yard were all shut, save for one. A small girl of about six in a dirty dress was walking up and down the alleyway and crying softly to herself.

Ruby put her hands around two of the fence posts and peered through the gap between them.

'Hello,' she called gently.

The girl jumped. She was clearly so lost in her misery that she hadn't seen or heard Ruby approach.

'Are you all right?' asked Ruby.

The small girl shook her head. 'It's Archie's birthday,' she said sadly.

'Oh. Well, isn't that a good thing? For Archie at least?'

Although Ruby couldn't help but understand the little girl's reaction. She could all too clearly remember feeling eaten up with jealousy when it was Harry's birthday. All those presents, all those cards, all that *fuss* . . . and none of it for her.

'It would be a good thing,' the little girl agreed. 'But he hasn't come home. And I didn't see him last night neither.'

'Oh.' Ruby had assumed that Archie was a brother. But this seemed now unlikely. Maybe . . . maybe . . .

'Is Archie a cat?' she ventured.

'He's *my* cat,' the little girl said fiercely.

Ruby felt a tightening behind her breastbone. 'What does Archie look like?' she asked gently.

'He's grey and very furry.'

'Fluffy!'

The small girl gave Ruby a strange look. 'Very fluffy,' she said.

'No. I mean . . . never mind. I've seen Archie before. Do you own any of the other cats who come through the fence? The black ones with the white markings, for instance.'

Ruby's particular favourites. It would be nice to know that Tess and Jess had a loving home when they weren't scavenging around the canteen kitchen.

But the little girl was shaking her head. 'No. No one owns them,' she said. 'They used to live with the horrible Harrises, but they moved away to the country and left them behind.'

Oh.

Tess and Jess were strays.

'Do you make shells in there?' the girl asked suddenly.

'Sort of,' said Ruby. 'Mostly I just carry things around.'

'Ma says they're not like the shells by the river,' said the girl, her eyes filling with tears. 'They're to *kill* people. Pa said not to tell me, but Ma said I ought to know and now I'm worried one of the shells has killed Archie.'

'No, no,' said Ruby. 'He'll be perfectly safe, I promise you. I'll keep an eye out for him, if you like?'

'What's going on over here, then?'

A sharp voice behind her made Ruby turn around.

A policeman and policewoman were walking briskly towards her, their faces grave. Belatedly, Ruby vaguely recalled that workers were banned from approaching the perimeter fence and that they were expressly forbidden from engaging in any type of communication with anyone on the other side. It was a matter of national security.

Oh, Lordy – and she had marched straight up to the fence and actively engaged someone in conversation.

But, in this case, the 'someone' had been a distressed child.

Surely that didn't count.

Ruby plastered a cheery smile on to her face. 'Good morning,' she said pleasantly as the police approached. 'This little girl's upset because she's lost her cat. She's wondering if it might have wandered on to the site.'

There.

That sounded so innocent.

That *was* so innocent.

Surely she couldn't get into trouble for trying to help a child.

But if Ruby had expected the police officers to relax into smiles and bonhomie, she would have been sorely mistaken. Both remained stony-faced as they approached the perimeter fence. Then the woman crouched down so that she was directly facing the little girl.

'If you've got questions about your cat, you need to tell your ma or pa to come to the visitors' entrance on Swann Street,' she said. 'Do you understand? You mustn't stand here, trying to talk to people through the fence. You could both get into lots of trouble.'

'I didn't try to talk to people,' said the girl, dissolving into floods of tears again.

'She didn't,' confirmed Ruby. 'It were me. I wanted to . . .'

But the policeman had taken firm hold of Ruby's elbow and was practically frogmarching her away from the fence.

Oh goodness!

Two transgressions in one day. She'd be out on her ear for sure.

'I'm so sorry,' Ruby gabbled. 'I didn't mean to cause no harm. It were just a little girl and she were so upset about her cat. Please don't report me . . .'

The policeman released her arm. 'Report you?' he said, with something approaching a smile. 'No one's going to report you for talking to a child. Although it is my duty to remind you to stay away from the perimeter of the site.'

'Yes, of course,' said Ruby fervently. 'Thank you ever so much. I won't do it again.'

The policewoman had caught up with them. 'Phew,' she said. 'That was close.'

'Blooming was,' replied her colleague. 'I didn't want to have to be the one to tell her. Best let the mother deal with it.'

'It's always sad when it's a pet.'

Ruby turned from one to the other in confusion. 'Tell her what?' she demanded. '*What's* sad?'

The police officers exchanged a glance but didn't say anything.

An icy chill ran down Ruby's spine.

'What's happened to that little girl's kitten?' she persisted. '*Tell* me.'

The policewoman sighed and laid a gentle hand on Ruby's arm. 'They came in with the lethal chamber last night,' she said. 'All the cats are dead.'

The words ran round and round Ruby's head as she slumped to her knees in shock.

In horror.

All the cats are dead.

Tess and Jess, Sir Marmaduke, Mr Darcy, Fluffy and all the others . . .

Dead.

She couldn't bear it.

Dead.

Ruby was vaguely aware of the police officers crouching on either side of her.

'Don't take on so, love,' said the man. 'They won't have suffered. It's the kindest thing, really.'

'Kind!' Ruby echoed. She concentrated very hard on the ground so that she wouldn't lash out. There was an ant laboriously making its way up a blade of grass and Ruby found herself irrationally thinking that at least *that* had been saved. 'How is it kind to have killed them?'

'Come along, let's get you a cup of tea in the canteen,' said the policewoman. 'I think once you calm down and catch your breath, you'll be able to see it was for the best.'

'How is it best for them to be dead?' said Ruby, resisting the woman's efforts to haul her to her feet.

'They're strays. *Vermin.* It's not right for them to be on

a government military site. Not safe for them either. A lot of those cats had toxic jaundice – you could see it on their noses.'

'A lot of *people* here have toxic jaundice,' shouted Ruby, hauling herself to her feet under her own steam and squaring up to the police officers. 'I don't see you killing *them*. Or does that come later?'

'Don't be daft . . .'

'I ain't being daft. And anyway, they weren't all strays. You saw that for yourself! Fluffy – Archie – belonged to that little girl. You killed her *pet*. How about if it were your son's or daughter's pet. How would you feel then?'

'My son is at the front,' the man said coldly. 'I'd say I have bigger things to worry about, don't you? And, if it's all the same with you, I don't really have time for this. If you're not going to faint, I need to get back to work.'

'I'm not going to faint,' said Ruby.

'Let me take you to the canteen and get you a cup of tea,' the policewoman persisted. 'You've had a shock.'

'I'm quite all right,' said Ruby, dusting herself down. 'Me shift is about to start, and I need to get back.'

Ruby would have been fine.

Or at least she'd have had a fair chance of being fine had she not had the misfortune to encounter Mr Briggs almost as soon as she walked back on to the factory floor. And, even then, all might have passed without incident, had Ruby not stumbled slightly as she walked past him. Nerves? Blurry eyes from crying? Ruby didn't know why it happened, and really it shouldn't have mattered, because she hadn't stumbled into anything, or against anyone, and there was no harm done. But Mr Briggs spotted it and, being Mr Briggs, decided to call her out on it.

'Come on, girl,' he bellowed. 'Pull yourself together. We haven't got room for lame ducks in here . . .'

Maybe it was Mr Briggs's choice of words hot on the heels of what had just happened. Or maybe it was because Ruby had been stretched as far as a piece of elastic that had nowhere left to go. Whatever it was, she simply couldn't take any more.

'What are you going to do with me, then?' she shouted. 'Put me in the lethal chamber same as those poor cats? Is that what happens round here? Anything not wanted is killed? Even if it's someone's pet? You're murderers. That's what you all are, murderers!'

As she finished her tirade, Ruby was aware of shocked faces straining in her direction. She had really gone and done it this time!

Mr Briggs, for his part, started with surprise, but immediately rallied.

'I have nothing to do with the munition factory's vermin control,' he said coldly. 'But if our policies distress you so much, might I suggest that this is not the place for you. We need reliable workers here – not silly little girls who get the vapours over a couple of stray cats.'

'They weren't all strays . . .'

'Gather your things, girl. I don't want you working for me any more.'

The shock didn't really set in until Ruby was back in the recruitment building where it had all begun.

As a middle-aged woman shuffled papers, all Ruby

could see were the faces of the cats who had been so cruelly destroyed. They hadn't been vermin to her. They had each had their own personality, their own little quirks. Sir Marmaduke liked to have his tummy rubbed, Mr Darcy had a penchant for kneading his claws into her thighs and Fluffy would run round and round in circles chasing his voluminous tail until he collapsed in a little heap.

Dully, Ruby signed the forms that the recruitment lady pushed in front of her. She observed – as though from a very long way away – that the papers were becoming splashed with tears. She hadn't really heard of the lethal chamber before – save that throwaway comment from Nellie at the market the other day – and she had no idea how the poor animals would have been dispatched. She hoped at least that it had been quick and humane. Suddenly, the plaintive cries of the kittens in the Thames came back to her across the years. She had saved some of those, but she had certainly been found wanting here.

It was all so *awful*!

'What's going on here, then?'

Ruby glanced up, recognising Miss Richardson's voice.

The same words that the police officer had used.

Had Miss Richardson known about the cats?

Had she been *part* of it?

'Lass here has been dismissed from the factory floor,' said Miss Richardson's colleague briskly.

'Oh, goodness,' said Miss Richardson. 'Why?'

'Gather she gave Mr Briggs a piece of her mind. A braver girl than me!'

Miss Richardson sat down on the opposite side of the

counter from Ruby. 'What happened?' she asked sympathetically, eyes kind.

'Did you know?' Ruby demanded. 'Is that why you weren't there this lunchtime?'

'Know? Know what?' asked Miss Richardson. 'That you gave Mr Briggs some lip?'

'No, that the cats have . . . gone.' Ruby choked on the words, her eyes filling with tears again.

'The cats? Gone *where*?' said Miss Richardson, looking utterly bewildered.

It was at least some comfort that she hadn't betrayed them all. But it was still too much to cope with. Ruby thumped both hands down on the desk.

'They've been *killed*,' she shouted. 'They got a lethal chamber in – whatever that is – and now they're all dead. And Mr Briggs said that if I didn't like that, then there were no place for me at the factory.'

'Oh, Lordy,' said Miss Richardson heavily. She put her elbows on the table and cupped her face in her hands, shutting her eyes. When she opened them again, Ruby could see that they were shiny with tears. 'All of them?' she added, almost in a whisper.

'Yes,' said Ruby, sitting down again. 'And some of them was pets too. There was a little girl at the fence looking for Fluffy.'

Miss Richardson reached out and squeezed Ruby's hand. 'This is horrible,' she said. 'Let's sort out what we can first and then we'll grab a cuppa. Do you want to stay at the factory? Despite what's happened?'

'I do,' said Ruby, suddenly realising that she very much did. 'But Mr Briggs said . . .'

'Mr Briggs has *sacked* her,' the other woman confirmed, her voice going up an octave.

'Mr Briggs has every right to dismiss Miss Archer from the factory floor,' said Miss Richardson. 'Just as we have every right to redeploy a member of staff should we see fit. Isn't that right, Mrs Clark?'

Mrs Clark's mouth opened and shut like a goldfish. 'Yes, that's right,' she conceded. 'But a troublemaker like this . . .'

'Mrs Clark, perhaps you would leave this to me?' said Miss Richardson. 'I believe there are some potential new recruits who will be finishing their medicals just about now. Perhaps you could go and see to them?'

Mrs Clark huffed off and Miss Richardson turned to Ruby. 'Is there anywhere in particular that you would like to be redeployed?' she asked gently.

Ruby paused. She wasn't really thinking straight. 'I don't know,' she said. 'But maybe somewhere a little *quieter*?'

Miss Richardson smiled. 'There's an awful racket on the factory floor, isn't there?' she said sympathetically. 'What about the canteen? I know they're recruiting in the kitchens.'

Ruby shrugged apathetically. 'I'll go wherever you put me, of course,' she said. 'But the kitchen might be a bit too much like being in service, if you know what I mean. And I'd like to carry on helping to make the shells if I can. You know, to do me bit?'

Miss Richardson nodded. 'I'll put you on assembling detonators,' she said decisively. 'Fiddly work, but a nice team and, most importantly, *quiet*. I think you'll be happy there.'

'Thank you,' said Ruby. 'Will I start there now?'

'Tomorrow will be fine,' said Miss Richardson. 'Take the rest of the day off and report for duty here at nine. In the meantime, shall we have that cuppa?'

Despite it reminding them of the cats, Ruby and Miss Richardson ended up taking their tea over to 'their' patch of grass. To have gone into either canteen, whilst not prohibited, would certainly have invited comment – or at least raised eyebrows – and neither woman felt able to deal with that at the moment. So Ruby nipped into 'her' canteen, bought two mugs of tea and carried them carefully outside. Sitting on the bank, they sipped their brews in sad, companionable silence.

'I can't believe they've gone,' said Ruby, after a while. 'I keep expecting one or other of them to come over and push against me for attention. Oh, it's just too awful.'

'I should have known,' Miss Richardson said morosely. 'I'm management and I should've ruddy known.'

Ruby made a little face. 'I suppose the only thing you can do now is to make sure it never happens again,' she said.

Miss Richardson shook her head. 'How can I do that? This is nothing to do with me. I'm personnel and this is maintenance – a completely different department. I didn't even know it was happening.'

'But next time,' Ruby persisted. 'Now that you *do* know, there must be something you can do.'

'There isn't,' Miss Richardson said shortly. 'The men don't think much of us as it is – and I can't really go around poking my nose in where it's not wanted. My influence is very narrow and I have far less power than you seem to think. Like Dot and the East London Federation of the Suffragettes yesterday. There's no way on God's earth that poor girl will be able to persuade them to open an animal charity.'

'She couldn't,' Ruby confirmed morosely. 'She told me this morning.'

'Of course she couldn't. It was a ridiculous idea.'

Ruby bristled. 'How can you possibly say an animal clinic is a ridiculous idea?'

'I didn't say that,' said Miss Richardson. 'I said sending Dot on a fool's errand to ask ELFS was ridiculous.'

'It wasn't a fool's errand. Have you seen the state of the animals around here? How can you think it's foolish to try and help?'

'Because there's a war on,' said Miss Richardson simply. 'Everyone and everything is focused on winning that and on the boys at the front. As it should be.'

Ruby exhaled noisily. Why was Miss Richardson being so difficult? 'So, by the same token, you think ELFS shouldn't be doing their baby clinic and all the rest, do you?' she said hotly. 'After all, that ain't exactly helping the boys at the front either, is it?'

Miss Richardson wrinkled her nose. 'I didn't say that,' she said testily. 'And of course, with so much dreadful poverty, we should all be doing everything we can to help people in need. Especially children. That's what people will give their time and money to. Not animals. I'm sorry, Ruby – but that's the truth of it.'

Ruby could feel the red mist rising. 'There's a hundred and one charities for children,' she snapped. 'The

Suffragettes, the church missions and the Oxbridge-bleeding-colleges are all in the East End – along with every other well-to-do lady in London. And I ain't saying it's not needed. Of course it is. And I'm not saying that people shouldn't come first. Of course they should. But shouldn't the animals come second? Not nowhere at all. There is no help at all at the moment, Miss Richardson.'

Miss Richardson made a little face. 'I do understand what you're saying. But I just don't think people would get behind it. And I certainly don't think that the vets would support it – so don't you start asking me to contact the vet that I know! I don't want to be rude, but lots of folk think poor people shouldn't even be allowed to keep animals when they haven't got the means to look after them.'

'And is that what you think?' Ruby demanded hotly.

Miss Richardson gave an infinitesimal shrug and, with that, Ruby was reminded of the gulf between them. Despite their tentative friendship, they were from different classes with different perspectives and different values, and nothing could change that.

Maybe the war simply wasn't enough to paper over the gaps.

Maybe *they* had been the fools to even try.

Ruby got to her feet and dusted down her trousers. '"Poor people" might not have money, but we do care for our animals as best we can, Miss,' she said coldly. 'And we need animals too – to keep vermin under control, to guard our houses, to pull our carts and barrows and to run dunnage. How dare you say we shouldn't be allowed to keep them?'

Miss Richardson stood up too. 'Please let's not fall out

over this,' she said. 'I really have tried to help you. I've befriended you and I've also just secured you a new position. I do understand your wish to make something good come out of what's happened, I really do, but a thousand animal hospitals wouldn't have helped the factory cats, would they? You're upset and you're not thinking straight.'

'Neither are you. Just leave me be. If you please, *Miss*.'

'Very well,' snapped Miss Richardson, two bright spots of colour appearing in her cheeks. 'I will do. I'll be off, then.'

She turned and was gone in a swish of skirts.

Suddenly exhausted, Ruby sat down again. She buried her head in her hands and exhaled slowly. What had that been all about? How dare Miss Richardson dismiss her ideas – dismiss *her* – so lightly and casually? Was that how Miss Richardson saw her?

As a joke?

An insignificant, vaguely amusing nobody?

Well, that was that, then!

Besides, helping the animals of the East End could *never* be a bad idea. Animals shouldn't count for less than nothing. The authorities *shouldn't* be allowed to kill people's pets with impunity and there *should* be somewhere affordable for people to take their sick animals – war or no war. That much was just common sense and basic humanity, and no one was going to dissuade her of that. And if no one – not even her friends – was going to help her, well, maybe Ruby should have a good think about what she could do on her own. After all, she had saved those kittens back when she was a child and . . .

But – wait – what was that?

The faintest of mews coming from the nearby shrubbery.

She must be imagining it.

As Miss Richardson had said, the stress and trauma of the day was playing havoc with her mind.

But no.

There it was again.

A quiet but very definite mew.

Heart thumping, Ruby got up and went over to the bushes. Bending over, she peered into the gloom.

Nothing but wishful thinking.

She straightened up, preparing to finally head for home, leaden disappointment in her chest. And then she heard it again.

And this time, there was no doubt.

She crouched down again, looked a little harder – and there was Tess.

A Tess who was very much alive!

Heart soaring, Ruby picked up the kitten and hugged her tight, breathing in Tess's warm-earth fragrance. Tess gave an answering purr which set her little body vibrating.

'Oh, Tess,' Ruby murmured. 'I'm so sorry about your sister. Now, what are we going to do with you?'

It was a rhetorical question. Ruby already knew exactly what she was going to do. For the briefest moment, she toyed with the idea of giving Tess to the girl who had lost Archie; that would perhaps be the kind and charitable thing to do. But she couldn't. It wouldn't be safe; Tess would only squeeze through the railings as soon as she got the chance and the next time the lethal chamber was brought on site, the little cat almost certainly wouldn't be so lucky.

No, Tess was coming home with Ruby, to a new life in Sanctuary Lane, and that was that.

As Ruby headed off to the shifting shed to get changed and to beg, steal or borrow a box to carry Tess home, she was suddenly full of optimism and excitement.

Tess had survived and that felt like a sign.

She had Mac and now she had Tess.

Anything was possible now.

12

'No,' said Ma. 'Absolutely not. Tess is welcome to stay. But no more animals.'

Ruby crossed her arms and stepped forward, ready for battle. Ready to cajole her mother into allowing her to bring more cats from the munitions factory home. And there would be more cats, Ruby was sure of it. Even now, more little figures could be squeezing through the fence, sitting targets for the next time the lethal chamber was wheeled in.

She couldn't bear it.

'Please, Ma,' she said. 'I can't just let them all die.'

'And you can't bring them all home, neither,' said Ma. 'I'm sorry about what happened at the factory, but from what you've said, some of them cats was pets anyway. They're not yours to bring home, like it or not.'

'But I've got to do something.'

'Well, it will have to be a different something,' said Ma. 'This might be called Sanctuary Lane but I'm not having me house filled up with every waif and stray and with angry owners knocking at me door, to boot. I'm sorry, Ruby, but that's that. Don't give me a reason to change my mind about Tess.'

Ruby dropped her arms to her sides and stepped back. There was just something about the set of Ma's mouth that told her argument was futile. Besides, Ruby knew in her heart of hearts that it would never work. There was barely room for the humans in Sanctuary Lane, let alone a whole menagerie of animals.

She needed to explore other ways of saving the factory cats, and she wouldn't give up on her idea of an animal hospital either.

But in the meantime, there were cats to mourn and a whole new role to get used to.

Ruby duly reported for duty in the reception building at nine o'clock the next morning.

It was packed to the gills with people, mainly women, either queuing up or bent over clipboards, scribbling furiously. How long ago it seemed since she had been one of them. And how much had happened in the weeks since.

Ruby took her place in the queue and scoured the room for Miss Richardson. There was no sign of her, and Ruby was surprised at just how disappointed she felt. She hadn't slept much the night before, and it had given her a chance to realise just how much she wanted to apologise to Miss Richardson. She blushed to think how she had flown off the handle at her quite reasonable comments and had all but thrown a tantrum when she had voiced the mildest of reservations about the animal hospital idea. Honestly, if Ruby couldn't keep her temper and her wits about her when someone she knew challenged her, what chance did she have when she was slapped down by those in authority?

'Can I help you?'

Ruby had been so lost in her own thoughts that she hadn't noticed she was at the front of the queue and that Mrs Clark was staring at her with barely disguised disapproval.

'Yes. Good morning,' said Ruby, determined to be polite. 'Ruby Archer reporting for duty in the detonation shop.'

Mrs Clark shuffled some papers in front of her. 'It says here you're not clocking on until six p.m. this evening,' she said.

'Oh, there must be some misunderstanding,' said Ruby. 'Miss Richardson specifically said that I should . . .'

'No misunderstanding,' Mrs Clark interrupted smoothly. 'Miss Richardson has specifically asked me to let you know that you'll be working the six p.m. to six a.m. shift from now on. So sorry you've had a wasted journey. There was no chance to get a message to you.'

Mrs Clark wasn't sorry.

In fact, her expression was bordering on a smirk. And there was *always* an opportunity to get a message to someone. Several times, Ruby herself had been asked to knock on so-and-so's door on the way home to let them know that a shift had been changed or that they were to report to a different department or something to do with a football match. The point was that Ruby didn't exactly live in the middle of nowhere and it would have been perfectly possible to have got a message to her if Miss Richardson or Mrs Clark had been so inclined. Still, Ruby was in no mood for an argument, so she just nodded at Mrs Clark, scanned the room one more time for any sign of Miss Richardson and headed home.

Ruby didn't mind the change in hours as such and it was certainly a small price to pay to help the war effort. Oh, it was annoying that she hadn't had advance notice and that she would now effectively have to stay awake for a whole day and night – unless she managed to grab some sleep during the day. But that didn't really matter. In fact, Ruby quite *liked* the idea of living her life in a topsy-turvy manner, out of sync with everyone else. Besides, there wouldn't be the constant temptation to lie on the bank during a sunny break and thus be constantly reminded about the cats.

What Ruby didn't like was the feeling that all this was some sort of punishment. Of course, there were all sorts of reasons why she could – and even perhaps *should* – be punished. She had approached the perimeter fence without permission and given lip to Mr Briggs. The trouble was that Ruby had a sneaky feeling it was Miss Richardson who was punishing her, and that made her feel sad and, perversely, rather angry. Never mind that a few minutes ago she had been planning to apologise to Miss Richardson. This changed *everything*. Moving her shifts without notice was childish and vindictive and obviously had something to do with Ruby getting ideas above her station. Well, if that was what Miss Richardson thought, she simply wasn't a friend, was she? Ruby was grateful to Miss Richardson for finding her a new role when she had been so abruptly dismissed from her old one, but that was that. No doubt Miss Richardson had moved her to the night shift so the two of them wouldn't be constantly bumping into each other – and that was perfectly fine by Ruby.

It was time to move on.

Ma was sanguine about the change in Ruby's working hours. A job was a job, and everyone had to fit in and do their bit nowadays. Ruby could eat her main meal before she went to work in the evening, and Ma would leave her something light in the morning before she turned in for the day. There were thousands all over the East End who had always worked this way and it was nothing to get their knickers in a twist about.

But in the meantime Ruby had a day to kill.

She wasn't tired enough to go back to sleep – she had only just got up! – and she had no real wish to hang around the house and be given a mountain of chores to do by Ma and Aunt Maggie. So she did something she had never done before.

She took Mac and went to the library.

The library was a short bus ride away on the Barking Road in Canning Town. Well, it would have been a short bus ride if it hadn't been for the dozens of soldiers marching in formation in the middle of the street. They slowed everything down and reminded Ruby that, despite the current stalemate, the war was still gearing up and that no one was really safe. The weather was getting clearer and warmer . . . another Zeppelin attack was surely imminent. And now there was all the news coming out of Dublin where the Irish republicans were staging a rebellion against British rule in Ireland. Honestly, it sometimes seemed that the whole world was going mad.

Ruby shook her head in frustration.

Worrying about things she had no control over wasn't going to help anyone. She braced herself: she was a woman on a mission.

Ruby had passed the imposing grey stone library building countless times, but she had never been inside. It just wasn't the sort of place a girl from Sanctuary Lane typically frequented and, as she climbed the short flight of stairs to the big wooden doors, Ruby half-expected to be swiftly escorted back down them again. Sure enough, the middle-aged woman behind the desk immediately stood up and pointed at her.

Ruby's heart plummeted.

It seemed that some things never changed.

'No dogs,' said the woman, mildly enough. And then, spotting Ruby's crestfallen face, 'Sorry. I don't make the rules around here.'

'He's ever so good,' Ruby pleaded, patting the top of Mac's head.

She could leave Mac tied up outside, of course, but she preferred not to do so. Poor Mac had already spent enough of his life attached to lampposts.

'Oh, very well, then,' said the librarian. 'It's empty in here and the poor little chap looks like he's been in the wars.'

Ruby nodded her thanks and the librarian turned back to her work. Ruby and Mac were alone in the dark, dusty silence.

Ruby looked around herself in wonderment whilst Mac flopped underneath a table.

All those books! Even more than at the Hendersons'!

Stories from floor to ceiling waiting to transport her to a different time and place.

But she mustn't – wouldn't – let herself get distracted.

Twenty minutes later, Ruby found herself thoroughly frustrated.

She didn't really have any idea what she had hoped to find, but she had hoped to find . . . something. A weighty tome on how to set up an animal charity? A slim tome on setting up *any* charity? A pamphlet on how to treat common ailments in dogs and cats?

There was nothing.

'There's not much call for things like that round here,' the kindly but slightly bemused librarian explained. 'The less salubrious medicine suppliers sometimes produce publications for the general public, and they might be your best bet. They're of variable quality, though. And usually not cheap.'

Ruby made a face. 'Not cheap' and of 'variable quality' was hardly an ideal place to start.

'What about veterinary organisations?' she asked.

After all, any animal hospital worth its salt was going to need vets, so this was probably the best place to start.

'There's the Royal Veterinary College,' said the librarian, brightening up at the prospect of being able to help. 'I could dig out an address if you'd like?'

'Yes, please,' said Ruby. 'And the addresses for a couple of local veterinary practitioners too, if you wouldn't mind.'

Armed with this information, Ruby stationed herself at a quiet table, Mac at her feet, to compose some letters. It was, of course, despicable that no one had done anything about the desperate plight of animals in the East End to date, but Ruby was prepared to be charitable. Maybe, as Miss Richardson had suggested, the war meant they simply didn't have people on the ground to see how dreadful things had become. Well, that wasn't an excuse and she was going to make sure they knew *exactly* how bad things were. She wrote three brief letters outlining her idea for a small animal clinic in Silvertown before she had a chance to change her mind. She also asked the local veterinary practitioners if she might volunteer her services in order to learn more about animal care.

How could any of them possibly refuse?

Next, Ruby turned her attention to helping the cats at the factory.

'Any books for keeping unwanted animals off your land?' she asked the librarian.

The librarian looked disappointed. 'Little call for that bang slap in the middle of London,' she said. 'But there are a couple of books on gardening over there which might be worth a look.'

Ruby started rifling through the threadbare books.

One way or another, she would make a difference.

She owed it to Jess and Mr Darcy and all the others.

She wouldn't be found wanting again.

13

Ruby took to her new role in the detonation shed straight away.

Everything about it was better.

For starters, there was no need to wear the wooden clogs which rubbed nor the tight cap with strings which often gave her a thumping headache. There was no need to wear the trousers and tunic, for that matter, but Ruby hadn't particularly minded those. Instead, like the other women, she simply pulled cotton overalls over her regular clothes, made sure that her hair was neatly tied back and she was ready to go.

Secondly, there was no chance of bumping into either Miss Richardson or Mr Briggs as both of them were now on different shifts. Ruby didn't mind at all about the latter – in fact she didn't care if she never saw Mr Briggs again – but she couldn't help regretting that things had ended the way they had with Miss Richardson. And it looked like her budding friendship with Dot might also be a casualty of the events of the past few days. Dot, still no doubt smarting at being laughed at on Ruby's behalf at ELFS, had looked thoroughly aghast at Ruby's outburst at Mr Briggs. There had been no attempt at communication since and Ruby could only sadly surmise that Dot wanted nothing more to do with her. She couldn't really blame her. Ruby had been used to her own company ever since her schooldays, but she had hoped that things might be different at the factory. It was a shame that things hadn't worked out.

More positively, however, Mrs Mason – the well-to-do, middle-aged woman in charge of the detonation shed – was a big improvement on Mr Briggs. Where Mr Briggs had been all barked commandments, condescension and nigh-on bullying, Mrs Mason had a soft Scottish burr and seemed to run her team with kindness and consideration. Something about the set of her mouth told Ruby she would be able to lay down the law with absolute authority when called on to do so, but her warm welcome and general demeanour couldn't have been more in contrast to Mr Briggs's.

Fourthly, Ruby could sit down.

The detonation shop consisted of eight or so huge wooden tables with ten women perched on stout wooden stools around each, busy with their tasks. No thumping machinery, no clanging trolleys, no shouts and shrieks. After the main factory floor, it was blessedly peaceful. Not that it was *quiet* as such – but the sound of nearly a hundred women chatting and laughing was certainly much more bearable.

Ruby was shown to a seat at the end of one of the tables and Mary – the plump, comfortable woman who was in charge of the table – sat next to her to show her the ropes.

'It's all very straightforward,' said Mary. 'A detonator is comprised of lots of different things – little springs, little this, little that – all packed in together. On some of the other tables they're weighing and measuring the springs and whatnot to make sure they can take the right pressure, but you don't need to bother yourself with that. On this table, we're putting them all together. Each person has a particular task, and you complete a boxload of whatever you're assigned to do and then pass it on to the next woman – and so it goes on, all the way round the table. You'll get the chance to try all the positions eventually, but we always start the new girls at the end so there won't be a backlog building up whilst you get up to speed. Your job this week will be to screw the cap on the finished detonator using these screws. Make sense?'

Ruby nodded.

As Mary had said, it did all sound very straightforward.

Mary slowly demonstrated what she needed to do and Ruby watched carefully.

'Let me see you do a couple,' said Mary, when she had screwed two caps into place.

Ruby took a deep breath, picked up an empty cap and held it over an assembled detonator. It was a bit fiddly lining everything up so that the screws slotted in easily, but she soon had them aligned and tightened.

Mary nodded her approval. 'Not bad at all,' she said.

She showed Ruby what tension she should be aiming for – 'not too tight, not too loose and about eight turns of the screwdriver' – and then sat down and carried on with something else.

Ruby was, apparently, fully trained and on her own.

The first few nights started pleasantly enough.

The work was easy and repetitive and Ruby was soon working as quickly as everyone else. After a couple of nights, Mary let her move position and she was put on springs. Now she was right in the heart of the production line and the pressure mounted a little because, if she fell behind, the woman in front of her would have nothing to do and then the woman in front of *her* would grind to a halt and Mary would get all agitated and start fussing about quotas and shipments. But in less than an hour Ruby was more than holding her own and was able to insert the little springs and adjust them just so without really thinking about it.

This was perfect.

Even better, the other women were mostly at least as old as Ma and didn't demand anything of her. For the most part, Ruby was happy to just sit there and let their conversation wash over her and, whilst no one made a huge effort to draw her out, they were all kind and friendly enough towards her. Over time, Ruby learned that many of the women had husbands and sons at the front and lived in constant fear of a telegram. Their fears weren't misplaced – a woman two tables over had lost her son a couple of months before and another's husband was on his way home without a leg – and Ruby could only wonder that they were able to laugh and joke at all. She felt worried enough about Harry – and he was still in Blighty and apparently having the time of his life with the other conscripts. Ruby's admiration for her co-workers only grew when she learned that most of the women also had children at home and were cooking and cleaning and generally keeping the home fires burning both before and after their shifts.

How on earth did they manage to do it?

Each break time, Ruby was happy to tag along and share a table with them in the canteen. Although it was now May, it was still too dark and cold to sit on the bank, and besides, Ruby had no wish to encourage any other cats to hang around the site. It was only now dawning on her that she and Miss Richardson had been part of the problem. It was dreadful to have to admit it, even to herself, but it was true: by lavishing titbits and attention on 'their' cats, they had, in effect, been partially responsible for sealing their fate. It was obviously too late to save Mr Darcy and all the others, but Ruby felt keenly that she had a responsibility to stop it happening again. She had no idea how often the lethal chamber was brought on to the site, but she knew that time must be of the essence. More than once, she had seen a feline streak near the old canteen doors or caught a pair of green eyes regarding her solemnly from the undergrowth, and she knew that a new generation of cats was already taking up residence there.

She had to help them.

The trouble was, where to start?

14

A week later, there had been no reply to any of Ruby's letters.

At first, she had assumed that her letters were just taking ages to reach the right people, given the shift in priorities to support the war effort. Mrs Henderson had always grumbled about the wartime post – and how the five daily deliveries had dropped down to only two – and just look at the problems Ma was having getting separation allowance now that Harry had enlisted. There simply weren't enough people left in Blighty to do all the jobs that needed doing.

But as the days went on, Ruby began to get more and more frustrated. She couldn't wait forever! Maybe it would be better just to turn up in person and talk to someone face to face. Yes, that was exactly what she would do. She would take matters into her own hands and start with the Royal Veterinary College in Camden Town. It was just down the road and across the park from Hampstead and, whilst Ruby couldn't picture the college itself, she must have walked nearby countless times during her time in service.

She would go straight after her shift the very next morning.

Ruby was at Silvertown Station by eight o'clock the next morning, dressed in her smartest skirt and blouse, her hair neatly pinned back and her handwritten notes for the meeting stacked just-so in her basket. She had been tempted to bring Mac along with her – he was the inspiration behind her idea – but she decided against it. If dogs weren't allowed in the RVC, he would just be an unnecessary complication and she could do without any of those. It was a blustery day and the wind was in danger of blowing away more than Ruby's hat; in fact, she could feel her bravado ebbing away with every gust. She was just a girl from the East End of London, a girl who until a few months ago had been destined for a life in service. Was she, as Miss Richardson had implied, getting ideas above her station? Was she meddling where she had no right to meddle, interfering in matters that she had no real knowledge of? Did she, in fact, have a cat in hell's chance of making the slightest bit of difference?

The answer to the last question, at least, was probably not. But then again, there didn't seem to be anyone else stepping forward.

Surely she owed it to the animals and their owners to at least try?

With a deep breath, Ruby bought her ticket and headed for the London platform. She rounded the corner ready to go down the stairs and . . .

Ooof!

Suddenly, Ruby was on her knees, hat askew. Her basket had been knocked from her hands and the papers inside had been caught by the wind whistling up the staircase and were already flying around.

'Damn it!' Ruby muttered vehemently.

This was not a good start.

'I'm so sorry,' said a male voice as Ruby staggered to her feet. 'We came round the corner at the same time and . . . here, let me help you.'

The man set off down the stairs in hot pursuit of Ruby's papers and she saw that it was a soldier wearing an army greatcoat. Back on leave, no doubt, and already drunk at eight in the morning. Ruby had seen them on the high street, making the most of their freedom back in Blighty or drinking away their demons. Then she chided herself for such an uncharitable thought; she didn't *know* that this particular soldier was drunk – although the collision had definitely been his fault. They might have come round the corner at the same time, but he was the one who hadn't been looking where he was going.

Ruby straightened her hat and smoothed down her skirts as the soldier climbed back up the stairs.

'Here we are,' he said, holding out a ragged sheaf of papers. 'I think I've got them all . . . and at least the stairs ain't wet today.'

'Thank you,' said Ruby, taking her notes and tucking them back into her basket.

The man didn't *look* drunk . . . and he was also very handsome, if a girl cared to notice that sort of thing. He was probably a little older than she was and he had brown, wavy hair, a broad face with high cheekbones and eyes that were at once green and hazel. His expression was serious – almost stern – and he had a little groove between his eyebrows. Ruby wasn't much given to swooning over men she had just clapped eyes on – in fact she wasn't much given to swooning over men at all – but there was no doubting the involuntary swoop of her stomach and the fact that her cheeks were suddenly burning hot.

Oh, Lordy.

'You seem in an awful rush,' she said conversationally, thanking her lucky stars that her words came out in the right order and with the minimum of stuttering.

Stop it, Ruby!

Stop talking to strange men you've only just met.

What's got into you?

The man gave a little grimace. 'I'm just looking for a dog,' he said.

'Any particular dog or just a dog in general?'

She hadn't intended it as a joke, but suddenly the man's face creased up in merriment and his whole countenance changed. Gone was the furrow between the eyes, replaced now by a lopsided grin, a dimple in one cheek and a sparkle in his eyes. His laughter was infectious and suddenly Ruby found that she was laughing along with him. Goodness, he was handsome. His wife or sweetheart – because men like him *always* had a wife or sweetheart – was a lucky woman indeed.

'I want to buy a dog,' the soldier clarified. 'And someone said that Club Row were a good place to start.'

'I see.' It was on the tip of Ruby's tongue to point out that there were dozens of strays on the streets of Silvertown, all desperate for a home, and that Club Row was full of charlatans, but . . .

'Where are you off to with all your notes?' the man asked as the two descended the steps together. 'They look *très bon*!'

Ruby smiled. She had no idea what *très bon* meant – but

it didn't sound like an insult. The man had a Silvertown accent – so maybe it was some sort of coster-slang she hadn't come across. 'Funnily enough, I'm off to see a man about a dog too,' she said archly. 'Well, hundreds of dogs, to be precise.'

There!

That would give the soldier something to unpick; something for the two of them to talk about on the train together. Because Ruby found that she very much wanted the two of them to sit together, to carry on their conversation and to see where it led them . . .

The train pulled into the station with a loud squeal of brakes.

'Actually,' said the soldier, 'I've decided not to go up to Whitechapel after all. I – er – need to go. I'll bid you good day, Miss.'

He touched his cap and, just like that, he was gone.

Ruby got on to the train, not sure whether to laugh or cry.

It was the first time she had met a chap she'd taken a shine to and . . . she had frightened him off!

That comment about hundreds of dogs *had* been a bit strange, now she came to think about it, but had it really been strange enough for someone to abruptly change their travel plans over it?

Well, justified or not, that was what the chap had done and there was nothing she could do about it now.

Shame, though.

He really had been *très bon*.

The austere red-brick façade of the Royal Veterinary College did nothing to calm Ruby's nerves. Everything – from the huge coat of arms above the door to the young rakes in their frock coats and suits milling around outside – reeked of class and privilege. Horribly aware that even her best navy skirt had a ragged hem and that her hair was already escaping from its bun, Ruby drew herself to her full height. Shoulders back and chin erect, she walked inside.

There was a large entrance hall with a grand sweeping staircase and, off to the left, a door with 'Reception' written above it. Ruby strode in with a confidence she didn't feel. An elderly woman sitting behind a desk, and busy on a typewriter, looked up at her enquiringly.

'Can I help you?' she asked.

Ruby fancied that the lines around her mouth were already radiating disapproval; Ruby was clearly the wrong class, the wrong sex . . . the wrong everything.

'Yes, please,' she said briskly. 'I'm Ruby Archer. I'd like to speak to . . .' Oh goodness. Who exactly did she want to speak to? Her letter had just been addressed 'to whom it may concern', as Mrs Henderson had taught her. 'I'd like to speak to the head,' she said firmly.

That should do.

'The head?' echoed the receptionist with a patronising smile. 'This isn't a boarding school, you know.'

'Ruddy feels like it sometimes,' muttered a young rake lounging on a bench behind her and Ruby suppressed a smile. Problems persisted whatever your class, it seemed, even if you were lucky enough to be training to be a vet.

She tried again. 'I'd like to speak to the person in charge,' she said crisply.

The receptionist sighed. 'And do you have an appointment?'

Of course she didn't. That would make life far too easy!

'Not as such,' she said. The receptionist raised an impeccably arched eyebrow. 'All right, not at all,' Ruby admitted. 'But . . .'

'But without an appointment, it is entirely out of the question,' the receptionist finished for her. 'The schedules are set weeks in advance.'

Ruby was being fobbed off. She knew it, but she wasn't sure how to turn things around. Miss Richardson wouldn't be dismissed out of hand like this. Miss Richardson would be taken seriously because she was upper class. And even the soldier would be taken more seriously, simply because he was a man. It was all so unfair. But she couldn't give up. Even though she could not have felt more out of place if she'd arrived at Buckingham Palace and asked for an audience with the King, she would carry on until she was physically thrown out of the place.

'I've already written, outlining a proposal,' she said, trying to keep a note of desperation out of her voice. 'I'd be grateful for the opportunity to discuss it with someone. It's – er – in our mutual interest.'

Ruby wasn't sure that the last bit was entirely true, but hopefully it sounded convincing. The receptionist, however, looked as though she was trying not to laugh.

'What sort of proposal?' she asked.

'It's for an animal hospital in Silvertown,' said Ruby. 'Somewhere where people only pay what they can afford. Everyone is really struggling to care for their sick and injured animals and we desperately need veterinary help . . .'

Just then, an office door burst open and a small, neat

man with a luxuriant moustache and a full head of shiny dark hair came out. He was followed by a tall, good-looking young chap with a petulant expression. It was clear that the older man had just given the younger a right good carpeting.

'This is your final warning, Coleman,' said the older man. 'Please don't let me have cause to talk to you again.'

'No, Sir,' said Coleman contritely. His eyes roamed casually over Ruby before he strode out. Through the open door, she could see him being swallowed up by a group of braying young men in the entrance hall.

The older man turned his attention to the young man sitting on the bench. 'Right, Wilson. Your turn,' he said, jerking a thumb towards his office.

The receptionist got to her feet. 'As I've said, Miss Archer, I'm afraid it's totally out of the question to demand to speak to Mr Cotter,' she said. 'I am more than capable of dealing with this matter on my own.'

Ruby opened and shut her mouth in surprise. She hadn't demanded to speak to Mr Cotter. She had never even heard of him, for heaven's sake.

What on earth was going on?

Mr Cotter spun on his heel. 'What matter, Mrs Coleman?' he said, with icy politeness.

'No need to trouble yourself, Mr Cotter,' said Mrs Coleman smoothly. 'I've already told Miss Archer you're too busy to see her and that I will deal with her application.'

The penny began to drop.

Oh, Mrs Coleman was a wily one.

The only question was whether Mr Cotter would take the bait.

'I think you'll find I have complete jurisdiction over my morning, thank you, Mrs Coleman,' he said stiffly. 'It's for me to decide whom I wish to see.'

'But . . .' started Mrs Coleman.

'If you'd like to come this way, my dear,' said Mr Cotter to Ruby, rudely turning his back on Mrs Coleman and pushing the door to his office open with an elaborate flourish. Ruby shot the receptionist a grateful glance and followed him inside.

A face-to-face meeting with someone important at the Royal Veterinary College.

She mustn't mess it up.

'I take it you've come about the secretarial role,' said Mr Cotter before Ruby had even had a chance to sit down.

Oh goodness!

'Mrs Coleman does rather like to think that the whole thing is down to her,' Mr Cotter continued with an oily laugh. 'But as you would ultimately report to me, I like to take, shall we say, an active role in proceedings.'

The look he gave Ruby made her skin crawl and she suddenly realised who Mr Cotter reminded her of.

It was Sir Emrys.

She took a deep breath. 'I'm not here about the secretarial role, Mr Cotter,' she said politely.

It didn't matter who Mr Cotter did or did not remind her of.

She had to get him on side.

Mr Cotter looked confused. 'Then how can I help you?' he asked, spreading his fingers wide.

Ruby pulled her slightly crumpled sheaf of notes out

of her basket. Her cause was just and her reason for the meeting watertight. Tentatively, she started to outline her vision. She wasn't sure what sort of response she was expecting, but even she was surprised when Mr Cotter threw his head back and let rip with a bark of laughter.

'My dear, there is a war on,' he said, amusement written all over his face.

As if she didn't know!

'Yes,' said Ruby. 'And that's part of the problem. It's making poor people poorer.'

'Miss Archer,' said Mr Cotter with exaggerated courtesy. 'At times like this, we all need to concentrate on keeping the home fires burning. Even spinsters like you have a role to play.'

Ruby paused and bit the inside of her lip until she could trust herself to speak. If only Mac were here. There was nothing like stroking his silky head to calm herself down.

'I *am* playing my role,' she said, mildly. 'I'm working at the government's munition factory in Silvertown.'

Mr Cotter reached across the table and patted Ruby's hand, leaving his hand on top of hers. 'A most admirable occupation,' he said. 'So why this silly talk of setting up a hospital for companion animals when you are patently not qualified?'

Ruby smiled at Mr Cotter, resisting the temptation to snatch her hand away.

'Oh, goodness,' she said. 'Not me. You're right – I don't know the first thing about looking after animals. But *you* do, don't you? It's something that you could – and some would say you *should* – be doing.'

Mr Cotter removed his hand. 'Don't be ridiculous,' he

said. 'Most veterinary practices are already over-stretched, or even closed, because most of the veterinary practitioners are helping the war effort in France.'

'But not all of them,' said Ruby. 'Not the ones who are training here, for instance. Surely you want to do your bit for animals in need?'

'Do our bit?' Mr Cotter echoed incredulously. '*Do our bit?* I'll have you know, young lady, that forty odd years ago, the Royal Veterinary College set up the Poor People's Out-Patients Clinic for just the need you describe.'

Goodness!

Had they?

'Well, there ain't one in Silvertown,' said Ruby. 'Everywhere you look there's dogs and cats limping around, eating in the gutters. It's terrible.'

'Dogs? Cats?' Mr Cotter sniffed. 'Oh, I'm not talking about companion animals. You can't expect vets to train for years and then to work with small fluffies.'

'They're not just companion animals,' said Ruby hotly. 'Besides, don't you think if you carry on only working with horses, you'll soon all be out of a job? When I walked up from the station just now, there was almost as many motors as horses . . .'

But Mr Cotter was standing up.

'There are plenty of charities which deal with small animals,' he said. 'I know for a fact that the Elizabeth Street Veterinary Centre provides pro bono veterinary care to both the Battersea Dogs Home and Our Dumb Friends League.'

'But they ain't in Silvertown . . .'

'Good day, Miss Archer.'

Mr Cotter was already holding open the door and the meeting was clearly over. Ruby stalked out with her head held high.

She had tried.

And now all she wanted to do was to get back to Sanctuary Road and bed.

'Thank you,' she said to Mrs Coleman as she passed the front counter. 'I know what you did back then and I'm ever so grateful.'

Mrs Coleman smiled. 'How did you get on?' she asked. 'By the look of you, the idea went down like a lead balloon.'

'It did,' said Ruby ruefully. 'Mr Cotter wouldn't even consider it. Maybe it's all a waste of time.'

Mrs Coleman tutted. 'Don't be disheartened by the likes of him,' she said, nodding her chin in the direction of Mr Cotter's office. 'You and I both know that it's a perfectly marvellous idea and one that's long overdue. Don't let a load of old ostriches with their heads buried in the sand put you off. You'll find some other way of making it work, you'll see.'

'Really?' said Ruby, hope flaring in her chest. 'Everyone seems to be telling me it's a terrible idea.'

'A difficult idea, not a terrible idea,' said Mrs Coleman. 'And if I wasn't a widow with children to support, I'd come out from behind this desk and help you, believe you me. Good luck to you, my dear.'

Ruby fairly skipped her way down the grey, windswept streets towards Mornington Crescent Underground Station.

It was as though a touchpaper had been lit inside her.

Far from being discouraged, everything suddenly seemed crystal clear. If neither the charities nor the vets were going to help her get an animal hospital off the ground – well, there was only one thing for it.

She was ruddy well going to have to do it on her own.

There was just one other person she needed to talk to first.

15

Now she knew where she was going, navigating the busy stalls didn't seem nearly as daunting as it had three weeks ago when Ruby had last been to the market. There was Schmidt's, still boarded up and apparently empty. And there was the barrow piled high with grisly bones, there was the attendant cloud of flies, and there was Nellie – headscarf on, sleeves rolled back to reveal muscular forearms – weighing and wrapping and taking money from the small queue of customers clustered around. She looked to be on her own this time, and Ruby hung back until there was a lull in business.

Goodness, she was tired.

It wasn't surprising: a night shift and then the meeting and the travel there and back and meeting 'him' . . . Maybe he was at the market himself. He clearly lived in Silvertown and . . .

'How's your boy's face?' asked Nellie, finally turning in her direction. 'Not here with you?'

'Not today,' said Ruby, impressed that Nellie remembered Mac. 'I've just been up to London. But it's cleared up nicely, ta.'

'Glad to hear it. And what can I get you today?'

'I've really come here to ask you a couple of questions, if that's all right?' said Ruby. 'But I'll take a couple of pounds without knobs on, please, while I'm about it.'

Nellie nodded. 'Fire away,' she said, deftly wrapping the meat in waxed paper and handing Ruby the already-oozing package.

'I were wondering if I could help you some mornings after me shift at the factory ends,' said Ruby, the words falling over each other in their rush to get out. 'Or maybe on me days off. I wouldn't charge you nothing, and in return, I were wondering if you could teach me all about caring for different types of animals.'

Nellie held up a gnarled hand. 'Hold your horses,' she said. 'I ain't no expert; I just likes to take an interest. And why do you want to know anyway? Got a menagerie at home, have you? Come from the circus?'

And she broke off into wheezing laughter.

'No,' said Ruby. 'But that brings me on to the second question.'

She hesitated, because she suddenly realised how much Nellie's answer mattered to her.

'Go ahead,' said Nellie.

'I'm thinking about trying to set up an animal hospital in Silvertown,' said Ruby. 'After what happened to Mac and seeing how little help there is and . . .'

She paused.

Would Nellie laugh?

Shut her down?

Please, please don't let her do either of those things . . .

But Nellie just put her head on one side. 'That ain't a question, is it?' she said. 'What did you actually want to ask me?'

Ruby paused, then dived in. 'Well, do you think people would come?' she said. 'If it were affordable – or even free – that is? Cos everyone I've spoken to seems to think the poor shouldn't be allowed to own animals or that we don't care for our animals or . . .'

'You and I both know that neither of those things is true,' interrupted Nellie. 'Of course we care for our animals. And of course people would come.'

'Thank you,' said Ruby. 'I just wanted to hear you say that. So you don't think I'm mad?'

Nellie patted Ruby's shoulder. 'You're mad as a hatter,' she said. 'But it takes a bit of madness to get anything done in this world. It won't be easy . . .'

'I know that,' said Ruby with a laugh. 'I've asked the vets and the charities but no one is interested . . .'

'I ain't surprised,' said Nellie. 'It always ends up with East Enders having to do things for themselves. It's just the way things are.'

East Enders doing things for themselves.

Yes!

Nellie had hit the nail on the head. The people who mattered thought the animal hospital was a good idea – and to hell with the rest of them.

East Enders doing things for themselves.

It had taken Ruby a while to work it out, but that was really what this was all about.

'And I'm happy to teach you everything I know,' said Nellie, pre-empting exactly what Ruby was thinking. 'Now, I do need a little extra help as it happens, because me daughter has just had a baby. And whilst I'm no expert, I have picked up a thing or two over the years.'

'How do you know so much about animals?' asked Ruby curiously. 'Is it just from working here?'

'Not likely,' said Nellie. 'Both sides of me family worked with dogs growing up. And as there weren't no one else to care for them if they got hurt or sick, we had to get smart pretty quick.'

'Did you breed dogs?' asked Ruby. 'Work on a farm? At the circus?'

'Mind your own beeswax,' said Nellie, with a laugh. 'No, I don't mind telling you this, but I don't want it going no further. Both me father's and me mother's family bred dogs to fight. I saw some pretty horrific injuries growing up, but I also learned the best way to care for them.'

'Oh,' breathed Ruby.

Dog fighting had been banned over eighty years ago – and quite rightly too, because it was cruel and hateful – but everyone knew that it still took place in secret all over the East End. In fact, Ruby was pretty sure that Pa had been along and placed bets from time to time. Nellie was a widow now, but Ruby wondered if her husband had carried on the family business . . .

'Either way, the customers chat about their animals all the time,' Nellie was saying, cutting across her thoughts. 'You'll learn as much about the right ways – and the wrong ways – of doing things from them as you will from me.'

'When can I start?' Ruby asked eagerly.

'Tomorrow do you?' asked Nellie. 'And I won't hear no nonsense about not being paid. I'll pay you the regular wage; it's not much compared to what you're getting at the Brunner Mond, but you're going to need all the money you can get for this clinic of yours.'

Nellie patted Ruby on the shoulder again and then

darted back behind the barrow to serve a patiently waiting customer.

Ruby wandered home, deep in thought.

Somehow, despite everything, it really had been a marvellous morning.

If she could only see 'him' again, it would have been absolutely perfect.

Ma and Aunt Maggie were both incredulous about Ruby's latest plan, and the conversation over supper that night was about little else.

'I'll never understand you, that I won't,' said Ma. 'You get yourself a well-paid job at the munitions factory and then choose to spend your spare time earning tuppence ha'penny up the market. But the animal clinic is a marvellous idea. Your pa would be proud of you.'

Aunt Maggie was, predictably, less charitable. 'Pie in the sky, more like,' she sniffed, spearing a circle of carrot with unnecessary force. 'An animal hospital, my arse. You'll be working with a bunch of ne'er-do-wells selling stinking offcuts from the abattoir and your pa's more likely to be turning in his grave. Bleeding ridiculous.'

'What do you think, Charlie?' asked Ruby. Her brother had backed her over Mac and it would be good to get a bit more familial support.

Charlie swallowed an enormous mouthful of stew and then nodded. 'I think it's a good idea,' he said. 'I hate seeing all the hurt animals on the street.'

Ruby patted his hand. 'Thank you,' she said. She suddenly felt a pang of regret; despite her intentions, she hadn't succeeded in getting any closer to her brother since she'd been home. 'How's your friend Joe?' she added. 'Are you still seeing a lot of him?'

Charlie shrugged. 'Suppose so,' he said.

Ma laughed. 'You see him all the time, love,' she said. 'I can't remember the last time you came straight home from school.'

Charlie just shrugged again.

'And how is he coping with his pa gone?' asked Ruby. 'It can't be easy for him.'

'Charlie is *such* a good friend to him,' said Ma, doling more stew on to Charlie's plate. 'After all, he knows what it's like to lose a father . . .'

She trailed off and Charlie looked as though he was about to shrug for the third time. But then he put down his knife and fork.

'Joe hates the Germans,' he said, to no one in particular.

'I ain't surprised,' said Ruby, surreptitiously dropping Mac a little piece of meat from her plate. 'I ain't too keen on them neither and they ain't killed me father.'

'No, but he really, *really* hates them,' said Charlie. 'He wants to get out there and fight them.'

'That's natural, love,' said Ma. 'Let's just hope that the war ends and we can all go back to normal before he has to go out there and do just that.'

'Nice attempt to change the conversation, Ruby,' said Aunt Maggie sourly. 'So, when exactly are you starting at the market?'

16

Several times over the next couple of weeks, Ruby was inclined to agree that working at Nellie's *was* 'bleeding ridiculous'.

She was so tired after her night at work that she could barely function at the barrow, and that horrible, detached 'looking at the world through a smeary windowpane' feeling lasted throughout the whole shift. Things weren't helped by the introduction of the government's latest initiative, the Daylight Saving Bill, in May when all clocks and watches had to move forward an hour. This not only made everyone lose an hour's sleep but meant that it was much darker and gloomier after Ruby's night shift.

And everything at the barrow was so smelly and messy and sticky. Worse, it felt that she was picking up precisely nothing about how to care for or treat sick animals. At first, Nellie had Ruby making up cat kebabs – grisly bits of meat and offal threaded on to wooden skewers to sell for a farthing – so she wasn't actually interacting with the customers at all.

The whole thing seemed to be a mistake of the hugest proportions.

Why on earth had Ruby thought it would be a good idea to work at the animal barrow purely to glean the odd nugget of information? It was such a roundabout route to increase her knowledge. She should have just taken Nellie out for a slap-up lunch, pumped her for everything she knew and been done with it.

Far better and far easier.

Gah.

Gradually, though, things began to get a bit easier. Ruby took to taking Mac up to the market with her, she was 'promoted' to serving customers and she began to see how it all worked. Her first, somewhat sobering observation was that many of the very poorest customers seemed to be buying the bones and entrails to feed their human families. On several occasions, she overheard women dressed in little more than rags swapping recipes and tips on how to make the resultant broths and stews more palatable for their husbands and children. Ruby's heart ached for them and she always endeavoured to give them extra. She vowed then and there that she would never turn her nose up at Ma's pork chops and hearty beef stews ever again.

Ruby's second observation was that the dogfood barrow really *was* being used as an informal animal clinic. Nellie had already alluded to this, of course, but it was fascinating to see how it actually worked in practice. People would come to the stall to buy their offcuts and their bones, but then they would stop to talk to Nellie and each other about their animals, their ailments and the various remedies and treatments that might be available to them. Often, they didn't even bother to buy anything – but just arrived looking for advice and reassurance. Sometimes they even brought their animals along for a more accurate 'diagnosis'.

In fact, the very first morning that Ruby was let loose

on the customers, a stooped and weather-beaten old man approached the barrow, leading a scrawny donkey with a swollen stomach. The donkey had been losing weight, the old man said, and no longer had the energy to pull his cart. As he made a living from carting seamen's belongings from ship to lodging house, this was naturally a potential disaster. Nellie had popped off on an errand and Ruby was powerless to advise, but the little crowd around the barrow soon sprang into action, patting and pressing the little donkey's flanks, inspecting the contents of her nosebag, and plying her owner with questions. Within minutes, a diagnosis had been made. In a bid to save money, the old man had been feeding his donkey packing straw he had picked up at the docks, unaware that it contained no nutritional value and was giving his poor donkey an acute case of indigestion – to say nothing of malnutrition. The best thing about it all was that there didn't seem to be any judgement or criticism of the old man – just an understanding that times were hard together with a genuine desire to help. Several people made suggestions on where the man might buy reasonably priced hay in future, and one man even offered to give him some tonic to help settle the poor donkey's stomach.

It was all rather lovely.

It wasn't all donkeys, of course. Over the next week, Ruby saw a variety of dogs and cats with all manner of ailments – to say nothing of the odd pet squirrel, badger, owl and monkey. And, again, if Nellie couldn't help with advice and remedies, there often seemed to be someone around who could. Ruby quickly learned that Dr Barker's Remedy was worth the money for colic if you could afford it, but that Young's Embrocation was nothing more than turpentine, oil and eggs and should be avoided like the plague. Garlic and honey were both a good cure-all and didn't cost the earth – and Nellie's salve was definitely worth saving up for. Alcohol or even a simple saline solution were both excellent in caring for wounds – a weak solution would irrigate and clean and a stronger one worked well as a disinfectant. On the other hand, putting a lump of pure sulphur in a dog's water bowl, as was the trend, was totally pointless as sulphur was insoluble in cold water. At least that one did no harm, because some people really did have the strangest ideas. One woman arrived saying she had been advised to put a length of wire up her dog's back passage and then tie it around his tail in order to deworm him. Ruby was relieved when Nellie roundly debunked that idea and suggested the woman try parsley water instead.

If only someone had put Mrs Driscoll right about setting fire to Mac's ear.

Ruby lapped all this information up and took to keeping a book in her apron pocket to make notes whenever she had a chance. If she was really going to open an animal clinic without veterinary support, she needed to know what worked and what didn't. And the afternoon she took the plunge and sent off for Day & Son's Dog Medicine Chest, felt like a red-letter occasion indeed. It cost twenty shillings – a whole pound! – but Nellie had given it the seal of approval and Ruby had to start somewhere. Besides, it contained everything she could think of and more – from lice killers to worm pills and liver pills to cough drops. There were various tonics to enable an animal to better fight off illness and infection, a black oil for wounds, cuts and bruises and a white oil for sprains, swellings and weak joints. And, on top of all that, there were *two* products to treat canker; if only Mrs Driscoll had had had access to either of those, Mac would have been saved an awful lot of pain and suffering. Almost best of all, the medicine chest came with a pamphlet entitled *Treatment of Dog Ailments*, which Ruby hoped would turn out to be as valuable as gold dust. Oh, she knew that – like Mrs Henderson's Milk Tray chocolates last Christmas – some of the selection would prove popular and some would be left languishing in the box for months, but at least there was the option to repurchase individual items as they ran out.

She was on her way!

Emboldened, Ruby decided to stock up on bandages as well, but here she drew a blank. It was impossible to get bandages for humans – they had all been sent to France – let alone anything specifically aimed at animals. Ruby vowed then and there to start making her own; her knitting skills had come on no end since Ma had reminded her how to knit socks for Harry, and bandages, by contrast, would be a piece of cake. She wondered if she would ever be brave enough to ask her colleagues at work to do the same.

In the meantime, she pumped Nellie for information for all she was worth. For the most part, Nellie answered Ruby's questions fully and good-humouredly, although occasionally she would sigh and say, 'Me ears hurt, girl. Give it a rest for a few minutes, eh?'

And Ruby would smile and do as she was told. Often-times, in those quieter moments, she would find her thoughts straying to 'him'. Sometimes she even thought she spotted him in the market crowd but was quickly disappointed. Silvertown Station was only a hop, skip and a jump away from the market, so there was every possibility that he might be there. Indeed, he might just turn up at the barrow one day. After all, he had been off to buy a dog and dogs needed to be fed . . . In fact, Ruby sometimes wondered if she had even taken the job at Nellie's because, deep down, she had deemed it the most likely place to bump into 'him' again.

Then she gave herself a little shake and told herself not to be so silly.

Hadn't the soldier all but run away from her after chatting for less than five minutes?

It was a ridiculous notion.

Of course, not every animal that came to Nellie's barrow could be saved.

There were some poor creatures who were simply too old or too ill or too injured to be cured, no matter how sound and well-meaning the advice. Ruby understood that; it was just part of the circle of life, and even the Bible talked about 'a time to live and a time to die'. Nonetheless, when Nellie first suggested that the kindest thing to do would be to destroy a cat that had been struck by a horse and cart, Ruby found herself shocked and upset.

'Come on, Ruby; you don't want the poor creature to suffer, do you?' said Nellie after the weeping owner had walked away.

'No, of course not,' said Ruby, although she rather felt like crying herself.

'We're very lucky to have a lethal chamber in Silvertown,' said Nellie. 'Father Murphy don't even charge if the owner is poor enough.'

Ruby exhaled, wondering if it was Father Murphy who had brought his lethal chamber into the munitions factory. And then, remembering all the cats that had lost their lives and that she hadn't really had a chance to mourn, Ruby found that she *was* crying; huge, tearing sobs that seemed to appear from nowhere and soon had her gasping for breath.

'Oh, Ruby; you mustn't take on so,' said Nellie, putting an arm around her. 'You can't save every stray or injured animal in Silvertown, you know.'

'I know,' said Ruby. 'But at work they kill people's perfectly healthy *pets* in the lethal chamber.'

And she told Nellie all about Mr Darcy and Sir Marmaduke and Fluffy and Jess.

'That's totally different,' Nellie agreed. 'Killing someone's pet with no warning *is* a dreadful thing to do.'

'I want to do something to change things,' said Ruby, wiping her eyes. 'I can't save the cats we lost but I can try to make sure it don't happen again. I had a look at some books in the library, but I don't really know where to begin.'

'Well, two heads is better than one,' said Nellie. 'I doubt they'll stop bringing the lethal chamber into the factory altogether, so let's see if we can hatch a plan.'

Ruby smiled at her gratefully. 'Well, I suppose the first thing is stopping the cats from getting in in the first place,' she said. 'They're squeezing through the metal fence posts at the moment. It showed you how to make a chicken coop in one of the books and I thought that sort of wire might help . . .'

'Yes. It's actually called chicken wire,' said Nellie. 'Cats might be able to scramble up it, of course, but at least it would make things more difficult for them. And what about planting things like lemon balm and curry herb? Cats absolutely hate them. If you planted them around the edge of the site – especially where the houses are – and also added some dense prickly bushes, it might put them off even more.'

'That's a marvellous idea,' said Ruby, perking up. 'And, of course, we'd have to discourage people from petting and feeding the ones that *do* get in. We could even put signs forbidding it around the site.'

Nellie nodded. 'With all that going on, I can't see a single cat either wanting or being able to come in,' she said with a smile.

'The trouble is, though, that the cats are also used as mousers,' said Ruby. 'If we're too successful and keep *all* the cats out, there would be a huge vermin problem. I can't see management standing for *that*.'

'What about official mousers, then?' said Nellie. 'They could live on site and wear special collars so that they're spared if the lethal chambers do still come in.'

'That's a wonderful idea,' said Ruby. 'And we'd give them all names so that everyone knows who they are . . .'

'Saints' names,' added Nellie with a wheezy cackle. 'Really fancy ones. No one would dare mess with them then . . .'

'Balthazar,' said Ruby with a giggle, trying to remember what she had been taught at Sunday school.

'Adjutor.'

'Erasmus. Is that even a saint?'

'Who knows?' said Nellie. 'You'd have fooled me, anyway.'

The two collapsed into giggles and Ruby suddenly felt much more positive. They weren't bad ideas, and in any case, they were a start. She would write them up and then work out who best to hand them on to.

Thanks to Nellie and the notion of East Enders doing things for themselves, she was well on her way.

17

Meanwhile, life at the munitions factory went on.

By now, Ruby knew all the tasks on the production line well enough to do them with her eyes closed. Once, in fact, she *had* tried to fit a detonator cap with her eyes closed and had managed to do quite a passable job – even if Mary had asked if she was feeling quite all right?

Ruby knew the names of all the women at her table as well as the names of their husbands and children and pets. She joined in with the chatter and even with the impromptu singalongs which started out of nowhere from time to time. The workers sang all sorts. Sometimes the songs were sentimental and nostalgic like 'Roses of Picardy', sometimes they encouraged a positive attitude despite the hardships of war, like 'Pack Up Your Troubles in Your Old Kit-Bag' and sometimes they were even humorous like 'Goodbye-ee', which never failed to lighten the mood and to get them all giggling.

Ruby even tentatively started making suggestions about how the women might care for their animals if problems and issues ever came up in conversation.

She suggested that Irene try a mixture of honey and garlic when her old tomcat was wounded in a scrap.

She cautioned Mary against buying a particular brand of herbal digestive for her dog because she had heard it regularly pooh poohed up at the barrow.

She was even able to pass on the tip about not feeding old packing straw to mules to a docker's wife who really should have known better.

And the first time someone specifically came up to her and asked for advice on a poorly cat felt like an important day indeed.

Meanwhile, Ruby finished carefully writing up her ideas for protecting the cats who wandered on to the Brunner Mond factory grounds. Then she spent an extra day debating who to give it to. She could – and perhaps *should* – give it straight to the head of maintenance, but somehow she felt that Miss Richardson might be a good intermediary. After all, Miss Richardson had loved the cats just as much as Ruby, and so surely she would be keen to make sure the same thing never happened again. The trouble was that she and Miss Richardson hadn't seen each other for weeks and had hardly parted on the best of terms. There was every possibility that Miss Richardson would simply throw out her notes.

Eventually, though, Ruby decided it was worth the risk. Despite their falling-out, she was sure that Miss Richardson would choose to do the right thing – whatever she deemed that to be. So she wrote a short note explaining what she had done and left it, together with her neatly written notes, clearly labelled in the reception building.

That evening, Ruby was particularly exhausted.

The night shifts, working at Nellie's, writing up her notes . . . it had all been too much. Bent over her boxes of little springs and half-assembled detonators, it was all she could do to keep her eyes open.

And then, around 11 p.m., the factory sirens went off.

Ruby had never heard the ear-splitting noise close-up before and, in her befuddled state, it took a moment for her to work out what was going on. But then the electric lights went out, someone yelled 'Zeppelins' and suddenly every muscle, every fibre was on high alert.

Zeppelins!

Ruby would never forget the first Zeppelin raid the year before, when she'd been living in Hampstead. She remembered the fear crackling through her body as the first sleek 'baby killer' slid into the skies, silently opened a trapdoor and unleashed bombs, carnage and panic on to the city below. It had been the first time the Great War had truly come to the home front and it had seemed so fantastical, so futuristic . . . so utterly terrifying. She had hidden in the mansion basement with everyone else, and even though the Zeppelins hadn't come within ten miles of Hampstead, it had felt like days until her heart rate had returned to normal.

Since then, things had calmed down; good old Blighty fog and general bad weather had seen to that. There had been other attempted raids, of course – some successful – but all those targeting London had ended without incident. Despite Ma's warnings when she had first moved home about the East End being a likely target, Ruby had allowed herself to be lulled into a false sense of security and had been sleeping as soundly as a baby . . .

More fool her!

Nervously, Ruby followed the other women streaming from the detonation shop and into the cold night air. Maybe it was a false alarm. Or the Zeppelin would be miles away . . . or the raid would end in failure as so many had done before. Maybe they would all shelter somewhere together without any real fear . . . and it would even be quite fun.

With a bit of luck, she might even be able to catch up on some sleep.

There were no lights outside and it was eerily dark.

It was a clear, moonless night; the ideal conditions for a strike. Dozens of faces anxiously scanned the sky. And there they were. One . . . two . . . three . . . four . . . no, five . . . *five*! . . . huge airships over to the west and silently heading in their direction.

Oh God.

Frightened voices began to ring out, barely audible above the sirens.

'They're following the direction of the Thames.'

'They're heading in this direction.'

'We might well be the target this time.'

'Run, everyone, *run*!'

The last was Mrs Mason – authoritative rather than frightened – punctuating her command by blowing loudly on a whistle. 'Run, everyone,' she shouted again. 'Stay calm, remember your training. Muster back here when the all-clear sounds. And good luck.'

She blew her whistle again and everyone started running helter-skelter. Ruby tried to remember the quick safety briefing. The main thing was to get well away from the Brunner Mond building; it didn't matter in what direction, you just had to try and put as much distance between yourself and all that TNT as you possibly could . . .

Ruby followed a stream of workers to the nearest exit, thanking her lucky stars that she wasn't hobbling along in wooden clogs as so many were. Once on the street outside, she hesitated and glanced up at the sky again. The Zeppelins were very close now – and closing in all the time. Could the pilots see them all, running like rats from a ship? For the first time since the war started, Ruby felt genuine fear. There was a very real chance the Zeppelins were specifically targeting the factory, and if they scored a direct hit, the place would go sky high, destroying everything within a half-mile radius.

Where should she go?

What should she do?

Ruby resisted the urge to run home. She wanted nothing more than to be back on Sanctuary Lane with Ma and her arms around Mac's neck and her face buried into Tess's fragrant fur. Even Aunt Maggie would be a comfort at a time like this! But it wasn't a good idea. She had come out of the factory on the far side from Sanctuary Lane, a good twenty minutes away. And Ma and the others might not even be at home. There was no basement and they might have judged it just too risky to stay put.

But what would happen to Mac and Tess if they were left alone?

Maybe she *should* try to get back . . .

A whistle blown from behind shocked Ruby out of her thoughts. It was a bobby on a bike, pointing directly at her.

'Don't stop,' he shouted. 'Take cover.'

And he was gone.

Ruby looked blindly around at the scores of people seemingly running in different directions. Where exactly should she take cover? All over London, people would be sheltering deep below ground in Tube stations, but Silvertown Station was part of the North London line, its tracks defiantly above ground. There was the Woolwich foot tunnel under the Thames, of course – but that was dangerously close to the Woolwich munitions factory and was also in the very direction the Zeppelins were heading . . .

'The foot tunnel under the old docks road,' panted a voice behind her.

Ruby swung around.

It was Mary.

Of course. The foot tunnel.

Ruby rarely had cause to go to that part of town but she knew exactly where it was – and it wasn't too far away. Impulsively, she reached out and grabbed Mary's hand.

'Come on,' she said, with another fearful glance to the sky. 'No time to lose!'

Hand in hand, the two women ran through the streets. Where once there would have been the spit and crackle of gaslights, all was darkness and it was hard to see where the pavement ended and the road began. More than once they stumbled over the kerb, so in the end they ran down the middle of the road instead. But then Mary started hobbling and slowing right down. For a second, Ruby was tempted to leave her and run to safety – every woman for herself – but, somehow, she couldn't. Or, more to the point, she *wouldn't*. Mary had been very kind to her over the past few weeks and it simply wouldn't do to abandon her.

'Come on, Mary. Nearly there.'

If one of the Zeppelins dropped its load now and hit

the munitions factory, that would be that. They needed to speed up, no two ways about it.

'Leave me, pet, and get yourself to safety.'

'I'm not leaving you.'

Come on.

Nearly there.

And there, finally, was the entrance to the tunnel with people streaming into it from all directions. Ruby slowed down and let go of Mary's hand and the two women were immediately separated from each other by the crowd. Ruby was swept along in the crush – through the mouth of the tunnel and down the slope under the road. Here, it really was pitch black. Only the occasional beam from a flashlight punctuated the darkness, and most of the time Ruby had to put her hands in front of her head to protect herself as she shuffled forwards.

But at least it was safe.

If the Zeppelin discharged its deadly load now – even if it was directly on top of them – hopefully the tunnel would hold and they would be protected. And, because there were two entrances, hopefully they would not get trapped inside.

The ground in front of Ruby started climbing slightly and she stopped walking. There was no point in inching forwards until she emerged right out the other side of the tunnel – no point at all. Besides, there were people coming in the other direction and walking towards her and everything was grinding to a halt anyway. She could hear shouts of 'move up' both in front of *and* behind her.

Then Ruby sensed – rather than saw – people beginning to sit down around her. She hesitated, wondering if she should do the same. If she sat down, she would be better able to protect a space around her, but on the other hand, if there was a crush, it might prove dangerously difficult to get up again. It was like being on the Tube, she thought incongruously; there could be the devil of a crush near the entrances whilst the people standing between the seats remained widely spaced. Either way, she judged it safe enough to slide down the tunnel wall and sit down. The bricks were cold and clammy against her back and she began to seriously regret not bringing her coat.

Where the Dickens was Mary?

Where were her family?

Please let everyone be safe.

Ruby wasn't sure how long she sat there – knees to chin, hands clasped around her legs – before the explosions started. Her sopping back and numb bottom suggested it was hours, but it was probably only a matter of minutes. Either way, the first boom almost made her jump out of her skin and a strangled cry escaped her lips – one that was echoed up and down the tunnel. The explosion was muffled and sounded like it came from a fair distance – further than the factory or Sanctuary Lane – and it was quickly followed by a second and then a third. There was no immediate way of knowing whether the Zeppelin was coming closer or heading further away.

'Bleeding heck; that's a Jack Johnson,' came a voice.

'A Jack . . . what?' another voice replied.

'Largest shell used by the Germans.'

Well, that was reassuring!

Ruby buried her face in her hands and willed it all to

stop. Then, as the explosions died away, she became aware of someone moaning in fear next to her. It was quiet – so quiet she had to strain to hear it – but it was definitely there. What was more, Ruby was pretty sure it was a *man*, and for some reason, that shocked her more than anything. Women cried all the time, but men were brought up not to show their emotions. She had *never* heard Pa cry, not even when his own father, Grandpa Wilf, had died.

Another explosion echoed through the tunnel and Ruby felt as much as heard the man next to her whimper. It was an involuntary, almost animal cry of distress, hastily smothered, and it cut Ruby to the quick. Whatever terror she might be feeling, her neighbour was feeling it ten times over and was clearly in acute distress. Ruby was just wondering how to respond when another explosion rocked the tunnel.

'Duck!' the man shouted. 'Shell incoming. Get back in the bloody trench!'

Ruby couldn't ignore it any longer.

She reached out and groped in the darkness for the stranger's hand and, on finding it, held it firmly in her own. At first, the man flinched, but Ruby hung on tight, hoping he would think that it was she who was seeking comfort. Eventually she felt the man's hand relax and his fingers – warm and dry – enveloped hers. Ruby realised instinctively that the fellow's mind had been far, far away – caught somewhere between the trenches of war and the horrors in his own head.

She leaned over towards him. 'Don't worry,' she whispered. 'It will be all right.'

It was a meaningless thing to say, because how could she possibly be sure that everything *would* be all right?

They were sheltering with dozens – probably hundreds – of other folk whilst the Germans tried their damnedest to hit a munitions factory which would blast them all to kingdom come. Still, she had to try and keep the man calm – both because it was the kind thing to do and because panic could be contagious and the last thing any of them needed was a wild stampede.

The man leaned closer to her, so close that their shoulders were touching. 'Did I shout out?' he murmured, his breath hot against her cheek.

Ruby hesitated. 'We all did,' she replied carefully.

'No. I mean, did I shout any words? Anything . . . unusual?'

Ruby paused again. But if she couldn't be honest now, in the dark, with a stranger, whilst innocent Londoners were, no doubt, being killed and maimed all around them, then when could she be?

'You said something about ducking from the shells and getting back into the trench,' she said. 'But there was that much noise going on around us I doubt if anyone else heard.'

The last bit was probably true; a lot of people had shouted out at the last blast, and besides, everyone was, no doubt, absorbed with their own worries.

The man exhaled a raggedy sigh. 'I thought I might have done,' he said. 'Feels like I've been going bleeding mad ever since that shell blew me off me horse.'

'You've been at the front, then?'

'Yes,' the man said shortly.

Ruby stretched out a leg. 'Me brother's in the army,' she said. 'He joined up nearly three months ago now.'

She wondered about asking if the man had come across Harry – but she knew that that would be ridiculous. Harry hadn't been anywhere near the various fronts. He hadn't even left Blighty yet, for goodness' sake!

'Ah. Part of Kitchener's new army,' the soldier was saying.

'Yes,' said Ruby. 'He were conscripted to the forty-seventh Division.'

'Where is he now?' asked the soldier.

'Somewhere in Buckinghamshire.'

They had received Harry's latest letter, short and to the point, a few days previously and Ruby had already replied and sent him the socks she'd made him in between knitting animal bandages.

'Basic training, then,' said the soldier. 'He's got a while to go. He'll probably be transferred to Witley Camp or somewhere else in Surrey for final preparations before being deployed.'

Ruby breathed a sigh of relief. 'Is it really terrible out there?' she ventured.

The man hesitated. 'Do you want me to whitewash it for you?' he asked.

'No,' said Ruby. '*No.*'

If Harry was about to join the fighting, the very least she could do was hear what he might have to go through.

'It's hell on earth,' said the soldier.

Despite the subject matter, they were speaking more easily, unconcerned that they might be overheard. There was something very freeing about the darkness, and besides, there was a little chatter all around them now.

'Tell me.'

And so the soldier told Ruby all about the mud and the vermin and the disease and going over the top and the shells and the terror. The bombs were still falling around them, but he was no longer shouting out. He was totally absorbed in telling her what he had lived through and where he would presumably be returning once his leave was over.

How could he bear it?

How could *she* bear it for Harry?

'I'm so sorry,' she said. 'I . . . didn't really have any idea. Your poor family must have gone through hell.'

'They didn't know,' said the soldier simply. 'We promise that we won't tell the truth in our letters. In any case, they get read and censored, if necessary.'

'But why?' Ruby was so outraged, she was quite forgetting where she was and her voice had risen. Someone nearby shushed her, although to do so seemed a little ridiculous. The men in the Zeppelins would hardly be able to hear them.

'Because the powers that be think that if people know what it's really like out there, it would all be over,' said the man, his voice back to a whisper. 'Public opinion would turn against it, men and boys would avoid the draft and the war would end in a heartbeat.'

'I wish it would,' said Ruby fervently.

'Me too,' said the soldier. 'Funny, it takes sitting in the dark holding hands with someone you ain't never going to see again, to get you to open out. I've never spoken about it like this to anyone before.'

'I'm going to be reading Harry's letters in a different light now,' said Ruby.

170

'He's in Buckinghamshire, for goodness' sake!' said the soldier.

There was a laugh in his voice and it was a lovely voice, Ruby realised. The same accent as her, but deep and rich and resonant.

'True!' she said with a little giggle. 'He's probably safer there than he were working at the docks!'

A strong wind whipped along the tunnel and she shivered. 'Lordy, I wish I'd brought me coat,' she said.

'I'm so sorry.' The soldier dropped her hand and started staggering to his feet. 'Please, you must take mine.'

'No! I didn't mean that,' said Ruby, pulling on him to sit down again.

'I can't believe I didn't offer before.'

'To be fair, you can't see I ain't wearing one, unless you can see in the dark.'

Suddenly, against all odds, the pair were snuffling with laughter together. And then the soldier took his coat off anyway and laid it across Ruby's shoulders and, despite having said she didn't want it, Ruby wriggled into it anyway. It was lovely and warm and several sizes too big.

'There now. You're wearing my coat, but we ain't been introduced,' said the soldier. 'I'm Jack.'

'Hello, Jack. I'm Ruby.'

Ruby liked the name Jack. It was down-to-earth, honest and friendly – rather like the soldier himself. And just sharing their first names somehow seemed appropriate. Down here, everyone was stripped of their identity, everything reduced to the bare essentials. It didn't matter where people lived or how much money they had.

Everyone was united in sheltering from a common foe.

There was another explosion and then some kind of commotion nearby. It was hard to work out what was going on in the darkness, but Ruby felt the crowd surging. Someone staggered against her knees and then moved away. Once the ringing from the blast had died away, there was also the babble of alarmed voices.

'Everyone all right back there?'

The authoritative voice came from the river side of the tunnel, the way Ruby had come in. Then a torch started playing around. It shone right into Ruby's eyes before playing over the crowd, moving to the tunnel ceiling, and going out.

'We've got a fainter,' someone near Ruby called back.

So that was what had happened.

'Need any help?' came the original voice. 'We've got smelling salts here.'

'No need. We're too wedged in for her to have done much damage.'

'Hang tight. Shouldn't be long now. Folks near the entrance say the Zeps are moving away to the east.'

Jack took Ruby's hand again and squeezed it tight. The gesture would have been impossibly forward in the cold light of day, but somehow seemed entirely appropriate given the current circumstances.

'*Oh là là.* Thank the heavens for that,' he said fervently. 'We'll all live to fight another day.'

Ruby didn't reply.

'Did you hear the man?' Jack persisted. 'Looks like we're out of the woods.'

Ruby still didn't answer.

She *couldn't*.

In fact, she felt as though she was rooted to the floor in shock.

Because, when the torch had briefly illuminated the tunnel, she had caught a glimpse of the man squeezing her hand. He had been partially turned away from her, facing the torch beam, as she was, so she had only seen his face in profile. A strong nose, firm chin, wavy, light brown hair . . .

She was almost sure it was him.

The soldier from the station.

Him.

18

Ruby sat there, thoughts awhirl.

Should she say something?

Tell Jack they had already met at Silvertown Station?

No, what was the point?

It had been the very briefest of meetings – in fact, they had hardly spoken. Jack probably wouldn't remember it at all – and that would be embarrassing, as well as making it blatantly clear that he had certainly left an impression on her.

But then again, he had run away from her, for goodness' sake! One moment he'd been saying he was going to get a train, and the next he'd been fairly running back up the stairs to the ticket office to get away from her. Whatever impression she'd made on him, it certainly hadn't been a favourable one.

Oh, this was all so embarrassing!

Ruby exhaled noisily, trying to process her thoughts. It didn't really matter what she did, one way or another. Jack had made a point of saying he'd only unburdened himself to her because he knew he was never going to see her again, and so that was that. He would be heading back to the front soon enough anyway, and no doubt he had a wife or a sweetheart to boot. There was nothing to lose by casually mentioning they'd met before at Silvertown Station.

But then again . . .

Gah!

Ruby was no closer to deciding what to do, when the all-clear sounded. The murmur of relieved voices broke out all around them, interspersed with one or two cheers. And then Jack was helping her to her feet and the stretching of limbs and the slow shuffle out of the tunnel began. Ruby lost Jack almost at once in the melee and inched forward alone. Lost in her thoughts, she let chattering voices wash over her from all sides.

Finally, outside, Ruby blinked, her eyes getting used to the relative brightness. People milled around, greeting and hugging each other and reuniting with those they'd become separated from. It was a strange atmosphere, almost one of tempered celebration – except that the sky was stained a grotesque red and orange across the river and the Zeppelins could still be seen in the distance and it really wasn't a celebration at all.

Ruby saw Jack straight away. Side on to her, hands behind his back, he seemed even more handsome than when she'd seen him at the station. He was glancing around – obviously looking for *her* – and, almost shyly, she made her way over to him.

'Jack,' she called, when she was nearly up to him. He didn't reply so she said his name again, a little louder this time. '*Jack.*'

Jack turned. He registered his army greatcoat and then looked at her face. And, to Ruby's dismay, the little smile that had been on his lips died away and he suddenly looked thoroughly discomfited.

Oh goodness.

What on earth was it about her that invited such a response?

'Hello,' said Ruby, when she drew level.

'Hello,' said Jack. 'We've met before, haven't we? At the railway station. I hadn't realised it was you.'

'No,' said Ruby. 'I don't expect you had. I hadn't either . . .'

Her mouth was suddenly dry and she couldn't think of what else to say.

Jack ran a hand over his face. 'I were very rude that day,' he said. 'Might I see you home and then I might explain along the way?'

He sounded so formal after the intimacy of their conversation in the tunnel that, despite everything, Ruby had to smother a laugh.

'Thank you, but I'm not going home,' she replied. 'I've got to report back on duty now we've been given the all-clear.'

'On duty?' Jack echoed.

'I work at the munitions factory,' said Ruby, gesturing to her overalls, and fancied, to her satisfaction, that Jack looked suitably impressed.

'I see,' he said. 'Well . . . might I see you back there, then?'

Even though there would be safety in numbers in the dozens of munitions workers returning to the factory, Ruby found that she would very much like to be escorted back to work.

But just then, a voice floated over to them.

'Our Ruby's a fast worker, ain't she? Look at her over there with that soldier. She's already wearing his coat and all!'

Ruby stiffened. She didn't even have to look across to know that the voice belonged to Elspeth. Ruby hadn't thought about her for weeks – hadn't realised she'd also transferred to the night shift – and now, here she was, ruining everything. One glance at Jack's face, and the muscle pulsating in his cheek, showed that he had heard every word as well.

Damn Elspeth, her careless comments and her piercing voice.

Damn her for making everything seem cheap and tawdry.

Damn, damn, *damn* her.

'Don't be beastly, Elspeth,' came another voice which Ruby recognised as Dot's. 'There's no reason to think that she's on the make.'

'She's a nutjob, Dot,' said Elspeth. 'She spent all her time with the cats and sucking up to that boring manager! You was just about her only friend and she even ignored *your* note after she was moved off the factory floor. But look at her moving in on that soldier! Still, they say the quietest ones are the worst.'

This time, Ruby couldn't even look at Jack.

She was just too humiliated.

She stared at the ground, wishing that it would open and swallow her whole.

'There you are, dear!' It was Mary – lovely Mary – appearing silently at her shoulder. 'I lost you as soon as we went in. Goodness, I'm feeling *very* shaky. Would you be so kind as to walk me back to the factory?'

Ruby was almost – *almost* – relieved.

'Of course, Mary,' she said, shrugging herself out of

the greatcoat and passing it over to Jack. 'Much obliged to you for lending me this,' she added politely, offering him no eye contact at all. 'I do hope the rest of your leave is less eventful.'

Jack looked like he was about to say something, but Ruby didn't wait to hear what it was. Blinking back tears, she linked arms with Mary, and walked resolutely away.

She wouldn't look back.

And she would probably never see him again.

Mary started up an almost immediate stream of chatter about the drama and horror of the night, but Ruby found that she couldn't respond. She couldn't even concentrate on what Mary was saying; there were just too many thoughts going around and around in her head and too many emotions jostling for supremacy. Most of them, of course, revolved around Jack, and just wanted to make her cry. After a while, Mary – clearly suddenly feeling a lot less shaky – gave up and peeled off to join a couple of other women from the factory.

Ruby was left on her own.

Maybe she should retrace her steps.

Look for Jack . . .

'Ruby!'

A woman's voice.

Not Jack.

It took a moment for Ruby to realise that the woman with the light brown hair who had drawn level with her was Miss Richardson. Panting from exertion and with her hair falling any old how, she was almost unrecognisable from the prim, buttoned-up manager at work. For a start, she looked much younger – she probably wasn't actually much older than Ruby.

'Good evening, Miss,' said Ruby, trying to put thoughts of Jack firmly behind her. 'Was you in the tunnel and all?'

'I was,' said Miss Richardson. 'Our lodgings aren't far away and it was the obvious place to come. Goodness, what a night! Those poor people over the river who got caught up in it all.'

'I know, Miss,' said Ruby. 'It don't bear thinking about.'

She glanced around, wondering if Elspeth had noticed her walking with Miss Richardson and what she might have to say about that. But then she realised that she just didn't care what Elspeth thought.

'I just wanted to let you know that I got your notes about the cats,' said Miss Richardson.

'Oh!' Ruby was confused. 'But I only dropped them off this evening.'

'I was working late,' said Miss Richardson. 'I picked them up before I went home and read them in bed. I can't say how impressed I am by them, Ruby, and by all the thought you've put into them.'

'Really, Miss?' Ruby could feel herself flushing with pleasure. 'Nellie from the barrow helped me with some of the ideas.'

'Well, whoever helped you, I think they're marvellous,' said Miss Richardson. 'I'll read them through properly in the morning and let you know if I can suggest any changes. And then, when we're both happy, we'll send them on to Mr Armstrong who oversees maintenance and keep our fingers crossed that he takes them – or at least some of them – on board.'

'Thank you, Miss,' said Ruby fervently. And then she added, for it had never been addressed, 'I'm ever so sorry about what happened the day the cats died. I overreacted something dreadful and I were terribly rude. Especially when you'd just saved me job.'

'And *I* was a pompous nincompoop,' said Miss Richardson ruefully. 'I'm so sorry I dismissed what you were saying – especially considering the ideas you've just come up with. I promise that I will never underestimate you again. And I didn't save your job; I don't have nearly that sort of authority, I'm afraid. Mr Briggs said he didn't want you in his department so I just made sure you were re-allocated somewhere that might suit you better.'

Ruby nodded. 'It does suit me better,' she said. 'So I'm ever so grateful, really, I am. Although I did think you must be furious with me, packing me off to the night shift like that!'

'Furious with you?' echoed Miss Richardson. 'Of course I wasn't furious. I just hadn't realised all the day-shift positions in the detonation shed had already been filled. And, to be honest, I thought it might be easier if you weren't bumping into Mr Briggs all the time.'

'Right, Miss,' said Ruby, feeling much happier.

Miss Richardson had stopped walking. 'I go this way,' she said, pointing down a side street. 'Back to bed for me.'

'Goodnight, Miss,' said Ruby. 'I'm ever so glad we had this chat.'

'Me too,' said Miss Richardson. She paused. 'There's just one more thing,' she added. 'If I'm being perfectly honest, the other reason I moved you to the night shift is that there had been some comment about the two of us chatting together on the grass. I thought it might be easier for you – for both of us – if we couldn't do it any more.'

Ruby wasn't sure how to respond. 'I'm sorry if talking to me caused you any embarrassment, Miss,' she said carefully. 'I'd hate for you to get in trouble on my account.'

'I wouldn't have got into trouble, as such,' said Miss Richardson. 'It was just some people might not have found it very seemly. And, to be perfectly frank, I did initially wonder if us becoming friends was entirely appropriate given our different upbringings and my managerial position at the factory.'

'I understand, Miss,' said Ruby.

And she did.

Entirely.

It was rotten but it was just the way things were.

'But then, to be honest, I changed my mind,' said Miss Richardson. 'Seeing you with the cats made me realise how much we've got in common, and these notes have quite sealed things for me. We both love animals and we both want to make a difference. Why shouldn't we be able to chat and be friends if we both want to be?'

'Because it don't work like that, Miss,' said Ruby simply. 'I've loved chatting to you too, but I've heard the odd comment as well. People just don't like it.'

'It's stuff and nonsense,' said Miss Richardson. 'I'm not even that senior, for goodness' sake. Just a personnel manager for the duration.'

Everyone had disappeared and the street was almost deserted by this time.

'I need to be getting back to work, Miss,' said Ruby gently.

'Of course you do,' said Miss Richardson. 'I'm sorry. But I just wonder – how would you feel about meeting *out* of work? I've taken to feeding the strays under the arches from time to time. Perhaps you would care to join me?'

'I would like that very much, Miss,' said Ruby.

And she meant it.

She had occasionally fed the strays herself – even though you weren't really meant to any more – but she hadn't yet ventured under the arches.

'Marvellous,' said Miss Richardson. 'Perhaps we could have tea afterwards. I'd love to hear more about how you think an animal hospital might work and what I might do to help get it up and running.'

'That would be lovely, Miss,' said Ruby. 'And I can think of one thing right off the bat that you could do to help. What's your knitting like?'

Miss Richardson laughed. 'Not bad at all,' she said. 'I'm already knitting socks for the soldiers but I'm happy to knit something for you too. What would you like?'

'Bandages,' said Ruby promptly. 'I don't want you to stop knitting for the soldiers, but the odd bandage would be marvellous.'

'Of course,' said Miss Richardson. 'I'll ask some of the other managers to do the same thing too. But all this is on one condition.'

'What's that, Miss?'

'That you stop calling me Miss! As I've already told you, my name is Leah.'

That felt very strange – rather like Mrs Henderson suddenly inviting all the servants to call her Fanny.

But then Ruby gave a little shrug.

Why not?

'Very well,' she said. 'But I'd like to set a condition of me own, if you don't mind.'

'Go on,' said Leah, with a little smile.

'We take it in turns to pay,' said Ruby, anxious to establish the rules of their friendship from the outset.

'Done!' said Leah. 'Let's meet in the next week or two. I'll check our respective days off and get a message to you.'

'Done,' echoed Ruby.

'Oh, and by the way,' added Leah with a grin. 'That was a very handsome soldier you were talking to outside the tunnel just now. I look forward to hearing all about *him*!'

If only there would be something to say.

As soon as Ruby got back to the factory, she went in search of Dot.

The comment that Elspeth had made about Dot leaving her a message had piqued her interest. The point was that Ruby hadn't received a note; indeed, she hadn't even known that such a message existed. She had just assumed that Dot wanted nothing more to do with her and had, regretfully, tried to put their budding friendship from her mind. The note put everything in a different light . . .

Ruby managed to find Dot by the lavvies before either of them reported back on duty.

'Hello,' she said with a wary smile, unsure of the reception that she would get. 'What a night!'

'Too right,' replied Dot, looking equally wary. 'It's only me second shift on nights so it's all been quite a shock.'

There was a slightly awkward pause and then Ruby took a deep breath.

'I heard what Elspeth said outside the tunnel . . .' she started.

Dot pulled a face. 'I'm sorry,' she interrupted. 'She had no right . . .'

'Don't worry, I ain't bothered. But she mentioned a note . . .'

The wary look on Dot's face was back. 'Yes,' she said. 'The note I put through your door the day after . . .'

'I never received it. I don't know what it said, but whatever it was, I never got it.'

'Oh!' Dot looked completely nonplussed. 'It just said that I were really sorry about the factory cats and about not being able to convince Miss Pankhurst to support an animal hospital, but that I thought your idea a perfectly marvellous one and I wanted to help in any way I could. And then, when I didn't hear back, I assumed you thought I hadn't tried hard enough and that you didn't want to be friends no more . . .'

'No. *No*,' said Ruby. 'It were a huge thing for you to even ask Miss Pankhurst and I'm ever so grateful that you tried. But I didn't get the note – it's probably been tucked behind Harry's picture on the mantelpiece by someone and then forgotten about – and I just assumed you were angry with *me* for asking such a big favour of you. That and for behaving like such a chump in front of Mr Briggs.'

'I were in *awe* of you for standing up to Mr Briggs,' said Dot simply. 'Oh, hark at the pair of us. It's a good thing we ain't in charge of the war effort with us getting crossed wires over something so simple.'

'Ain't it just?' said Ruby. 'Walk home together after our shift?'

'Of course,' said Dot. 'If I can stay awake until then. By the way, who *was* the soldier in the tunnel? He looked jolly nice if I might say so meself.'

19

Nine dead.

Forty injured.

And that was just in London.

The news spread up and down the factory as the sun rose and the night shift finally ended.

Thirteen Zeppelins had set out from Germany and, although only five had reached London, they had managed to drop thirty-six bombs south of the river in a ten-minute window.

'*Ten minutes!*' said Dot to Ruby as they walked home together. 'I felt like we was in that tunnel for *hours*.'

'Me too,' agreed Ruby. Her little cocoon with Jack seemed to have lasted forever. 'But nine people dead,' she added morosely. 'Nine people heard the same air-raid sirens we did – and now they're dead. It just ain't fair.'

'It really ain't,' said Dot. 'Let's talk about something more cheerful. What can I do to help with the animal hospital?'

Ruby perked up. 'Store things. Make bandages. Fundraise,' she said with a laugh, counting them off on her fingers. 'Is that enough to be going on with?'

'Consider them all done,' said Dot. 'Well, the bandages I can speak for now and I'm sure Ma and Pa will say yes to the others. There's a big cupboard out the back which is nearly empty and I'll persuade Ma to let me leave a fundraising tin in the shop.'

That would do nicely.

Yes, that would do very nicely indeed.

Ruby arrived home determined to discover who had absent-mindedly hidden or disposed of Dot's note, but no sooner had she set foot through the front door than Charlie appeared looking worried. 'Mac's hurt,' he said.

Her heart rate suddenly going like the clappers, Ruby ran into the kitchen. Everything looked as it always did at this time of the morning. Her mother was tending the range; in fact, Ma had always spent so much time in front of the big, black beast that Pa used to joke he saw more of her backside than her face! Aunt Maggie was taking the dirty breakfast plates through to the scullery. That was perfectly normal too, as was her sour expression at clapping eyes on Ruby. What was more unusual was that Mac was in the kitchen too. He'd usually be outside in the yard whilst everyone else was scurrying about. But there he was, lying on the hearth rug, with Tess cuddled against him and his back to Ruby. He hadn't heard her come in, but when she bent down to stroke him, he turned about, nearly squashing Tess, and . . .

Oh!

Despite what Charlie had already told her, Ruby couldn't help but cry out in shock. There was a huge, oozing cut on the left side of Mac's face – the side that had been burned. Blood had dripped on to his chest and paws and the white fur was stained a watery crimson.

Ruby fell to her knees and took Mac's head in her hands. 'Oh, no!' she cried.

Ma came and laid her hand on Ruby's shoulders. 'Don't

fret so,' she said. 'It's not too deep and it's just about stopped bleeding.'

'But what happened?'

Ma sighed. 'To be honest, we don't know for sure, love,' she said. 'We found him like this when we got back after our night out.'

'Night out?' Despite the situation, Ruby gave her mother the ghost of a grin. 'You make it sound like you've been to one of Mr and Mrs Henderson's soirées – not hiding from the Zeppelins!' she said.

Ma's answering smile lit up her pale, drawn face. 'Well. I'm not sure which I would have hated more,' she said. 'There certainly weren't no oyster soufflés in the laundry basement, but nor were there any men putting their hands where they've got no right to be.'

Ruby grinned again. 'I wish you'd taken Mac with you,' she said, kissing the dog's furry head.

'I know, love,' said Ma. 'But there's no animals allowed in the laundry basement.'

'I'd have stayed at home,' said Ruby staunchly. 'I'd have hidden under the table with him and taken me chances.'

'Well, more fool you.' Aunt Maggie, who had clearly been listening to every word, stepped in from the scullery, arms lacy with suds. 'Your mother did the right thing leaving Mac in the yard. The robbers had a field day in the empty houses. Mac were just doing his duty keeping everything safe, and a very good job he did of it, too.'

'Is that what happened?' asked Ruby. 'Did Mac get injured fighting off an intruder?'

'Very probably,' said Ma. 'There were a piece of wood in the yard with a nail in it and a bit of cloth which looked like it might've come from some fellow's trousers. I reckon some ne'er-do-well jumped into the yard, got set on by Mac and clobbered him with the piece of wood. But Mac fought back, and as the fella scarpered empty-handed, he had a big bite taken out of his backside for his troubles.'

'Oh, Mac!' Ruby found that she was half-laughing and half-crying. 'You brave darling. I love you so much.'

'We all love him this morning,' said Aunt Maggie. 'Turns out two doors down were broken into *and* the house next to them. Broke the kitchen windows and took everything they could get their hands on.'

'Looks like your Mac saved us from that,' added Ma. 'He's *our* hero.'

Ruby beamed at both women, her heart swelling with pride. Then she crouched down and looked at Mac's wound more closely. The dog flinched and whimpered but didn't snap or move away. Ruby judged that the ragged cut was nothing to worry about. As Ma had said, it didn't look too deep and, whilst still a little oozy, it had mostly stopped bleeding.

'We've already cleaned the wound,' Ma said. 'But you might like to give it another going over. There's hot water in the kettle and bicarb in the cupboard.'

Ruby got a bowl and filled it with hot water. Then she sprinkled in the bicarbonate of soda – just as Ma had always done whenever she or her brothers had grazed their knees or elbows.

If only it worked as well for broken hearts.

Oh, stop it, Ruby.

Stop being so sentimental.

She had known Jack for no more than an hour and she was being ridiculously melodramatic.

Besides, it was over.

Whatever 'it' was or might have been.

Ruby finished off cleaning Mac's wound as best she could, washing down his chest and paws for good measure.

And then she sneezed.

Three times.

'Quick. Make a wish,' said Ma.

Ruby duly shut her eyes. She should, of course, wish for Mac's full and speedy recovery. But Mac was fine and, almost against her will, Ruby found herself making a fervent plea that – somehow, somewhere – she would see Jack again.

'And now to bed with you,' said Ma. 'I hope you're not coming down with something.'

Ruby suddenly realised she was exhausted and chilled to the bone. She had never properly warmed up or dried out after sitting in the damp tunnel and she wanted nothing more than to strip her wet clothes off, slip on her nightie and cuddle down beneath her warm eiderdown.

'Mac will be all right, won't he, Ma?'

'Yes. You'll see. He'll be better before you know it.'

But Mac didn't get better.

In fact, he got worse.

Over the next couple of days, his poor face resolutely refused to heal. The red oozing cut, far from scabbing over, began to turn yellow and green and Mac wasn't himself at all. He was tired and lethargic and he whined in pain whenever anyone touched his face. It was heart-breaking to see.

Ruby and Charlie tried everything.

As well as more bicarbonate of soda, they carefully applied honey from the store cupboard and then got stuck in to the contents of the Day & Son's Dog Medicine Chest. They gave Mac various tonics and carefully applied the black oil, but none of them seemed to help. So, the next morning when she was working at the barrow, Ruby bought one of Nellie's salves. She trusted Nellie implicitly now – probably even more than Day & Son – and she kept her fingers firmly crossed that the thick, pale paste would do the trick.

It didn't.

Nobody else seemed to realise the potential gravity of the situation. Ma and Aunt Maggie were caught up with the dreadful news coming from the North Sea where the Germans had sunk – amongst others – the splendid *Queen Mary* with the consequent loss of well over a thousand lives. It was just too much to bear, Ma kept saying.

When was the wretched government going to do more than wrangle and procrastinate?

When would all the butchery and the carnage be over?

When would they all be able to go back to normal?

Ruby wasn't blind to what was going on in the war – of course she wasn't. She was desperately sorry for all the poor sailors who must have gone through veritable hell on their ships. Closer to home, she read and reread all Harry's weekly letters, trying to work out if there was a hidden message behind the cheerful, reassuring words. (There didn't seem to be, but, then again, he was still in

Buckinghamshire!) In the meantime, there was a potential tragedy unfolding in Sanctuary Lane and no one seemed to much care. It was down to Ruby. Mac had been hurt protecting the family home and she had done a dreadful thing by not using her wish on him. Ruby promised him then and there that she would do anything in her power to make him better.

She would not let him die.

By the next day, Ruby was frantic.

She got back from work in the early morning, sat with Mac for a couple of hours getting more and more het up that his breathing seemed to have become laboured – and then knew exactly what she needed to do.

Of course!

She'd take Mac up to the market to see Nellie.

No sooner had the thought come into Ruby's head than she sprang into action.

No one else was around. It was one of Ma's days at the laundry, Charlie was at school and Aunt Maggie was out and about, so there was no one to help her.

No matter.

Ruby slipped Mac's halter over his head and half-pulled, half-cajoled him out of the scullery door, along the back alleyway and round the corner to Victory Lane.

And there Mac refused to budge.

He simply lay down on the pavement with a deep groan and looked up at Ruby with mournful eyes.

What now?

Ruby pulled gently on the rope a couple of times, but it was no good. Mac either wouldn't or couldn't move. With panic bubbling in her chest, Ruby picked him up. It was no easy task; Mac lay limp in her arms, making no attempt to struggle, but he was heavy and awkward to carry. Ruby staggered along Victory Lane, wondering how long she could keep going. Her arms were lead weights, her hands were going numb, Mac was slowly slipping from her grasp . . .

If only Jack would suddenly appear from somewhere and . . .

'Ruby!'

Ruby turned in the direction of the woman's voice but didn't stop walking. It was Daisy from work, standing in the doorway to one of the houses, looking at her with a mixture of confusion and amusement.

'Whatever are you doing?' she asked, with a little giggle. 'Do I need to report you for stealing that dog?'

'It ain't funny.' Ruby knew that Daisy was only pulling her leg, but this wasn't a joke. 'Me dog's really poorly and I'm taking him to get help.'

'Goodness. I'm so sorry.' Daisy was all contrition. 'Here, let me help you.'

Ruby lowered Mac gently to the ground. One arm had totally gone to sleep and she couldn't really go any further on her own, anyway.

'Thank you,' she said. 'I'm taking him to Nellie at the dogfood barrow.'

'The dogfood barrow?' Daisy wrinkled her nose in confusion.

'Do *not* make any jokes about him being sold off as cheap meat or made into cat kebabs. Nellie knows all there is to know about animals. I'd be ever so grateful if you would help me carry him there.'

'I can do one better,' said Daisy. 'Stay there one minute.'

She disappeared back inside her house and, exhausted, Ruby sat down on the filthy kerb, one hand cupping her chin and the other stroking Mac's head. She would rest here for exactly one minute – she would count to sixty – and if Daisy hadn't come back, she should have regained enough energy to set off on her own again.

Daisy reappeared when Ruby had counted to fifty-six, manhandling a large black perambulator.

Despite herself, Ruby almost laughed.

'We can't,' she said. 'Can we? Won't your mother mind? Won't the *baby* mind?'

'It ain't my mother's,' said Daisy with a grin. 'And there ain't no baby. Not yet, anyway. Me sister's in the family way and someone has lent her this for when she needs it. Besides, everyone's out now, so if we're quick, no one will ever know.'

'Let's go, then,' said Ruby.

Between them, the two women lifted Mac carefully into the pram. It was a tight squeeze and he gave an initial little whimper of discomfort, but he soon settled down.

And then they were off, running along the pavement towards the market.

If this was the films, Ruby thought, Nellie would take one look at the two women skedaddling towards her and come out to meet them. She would put a gentle hand under Mac's chin, scrutinise his wound and then straighten up with a smile. It was nothing to worry about, she'd say; she had just the potion or just the ointment to make it better. Give it a couple of days and Mac would be right as rain.

Well, the first part went as Ruby had imagined.

As she had *hoped*.

Nellie *was* at her dogfood barrow and she *did* come out to meet them.

'Whose little 'un is it?' she asked curiously, peering into the pram. Then she stepped back, hand to heart, with a little laugh. 'Well, I've seen all sorts now,' she added. 'What's your boy doing in there, then?'

'He's poorly, Nellie. Really poorly,' said Ruby, her words falling over each other. 'It's his face. I've tried everything – honey, the stuff from Day's Medicine Chest, your salve . . . He's been like this for a few days, nothing is making any difference and I think he's getting worse. Please help me.'

Nellie peered back into the pram for a long time, gently turning Mac's face this way and that, cooing to him softly like a baby when he protested. When she straightened up for a second time, her expression was grave.

'That's a bad infection and no two ways about it,' she said. 'Poor little chap.'

'I know,' said Ruby impatiently. *Desperately.* 'What can I do?'

Nellie laid her filthy, gnarled hand on Ruby's arm. 'Just keep doing what you're doing, sweetheart,' she said. 'And maybe say a little prayer.'

For a second, Nellie's words didn't make sense.

Then the awful realisation dawned.

'But there must be something else you can give me,' Ruby stammered.

'There ain't, I'm afraid, sweetheart,' Nellie said gently. 'You can start giving him aspirin for the fever and pain if you like, but that won't help the infection. Just keep cleaning the wound, keep applying the salve and keep your fingers crossed. It's all you can do at this stage.'

Ruby's head was swimming and she began to feel sick.

She couldn't lose Mac.

She *couldn't*.

'There must be something,' she repeated, almost to herself. 'What about a vet?' she asked Nellie.

Nellie gave a little shrug. 'If you could find one,' she said, doubtfully. 'But . . .'

The 'if' was good enough for Ruby.

'Let's go,' she said shortly. 'Come on, Daisy.'

'Where to?' asked Daisy who, until now, had stood by Ruby's side and not said a word.

Ruby wheeled the pram around. 'I've got to go back to the munitions factory,' she said. 'I've got to see Leah.'

As they ran, Ruby and Daisy agreed that Ruby would take Mac back to Sanctuary Lane in the pram and, from there, head off to the munitions factory. Daisy had to run some errands before she headed to the factory later in the morning to start her own shift, so Ruby would return the pram to Daisy's house in Victory Lane over the next day or two once she had given it a good clean.

Ruby dumped Mac and the pram at home, hurled a garbled explanation at Aunt Maggie, who was back from wherever she'd been, and – trying to ignore how exhausted she was – set off at a run towards the factory. As she approached the site, she started praying that the daytime recognisers hadn't totally forgotten her but, on the other hand, didn't remember her well enough to know that she had left the factory barely two hours ago and wasn't due back on duty until that evening. All was well and she was handed a pass without comment. The policewoman at the barrier merely raised one eyebrow at Ruby's sweaty and dishevelled appearance – she hadn't had a chance to get changed since her night shift – and said dryly, 'Running late, are we?'

Ruby gave a weak smile and kept running. Through the site, past the main factory floor and the canteen and the detonation shop, all the way over to the reception building on the other side of the site. She flung the door wide, trying to catch her breath, and scanned the room. A dozen faces turned to stare at her but none of them belonged to Leah.

'Can I help you?' asked Mrs Clark, looking indignant at Ruby's abrupt entrance.

'Miss Richardson?' asked Ruby. Maybe Leah was in one of the offices.

Mrs Clark gestured outside, but Ruby didn't stop to hear the details. She turned tail and fled, not bothering to shut the door behind her.

Where was Leah most likely to be?

Maybe she should retrace her steps and ask Mrs Clark. No, that would waste valuable time and might prompt awkward questions about why she wanted Leah. She was far better off trying to find her friend on her own. The lavvies was one possibility, of course, as was the canteen. But it was far more likely – particularly at this time in the morning – that Leah would be at the medical checks.

Yes, of course.

Ruby was there in a matter of seconds. She smiled sweetly at a young woman with a clipboard just inside the door.

'I'm here to help Miss Richardson,' she said confidently.

The young woman looked her up and down. 'And you are?' she said.

'Miss Archer.' Ruby crossed her fingers behind her back. 'Miss Richardson is expecting me.'

The woman nodded and Ruby strode briskly away before she could be further challenged. Across the hallway, up the stairs and . . .

'Drop skirts, please!'

Ruby paused halfway up the stairs, her hand to her mouth. Of all the times to turn up! It was so ridiculous as to be almost funny. Meanwhile, what to do? Maybe she should come back when Leah had finished the inspections. No, Leah would be swept straight up into the briefing and then there was the trip to the shifting shed to get kitted out and . . .

Ruby marched up the stairs and into the ward. Dr Welch, busy with paperwork at one end, didn't even look up, but Leah started – hand to heart – when she saw Ruby.

'What are you doing here?' she hissed as Ruby approached. 'This isn't the best time.'

'It's Mac,' Ruby blurted out without preamble. 'He's badly hurt and I'm scared he's going to die.'

The curtain nearest to them twitched and a flame-headed girl poked her head out.

'Excuse me, Miss,' she whispered. 'Do you mean to drop our skirts *right* down?'

'Right down, please, Miss Hesketh,' said Leah briskly.

Looking dubious, Miss Hesketh shut the curtains and Leah turned back to Ruby.

'Whatever's happened?' she asked.

'Mac's wound is badly infected,' said Ruby, tears pricking at her eyelids. 'Even Nellie from the barrow says she can't help.'

Another curtain twitched open.

'You mean you want to see our . . . unmentionables?' a pretty, dark-haired girl asked.

'Precisely, Mrs Lovell,' said Leah. 'I'll be with you in one minute.'

Once again, Leah turned to Ruby. 'I'm assuming you didn't come here for tea and sympathy,' she said briskly. 'How can I help?'

Relief surged through Ruby.

Leah was going to help.

'I haven't got all day, ladies,' a voice rang out. It was the doctor, shuffling paperwork and glaring at them with disapproval.

'Sorry, Dr Welch,' said Leah. 'I'll get straight on with the checks now.'

'And who is this with you?'

'This is Miss Archer,' said Leah calmly. 'She's helping me whilst she learns the ropes.'

'Well, get on with it, then,' the doctor said tetchily.

'Of course,' said Leah. She thrust her clipboard at Ruby. 'Follow me,' she said, sotto voce. 'Tick the names off as I call them out and quietly tell me what you'd like me to do.'

She stepped up to the first cubicle and tweaked open the curtains. Ruby quickly averted her eyes.

'Thank you, Miss Hesketh,' said Leah matter-of-factly. 'Please put on your skirt but unbutton your blouse so the doctor can listen to your chest.'

199

'Yes, Miss.'

Ruby duly put a tick next to 'Amelia Hesketh' and followed Leah to the next cubicle. 'Mac needs a vet,' she said as Leah swung the curtains open. 'And I remembered you saying you knew one who worked nearby. One who has flat feet?'

'Robert Smith. Yes.'

Smith. Not one of the vets she had sent a letter to.

'I need him to come round to my house,' said Ruby.

'Thank you, Mrs Slack; you can get dressed now,' interrupted Leah, pulling the curtains shut. 'It isn't that simple,' she said to Ruby. 'I only know him socially, and I don't think he'll be able to help.'

'Why not?' Ruby demanded.

'Mark Eva Slack on the form and keep your voice down,' said Leah, busy at the next cubicle. 'I think he only treats horses.' She took the clipboard from Ruby, crossed out 'Ida Windsor' and gave the clipboard back to Ruby.

'He treated your dog,' Ruby pointed out.

'That was a favour.'

'Well, this could be a favour too.'

Leah sighed. 'Look, I'm sorry about Mac,' she said. 'But Robert Smith is just a family friend and my mother is already trying to marry me off to him. I can't just start asking him for favours. There must be other vets you can telephone.'

'I ain't got no telephone,' said Ruby. 'Please. This is my last chance and this is Mac's *life* we're talking about.'

There was a long pause. Leah swished two sets of curtains open and shut without saying a word. Then she turned to Ruby, her expression inscrutable.

'Listen to me,' she said. 'This is what I'm going to do. I am going to finish processing this batch of recruits and then I will go to my office and telephone Robert's number. If I can get through to someone – a big if, mind, because he might be out on his rounds – I will ask him if he might visit Mac late this afternoon. Understood?'

'Understood,' said Ruby fervently. 'And thank you. Thank you, thank you, thank you.'

The last curtain opened. A tall, well-built woman came out and without a word, thumped towards the stairs in a swish of skirts and was gone.

Ruby and Leah locked eyes.

'Was that . . . a man?' Ruby asked incredulously.

'I don't suppose we will ever know,' Leah replied dryly. 'Now, go and get some sleep and I'll see what I can do.'

20

Ruby returned home to Sanctuary Lane feeling slightly more optimistic – and absolutely bone tired. Too exhausted to return the pram to Daisy, too exhausted to explain what might happen later that afternoon, she collapsed into bed beside Mac. He didn't seem any better but, encouragingly, neither was he any worse. Ruby kissed the top of his head, put her arm around him and quickly fell into a deep sleep.

She awoke feeling anxious. Her room was hot and stuffy in the early June sunshine and she had the beginnings of a headache tightening across her temples. As she got dressed ready for her night shift, her earlier optimism had quite drained away, leaving a gnawing ache under her breastbone. There was absolutely no guarantee that Robert Smith would have answered the telephone, let alone turn up; in fact, the more Ruby thought – *agonised*! – about it, the more unlikely it seemed. So many things would have had to go her way to make it even remotely a possibility. Robert Smith would have to get the message, he would have to be free and roughly in the right locality – to say nothing of being amenable to the whole venture. If just one of those things wasn't in place, the whole idea would collapse like a house of cards. If Robert was sick, taking the country air, working the other side of London, or had suddenly developed a conscience and signed up, it was all over.

A loud knocking at the door shocked Ruby out of her reverie.

Oh goodness.

Could it be . . . ?

Dare she believe it . . . ?

Ruby shot off the bed and bolted down the stairs two at a time, flinging the front door wide.

Two policemen were standing there, staring back at her impassively.

You stupid, stupid *girl.*

You selfish, blinkered, misguided fool.

Focused to the point of obsession on your own concerns, blind to everything else – and now the police are at the door to tell you that your brother has been killed in action.

Ruby had sagged against the bottom of the banisters in shock, but Ma and Aunt Maggie had obviously heard the front door and were bustling up the passage.

'Can I help you?' Ma asked the policemen calmly.

Ruby turned in surprise.

Ma sounded – *looked* – calm enough. In fact, she appeared curious more than anything. Even Aunt Maggie looked concerned rather than panicked – and she was never one to pass up a fit of histrionics lightly. Then Ruby remembered, with a jolt of blessed relief, that it wasn't the police who announced a death far away at the front. It was the young telegram boys and girls – the angels of death – who moved silently around town delivering the most heartbreaking of news.

Besides, hadn't Harry's last letter said he was still in Buckinghamshire?

Ruby was still catching her breath when the older of the two policemen said, 'Does Charlie Archer live here?'

Another sigh of relief.

For once, Charlie was at home; Ruby could hear him playing with Tess in the kitchen. At least he hadn't been hit by a horse or run over by one of the new-fangled motors driving too fast through town . . .

Charlie was duly summoned and Ruby scanned his face for any obvious signs of guilt. Shifty eye contact . . . downturned expression . . . what on earth had he been up to?

'You go back to bed, love,' said Ma to Ruby. 'You'll be back on duty before you know it and you need your sleep. Our Ruby works nights at the Brunner Mond munitions factory,' she added to the policemen. 'Ever such dangerous work, but we feel it's important to support the war effort, especially as my other son is in the army and soon on his way to France.'

It was such a blatant attempt to curry favour that Ruby was smiling to herself as she scampered upstairs. Curiosity got the better of her and, instead of going back into her bedroom, she sat down on the top step to eavesdrop.

She didn't have long to wait.

One of the policemen started telling them that ever since the last Zeppelin attack and the naval battle in the North Sea, German businesses around London had been attacked by angry mobs. Ruby knew this – it had been in all the papers and the subject of much discussion in the detonation shed and, of course, she had seen Schmidt's up the market with her own eyes. What she *didn't* know was that Muller's haberdashery at the top of Sanctuary

Lane had been the target of such action. A brick had recently been thrown through a window and the police had reason to believe that Charlie had been one of the culprits.

Ruby was shocked all round.

For one thing, she hadn't realised that Muller's was owned or run by Germans, although perhaps given the name, that much had always been obvious.

But . . . Charlie?

Throwing bricks?

Surely not!

Then again, Charlie had been spending a lot of time with his friend Joe and he had made a point of saying that Joe hated the Germans with a passion, so maybe anything was possible. Ruby had, she realised, no idea of what Charlie was capable of and, once again, she regretted the fact that she hadn't invested the time in getting to know her brother better.

In the meantime, Charlie was loudly protesting his innocence, but Ruby couldn't tell whether or not he was lying. In either case, the police were clearly there to caution rather than to arrest, and after a dressing-down and threats of further action if the offence was repeated, they duly departed.

'Did you do it?' demanded Ma, as soon as the footsteps had disappeared down the street.

Ruby couldn't hear a reply, but presumably Charlie had nodded or mumbled an affirmative because the next voice to float upstairs was Aunt Maggie's.

'Good for you, lad,' she said. 'Got to show Jerry who's boss.'

Wow!

'*Maggie*,' said Ma. 'Violence ain't never acceptable.'

'Course it is,' said Aunt Maggie. 'The boys ain't hurt no one and these are the *Germans* we're talking about. They've just killed Joe's father.'

'Not these particular Germans. Not the Mullers.'

'Still . . .'

The voices were getting quieter as the three, presumably, headed back to the kitchen, but Ruby stayed sitting on the top step deep in thought. She really wasn't sure what to think. The Mullers had had the haberdashery shop at the top of Sanctuary Lane for what seemed like forever and they had always seemed very pleasant and perfectly English to Ruby. But, even if they weren't, was it really acceptable to attack their property because they happened to have been born in Germany?

Ruby found that she didn't have an immediate answer to that.

She simply couldn't think straight.

If only Mac would get better.

Five o'clock duly came and went with no further knock on the door.

By now, Ruby just felt numb.

She was beginning to realise that the idea of asking a veterinary surgeon to attend them on Sanctuary Lane was as preposterous as asking one of the King's pages to come and serve them their supper. Her plan was never going to have worked. In fact, maybe Leah hadn't even tried. Maybe she had just promised to give Ruby a glimmer of hope – or to get Ruby off her back. And, frankly, who could blame her? What had Ruby been thinking, barging in like that in the middle of the inspections and demanding Leah's attention?

Anyway, none of that mattered now.

The point was that there was no help coming for Mac and, as bleak and as hopeless as it might seem, she had to face facts. It might not be tonight – it might be days or even weeks – but Mac was dying and there was absolutely nothing she could do about it. Nothing except show him how much he was loved. And, if he was in great pain, maybe she should consider taking him to Father Murphy who was doing such a sterling job with his lethal chamber . . .

There was a loud knocking on the door.

Ruby didn't dare get her hopes up this time. She walked sedately down the stairs and opened the front door almost casually. And there, on the doorstep, was Leah together with a man in overalls.

'Hello,' said Leah, with a broad smile. 'This is Robert Smith. May we come in?'

Oh, thank goodness.

Thank goodness for that.

Somewhat overwhelmed – it *had* happened, after all – Ruby stood blinking into the afternoon sun, trying to take it all in.

'Thank you so much for coming,' she babbled. 'I'm ever so grateful, really I am.'

Leah was looking lovely. She had changed out of her work clothes into a navy silk dress, her hair was nicely styled and there was even a touch of rouge on her usually pale cheeks.

By contrast, Robert Smith was a big disappointment.

In Ruby's mind, vets were a rarefied and almost godlike species and she had duly built Mr Smith up to be impossibly tall and handsome with an impeccably suave and sophisticated manner to match. The man standing in front of her was disappointingly human. He might have been dark – straight, springy hair brushed forwards into a peak – but he was barely taller than Leah and he had a narrow face with deep, close-set eyes which somewhat reminded Ruby of a ferret. He was also wearing an expression which could curdle milk.

'Will my motor be safe here?' he asked tetchily.

Ruby's eye went to the shiny green and gold motorcar parked on the kerb behind him. Motors were common enough these days, of course – the Hendersons in Hampstead had had three, for goodness' sake – but smart ones like this one didn't often drive down Sanctuary Lane and it had already become the subject of much curiosity. A small group of boys and young men had gathered around it, including Charlie. Far from being in disgrace, the little tinker was already outside, standing on the running board and looking very much like he was about to lean inside . . .

Ruby didn't directly answer Mr Smith. 'Charlie,' she called out. 'I'm leaving you in charge out here. Absolutely *no* touching.'

Her attention was caught by a man further up the street. He looked about the same height and size as Jack and he was walking with his hands behind his back just as . . .

The man turned . . . and it was someone else. This man was older, darker . . . nothing like Jack.

Oh, Ruby.

Stop it!

Jack would be back at the front by now and would certainly have forgotten all about *her*.

And here was Ma – Aunt Maggie in tow – bustling down the passage for the second time in as many hours. 'What's going on here, *now*, then?' Ma asked impatiently, coming up short when she saw the visitors.

'This is Miss Richardson, one of the managers from work,' said Ruby. 'And this is Mr Smith, a veterinary practitioner, who has kindly come to take a look at Mac.'

Ruby, frankly, had no idea if vets should be addressed thus – maybe they were doctors – and very much hoped she hadn't made too much of a hash of the introductions. But Ma and Aunt Maggie were just looking overawed and Aunt Maggie's mouth was literally hanging open.

And then Ma was waving them in, all a-fluster. 'Much obliged to you both, I'm sure,' she gabbled. 'Mac is upstairs in Ruby's room; shall we bring him down?'

'No, no. Leave him be,' said Mr Smith. 'I can examine him up there.'

'Very good,' said Ma. 'And might I bring you up some tea?'

'Please,' said Mr Smith. 'It's been a long day.'

Heart in her mouth, Ruby led the way upstairs. She paused momentarily in the doorway and tried to see the room through Leah's eyes. She hadn't considered this before – whether the house was ready for visitors – as she'd been so worried about Mac. Clean and tidy enough, it was nonetheless a tiny box room, sparsely furnished and without electricity. What, she wondered, was Leah's bedroom like? Ten times the size, no doubt and . . .

Stop it, Ruby.

Stop it!

'Why don't I go and give your mother a hand with the tea?' said Leah. 'It will be a bit of a squeeze with us all in there.'

And, without waiting for an answer, she headed back down the stairs.

Mr Smith had already gone over to Mac, lying inert on the bed, and his whole demeanour had changed. Talking softly under his breath, he stroked Mac's head with such tenderness that Ruby suddenly had a lump in her throat. Mac, for his part, lifted his head slightly and gave a weary thump of his tail by way of reply.

'Tell me what's happened to this old fella, then,' said Mr Smith, in his normal voice.

'He were hit by a piece of wood with a nail in it,' said Ruby. 'We think he were fighting off someone trying to break in the night the Zeps came across.'

'Brave boy,' said Mr Smith, patting Mac on the head. 'So, four days ago, then? Well, it's a nasty infection, to be sure, not at all helped by all this scar tissue underneath. What happened there?'

'The person who owned him before put paraffin in his ear to try and cure his canker,' said Ruby, matter-of-factly.

Mr Smith shot her an incredulous glance. 'Now I've heard it all,' he said. 'And people wonder why we say some people shouldn't be allowed to keep animals.'

He turned back to Mac and Ruby let the comment go. Now was neither the time nor the place.

'As I said, it's a nasty infection,' said Mr Smith, straightening up. 'And I'm very glad you haven't left it any longer before calling me in. The good news is that, with the right treatment, I'm pretty sure we'll be able to turn the old boy around.'

Relief, pure and simple, coursed through Ruby.

Mac was going to be all right.

Ruby flung herself on the bed and wrapped her arms around him, kissing him again and again on top of his head.

'Thank you,' she said to Mr Smith. 'You don't know what this means to me.'

'I think I have a good idea,' said Mr Smith, with a small smile. He sat down on Ruby's chair and pulled a smart mahogany box on to his lap.

And here was Leah, manoeuvring the tea tray into the cramped little room. Ruby smothered a giggle when she saw Ma and Aunt Maggie had tried to impress Leah and Mr Smith with the smart silver tea service. It was almost never used – reserved for high days and holidays – but today it seemed appropriately celebratory.

'I take it it's good news?' said Leah with a smile, putting the tray, with difficulty, on the tiny bedside table.

'The very best,' said Ruby, from her position on the bed. 'Mac's going to get better.'

'That's marvellous news,' said Leah. 'Huzzah!'

'There's a bit of work to do first, ladies,' said Mr Smith dryly, pulling various containers out of his box.

'How are you going to treat him?' asked Ruby, scrambling to a sitting position.

Mr Smith glanced at her. 'Firstly, I'm going to wash the wound with a solution of potassium permanganate and then I'll leave you with an embrocation to apply twice daily,' he said. 'I'll need one of you to pop down and get me some water – preferably warm – to make up the pot permang.'

'I'm nearest the door,' said Leah. 'I'll leave you to be mum with the tea, Ruby.'

She said the last bit rather pointedly and Ruby suddenly realised that sprawling on her bed when there was a gentleman present was hardly the done thing – whatever the circumstances. Blushing furiously, she stood up, wriggled past Mr Smith and started pouring the tea.

'I'd be interested to know what the embrocation is,' she said, handing Mr Smith a cup. 'The ointment I've been using has all manner of things in it, but none of them seem to have done the trick.'

She started rattling off the ingredients in Nellie's salve – at least those that she could remember – and then paused, half-waiting for Mr Smith to dismiss them all out of hand.

But Mr Smith just took a leisurely sip of his tea, flickering another glance in her direction. 'You seem very informed on such matters,' he remarked with what almost seemed like amusement.

Ruby nodded enthusiastically. 'I'm really interested in caring for animals, Sir,' she said. 'In fact, it's my dream to set up a small animal hospital in Silvertown.'

The words were out of Ruby's mouth before she had a chance to ask herself if she really wanted to tell Mr Smith about her plans. But it felt good saying it out loud and, after all, why not? It *was* what she intended to do – had already *started* doing by being somewhat trained by Nellie – and, even though she had been dismissed out of hand by the Royal Veterinary College, there was always a chance that an individual vet might be open-minded to the idea.

But, across the small room, Ruby saw Mr Smith stiffen.

'Is it, now?' he said mildly enough. 'And how, might I ask, are you qualified for such a venture?'

'Well, I'm not,' admitted Ruby, suddenly feeling defensive. 'I mean, I'm not a vet or anything, but I've been helping Nellie at the dogfood barrow for a few weeks now and I've picked up ever such a lot over there . . .'

Mr Smith laughed – not a terribly kind laugh at that. 'I almost wish I hadn't bothered with five years' training at the RVC,' he said. 'Maybe I should just have had a little chat with Nellie and saved myself the trouble.'

Mr Smith was poking fun at her and Ruby's defensiveness coalesced into humiliation.

'I would love to have a vet on board, Sir,' she said. 'But, so far, I haven't had any success in attracting any. It would make all the difference to have someone like you helping us out.'

Leah arrived back with a glass bowl of water before Mr Smith could answer.

'Is everything quite all right in here?' she asked.

'Yes, thank you,' said Ruby. There was no point in letting anger get the better of her.

Mr Smith didn't answer. He took the bowl of water and tipped some powder into it. The water turned purple – an almost regal shade.

'If you don't want to be actively involved in the animal hospital, perhaps I could follow you on your rounds and learn that way?' Ruby asked politely.

'When you're not busy working at the dogfood barrow?' replied Mr Smith caustically, dabbing Mac's face with the solution.

'Robert!' said Leah, looking shocked.

'I wouldn't charge you,' persisted Ruby.

'The answer is still no,' said Mr Smith. 'Absolutely not.'

'One last thing,' Ruby persisted. 'I understand you ain't got time to help us. But we're going to need access to the ointments you use – and quite a lot of them. That's why I were asking what's in the embrocation you're leaving behind for Mac. Can you help there? Maybe donate some ingredients or, at least, show us how to make them up?'

'This is getting ridiculous,' said Mr Smith, smearing an almost metallic-looking ointment on to Mac's face. 'I've tried to be polite but – really! Vets don't train for years to simply hand out their knowledge, their expertise and their *products* to every silly girl who gets ideas above her station.'

'Robert!' exploded Leah. 'Times are changing and, whether you like it or not, women like Ruby are part of that change.'

'Well, I *don't* like,' said Mr Smith, packing up his box. 'When the soldiers get back from war, hopefully she and her type will be back below stairs where they belong. Now, I will leave you the ointment, Miss Archer – twice a day: no more, no less – and I will bid you good evening.'

Despite her joy at knowing Mac would get better, Ruby felt tears pricking at her eyelids. She had been humiliated in nearly every way possible – in front of Leah, too – and now she just wanted the two of them to leave.

'If I could just have your bill?' she said, with as much dignity as she could muster.

'That's all been taken care of,' said Mr Smith shortly.

Oh, for goodness' sake.

Ruby rounded on Leah. 'Have *you* offered to pay?' she said. 'Because I would really rather you didn't. I have the money.'

She didn't.

Not really.

But she would find it.

Somehow.

Leah, looking furious, shook her head.

'I have agreed to waive my fee,' said Mr Smith. 'It's a small price to pay for an evening of Miss Richardson's company.'

'Pardon me?'

'Miss Richardson has kindly agreed to accompany me to the theatre tonight,' clarified Mr Smith. 'And, now I think about it, time is marching on. Come, my dear,' he added to Leah. 'We really should be on our way if we're to grab a bite to eat beforehand.'

The theatre?

A bite to eat?

My dear?

'No,' cried Ruby. 'Please let me pay. I *want* to pay.'

'Really no need, Ruby,' said Leah neutrally. 'Mr Smith has offered to donate his services for free and I think we should accept his gesture. Besides, I'm looking forward to seeing *Pell-Mell* this evening.'

Goodness, Leah really *had* gone above and beyond the call of duty. Ruby was suddenly filled with a wave of gratitude for her friend and only hoped Leah hadn't bitten off more than she could chew. She comforted herself with the thought that Leah could surely feign a headache if the thought of Mr Smith's company was too much to bear.

Ruby preceded the other two down the stairs and opened the front door for them.

'Well, thank you, both,' she said. 'Thank you ever so much.'

On impulse – and totally against convention – she reached up and kissed Leah on the cheek.

'I say,' said Mr Smith. 'That is an extremely impertinent way to treat your manager.'

Ruby bobbed a little curtsey. 'I'm so sorry, Miss Richardson,' she said. 'I'm just so grateful and so excited that Mac's going to get better.'

'That's quite all right,' said Leah. 'Just don't be doing it at work! Please thank your mother for the tea.'

'I will,' said Ruby. 'Thank *you*, Sir, and all. And here's your motor – all safe and sound.'

'Good evening to you,' said Mr Smith, opening the passenger door for Leah and then walking around to the driver's side.

'Funny,' said Ruby, almost to herself. 'You don't look flat-footed at all.'

21

Mac did get better.

Not that day, or even the next, but Ruby kept the faith and kept applying Mr Smith's ointment and a couple of days later, Mac began to show some improvement. Slowly, slowly, the wound on his face began to dry up and scab over. Slowly, slowly, the puffiness and redness started to disappear. And slowly, slowly, the little dog began to get his appetite and his energy back. He was less unsteady when he walked. He didn't groan when he lay down. And the first time Mac managed to eat every scrap of meat from one of Nellie's cat-sticks was truly a red-letter day – even though, back in the day, he had been known to demolish four!

Ruby, of course, was ecstatic. She knew how dangerously close she had come to losing Mac and the fact that he was getting better seemed almost miraculous. The rest of the family were relieved too but they – and the whole country – were soon reeling from the worst shock since the war began. Lord Kitchener – that trusted, fine leader who had raised an army of five million volunteers – had been lost at sea off the Orkneys, his ship torpedoed by a treacherous German submarine. It had been the talk of the munitions factory, of course, and Ruby had then read all about it in the *Daily Sketch*. What made it all almost worse was that several hours after the dreadful news reached England, the reports were suddenly contradicted and declared to be a mistake – cue a celebratory tea party in Annie-Next-Door's kitchen – which made the whole thing seem twice as bad when the original announcement proved to be true after all.

One dreadful piece of news after another and nothing any of them could do about it.

It all just seemed too much to bear and Ruby quickly decided that the only way she could get through it was to concentrate on the things that she *did* have some agency over. Like, the fact that it wasn't, of course, a miracle that Mac had got better. He had turned the corner purely because of the treatment prescribed by Mr Smith. Not Day & Son's Dog Medicine Chest. Not even Nellie's salve. And the trouble was that the ointment could only be obtained from vets and, as such, was so prohibitively expensive to ordinary people that it might as well not exist. Ruby knew how fortunate she had been to get her hands on some of it, but most people didn't have those advantages and it all seemed so unfair.

What was even worse was that it seemed that her plans for the animal hospital might have to be put on ice. How could she, in good faith, offer to treat people's animals with products which she now knew for a fact were not a patch on those offered by veterinary practitioners? Products that, to be blunt, didn't even seem to work. She might have already started planning the hospital – might even have roped in her friends to help – but it looked like she would have to think again.

In the meantime, the very least she could do would be to try and get hold of some more of Mr Smith's ointment and share it where it was most needed. Mr Smith had already made it perfectly clear that he would not simply give – or even sell – her more, so she would have to resort to more nefarious ways. So, once it was clear that Mac was on the road to recovery, Ruby wrote a letter to Mr Smith. Firstly, she thanked him very much for all his help. Then she informed him that, whilst Mac was starting to get better, she had already run out of ointment and she hoped very much that Mr Smith would be able to provide her with another jar in order to ensure his full recovery. She took the letter to the reception office and, on finding that Leah wasn't there, put it into a larger envelope addressed to Leah and added a short note asking that Leah forward it on to Mr Smith.

It might not work, of course.

Leah might decline to send the letter on. Or, for his part, Mr Smith might see through Ruby's ruse and refuse to comply. Or he might demand to examine Mac again and Ruby's duplicity would thus be exposed.

But, despite these potential pitfalls, surely it was worth a try?

'Present for you!' said Leah.

It was a couple of days later and, as agreed, Ruby and Leah had met by Silvertown Station to feed the stray cats who lived underneath the railway arches. Ruby had judged it far too soon to have heard back from Mr Smith and yet here was Leah triumphantly brandishing a bulky parcel wrapped in brown paper.

Ruby took the package and tore it open with impatient fingers. And inside – yes! – were another *two* jars of ointment, both identical in size and shape to the one at home. With it, there was a short note from Mr Smith which Ruby read out loud to Leah:

Dear Miss Archer.

Thank you for your note. I enclose two jars of ointment which should be more than enough to complete Mac's course of treatment. Use sparingly; each application should be no more than pea-sized. Glad to hear he continues making progress.

Regards, Robert Smith.

Ruby put everything back into the envelope and hugged the package to her chest in excitement. Shutting her eyes, she let out a little squeal.

Two jars!

More than she had dared hope for.

Not a long-term solution but, with a bit of luck, more than enough to help several other animals in need.

When Ruby opened her eyes, she saw that Leah was laughing.

'Very crafty, little Miss,' she said as Ruby popped the jars into her bag and the two of them headed up the street towards the railway arches. 'Of course, I knew exactly what you were up to the moment I saw your letter.'

'Did you?' said Ruby. 'Oh dear, I hope you didn't think it were a terrible thing to do.'

'Of course not,' said Leah. 'It's exactly what I would have done.'

The two women laughed easily together and Ruby marvelled at how natural all this seemed. It was partly, of course, that the war had changed things, and situations that were unimaginable a few years ago were now acceptable, but it was also that Leah seemed different out of work. Far less formal and much more relaxed, she was barely batting an eyelid that the bottom of her skirt was already covered in mud.

'Do you think Mr Smith cottoned on as well?' Ruby asked as they reached the railway arches.

Leah took out a torch and shone it into the first dark recess under the arches. 'I shouldn't think so for a minute,' she said. 'But he did ask me if I'd helped you write it so, sadly, I don't think he credits you with much intelligence or imagination.'

Ruby wasn't sure whether to laugh or cry. 'Wasn't you tempted to tell him what I was up to, Miss – I mean, Leah?'

Leah must be getting fed up with her trying – and failing – not to call her Miss. Often it came out as M'Leah.

'Of course not,' said Leah, playing the torch beam around. 'I'm on your side. Besides, Robert was an absolute *oaf* at your house, so as far as I'm concerned, he deserves everything he gets. I'm so sorry for the terrible things he said.'

'That's all right,' said Ruby. 'It ain't your fault.'

'It's not all right,' said Leah crossly. 'Robert's a dinosaur and he was unspeakably rude to you in your own home. I gave him a piece of my mind as we drove to the theatre, let me tell you.'

Ruby laughed. 'I just feel terrible you had to spend an evening in his company on my behalf,' she said. 'That really were going above and beyond the call of duty.'

Leah shrugged. 'At least he doesn't get ideas like some of them, and I'd wanted to see that play for ages,' she said. 'If I step out with him occasionally, it might get Mummy off my back, and anyway, I have a feeling that I might be able to educate him. He needs to realise the world is changing and stop trying to fight against it. Enough of that. I can see eyes shining in that beam of light and there were cats in here the last time I came by. Shall we take a look?'

For the next hour, the two women worked their way down one side of the railway arches and then around the scrubby piece of waste ground on the far side. It was difficult, dirty and uncomfortable work, and Ruby couldn't help but be impressed how Leah threw herself into the task. She ventured into the darkest, most unsavoury arches with only a thin, flickering beam to light the way. She wriggled on her stomach into the middle of a prickly gorse bush to reach a family of cats she thought had set up home there. And she clearly thought nothing of picking up the fiercest-looking feral cats to inspect them for disease and injury. More than once, Ruby had to remind herself that this dishevelled creature was the same rather la-di-da Miss Richardson who never had a hair out of place at work.

If only they could see her now.

This was the rough side of looking after the animals of the East End. Like Leah, Ruby threw herself into it all with gusto, distributing the large tin of offcuts she had bought from the barrow to various ravenous recipients. She even tried applying some ointment to a scrawny tomcat who had a cut under his eye but succeeded only in getting a scratched finger for her troubles.

'What do we do if the animals are really injured?' asked Ruby, sucking her finger and applying a little ointment for good measure.

Leah dusted down her skirt, a somewhat futile gesture. 'The vicar with the lethal chamber does the rounds fairly often,' she said. 'And he puts the worst of them out of their misery. But if we find an animal which is really injured and in pain, I'd probably take it around to him straight away.'

Ruby nodded. That made perfect sense to her. She was beginning to realise there was no place for sentimentality in truly caring for animals.

They made their way back down the other side of the arches with Ruby holding the torch and taking the lead this time. As they approached the last dark, dank entrance, she tried to ignore a strong, sickly smell which permeated her nostrils and made her feel slightly sick.

'There was a cat in here last time,' Leah said, picking her way in behind Ruby. 'A ginger moggie over on the right by that pile of rubble. I think she might have been pregnant.'

Ruby played the thin beam of light around and – yes – there was the ginger cat. She was lying on her side and, even from a distance, it was obvious that she had been dead for some time. Ruby swallowed hard on a wave of nausea.

'She doesn't look pregnant any more,' she said, trying to keep her voice matter-of-fact. 'I wonder if she died giving birth? Only there's no sign of no kittens.'

'Probably all picked off by foxes,' said Leah grimly. 'How very sad all round. I'm so sorry you had to see this, Ruby.'

'Nonsense,' said Ruby staunchly. 'I need to see it all. Good *and* bad.'

'Still, rotten luck your first time,' said Leah. 'Come on, let's call it a day. We can cheer ourselves up with tea and a cake at Fisher's.'

Suddenly, a noise punctuated the gloom.

A quiet, clear, unmistakable little mew.

'There's one left!' cried Ruby joyfully. 'Oh, thank goodness. Just like at the factory, there's one left.'

She cast the torch around, trying to follow the source of the sound. And there, standing on an old broken barrel, was a tiny kitten.

Leah picked her way over, scooped it up without difficulty and the two women went outside into the warmth and the light.

'It looks just like Fluffy,' said Ruby, tickling the little kitten between its ears.

It was true.

With its shaggy steel-grey fur and startled expression, the little kitten was the spitting image of the little bundle of fun who had been lost at the factory.

That somehow made the discovery seem even more poignant.

'The good news is that it doesn't look hurt,' said Leah, holding the kitten up and inspecting it all over. 'It's a boy, by the way.'

'He must be starving,' said Ruby. 'And he won't be weaned yet so we'll need to get him some milk as soon as possible.'

'We'll need to do more than that,' said Leah. 'He won't survive much longer if we leave him here on his own; he's simply not strong enough to fend for himself. We'll have to try and find someone to take him in. I'd try and smuggle him back to my lodgings but I was given a final warning the last time I tried to do that. And Mummy said . . .'

Ruby didn't hesitate. 'I'll take him home with me,' she said, stroking the kitten's silky flanks.

Leah grinned. 'I can't imagine your mother being anything but charming,' she said. 'But you did say she'd have your guts for garters if you tried to bring another animal home.'

'Trust me, she won't be able to resist Steel,' said Ruby with a giggle.

'Oh, it's Steel, is it?' said Leah, arching an eyebrow.

'It is.'

'No titles?'

'Not a single one,' said Ruby. 'It's perfect,' she added. 'With a bit of luck, Tess will nurse Steel for us. Even Ma will have to agree that it's meant to be. And if you come home with me, she won't even try to argue. I haven't heard the end of how gracious and poised you are – just because you offered to carry the bleeding tea tray.'

Leah laughed. 'Always offer to carry the bleeding tea tray,' she said.

Ruby and Leah walked briskly back to Sanctuary Lane with Steel safely ensconced in Ruby's basket.

As predicted, Ma only put up a token protest before Steel was allowed to stay. After giving the kitten a bowl of milk, the two women wasted no time in introducing him to Tess who was, as usual, curled up in her basket by the range.

'I think she likes him,' said Ruby excitedly, as Steel burrowed close to Tess and Tess, for her part, licked Steel on the top of his head.

'I think she does,' said Leah, sitting back on her heels. 'Oh, he *is* like Fluffy, isn't he?'

'They could be twins,' said Ruby. 'And I have a plan. If it's ever safe to do so, I intend to give him to the little girl who used to own Fluffy.'

'Hallelujah,' said Ma, from her spot on the sofa. 'You mean this might only be a fleeting visit?'

'You'll fall in love with him, you see if you don't, Mrs A,' said Leah with a grin.

'Don't you believe it!' said Ma and she and Leah laughed easily together.

It was amazing how relaxed they were with each other.

'You might be stuck with Steel for a while, though, because who knows when we'll be able to give him to that little girl,' said Ruby. 'We can't just go handing out kittens to little girls without their parents' permission, and besides, the factory site ain't any safer than it were so it wouldn't be the responsible thing to do.'

'Oh!' said Leah, slapping herself on the side of her head. 'I can't believe I didn't tell you!'

'Tell me what?' said Ruby.

'About the Cat Committee.'

'The Cat Committee?' echoed Ma. 'Is that what you girls are calling yourselves now?'

'No!' said Leah, hauling herself up on to the sofa beside Ma. 'I forwarded Ruby's ideas for protecting the cats on the factory site to Mr Armstrong a few days ago – I didn't change anything in the end. Anyway, Mr Armstrong loved it all and he's setting up a cat committee. He's promised there won't be any more visits from the lethal chamber until it's up and running and until we've implemented everything we decide to do.'

Ruby clapped her hands together in glee. 'Oh, how exciting,' she said. 'That's wonderful news. Are you on the committee?'

'Yes,' said Leah. 'But more to the point, so are you.'

'*Me?*' Ruby could hardly believe it.

'Yes, of course, you,' said Leah. 'You didn't think I would steal your thunder, did you? After all, they were your ideas and I made sure Mr Armstrong was perfectly aware of that.'

Ruby gave a little squeal of delight. 'Did you hear that, Ma?' she said. 'Your Ruby is on a committee.'

'I did,' said Ma with a smile. 'And I'm proud of you, love. But for now, might I suggest that Ruby-on-a-committee and her friend Leah-on-a-committee stir themselves and buy some more milk before this little beggar drinks us out of house and home.'

Ruby and Leah walked back up Sanctuary Lane together, had a quick cup of tea and a cake at Fisher's, and then went their separate ways.

Ruby bought some more milk and was just heading home when something – or rather some*one* – caught her eye. That man, approaching the end of the road and about to cross the street in the direction of the docks. She couldn't be sure – he was a fair distance away – but it *looked* like Jack. He was wearing civvies and had a cap pulled low across his forehead, but there just was something about the height and build and the way he was walking with his hands behind his back that made her think . . . maybe, just maybe.

Ruby's heart started hammering nineteen to the dozen. She had given up ever seeing him again after mistaking someone else for him the night that Leah and Mr Smith had come to her home. But then the man stopped at the kerb and looked in her direction.

No second glance, no start of recognition.

Nothing.

He just checked for horses and motors and carried on his way.

Maybe it wasn't Jack at all, or maybe he just hadn't recognised her – but it had certainly looked like him. Maybe she should run after him and tap him on the shoulder. At least she would know one way or another, then. Not that it mattered. It would just be nice to know.

But just then, the man turned and looked directly at her. It *was* Jack, looking startled and a little embarrassed to have been caught in the act of turning around. He looked her in the eye and Ruby knew without a doubt that he had recognised her. Her face broke into an involuntary beam; she felt her cheeks glowing red and her feet began to walk a little faster of their own accord . . .

Jack gave her a half-smile and a little wave that was more like a salute.

Then he spun round on his heel and strode briskly away in the opposite direction.

22

It didn't matter.

It really didn't.

Jack was just a soldier she had met precisely twice, and well, if he chose to ignore her, then Ruby wasn't going to get in a tizzy about it.

Besides, she had other things, much more important things, going on her in life and far more deserving of her attention.

She had munitions to make and a war to win.

An animal hospital idea to pursue.

Lovely new friends.

Ruby might have been smitten with Jack from the very minute she'd first set eyes on him, but that wasn't enough.

If he didn't have the courtesy to at least greet her properly when they met in the street . . . well, he simply didn't matter at all.

Now that she had two jars of precious ointment in her possession – and a dog that was very nearly recovered – Ruby knew that she needed to start making decisions. She could store the ointment away until such time as she was ready to find premises and make her animal hospital dream come true – or she could choose to start letting animals benefit from it straight away. She plumped for the latter. After failing to cure Mac on her own, she had started to have cold feet about her ability to credibly open an animal hospital – but what was the point of letting animals suffer in the meantime when she had the means to make them better?

So, after a sleepless night, Ruby started spreading the word that she was happy to share her embrocation with whoever needed it most. She began very gently by mentioning it to the women on her table in the detonation shed. But word quickly spread, and soon Ruby was inundated with requests. Mary's sister's moggie had been in a fight and had a nasty cut close to her eye that just wouldn't heal. Isobel's mother's dog had hurt his paw and could no longer weight-bear. And then, at breaktime, Dot told her that the family cat had been thrown against some railings by a group of urchins and had a nasty wound on its underbelly.

All those animals and all those owners needing help and nowhere for them to turn.

As she carefully inserted springs into partially assembled detonators, Ruby started to make plans. Rather than just dole out the precious elixir to all and sundry, she decided it would be better to visit the injured animals in their own homes. Not that she felt at all confident in her judgement or diagnosis skills after only a few weeks at Nellie's – but because it would be the best way for her to learn. She wouldn't charge anything for the salve, but if owners felt able to contribute anything – well, every little helped. If she ever did decide to go ahead with opening a premises – a 'proper' animal hospital – she was going to need all the money she could find.

She would start with Dot.

Of course she would. Dot was her friend and Ruby was forever grateful that she had thrown herself wholeheartedly behind the animal hospital idea. Dot had already given Ruby a little stack of hand-knitted bandages and a couple of hand-knitted cushions to boot, to say nothing of the three shillings that had been collected in the tin on Fisher's counter. She had also outlined to Ruby some ambitious plans for educating owners on how best to care for their animals to prevent illness and injuries – drawing on her experience of doing the same thing for mothers and babies at ELFS. It was a brilliant idea and Ruby would have been wholeheartedly behind it if she wasn't constantly plagued by the nagging fear that the whole animal hospital idea was a non-starter without access to medicines which actually worked.

Anyway, Dot was as keen as mustard to get her hands on some of Mr Smith's ointment. She and her family were worried out of their wits about Willow and had tried everything they could think of to help her wound heal – but to no avail. Always a little pale and solemn-looking, Dot now looked thoroughly drawn and pinched. Ruby could sympathise; after Mac's recent injury, she knew exactly how her friend must be feeling.

They agreed that Ruby would go to Dot's home early the following evening, before they both started their night shift at the factory. In the meantime, Ruby scurried around picking up bits and pieces from the pharmacy and was thrilled when she found some potassium permanganate crystals. Not that she was trying to pass herself off as a vet or anything . . . but they had certainly helped to do the trick with Mac. Besides, she did suddenly feel horribly out of her depth; she wasn't trained and she didn't even have any real experience of caring for animals. She comforted herself with the thought that all she was doing was carrying out a good deed and sharing Mr Smith's ointment.

Nothing more.

Nothing less.

At five o'clock the next evening, Ruby duly walked up Sanctuary Lane to Fisher's.

She had, of course, been into the bakery many times over the years – indeed, she had enjoyed a cup of tea there with Leah only the week before. It had changed, of course, since the war had started – ingredient shortages had led to a reduced range, labour shortages had led to shorter hours and there were heavily advertised special offers for military personnel – but it was essentially the same place. However, Ruby had never had cause to go to the private quarters where the family lived, and it took a little while to find her way in. The bakery was flanked by Muller's the haberdashery on the left and the side of a shop that opened on to Silvertown High Street on the right, and – curiously – there were no doors to the flat upstairs on either side. Or at least none that Ruby could see. She walked up and down a little, noticing with a twinge of guilt that Muller's front window was still boarded up. She was just about to give up and go into the bakery itself to ask for directions when she saw a small sign on a gate on the far side of Muller's: *Fisher's Bakery and Deliveries.*

Ruby rang the bell, and after a minute, the gate was opened and she was ushered in by a beaming Dot. The gate led to a large courtyard which ran the length of both

Muller's and Fisher's and which was flanked by various outbuildings. There was a smart Fisher's van with fancy green and gold lettering parked at one end and two horses poking their heads over the top of stable doors at the other. Ruby suppressed a grin; if anything demonstrated a world in transition more than this, she wasn't sure what it could be.

Dot led the way through a door at the back of the building which opened to a long corridor and a steep flight of stairs. The family obviously lived upstairs, literally above the shop.

'She's here, Ma,' Dot called, taking Ruby into a comfortably – but not grandly – furnished living room. Willow the cat – a short-haired white moggie with irregular black patches – was in a basket by the fire, apparently asleep.

Suddenly Ruby began to feel queasy with nerves again.

Supposing the wound was bad enough to need stitches?

Supposing the kindest thing to do would be to put Willow out of her misery?

Goodness, she felt like a fraud; this business really wasn't for the faint-hearted.

Maybe she *should* have started with someone she didn't know.

Dot's mother – as short, dark and freckled as her daughter – came clucking into the room. Ruby recognised her from the bakery, of course.

'Hello, Ruby,' she said warmly. 'How very kind of you to share your ointment with us. It's quite restored my faith in humanity.'

Together they tiptoed over to examine Willow. Most

conveniently, the cat was splayed out on her back, her undercarriage on full display. There was a puckered four-inch gash along her belly, oozing yellow and green. It looked nasty, but, to Ruby's largely untrained eye – and to her relief – the wound looked no worse than the one on Mac's face. It certainly didn't look deep enough to need stitches. Although Willow's breathing was high and rapid, Ruby judged that she was eminently treatable.

'What happened?' she asked, bending down and stroking Willow gently.

'It were those beastly youths,' Dot burst out. 'I'm sure they threw Willow against the railings. It's ... it's just *hateful*.'

'Come, dear, we don't know that were the case,' soothed Mrs Fisher. 'We didn't see what happened. Willow just came home like this so we're really none the wiser.'

'But we've seen those youths tormenting cats before,' said Dot. 'The same ones who probably threw the brick through Muller's window. It *must* have been them.'

Ruby's blood ran cold and her chest tightened.

She hadn't seen Charlie much since the police had come around – hadn't had a chance to question him – but surely he'd had nothing to do with this. Throwing a brick was one thing, but Charlie wouldn't deliberately hurt an animal, would he? Ruby didn't like to think he would even stand by whilst someone else manhandled a defenceless creature.

'Did you see who they were?' she asked, hoping against hope that her cheeks weren't flaming red and giving away her second-hand guilt.

'No,' said Mrs Fisher firmly. 'As I said, we didn't see

what happened to Willow. Besides, I'm not sure I would recognise any of the boys who've been hanging around Muller's anyway. They're always bundled up in coats and scarves.'

Of course they were, thought Ruby furiously. Why else would they be wearing coats and scarves on a warm June evening, even if the weather had recently turned a little cooler? The youths had clearly been hellbent on trouble and had planned it all in advance.

Please don't let Charlie have hurt Willow.

She took a deep breath. 'Shall we try and clean the wound first before we apply the ointment?' she suggested briskly, anxious to move things along. 'The vet used a potassium permanganate solution on Mac's wound so I thought we might try the same here.'

Mrs Fisher and Dot looked suitably impressed as Ruby made up the lilac solution and cleaned Willow's belly as well as she could. Willow flinched and then hissed, but Ruby held her down gently and persevered. Then she carefully applied the ointment on top of the wound.

'I hope that works,' she said, standing up and dusting herself down. 'It did the trick with me dog, so hopefully Willow's wound will heal well too. It will take a couple of days though; don't expect it to happen overnight. I'll leave the ointment with you; just apply it twice a day.'

With a wound of that size, Ruby realised there was unlikely to be any ointment over by the time Willow had finished her course of treatment. She would just have one jar left. Enough to help another animal or two – but that was it.

'We're so grateful,' said Mrs Fisher, as they showed

Ruby out. 'Whatever happens, it's just good to know that someone is on our side. Thank you, my dear. And whatever help you need with the animal hospital, please just let us know.'

Instead of going straight into work with Dot as she had planned, Ruby made her excuses and hurried home. Charlie wasn't in – of course he wasn't – but as Ruby was about to leave again for the factory, she spotted him coming into the backyard from the rear alleyway and hurried out to confront him.

'I'm disgusted at you,' she hissed without preamble.

Charlie recoiled. Shock, guilt, hurt flitted across his face – half-man, half-boy – but he quickly rallied. 'Ain't you always?' he replied flippantly.

'Don't be pert,' snapped Ruby. 'I know exactly what you or your precious friend Joe did to that cat.'

'What cat?' Charlie really did look impressively baffled.

'Don't lie to *me*, Charlie Archer.'

'I ain't lying,' said Charlie. 'What on earth are you talking about? What cat?'

'The cat you hurt, stupid. Or are there several?'

'I promise I ain't hurt no cats,' Charlie said vehemently. 'I give you me word.'

'Says the lad who lied to those policemen,' said Ruby. 'I'd say your word don't count for much, wouldn't you?'

'Oh, I just *knew* that you were listening upstairs that day,' said Charlie, trying to push his way past Ruby and into the house.

'Don't change the subject,' she said, shoving him back and then grabbing hold of his arm. 'The point is that if you're prepared to lie to the police, there's no reason that *I* should believe a word you say. So I'll just say this. If I hear of any more animals being deliberately hurt around here, I'm going straight to the police station to tell them that you've admitted to going around town, throwing bricks through people's businesses. Understood?'

'Loud and clear,' said Charlie coldly, wrenching his way free. 'Businesses belonging to Germans is one thing, but if you really think I'd hurt an animal, you don't know me at all.'

'I don't think I do, Charlie,' said Ruby to his departing back. 'No. I really don't think I do at all.'

To Ruby's relief and joy, Willow made a good recovery.

Dot came to find Ruby a couple of days later to tell her the wound was starting to heal nicely and that Willow was up and about. She gave Ruby a large currant cake, a shiny sixpence and a note from Mrs Fisher, fulsome in its praise and gratitude. Ruby couldn't help feeling guilty as she accepted these gifts. She hadn't really done *anything*; she hadn't even paid for the ointment, for goodness' sake.

It was all down to Mr Smith.

Still, the experience gave her the confidence to make a couple more house calls and both – to Ruby's relief – had also gone swimmingly. But one war-loaf and a beef broth in payments later, she was almost out of ointment. With word spreading around the factory about what she was doing, Ruby was inundated with more and more requests for help. Once, thrillingly, someone even stopped her outside the lavvies to ask if she was the 'animal lady'. If only she had access to the same products that Robert

237

Smith did. Without them, the whole project was in danger of grinding to a halt.

'Do you think Mr Smith would give me any more ointment?'

Ruby and Leah were chatting after the inaugural meeting of the Cat Committee a couple of days later. The meeting itself had gone exceedingly well; just about all Ruby's suggestions had been adopted and plans were being put in place for their implementation. Ruby was thrilled about that, but she couldn't help her frustration over everything else from bubbling up in front of Leah.

'Not a chance, I'm afraid.' Leah screwed her face up in sympathy. 'He made a point of telling me that that was your lot.'

It was on the tip of Ruby's tongue to point out that Leah seemed to be seeing rather a lot of the odious Mr Smith, but she resisted the temptation. None of this was Leah's fault, and besides, it was none of Ruby's business what Leah chose to do in her spare time.

'It's just a shame,' she grumbled. 'It somehow feels that he holds the key to making the animal hospital idea work and yet he refuses to get involved.'

'I'm sorry,' said Leah as the two women gathered up their papers and stood up. 'If it's any consolation, he did tell me that there's nothing really in his ointment that isn't in the salve Nellie sold you.'

'Pardon me?' Ruby was so taken aback that she sat down heavily on the seat she had just vacated. '*What* did you just say?'

Leah looked surprised. 'Well, just that,' she said. 'Robert

said that everything he uses is also on sale to the general public. Apart from a couple of very dangerous drugs, there are absolutely no regulations.'

Ruby paused, trying to work it all out. 'So, if I knew where to get it from, I could just buy that embrocation?' she said slowly.

'Absolutely,' said Leah. 'Although Robert also said that, judging from what you told him was in it, Nellie's salve would have worked pretty much as well.'

'Really?' said Ruby, excitement bubbling up in her chest. 'So he thinks Mac would have got better if I had just carried on doing what I'd been doing?'

'Yes,' said Leah. 'He said he was glad he hadn't charged you for the ointment because it would have been a waste of your money.'

Ruby exhaled noisily and slapped her hand down on to the table. 'Why didn't you tell me before?' she exclaimed.

'Robert only told me yesterday,' Leah replied mildly.

'But can't you see that this changes everything?' said Ruby.

Leah shrugged and shook her head. 'Not really,' she said. 'I thought the issue was money. Didn't you say even Nellie was charging you a shilling a pop?'

'She is, but that isn't the point,' said Ruby. 'Not the whole point, anyway. We can always raise the money.'

'So, what is the point?'

'The point *is* that I thought no matter how hard we tried, we would always be second best to what the vets had to offer,' said Ruby. 'That the medicines available to us would never be as good as theirs. Robert more or less said as much; maybe he were just trying to protect his job, but I believed him. And now I know that the medicines we can offer will be exactly the same. Oh, I know we ain't got the same experience or training as vets and I know we can't do surgery at the moment – but there's an awful lot that we *can* do and there's nothing stopping me from pressing ahead with the damn thing. So, thank you, Leah. Thank you.'

'Don't *thank* me,' said Leah, with a laugh. 'So, what are your next steps?'

Ruby had been thinking about this for weeks. 'Three things,' she said. 'Premises, money and staff.' She started counting them off on her fingers. 'Premises is a difficult one – I've asked around a little and there's not a lot available and everything is so expensive. Money's difficult too – we'll have to start fundraising soon. And staff – well, that's difficult too if people don't get involved. But apart from that, it's easy!'

Leah laughed, but it was a kind, supportive laugh.

'One step at a time,' she said. 'Get one of those three pillars sorted and the others will follow, I'm sure. And I've been thinking about how I might help and I'll get back to you on that as soon as I can. In the meantime, I'd better get back on duty and you had better get some sleep.'

She patted Ruby on the shoulder, picked up her paperwork and was gone.

Ruby looked after her thoughtfully.

Leah had certainly changed her tune.

23

After that, exciting things seemed to happen in quick succession.

The first was Mrs Mason, the detonation shop supervisor, taking Ruby to one side before her shift.

'You're doing well in here, Ruby,' she said. 'Mary has made a point of saying your work is quick and accurate and that you're a helpful and positive member of the team.'

'Thank you, Ma'am.'

Ruby was delighted, of course, and, it had to be said, somewhat surprised. She'd had very little to do with Mrs Mason since starting her new role and, as she spent much of the time on duty either exhausted or deep in thought about something else, it was a miracle she wasn't getting torn off a strip.

She was obviously doing something right.

Mrs Mason was still talking. 'Many of the women here are old enough to be your mother, but Mary and I have noticed that you always have your eye on the quotas, you encourage others to make sure that the targets are met and that, on occasion, you've stayed behind to help Mary make up any shortfall whilst others have clocked off immediately the shift finishes. I'm impressed, Ruby, and I've got my eye on you as a potential table supervisor,' she said.

'Really?' Ruby clapped her hands together in excitement. 'Me? A supervisor? That's marvellous . . .'

'Hold your horses!' interrupted Mrs Mason with a laugh. 'It hasn't happened yet. But Mary is taking some leave with immediate effect – one of her sons is heading to France and they want to spend some time together as a family before he goes off – and I would like you to take charge of her table whilst she's gone. If all goes well, I will give you your own table of new recruits when she returns.'

That sobered Ruby up no end. No one wanted to benefit from someone else's misfortune and of course she felt desperately sorry for poor Mary. But still, this was an opportunity that she simply couldn't pass up – even if she had any real choice in the matter.

Ruby felt ever so important and more than slightly petrified as the shift started that evening. To her relief, everything went smoothly enough.

Fancy!

All those older women accepting her as their manager. Not, to be fair, that there was an awful lot of 'managing' to do. By now, each woman knew all the tasks like the back of their own hands and they basically just got on with whichever one they had been allocated to do that week. The conversation was all about the huge numbers of young men that seemed to be on their way to France and the huge offensive that this no doubt heralded, and there were no disgruntled comments or sideways glances at Ruby – let alone open mutiny. Ruby took all that as a success and buried her own fears about Harry. As far as she knew, he was still safely ensconced in Buckinghamshire and there had been no mention of anything changing in his letters home.

She must make do with that.

The next unexpected thing happened during one of Ruby's shifts at Nellie's barrow a couple of days later.

Ruby was hard at work when Nellie suddenly turned to her and said, apropos of nothing, 'You still thinking of setting up that animal clinic, girl?'

Ruby paused, grisly offcut of meat in one hand, waxed paper in the other.

'Yes, I am,' she said cautiously. 'One day. I must admit I got cold feet, but . . .'

Nellie tutted. 'One day,' she echoed. 'One day? Empires are won and lost whilst folks talk about one day!'

Ruby turned to her in surprise. 'It ain't that easy,' she said defensively.

'Nothing worthwhile ever is,' said Nellie. 'But there's a space coming free at our depot next month. A lot of the stallholders here are based there and I thought it might do very well for you too.'

Lordy.

Ruby was so surprised that for a moment words eluded her.

'Don't just stand there with your mouth hanging open, girl,' said Nellie. 'It ain't nothing grand, but the rent is low. If you're interested, I'll show you next week after one of your shifts.'

Ruby found her tongue. 'Yes. *Yes*. Of course I'm interested,' she said. 'And I'm sure one day next week will be just fine an' all. It's just a case of which one. Only, on

Monday I've got a meeting of the Cat Committee and on Tuesday I'm going to take a look at Annie-Next-Door's cousin's dog and . . .'

Nellie gave a throaty chuckle. 'I'm going to make this easy for you,' she said. 'You're sacked. As of now. I don't want to see you here no more.'

Ruby turned to her in dismay.

In *confusion*.

'Nellie, *no*,' she protested. 'What have I done wrong?'

'Well, for one thing you're standing there waving that bone around rather than serving Miss Parker,' said Nellie.

'But that ain't fair. *You* were the one who started talking to me about the depot.'

'I'm joking, child,' said Nellie. 'You ain't done nothing wrong. But you've got more important things to do now than working here, so I'm letting you go.'

'But I *need* you,' Ruby stammered.

'No, you don't,' said Nellie briskly. 'I reckon you've learned just about all you're going to learn by standing around here all day. Besides, *I* ain't going anywhere. I'm always here if you've got a problem or want to ask summat, and if you do start renting that space in the depot, you'll end up seeing more of me than you do now anyway.'

'Oh, Nellie,' said Ruby. It made sense. In her heart, Ruby knew it did. It was just all so sudden. 'Won't I be leaving you in the lurch?'

'Not at all,' said Nellie. 'Me daughter will do the odd shift here now her baby's a little older – she ain't going back to the munitions factory just yet. Besides, if you carry on sending folk here to buy me salve, I'll be your

244

friend for life. I've sold more of it in the last couple of weeks than I have done in the last year.'

'Thank you, Nellie,' said Ruby. 'Thank you for everything.'

She reached over and gave Nellie a great big hug then pulled away with a little sigh.

She might not have money and she might not have staff, but now she might just have somewhere to base her hospital and that felt like a huge step in the right direction.

She was on her way and she was ready.

Maybe 'one day' was now.

Or, at least, next week.

'Just one more thing, Dolly Daydream,' Nellie was saying.

'What's that?'

'Hurry up and serve Miss Parker. She ain't got all day.'

The third unexpected thing happened just half an hour later.

Ruby had finished what had turned out to be her final shift at Nellie's and was walking home, ready to tumble into bed. Everything seemed fresh and newly minted – full of hope and possibility – and her mind was full of what the depot might be like and how well it might suit, when she rounded the corner into Victory Lane and saw Jack.

This time, he was only a few yards in front of her.

Bending down – trousers tight around a muscular bottom if a girl cared to notice – he was feeding chunks of meat from a pie to a stray dog. He was close enough for Ruby to hear him talking reassuringly to the dog, but he didn't seem to have heard Ruby approach.

She wasn't sure what to do.

The chap had already made it abundantly clear that he wanted absolutely nothing to do with her, so maybe the polite thing would be to cross the road before he saw her and just continue on her way home.

Then again . . . no!

Why should *she* creep around and alter her route just because *he* hadn't been polite enough to doff his cap and greet a lady the last time they'd met? No, she would walk right up to Jack, greet him civilly and show him that *she* knew what good manners were, even if he didn't, thank you very much.

'Oi!' shouted an indignant voice behind her. 'I should report you for that!'

Ruby swung around, bemused.

She wasn't sure what she had done wrong, nor why a middle-aged woman was marching up to her, hands on hips, eyes ablaze. Then she realised that the woman was bearing down on *Jack*. Jack, for his part, had straightened up and was now looking thoroughly befuddled to see both Ruby and the older woman standing there.

'Report me for *what*?' he said to the middle-aged woman in good-natured confusion, giving Ruby a brief nod at the same time. Curly brown hair, green eyes, lopsided grin . . . none of her attraction had gone away.

'Feeding that dog, that's what,' said the woman.

Jack shrugged. 'It's me own pie,' he said mildly.

'But feeding strays is illegal,' the woman said indignantly.

Jack glanced at Ruby as if for confirmation.

'We ain't meant to feed them no more,' Ruby confirmed quietly. 'I don't know if it's actually illegal . . .'

'We need the meat for the real men at the front,' said the woman, her tone hardening. 'Not the yellows like you.'

A bolt of pure outrage crackled through Ruby.

Had the woman really just called Jack a coward?

And him a serving soldier, to boot.

How *dare* she?

Ruby stepped towards the woman, with no regard for personal space. 'He ain't yellow,' she said. 'He's just got back from the front.'

'If you say so . . .' said the woman, sounding slightly uncertain.

'I do say so! Apologise to him at once.'

'You heading back to the front, soldier?'

'Tell her, Jack,' said Ruby. '*Tell* her.'

There was a silence which stretched until it threatened to become awkward.

'Say something, Jack,' said Ruby.

Say something!

Finally, he gave a little sigh.

'I've got to be honest,' he said. 'I ain't no soldier.'

Ruby stared at Jack in confusion.

What on earth was he talking about?

They'd talked at length about life at the front when they'd been packed like sardines in the tunnel – and she'd been wearing his army greatcoat, for goodness' sake . . .

'I knew it,' the woman said nastily. 'You can always tell a yellow from fifty paces.'

Jack ignored her and turned to Ruby. 'I were a soldier, but I ain't no more,' he explained. 'I've been invalided out.'

Really?

Ruby had a thousand and one questions, but the woman had taken a couple more steps towards Jack. 'Can't say you seem much like an invalid to me,' she said rudely.

Ruby stepped forward in exasperation. 'Not that it's any of your business,' she said hotly.

She wasn't entirely sure what Jack's Blighty wound was either, but that didn't matter. She somehow completely trusted that he was genuine.

'Don't take that tone with me, Miss,' the woman said, pointing her finger at Ruby. 'You're part of the problem, and all!'

'What problem?' Ruby grinned and shot Jack a 'can-you-believe-what-she's-saying-now?' look and he smiled and pulled a little face in return. 'I ain't no part of no problem.'

'You work at the munitions place, don't you?'

'And what if I do?'

Working for the war effort was something to be proud of. Everyone knew that.

'You work for cheaper rates and you're taking the work away from the men who *should* be doing that work,' the woman said.

Ruby sighed.

Like everyone, she had heard this from time to time at the factory. She had seen the hostile glances, heard the muttered comments, even overheard the odd confrontation. It was usually men who were unhappy, and Mrs Mason

248

always said it was because women had proved once and for all they could do just about any job as well as the men and that they were more than worthy of equal rights. Mrs Mason also said that the best reply was to smile sweetly and not get drawn into an argument, and by and large Ruby had taken that advice.

But this was different.

This was out of work.

And this was a *woman*.

A woman who had been unforgivably rude to Jack.

'We're working in the munitions factory because the men ain't here to *do* the work,' Ruby retorted tartly. 'Everybody knows that.'

'And what happens when the *real* men come home from the war needing a job?'

To be honest, Ruby didn't know.

Who knew what would happen when the war was over? Would they all just go back to how they had been before? Would Ruby head back to Hampstead and service?

Oh, she hoped not.

Too much had changed already.

In the event, Jack answered for her. 'When the men come back from the war, let's hope there'll be no need of munitions factories for a long, long time,' he said. 'And let's hope a fella will be able to give a starving animal a bite to eat without being called to task, eh?'

The woman gave a rude snort, looked from Ruby to Jack and then stalked off with her nose in the air. Ruby and Jack didn't say anything for a moment and then, as one, they burst out laughing.

'Oh goodness,' said Jack, throwing the rest of the pie down to the dog. 'I weren't expecting *that*. Thank you for coming to my rescue.'

'I can't believe how rude she were,' said Ruby. 'Some older people are horrified about what the war has done to young people . . . and then some of them come out with things like *that*.'

There was a short silence and Ruby wondered if Jack would make his excuses and shoot off down the road as he was wont to do.

But he didn't.

He crouched down and carried on petting the stray dog and Ruby wondered if she should take the obvious hint and leave. But then he looked up at her with a half-smile that made her stomach flip-flop and said, 'So . . . not the army.'

'You never said,' said Ruby, with a smile. 'And I thought . . . the coat . . . ?' She mimed pulling his army greatcoat around her shoulders and looked questioningly at him.

'You're allowed to keep it for a month,' said Jack, straightening up and hitching his hip on to a low wall. 'Then you need to return it to the nearest main station and a pound for your troubles. The month was up the morning after the Zeppelin raid – otherwise I'd have let you wear the coat back to the munitions factory. I really didn't feel like the walk to Liverpool Street after that night's sleep, I can tell you!'

'Walk? To Liverpool Street?' said Ruby. 'You could have got the Tube from Mile End.'

Jack gave her a lopsided grin. 'I think you saw what I'm

like trapped underground,' he said. 'And the Tube is far worse than the foot tunnel – what with all the noises and knowing that you can't get out. In fact, the first time I saw you – at Silvertown Station – I were intending to drop me coat off then as well as going to Club Row to buy a dog. I were trying to pluck up me courage to get on a train – I'd already missed three! – but I just couldn't face it.'

'Oh,' said Ruby, as the pieces slotted into place. 'I thought it were something to do with me.'

'Why on earth would you think that?' said Jack, looking genuinely puzzled. 'No, it were all me and what's going on in me head.'

Ruby touched him sympathetically on the arm. 'Is that why . . . ?' she started and then hesitated, unsure how to proceed diplomatically.

'Why I've been invalided out?' Jack finished for her. 'I weren't lying, by the way; it were all above board and I've got me silver war badge to prove it.' He rummaged in his pocket and produced the small badge which was presented at an honourable discharge. 'I couldn't be bothered to show it to that rude woman but, well, here you are.'

'You don't have to show me nothing!' said Ruby, horrified that Jack might think she had doubted him. 'I weren't implying . . .'

'I know you weren't,' said Jack. 'But I'll tell you anyway. Me leg were badly injured and I can't run very fast no more, and I know it ain't obvious – but I'm actually pretty deaf.'

He pointed, unnecessarily, at his ears and Ruby wrinkled up her nose.

'Are you?' she said doubtfully. 'You seemed to hear well enough in the tunnel.'

And then she could have kicked herself because it sounded very like she *was* doubting him.

'I'm almost completely deaf in one ear and me hearing comes and goes in the other,' Jack clarified. 'It were just lucky we was sitting the way we was in the tunnel, otherwise I wouldn't have been able to hear a word you were saying. In fact, the chap on the other side of me could have been talking away nineteen to the dozen and I wouldn't have had a clue.'

'He's saying to this day how rude you were!'

Jack laughed and, emboldened, Ruby asked, 'How did you go deaf?'

'A shell exploded very close to me and blew me off me horse,' he said. 'Buggered me leg too. I've been in hospital on the Isle of Wight for a while and me leg's now about as better as it's going to be, but me hearing ain't come back. So, here I am. Of no more use to the army. Of no more use to *anyone,* for that matter.'

He was smiling, but Ruby could hear the bitterness and the confusion in his words.

'That's not true,' she said, sitting down on the wall beside him and not caring what any passers-by might think. 'And at least you're out of there now. Hell on earth, you called it when we was in the tunnel.'

'I know,' said Jack, almost in wonderment. 'I ain't talked to anyone like that before. Not me ma, not me pals – no one. It were dark in there, and of course I thought I would never see you again.'

Ruby took a deep breath. 'Is that why you ignored me the other day?' she said.

She had to know. She had barely admitted it to

herself, but Jack turning his back on her like that had really hurt.

Jack flushed and ran a hand over his face. 'Sort of,' he admitted. 'Well, that and the baby.'

A baby!

Ruby made sure that her expression didn't change, but she was surprised by how devastated she felt.

In fact, it felt like all the warmth and excitement that had been bubbling up inside her since she had been talking to Jack was now being squeezed out by an unforgiving, iron fist.

Of *course,* someone as handsome as Jack was always going to have been spoken for. If not a baby, he would at least have had a wife or a sweetheart.

Ma always said that the good ones got snapped up straight away.

'I didn't realise you had a baby,' she said, hoping her voice didn't sound as flat as she suddenly felt.

'Not *my* baby,' said Jack, looking confused. '*Your* baby.'

The world spun for a moment . . . and then shuddered to a halt.

Ruby looked at Jack blankly. 'I beg your pardon?'

'Come now,' said Jack, with a little regretful smile. 'Don't play games. I *saw* you. I saw you with your baby.'

'But I ain't got no baby,' said Ruby, utterly confused. Maybe the shell exploding had damaged more than Jack's ears. 'I honestly don't know what you're talking about.'

Jack took a deep breath. 'I saw you wheeling your pram down this very street less than two weeks ago. And I thought that holding your hand in the tunnel when we was both frightened out of our wits was one thing but that I've got no business talking to a married woman with a child after that.'

Oh.

Oh!

Ruby threw her head back and started laughing.

And once she'd been laughing for a while, she found she couldn't stop.

'What's so funny?' asked Jack, looking half-annoyed and half-amused. 'Come on, what have I said?'

With a big effort, Ruby managed to compose herself. 'It weren't a baby in that pram,' she gasped, between more giggles. 'I'd been using it for me dog and I were just returning it.'

And she was off again, laughing until tears ran down her cheeks and her belly ached.

Jack pursed his lips and shook his head from side to side. 'I won't ask why your dog were in a pram,' he said, with the glimmer of a smile. 'But you're sure there ain't no baby?'

'Not even a little one,' said Ruby. 'Not even a sweetheart, for that matter. You?'

'None at all,' said Jack. He paused and swallowed hard. 'There ain't even a dog,' he added. 'Mine died whilst I was at the front and me ma hadn't wanted to tell me.'

'Oh. I'm ever so sorry.'

How beastly after everything else that he had been through.

Ruby leaned forward and touched Jack's arm. The two of them locked eyes for much longer than was strictly necessary. The green had hints of hazel in it and . . .

'Oh, reggub,' Jack blurted out, standing up. 'How long have we been sitting here?'

Ruby knew just enough of the old costermonger slang to know this was 'bugger' backwards. 'I don't know,' she said. 'It must be about half past nine.'

Jack hit himself lightly on the side of his head. 'I'm meant to be looking at a friend's mule,' he said. 'And I'm very, very late.'

'Reggub, indeed,' said Ruby, not caring if that sounded too forward.

Jack was walking backwards away from her. 'Well, Ruby-who-definitely-doesn't-have-a-baby, would you like to step out with me one day?'

Ruby's heart soared. 'Ruby-who-definitely-doesn't-have-a-baby would like that very much,' she replied.

Jack's face lit up with pleasure and relief. 'What about the football match next week?' he said. 'Unless you've already got plans for it?'

The football match?

What football match?

That hadn't been what Ruby had had in mind at all.

'That would be marvellous,' she said.

24

Ruby asked Leah to accompany her to look at the depot with Nellie.

She could have gone on her own – and perhaps, indeed, she *should* have done – but, on balance, she reckoned that two heads were better than one. Besides, someone as poised and well-spoken as Leah couldn't help but give a good impression to the landlord in a way that Ruby, on her own, might not.

It was just the way that things were.

'What's she doing here?' demanded Nellie when they met near the market as agreed. She jabbed a grubby finger towards Leah in a manner that was just shy of rude and Ruby felt a stab of embarrassment and discomfiture. She liked Nellie and she liked Leah and it had never occurred to her that they might not immediately get on with each other.

'This is Miss Richardson, my friend and a manager at the factory,' she said carefully. 'And this is Mrs Byrd, my friend and my former manager at the market.'

Nice and equal; hopefully that would do the trick.

Leah and Nellie nodded civilly enough at each other and Ruby exhaled a ragged sigh of relief.

Civil, she could work with.

Warmth might follow – but no matter if it didn't.

'It ain't nothing grand,' said Nellie, with a sideways

glance at Leah as she set off at a clip along the road, around a couple of corners and down a muddy alleyway. Ruby must have walked down that particular road dozens of times, but she had never really registered this particular alleyway. She'd had no reason to.

'I don't need grand,' said Ruby, taking in the rather dilapidated brick warehouse that stood in front of them. One of the windows was cracked, the door was slightly off its hinges and the ground outside was ankle deep in mud, even though it hadn't rained in weeks, and strewn with all manner of detritus.

'This certainly isn't grand,' Leah muttered so that only Ruby could hear.

She wiped her boot on the side of a discarded wheel with something approaching disgust. Ruby felt a stab of irritation; this was the woman who thought nothing of getting herself thoroughly grubby ferreting out strays from the most unsavoury parts of Silvertown – and here she was getting her knickers in a twist over a bit of mud.

'I don't need the Ritz,' Ruby said, more tartly than she had intended. 'Anyway, I couldn't afford it. I can't afford nothing really – but don't tell the landlord, Nellie!'

'Oh, the landlord ain't here, sweetheart,' said Nellie. 'He don't care who's in here, anyway. As long as he gets his rent each month, he wouldn't care if Beelzebub himself rented one of the stalls, believe you me.'

She gave a wheezy cackle and pushed open the rickety door, and the three women stepped inside.

Inside was a hive of concentrated activity.

It was clear that a dozen different types of business had their home there and the result was a veritable assault on the senses. In the cavernous central area, there was an old lady scrubbing turnips, another sorting old rags and a third making toffee-apples over a charcoal fire. And around the outside, there was a series of 'rooms' which were really little more than stalls. Some were open to the central area and obviously used as stables – a young man in the nearest one, busy harnessing a donkey to a cart, waved cheerfully as they passed – and some had been closed off with flimsy partitions and wooden doors. There was no doubt which stall belonged to Nellie; the grisly-looking meat offcuts, flies and the stench gave *that* away, good and proper. It didn't look the most hygienic, but at least there would be something convenient to feed the hospital patients . . .

Ruby and Leah followed Nellie across the warehouse, skirting their way carefully around an old man boiling oranges, and over to the far side of the building.

'Here we are,' said Nellie, throwing open a door. 'It's a nice double stall with its own door – so easy as pie to lock everything away when you ain't here. The previous owner has gone to the front and his wife tried to keep their coster business going but found it too hard on her own. It's yours if you want it, but no offence taken if you don't. Someone else will snap it up.'

Ruby cast her eye around the space, trying to imagine it all in practice. A large window in the far wall looked over tatty scrubland at the back of the building; it let in ample natural light and the sunshine streaming in and catching the swirling dust motes in a shower of gold somehow seemed to be a good omen . . .

Concentrate, Ruby!

What about practicalities?

There was no door allowing external access and that was a pity because, as it stood, the only way in and out of the room was directly through the warehouse. Maybe they could ask for one to be installed. And there was no electricity – but that was probably to be expected. There were a couple of old tables and chairs that looked sturdy enough and some shelves against a side wall that would, no doubt, prove useful and . . .

'Running water?' she asked.

That really would be make or break.

Nellie gestured back into the main warehouse. 'There's a tap out there,' she said. 'We all share it but it's right outside so you ain't got too far to walk.'

Ruby nodded. She put her hands on her hips and twirled slowly in a circle.

Was this what she had imagined?

More importantly, was this what she *needed*?

She realised she had absolutely no idea.

'What do you think, Leah?' she asked, the words sticking in her throat.

She dreaded the answer but she had to know. Somehow, she knew that whatever Leah said – whatever she *thought* – would determine what Ruby did next.

Leah didn't say anything for a moment.

Then she smiled brightly. 'Well, I must say there's a perfectly marvellous smell of oranges out there,' she said. 'To tell the truth, I'm quite tempted to buy a jar or two of marmalade from the gentleman before I leave.'

There was a short silence.

Ruby met Nellie's eye with the ghost of a grin.

'I'll take the room,' said Ruby. 'I'll pay you the deposit now.'

Because, completely without intending to, Leah had given her the very answer she needed.

'Oh Ruby,' said Leah. 'There's no need to rush into anything.'

'I think the animals would say there's every reason to rush into *everything*,' Ruby replied. 'I'll take it,' she repeated to Nellie, more firmly this time.

That casual comment about the marmalade had shown, once and for all, that Leah didn't know what she was talking about. She didn't belong in this world and she would never really understand its ways, and because of that, her opinion of the depot really counted for nothing. Because the 'gentleman' stirring the oranges over the charcoal brazier wasn't making marmalade. Of course, he wasn't. The old rogue was simply boiling his oranges – *ruining* them, in effect – to make them appear extra plump and juicy on his stall or barrow. It was an old costermonger trick. Ruby knew it and Nellie knew it, just as they both had grown up trying to dodge a hundred such scams. And the important thing was that Leah *didn't* know it. She was viewing everything through a completely different lens.

It was the same with the depot, Ruby realised.

Where Leah was just seeing the dirt and the squalor, Ruby saw dignified working-class people eking out a living any way they could.

These were *her* people.

More importantly, these were precisely the people she was trying to help.

'I'll take it,' she said for a third time and Nellie laughed.

'I heard you the first time, you daft ha'porth,' she said. 'And I'm very pleased to hear it. I'm sure you'll make a great success of it and I'm happy to help out where I can. I'll even put in the odd shift meself if you would like. Now, if you've got five quid, I'll get you signed up and it's all yours from the beginning of next month.'

Ruby had come prepared. Five pounds was quite a steep deposit, but she had money set aside from her wages, and after that, the rent seemed very reasonable. In a matter of seconds, Nellie had secreted Ruby's notes into her apron pocket and had pressed an illegible receipt into Ruby's hand.

'Thank you,' said Ruby. 'Right, I think we need to set a date for the grand opening of the animal hospital.'

'Steady,' said Leah, with a little laugh.

'No, it's important to have a rough target or we'll never get things off the ground,' Ruby insisted. 'Why don't we give ourselves six weeks to get things up and running – even if we start off small. We can set an actual date nearer the time.'

'Good for you, girl,' said Nellie emphatically.

Ruby smiled at her.

It was done!

'Congratulations,' said Leah.

She and Ruby were walking back to the centre of Silvertown together before they went their separate ways; Ruby back home to sleep off her night shift and Leah off to the factory to start her day.

'I know you didn't like it,' said Ruby, trying her darnedest not to sound sulky. 'That were clear right from the moment you got there.'

Leah stopped still on the pavement. 'I trust your judgement, Ruby,' she said softly.

'That ain't the same thing.'

'But surely that's the important thing? You know what you want – what will work – and you've made it happen. Besides, it was a very good idea to set a date for the opening. Never mind what I think.'

The sulky feeling evaporated.

'Thank you,' said Ruby. 'You don't know how much that means to me.'

'And now I'm in a position to tell you the things I mentioned the other day,' said Leah.

'What are they?' asked Ruby, curiosity piqued. 'I hope one is that you've finally told that Robert Smith exactly where he can sling his hook.'

Leah laughed. 'No,' she said, bending to stroke a skinny cat who was scavenging in the gutter. 'No, I rather think it's best to keep him on side, don't you? Although I certainly won't be letting him take any liberties.'

'Very pleased to hear it,' said Ruby with an exaggerated shudder. 'So, what did you want to tell me?'

They stopped walking. They had reached the corner of Sanctuary Lane where their paths would diverge. The front window of Muller's had been mended, Ruby noticed.

'I've pawned some of my twenty-first birthday jewellery,' said Leah, her eyes shining. 'And I want you – or rather the animal hospital – to have the money.'

Ruby was covered in confusion. Excitement, embarrassment and hope all jostled for supremacy.

'Oh Leah – you haven't!' she spluttered. 'You *can't*!'

'I can and I have,' said Leah matter-of-factly. 'I knew

you might react like this and that's why I didn't tell you until the deed was done.'

'But . . . but what will your parents say?'

It was the first thing that came to mind.

Leah shrugged. 'It's been a couple of years since my twenty-first and I don't think they remember everything I was given. We're a big family and I'm an only child and I got given a *lot*. Besides, this particular set was ghastly. They made me look like Queen Victoria! I was never going to wear them.'

'But it's part of your inheritance,' protested Ruby, thinking of the silver tea set at home which would one day be hers. Their only precious item, it hadn't even occurred to Ruby to sell or pawn it. Not that Ma would have countenanced such an idea, anyway. 'Aren't you meant to pass it down to your own children?'

'Oh, I'm never going to have children,' Leah said casually. 'And this piece was inherited from a great-aunt I really didn't like, so it's not as though there's any sentimental value attached to them. Luckily, although they were perfectly hideous, they turned out to be quite valuable so they fetched a tidy sum. I don't think Mummy and Daddy realised their value; in fact, Mummy once said they looked fake.'

She mentioned a sum and Ruby started with shock.

'I couldn't possibly accept that,' she said, a little stiffly.

It would be marvellous – of course it would – but it was all just too much.

'Oh, come on, Ruby,' said Leah. 'Of course you can. In fact, you *must*! Anyway, it's not for you – it's for the hospital – and it's taken from the upper classes (at least

Mummy would like to think we're upper class) and donated to help the poor. There's a certain elegance in that, don't you think?'

'Of course I do,' said Ruby. 'It's just like Robin Hood. But . . .'

'But Aunt Isabella would turn in her grave,' said Leah. 'It's such a marvellous plan. Please accept it.'

The two of them burst out laughing and Ruby felt the stirrings of real excitement. This money could – *would* – make all the difference. Even with premises lined up, Ruby had been worried about how she was going to make a weekly clinic function on a shoestring. She had some savings, but there was a limit to what anyone could do on the munitions factory wage – generous as it might be. Leah's money would mean she could fit the depot room out properly, buy the supplies they needed and give the whole thing the best chance of success.

'Are you sure, Leah?' she said, hardly daring to believe her luck. 'It's a lot of money and it hardly seems yesterday you was telling me what a daft idea the whole thing is. And that were when I thought I'd be getting someone else to run it!'

'Oh, I still think you're daft,' said Leah with a laugh. 'Daft as a brush, in fact. But I've realised we can't put everything on hold because of the war – after all, who knows how long the blasted thing is going to go on. You've told me about all the people at the factory who are desperate for help – and who have paid you in any way that they can – so I've had to eat my words about the working class not giving tuppence about their animals. In other words, you've won me around, my girl, and the money is yours. Or, rather, the Silvertown Animal Hospital's.'

Ruby rolled the name around her mind and then said it out loud.

'Ooh, I like that name,' she said. 'Yes, I like that very much. And thank you, Leah. That's ever such a lot of money.'

'It will barely touch the sides,' Leah countered. 'And, in that vein, there's something else I'd like to do to help.'

'Oh, Leah. The jewellery is more than enough.'

'But this is something fun. And we all need a bit of fun nowadays, don't we?'

'We do . . .' Ruby agreed cautiously.

'Well, one of my godmothers is a singer called Clara Williams . . .'

'*The* Clara Williams?' Ruby interrupted, shifting out of the way as a group of soldiers marched by.

'Well, yes,' said Leah with a laugh.

'But she's famous,' said Ruby. 'And she's bleeding *marvellous*. When I were in service, she were guest of honour at one of our soirées and she were absolutely wonderful.'

It had been her last evening in service, Ruby reflected. The evening when everything changed. The evening which had ultimately brought her . . . here.

'She *is* marvellous,' Leah was saying. 'And she's doubly marvellous because she's agreed in principle to allow us to be her "charity" for an exclusive concert in a couple of weeks' time.'

'No!' breathed Ruby. 'I can hardly believe it. Why on earth would she do that?'

'Because she's a good egg,' said Leah. 'Because she

loves animals. And because she's forgotten my birthday for the last umpteen years – including my twenty-first – so when she asked me what she could do to make up for it, I suggested this.'

'But ain't she booked up for months if not *years* in advance?'

'She is, usually,' said Leah. 'But she's just had a tour cancelled in America, and of course, what with these dratted Zeppelin raids and general war misery, people are less likely to go out than they used to be. Besides, between you and me, I think her star might be waning just a little bit.'

'Really?' Ruby was surprised. 'I thought she were still ever so popular?'

Leah shrugged. 'Mummy says her type of voice doesn't translate well to gramophone records so she's not quite as popular nowadays. But she still packs enough of a punch to sell out the Adelphi at short notice so I'd say we've got nothing to worry about.'

Ruby clapped her hands together in delight. 'The Adelphi!' she squealed. 'Ooh, that's ever so posh.'

'Please say yes,' said Leah. 'The concert is going ahead anyway; the only question is whether we're far enough along with our plans for Aunt Clara to credibly have the hospital as her charity. But now we've got some premises and a bit of funding, I'm sure everyone will be happy.'

'Yes, then!' said Ruby. '*Yes*! Can we sneak me ma in? She loves Clara Williams.'

'I'm sure we can do a lot of sneaking,' said Leah with a grin. 'But mainly we need to invite the great and the good who like to show off how much money they have by outdoing each other in their generosity. Leave that with me.'

'Thank you, Leah,' Ruby said earnestly. 'You're a real pal.'

'One more thing,' said Leah. 'You don't have to say yes to this and your answer doesn't affect either of the other things I've offered. But I'd love to get involved with the animal hospital in a more hands-on way as well. Maybe the fundraising or bookkeeping or the ordering or the general admin. Not to take over in any way, of course – just to help. You're in charge.'

Ruby leaned over and kissed Leah on the cheek. 'Of course,' she said. 'I were hoping that you would.'

New premises.

A fundraising concert.

And a generous donation.

Ruby couldn't believe how quickly things were suddenly beginning to come together. After a slow start, it looked like the Silvertown Animal Hospital would finally be getting off the ground.

25

Well, that certainly set things in motion!

It felt like the fuse had been lit a long time ago, but now – finally – everything was set up for the whole project to burst into flame.

And what a lot there was to do.

What a lot there was to *buy*!

To date, all they really had was Nellie's salve, the remnants of the Day & Son's Dog Medicine Chest and a handful of hand-knitted bandages and cushions. It was a start but there was a long, long way to go. They needed medicines and pills, powders and splints; gauze, cotton wool and adhesive tape; lamps and cages and filing cabinets and examination tables; stethoscopes, thermometers, scalpels and tweezers . . .

And so it went on.

Ruby had it all carefully itemised, of course. She even had lists of lists! But writing it all down and working out how to actually get her hands on everything were, she discovered, two entirely separate things.

The most straightforward items could be sourced close to home. The local apothecaries and dispensaries carried some of the medicines and ointments that they needed and, over the next few days, Ruby, Dot and Leah began befriending the pharmacists and trying to work out what they needed most.

Other items could be purchased direct from the suppliers, and Ruby started poring over catalogues and filling in order forms when she really should have been getting a good night's sleep so that she could function well at the factory come the evening.

But it quickly became clear that some purchases would require longer journeys to the veterinary supply shops and surgical instrument suppliers dotted around the capital – and these would require both more organisation and, ideally, a mode of transport capable of transporting bulky items. Ruby resigned herself to weeks of arriving home from work, bolting her porridge and heading straight out on some hospital-related errand. Luckily Leah and Dot were both fully committed and equally anxious to get the project off the ground.

It was thrilling, exhilarating and absolutely exhausting.

Despite Ruby's excitement at seeing Jack again – and it had felt like a very long week – she couldn't help but have misgivings that they were meeting at a football match.

She had never been to a match before and, to be honest, she had no real wish to watch a bunch of sweaty men charge around after a ball. And there was more to her antipathy than that. Back in the day, Annie-Next-Door's husband had occasionally taken his sons along to watch the Hammers at Upton Park. It had never ended well. Win or lose, he had invariably taken refuge in one of the local hostelries and had then arrived home drunk and belligerent. Ruby had heard the shouting through the wall and had decided, there and then, that she hated football. And so, more than once over the past few days, it had crossed her mind that if Jack was an ardent football fan, then maybe he wasn't the man for her.

Still, she had to give him a chance.

She certainly couldn't judge Jack by how her neighbour had chosen to behave. And whilst, of course, she could have suggested a different activity, it would be illuminating to see how Jack conducted himself under similar circumstances. Not that the circumstances were entirely the same; in fact, they couldn't have been more different. Far from being held in a teeming football stadium, this match was being played in the altogether more genteel environment of the Royal Victoria Gardens. Ruby knew them well, had grown up playing there with Harry. In fact, she had been playing hide and seek in that very park when she had witnessed those poor kittens being thrown into the Thames all those years ago . . .

Jack was waiting for Ruby at the entrance to the park as he had promised and looking just as handsome as she remembered, with his light-brown wavy hair, his green eyes and his lopsided grin. Wreathed in smiles, he held out his arm to her and Ruby duly tucked her hand under his elbow.

How lovely that felt.

Just like a real lady.

'Looking forward to it?' he asked, smiling down at her.

'*Rather*,' replied Ruby, trying to inject a note of enthusiasm into her voice. 'Who's playing?' she added. The names, of course, probably wouldn't mean a thing to her, but it would be polite to show an interest.

Jack stopped so suddenly that the two women walking behind them almost collided into them. 'You're pulling me leg, ain't you?' he said with a grin.

'I'm afraid I'm not,' said Ruby, with a self-deprecating laugh. 'I don't have the foggiest about football.'

And, to be honest, she didn't really care who was playing. Being with Jack was what mattered and, besides, one boring regional team was very much like another.

'But it's you chaps, of course,' said Jack, shaking his head in mock frustration. 'Or, should I say, you chapesses?'

'Chapesses?' echoed Ruby, none the wiser.

What on earth was he talking about?

'Your factory,' said Jack. 'The Brunner Babes. You're playing against the Hackney Harriers in the first round of the new Munitionettes' Cup.'

Oh, goodness.

How embarrassing.

There had been chatter about the upcoming women's match at work, of course – quite a lot of chatter, in fact – but Ruby just hadn't put two and two together. She'd had too many other things on her mind. Things like how to get an examination table from Totteridge back to Silvertown. Besides, it wouldn't have entered her head that Jack would be interested in *women* playing football.

Jack started to laugh. 'Your face!' he said. 'As if I'd have dragged you along to any old football match. But do say if you'd rather do something else?'

'Not at all,' said Ruby, suddenly realising that she wouldn't. 'This is marvellous.'

They had already walked past the pleasure gardens and the bowling alley and the crowds were getting denser as they approached the large field where the football match was taking place. Many of the spectators streaming in appeared to be women and Ruby started to recognise one or two faces from the factory. There was Alice from the detonation shed shepherding a brood of children. And over there was Mrs Mason arm in arm with a man who was presumably her husband. And was that really Mr Briggs, strolling along with his wife, and looking positively cheerful?

Oh, this really was wonderful.

The atmosphere was friendly and jolly, undercut by a pleasant frisson of anticipation and excitement. The sun was shining, the air was fragrant, and both the sky and the river were a radiant blue.

Even the Brunner Mond tower in the background looked positively regal.

It was just what they all needed after the horrors of the past few weeks.

As Jack bought two tickets for eightpence each and made an additional donation to the Soldiers' Benevolent Fund, Ruby wondered why she hadn't come to a friendly match before. She could have brought her family along – it would have done them all good and it might even have brought a touch of colour to Aunt Maggie's cheeks. They would have loved the little array of brightly coloured tents serving everything from meat pies to roasted chestnuts, they would have adored the jaunty brass band playing the 'Colonel Bogey March' and they might even have joined in with the crowd who were already singing lustily along.

And then Jack took hold of her hand and she stopped thinking about her family. She just laughed and enjoyed the moment as she let him pull her along to the front of the crowd standing six deep behind one of the goals.

'This all right for you?' Jack asked, letting go of her hand. 'Not too close?

Ruby laughed. 'This is perfect,' she said.

'It is, isn't it?' said Jack. 'There are no programmes, of course, but otherwise you could almost forget there's a ruddy war on.'

'Except that the match is between two teams of female Munitionettes who got their jobs precisely because there is a war on,' Ruby replied pertly.

Oh, goodness.

Was that too forward?

Maybe Jack was one of those men who liked women to agree with everything he said.

But he just threw his head back and started laughing. 'Good point,' he said. 'Hopefully we'll see some action here,' he added. 'But fingers crossed that it's only during one half.'

'And during the right half,' added Ruby with a little giggle.

There was something about Jack's enthusiasm and cheery demeanour that made Ruby, in turn, feel carefree and happy. Out here in the sunshine, he seemed so different from the man panicking in the foot tunnel that it was hard to believe they were the same person. In fact, it was difficult to know which one was the 'real' Jack. Maybe the war did that to a person.

'You like your football, do you?' Ruby asked rhetorically.

'Like it?' Jack grinned. 'It were me whole life when I were younger. In fact, fool that I was, I joined the army in a Pals Battalion.'

Pals Battalions had been a popular way to sign up

earlier in the war. They were made up of men who had enlisted together in local recruiting drives, with the understanding they'd be able to serve alongside their friends and neighbours as opposed to being arbitrarily allocated to a unit.

'Who were you with?' Ruby asked.

'The West Ham Pals. Signed up with me friends Leo and Fred in December '14. We'd followed the Hammers all our life and even taken trials for them too, so it seemed the obvious thing to do. Pretty quick out of the blocks, we was, thinking back. We didn't have no uniforms or rifles, and most of us had no military experience to speak of, but we was all desperate to give a good smacking to the Germans.'

Ruby wondered if she dared to ask what had happened to Leo and Fred, but suddenly the teams were running on to the pitch and everyone was clapping and cheering and, almost to Ruby's relief, the moment passed.

Two thoughts struck her almost simultaneously.

The first was that the women were wearing shorts . . . and very *short* shorts at that, the players' knees on full display to all and sundry. It didn't half look strange and it didn't half look *modern*. Perhaps it was better that Aunt Maggie wasn't there, after all.

The second thought was that one of the forwards looked very familiar. Ruby peered more closely and . . . yes. It was Elspeth. Silly little Elspeth running around in the Brunner Mond bright blue top and representing the factory at the very highest level.

She didn't look so silly now.

The game started and Ruby found herself swept along

in the drama and excitement of it all. She cheered along with everyone else every time the home team took possession and groaned along with everyone else when the Hackney Harriers scored two early goals. And, through it all, she was acutely aware of Jack by her side, standing so close that their shoulders were touching. She kept her hands firmly by her side; she had loved it when Jack had taken her hand earlier but she didn't want him to think that she was one of those girls who expected to have their hands held just because they were alone in a crowd.

When the half-time whistle sounded, the Brunner Babes were three goals down. But it didn't really matter. The afternoon was about far more than winning and losing. It was about teamwork, community, about women doing it for themselves and raising money for a common cause. For the first time, Ruby began to understand the thrill, the reward – the point – of following football and she told Jack as much when they went for a half-time wander along the river bank and treated themselves to sticky toffee apples and roasted chestnuts.

What a perfect day.

Despite only one substitution, the Brunner Babes upped their game during the second half and it was all much more evenly matched.

But – despite valiant cheering and shouting from the crowd – the home team still failed to score. It was looking as if this half was destined to be a goalless draw . . . but then the Brunner Babes made a break for it. It was Elspeth – *Elspeth* – streaking down the middle of the pitch, dodging not one, not two, but three defenders before sending the ball thundering into the goal right in front of Jack and Ruby.

The crowd duly went wild. Ruby turned with shining eyes to Jack and they gave each other an awkward hug. And then Elspeth dashed into the goal to pick up the ball. Throwing it back up the pitch, she straightened and her eyes went straight to Ruby's.

'Hello, Ruby,' she called, eyes widening in delighted surprise. 'How marvellous to see you here.'

There was a murmur in the crowd around them and Ruby felt a little thrill of self-importance at being on first-name terms with the star of the show.

Why on earth was Elspeth so pleased to see her?

'Wouldn't have missed it for the world,' Ruby shouted back from the front row. 'Marvellous goal.'

'We just need a few more of them,' yelled Elspeth with a rueful smile. 'Better get to it.'

She gave Ruby a beaming smile and she was off, running down the pitch to join her teammates.

'I recognise her,' said Jack, staring at Elspeth's departing back.

Ruby hesitated.

She knew exactly where Jack recognised Elspeth from.

Elspeth's crass, careless comments the night of the Zeppelin attack were still seared across Ruby's mind – together with the dreadful feeling that everything was ruined and that she would never see Jack again. But look at what had happened. She *had* seen Jack again, the two of them were having a lovely afternoon together and who knew what might happen next. Nothing had been ruined and she should probably just have laughed Elspeth's comments off at the time.

Meanwhile, why exactly had Elspeth been quite so friendly? There must have been a lot of people watching the match that she recognised . . . that she *liked*. Elspeth had barely said a friendly word to Ruby since the two of them had started at the factory together, and yet, here she was, being sweetness and light itself.

There *must* be an ulterior motive.

'It were the night in the tunnel,' said Ruby, turning her attention back to Jack. 'Well, outside the tunnel to be exact.'

'Ah, yes,' said Jack. 'The little miss with the very loud opinions.'

'The very same,' said Ruby. 'I could have ruddy killed her for what she said.'

'Me too,' said Jack.

Ruby turned to look at him. 'Really?' she said. 'But not nearly as much as I could have done, surely?'

'Why not?'

'Because I thought you was going back to the front,' Ruby exclaimed. 'I thought I were never going to see you again. Whereas you *knew* you weren't going back to the front and, at any time, you could have . . . you could have . . .'

She trailed off.

She was giving away too much.

But why, come to think of it, *hadn't* Jack come in search of her? He hadn't seen the pram by then; hadn't got the wrong end of the stick.

'I did,' said Jack softly, as though reading her mind.

'Pardon? Did what?'

'Did come looking for you. At the munitions factory.'

'Oh.'

The world shrank until it was a just a bubble enclosing the two of them, staring into each other's eyes. Even the cheering of the crowd around them – presumably another goal – went almost unnoticed.

Oh!

'But there are a lot of women working at the factory,' said Jack. 'And it turns out that there are also rather a lot of Ruby's.'

'Oh,' said Ruby. 'You didn't know my surname.'

'Still don't,' said Jack, with a grin. 'And I'm out in public with you. That's either terribly modern or just terribly terrible. I'm Jack Kennedy.'

'Ruby Archer.'

And the two shook hands with mock formality.

'Anyway, then I saw you with the pram and, well, that was that,' said Jack.

'Yes,' said Ruby. 'That was that. And I suppose we can't blame *that* on Elspeth!'

Jack smiled. 'I really disliked her for being so rude about you,' he said. 'And, to be honest, I still think she were bang out of order. But it just goes to show that first impressions ain't necessarily the full picture.'

'What do you mean?' asked Ruby.

'Well, look at her,' said Jack, waving over to where Elspeth was intercepting a much taller and stockier opponent before making another run for it. 'I had written her off as a silly loudmouth. But she's yellow as a canary from dealing with those dangerous chemicals so she's obviously brave. *And* she plays a mean game of football. I'd have thought twice about tackling that woman even before I buggered me leg and there she is, getting stuck in and winning the ball, to boot.'

The bubble seemed in danger of bursting. Was Jack sweet on Elspeth? It almost sounded as though he was, and frankly, Ruby wouldn't have blamed him for being attracted to her. Then she gave herself a little shake. She generally had no truck with jealous, petty women and she had no intention of turning into one herself. Not now. Not ever. Jack was at the match with *her* because he wanted to be, and she was with him because she wanted to be and that was all that mattered.

But now Ruby came to think about it, Elspeth *was* quite yellow.

'Do you know, I hadn't even noticed her skin had changed colour?' Ruby said idly. 'I suppose that's how used I am to it all.'

'Interesting,' said Jack. 'So, if you don't mind me saying so, you probably don't notice just how yellow you are, either?'

What?

'Am I?' said Ruby.

'Absolutely,' said Jack.

'No, I'm not!'

'Yes, you are,' replied Jack emphatically. 'Well, maybe not canary yellow,' he conceded. 'More a sort of top-of-the-milk yellow.'

Ruby's brain was going nineteen to the dozen. This was all most disconcerting. Not that it mattered as such – in fact, it didn't matter at all – but surely . . .

'Ma would have said. Aunt Maggie would *definitely* have said.'

And surely her brother would have ragged her mercilessly about the slightest tinge? Not that the two of them were really talking to each other.

'Ah, well,' said Jack. 'Maybe they didn't like to. You know, it's important work you're doing there and perhaps they didn't want to put you off. Or maybe they haven't noticed, either. You know, when something is right under your nose and you don't see it?'

'But . . . but . . .' Ruby blustered. 'But I don't even work with the chemicals no more. I'm in the detonation shed!'

Then she noticed the slightest tugging at the corner of Jack's mouth and the twinkling in his green eyes and the penny dropped.

'Oh!' she exclaimed, punching him on the shoulder in a most unladylike fashion. 'You're teasing me. I ain't yellow at all!'

Jack grinned and clutched his shoulder, pretending to stagger back in pain. 'You're not. Your face though!' said Jack. 'It was a picture!'

'At least it wasn't a *yellow* picture!' said Ruby. 'Oh, that was beastly.'

'Funny, though.'

'Yoo hoo. Ruby.'

Ruby had been so lost in the moment – so lost in *Jack* – that she hadn't seen Elspeth come over to them in her muddy kit. In fact, she hadn't really registered that the match had ended and that Elspeth had left her teammates in a little huddle to make a beeline for them. To be honest, she didn't even know what the score was, so she didn't know whether to congratulate or commiserate with Elspeth.

'Can I help you?' she asked instead, turning – reluctantly – from Jack.

Can I help you?

What sort of ridiculous question was that?

But Elspeth was nodding, a furrow forming between her eyebrows. 'Yes, you can, as it happens,' she said. 'Or, at least, I hope you can.'

So *that* was what was behind all the friendliness.

Ruby wrinkled up her nose. 'What can I do?' she asked warily.

'It's our cat, Bonnie,' said Elspeth. 'We think she's broken her leg and we haven't the faintest idea what to do. And everyone at the factory has been talking about you and everything you've been doing for their animals and, well, you don't know how pleased I were to see you here today.'

Ruby wasn't sure whether to be flattered or annoyed by this (and after all the things Elspeth had said to and about her, too!) and ended up being quite a bit of both.

'I'm sorry,' she said. 'I hate to think of an animal in need but I don't know the first thing about broken bones.'

'Oh,' said Elspeth, her face falling. 'It were just a thought.'

'Ruby might not know what to do,' interrupted Jack. 'But I know all about animal bones. And I'd be very happy to help.'

26

How on earth did Jack know about animal bones?

He had never mentioned what he'd done before the war, but, from what – admittedly little – Ruby had gleaned from their few conversations, she had assumed Jack and his family were either costermongers or worked at the docks. There was certainly nothing about him – from his accent to the way he dressed, and the fact that he obviously lived in Silvertown – to suggest that he had any sort of veterinary background.

More to the point, where did Elspeth's very unexpected intervention leave their afternoon together?

Elspeth had rushed off to join her team talk, but what would happen when she came back? Would she expect Jack to accompany her straight back to wherever she lived? Would Jack agree to go? Ruby had imagined another walk along the river or a cup of tea at Fisher's or maybe even a trip to a Lyons Coffee House – but it looked as though Elspeth might be spoiling things all over again.

How *did* Jack know about animal bones?

'It's not quite how we'd imagined the afternoon would pan out, is it?' said Jack as the crowds dissipated around them.

'It isn't,' said Ruby. 'But this is more important. You can't just leave an animal in pain.'

'No,' said Jack. 'We can't. But please would you come with me? It shouldn't take too long and I'd hate the afternoon to end like this.'

Ruby paused. Going to Elspeth's house felt rather like willingly entering the lion's den, but then again, she didn't want the afternoon with Jack to end, either.

'Of course,' she said simply.

Elspeth lived about half a mile away on the other side of the Old Woolwich Road.

It was less than a ten-minute walk away, but Ruby feared that it might feel much, much longer. After all, she and Elspeth were hardly friends so the atmosphere was highly likely to be, at best, on the awkward side.

But not a bit of it.

Elspeth re-joined them – back in her everyday clothes and the mud wiped from her cheeks – full of cheerful good humour and gushing gratitude. She kept up such a steady stream of inconsequential chatter about the match and the weather and her cat that it was impossible for anyone to feel awkward.

And then she linked arms with Ruby.

'You don't know how pleased I were to see you at the match,' she said. 'Everyone at the factory is really singing your praises. In fact, I heard someone in the shifting shed call you the "people's vet".'

'Oh, that's quite ridiculous,' said Ruby, flushing. 'What a lot of tosh!'

And it was.

Totally ridiculous and absolute tosh.

But she couldn't help but be quietly pleased. If people

were taking what she was doing seriously, well, surely that made all the difference?

She needed people to believe she knew what she was talking about.

But Elspeth – *Elspeth* – complimenting her like that?

Ruby could scarcely believe it.

'Well, ain't you a dark horse,' said Jack on Ruby's other side. 'And here were I thinking you "just" made shells.'

'Oh, our Ruby ain't "just" anything,' said Elspeth. 'She were the brightest in the year at school and now she's setting up an animal hospital. It's enough to make *anyone* feel inadequate by comparison.'

Ruby shot Elspeth a glance. Was that an apology? It was rather an oblique one, if so, but it definitely felt very like the holding out of an olive branch. Then again, Elspeth could just be buttering Ruby up because she was desperate for someone to help Bonnie – and it would be business as usual once they got back to the factory. It was hard to work out which way the wind was blowing – let alone how to reply – but Ruby was saved having to do either because they rounded a corner and Elspeth said, simply, 'Home.'

Armagh Street was altogether more genteel than Sanctuary Lane. The houses, whilst still terraced, were double-fronted and, rather than opening straight on to the street, each had a small garden in front. Ruby imagined that the gardens would usually be full of flowers at this time of year and that the whole effect would be very pretty, but this was wartime and, of course, most were currently planted with cabbages and runner beans. What was interesting was that this part of town was clearly more prosperous, but there had been no talk of Elspeth's family turning to a vet to look at Bonnie. Clearly vets were an unaffordable – or simply an elusive – prospect even here.

Damn Mr Smith and his ilk.

Damn them for doing nothing to help when they could be making such a difference.

Bonnie hadn't broken her leg after all.

'It's a sprain,' said Jack, straightening up after gently examining the very disgruntled cat on the kitchen table. Ruby had watched him, captivated by the way he gently but firmly prodded and massaged Bonnie's leg, talking to her reassuringly all the while. He certainly seemed to know exactly what he was doing, and Ruby found herself admiring how calm and collected he was under pressure.

'That's marvellous,' said Elspeth's mother, a glamorous redhead with curled hair and a wasp waist. 'I were convinced the little tinker had fractured it.'

'Most of the symptoms are the same, to be honest,' said Jack. 'Hiding away, walking on three legs, loss of appetite . . . you name it, it happens in both cases. She's got a nasty bite on her flank – she were probably in a fight and trying to escape – but I'm almost certain there are no broken bones.'

'How do you know?' asked Elspeth's younger brother, Bertie, who was hanging around the kitchen door and swinging on the handle.

Jack didn't answer. For a moment, Ruby wondered if he was unhappy to have had his credentials challenged, but then she realised that he simply hadn't heard. Ruby had already learned that Jack was generally so adept at presenting his 'good' ear that it was easy not to grasp that he was partially deaf.

'Jack can't hear in one ear,' Ruby explained. She touched Jack lightly on the arm. 'Bertie were asking you a question,' she said.

'Sorry, fella,' said Jack, turning towards the boy. 'I'm all ears now. Or, should I say, I'm all "ear".'

Everyone laughed.

'I just wondered how you know so much about cats,' Bertie repeated.

'Are you a vet?' asked Elspeth.

Yes. Ruby rather wanted to know this as well.

'Ha! If only!' said Jack. 'I helped out at a veterinary practice before the war – just fetching and carrying, mainly – but I've picked up most of what I know from the front. When they discovered I knew a fair bit about animals out there, they put me in charge of the dogs and cats – under the very vague supervision of a vet. My main job were helping out with the horses, and I loved that until a rogue shell blew me off the horse I were helping to rehabilitate.'

'There are cats at the front?' asked Elspeth, as she distributed cups of tea and thick buttered slices of bread. She was still being very pleasant to everyone – no sign of her usual airs and graces and belittling comments, and Ruby was, finally, beginning to relax.

'Thousands,' said Jack. Ruby was pleased to notice that the smile he gave Elspeth was warm but identical to the ones he'd already given to her mother and brother.

'Why are there cats?' asked Bertie.

'Well, mainly for killing mice and rats, of course,' said Jack. 'There are millions of the blighters in the trenches, spreading disease and eating the supplies. But we also used cats to help detect any gas that could spark fires and explosions. And some were used as mascots. We came to love them, just like you love old Bonnie here. And, talking of Bonnie, let's treat this sprain, shall we?'

'Will she need a splint?' asked Mrs Carson. 'Bandages?'

'Neither,' said Jack. 'The main thing she needs is lots of rest to give her leg a chance to heal. Bonnie might not like it much, but the best thing to do is to keep her in a pen or a cage so she's not tempted to jump around too much.'

'I'm not sure we have anything to use for that,' said Mrs Carson, looking around vaguely for inspiration.

'Crates? Boxes?' suggested Jack.

All three Carsons looked blank.

'Anyone nearby with a spare pram?' suggested Ruby.

It turned out that the neighbours two doors down had the very thing. Then it was just a matter of putting the hood up on the pram, fixing some chicken wire from the yard over the opening, and Bonnie was popped into her new temporary home.

'You're a marvel, Ruby,' said Elspeth in all apparent sincerity.

'Not at all,' said Ruby. 'I've just made it my business to learn as much as I can. Now, I suggest that you feed Bonnie with Lactol or milk puddings, give her a little castor oil and keep her topped up with aspirin to lower her temperature and reduce any pain over the next few days.'

It was all parroted from Nellie, but Ruby was gratified to see Jack give her a little approving nod.

'I'm ever so grateful, really I am,' said Elspeth, standing on the doorstep to see them off. 'You must promise to let me know if I can ever do anything for you in return. And Ruby, at the very least, I'll buy you a hot chocolate in the canteen the next time our shifts coincide.'

Ruby paused. She still had no idea what had caused Elspeth's volte-face, but Ma was always a great one for saying that you had to take people as you found them. Besides, if she thought about it honestly, she had also been rude and dismissive of Elspeth in the early days at the factory. Maybe they had each been as bad as the other. Everyone had good in them if you only looked for it, and ultimately in wartime nothing really mattered apart from looking after one another and putting any differences to one side.

So she linked her arm with Jack's and smiled at Elspeth over her shoulder as they set off down the street. 'I'd like that,' she said.

And she really meant it.

No sooner had Ruby and Jack got round the corner than Jack stopped walking.

'Phew, am I glad that were a sprain and not a break,' he said with an exaggerated sigh. 'I wouldn't have had a clue what to do if it were a nasty break.'

Ruby looked at him in surprise. 'I thought you said you knew all about animal bones? You certainly sounded the part.'

'Oh, I do,' said Jack. 'But only if I've got the right tools and equipment around me. Besides, sometimes the only thing with a bad break is to put the poor animal out of its misery. Out in the trenches, it was a quick bullet, but I suddenly realised I wouldn't have known where to go and what to do in Silvertown.'

'There's a priest on the high street with a lethal chamber,' said Ruby. 'Father Murphy, to be precise.'

Jack turned to her with a smile. 'I were right when I said you were a dark horse,' he said. 'Would you like some tea at Fisher's after all that excitement?'

'Yes, please,' said Ruby. 'I could think of nothing nicer.'

Ten minutes later, Jack and Ruby were installed in the little café at the back of the bakery.

Mrs Fisher spotted Ruby coming in and immediately swooped. It would be her pleasure to provide both her and Jack with a slap-up tea, she said, and, no, they weren't to pay for a thing. It was the least she could do after all Ruby's kindnesses to Willow.

'I could get used to this,' said Jack, rubbing his belly, when a veritable cornucopia of cakes had appeared in front of them. 'Now, tell me all about it,' he added. 'Tell me how you know so much about animals. I'm on the edge of me seat.'

In fact, he was sitting back, looking relaxed, but – it had to be said – he was looking gratifyingly interested.

Ruby took a deep breath. How to describe all that had happened in the last few months?

She started by telling Jack all about moving back from Hampstead and seeing the strays and the animals whose owners couldn't afford to care for them. She told him about saving Mac and Tess and little Steel – and discovering how prohibitively expensive vets were to the ordinary person. And then she told him about her idea for an animal

289

hospital, about how both a local vet *and* the Royal Veterinary College had pooh-poohed the notion and how she had decided to go it alone. She told him about helping at Nellie's barrow and discovering that vets didn't have access to any special medicines, and then tentatively starting to treat some animals herself. And, finally, she told him about the fundraising concert and Leah's gift, finding a home for the hospital and starting to buy the equipment.

It all sounded pretty good when she said it out loud, but she could feel her heart rate ratcheting up a gear as she waited for Jack's verdict. Not that it really mattered, of course. After all, she would be going ahead regardless of what he thought.

But actually, it did matter.

It mattered very much.

Because how could the two of them have a future if . . .

'The depot near the market?' asked Jack, apropos of nothing.

Ruby blinked. 'Yes,' she said. 'Why?'

Of all the things she had expected him to say, it certainly wasn't that.

'That's where me stepfather's business is based – at least it were before he were called up,' said Jack. 'And his old mare, Mayfair, is still stabled there. Me stepfather's pal Tarroc uses her for his fish round nowadays, and I'm using her to run dunnage a couple of times a week while I get meself sorted out.'

'Fancy!' said Ruby, almost choking on her bun.

So, Jack would be in and out of the depot all the time. What a wonderful bonus.

Or at least it would be if Jack didn't think her idea the most ridiculous thing he had ever heard . . .

'It's all just dilly,' said Jack.

'What is?' asked Ruby cautiously. 'The animal hospital or it being located in your depot?'

'Both, of course,' said Jack emphatically.

Ruby exhaled slowly and took a deep draught of tea. She hadn't even realised she'd been holding her breath.

'Really?' she said, wanting, for some reason, to test Jack. 'Everyone keeps reminding me there's a war on and that animals should be the last thing on anybody's mind.'

'Nonsense,' said Jack robustly. 'There's *such* a need for it; no one can argue with that. And I'd say the war is all the more reason for giving it a go.'

'The *more* reason?'

'Yes.' Jack took a huge bite of jammy bun. 'The war has shown us that women can do just about anything as well as men can. I mean, just look at all you lot making weapons – no one would have dreamed of getting women to do that before the war. So for one thing, no one now-adays should be doubting that you can set up an animal hospital just because you're a woman. And as for the veterinary college . . . have you heard the expression "lions led by donkeys"?'

'Of course,' said Ruby.

It was all over the papers – the inference being that valiant soldiers were being sent to their deaths by incapable and indifferent generals.

'I wouldn't be discouraged by them giving you short shrift. *They're* the donkeys. They don't know everything and they don't get everything right. And you, to my mind, are very much the lioness.'

'So you don't think I'm daft?' Ruby ventured.

'Oh, I think you're daft, all right,' said Jack with a laugh. 'It won't be easy. But I reckon being daft gets things done. And, if you wouldn't mind, I'd quite like to be daft right alongside you.'

It took a moment for Jack's words to sink in.

And then Ruby's face broke into a big grin.

'You mean you'll help me with the animal hospital?' she clarified.

Just to be sure.

'If you'll let me,' said Jack. 'The money I got from the army won't last forever so I'm going to have to work for a living. But, yes, as a volunteer – I'm in!'

Ruby clapped her hands together in glee and resisted the temptation to reach across the table and kiss Jack fully on the lips.

'Oh, that's perfectly marvellous,' she said, ignoring – unaware of – the curious stares all around her. 'I have money, a room, and now I have someone who knows about animals to work alongside me. It feels like it's all coming together.'

'In the meantime, though, would you do me the honour of stepping out with me again?' said Jack. 'This afternoon has been wonderful but not exactly what I planned, so . . .'

He trailed off, looking suddenly nervous, and Ruby swallowed a smile.

Did he even need to ask?

'Yes, I would,' she said simply. 'I'd love to.'

'Marvellous,' said Jack. 'And what would you like to do?'

'Would you think I was mad if I suggested going up to Totteridge to get a very expensive examination table that I've ordered?' said Ruby. 'Only I don't get many days off and . . .'

'Sounds good to me,' said Jack. 'What about I bring Mayfair and the cart along?'

'That would be wonderful,' said Ruby.

'It's a date, then.'

And, somehow, they sounded like the sweetest four words in the world.

27

And, suddenly, it was all change at work.

A very subdued Mary came back on duty the very next day and Ruby was, as promised, given her own table of new recruits to manage. It would be her responsibility to get everyone trained and up to speed as quickly as possible because she needed to be hitting a fairly ambitious quota of detonators each shift by the end of the following week.

Ruby was going to have her work cut out to meet it and she was determined not to fail.

To Ruby's surprise, one of the new recruits on her table – alongside eight much older women that she didn't recognise – was Dot. Ruby hadn't seen Dot for a few days, but she had certainly made no mention of wanting to move away from the factory floor at that point. More pertinently, Leah hadn't mentioned anything either, and Ruby had seen *her* several times over the past few days. In the usual course of events, none of that would have been an issue; staff were often moved between departments with very little notice, and she knew that Leah made a point of trying not to mix business and pleasure. Still, it would have been nice to have had a little advance warning. She and Dot were friends; they had started at the factory on the same day and Dot was older than her by a couple of years. It might feel a little awkward suddenly being in a position of authority over her.

For the first couple of days, Ruby had little time to think about all that because she was rushed off her feet teaching nine new recruits the intricacies of assembling a detonator. The women in her team were pleasant enough; like everyone else, they were all anxious to do their bit, to chat about the war and their families with like-minded folk, and to have a bit of a laugh whenever they got the chance. No one seemed to resent reporting to Ruby, but inevitably, it took a while to get the team off the ground. Ellen struggled with her joints and found some of the fiddlier tasks tricky to master. Mabel's attention to detail was laudable but it did mean that she was prone to falling behind. And Eliza was good enough at the job, *very* good at chatting – but didn't seem to be able to combine the two. It took Ruby a couple of days to work out how to whip them into shape, but soon Ellen was assigned a task that required less dexterity, Mabel was reassured that, whilst accuracy was important, there was no need to triple-check *every* detonator, and Eliza was kept at the other end of the table from her chief partner in crime, Mona.

And it all seemed to be working.

Most of the women were pulling their weight within a couple of days, output shot up and, whilst they weren't quite reaching their quota yet, Mrs Mason was full of praise for how Ruby had stepped up to her new role.

To Ruby's surprise, the weak link in the chain was Dot.

For one thing, Dot, always quiet and rather intense, now seemed miserable to the point of rudeness. There was a permanent furrow between her brows and Ruby almost never saw her smile. She rarely initiated a conversation, she answered in monosyllables and she never joined in with the singing that broke out from time to time. Ruby tried to remember how Dot had behaved on the main factory floor. It was, naturally, hard to compare the two because the work back then had been so physical, and the environment so noisy, that it had been well nigh impossible to chat, let alone to sing. But, nonetheless, Ruby seemed to recall that Dot had been sociable enough then; she had crammed into the canteen with the other girls and, needless to say, she had talked to anyone who would listen about the East London Federation of the Suffragettes.

Strictly speaking, of course, none of that mattered. None of them were being paid to socialise and make friends, and belting out 'It's a Long Way to Tipperary' was hardly, by itself, going to win the war. But the issue was far more fundamental than that, because Dot's work was slow and distracted in the extreme. No matter which task she was given, she quickly fell behind. And that was a nigh-on disaster because, if one woman lagged behind, the effect rippled through the entire production line. After a while, Ruby kept Dot in the final position, screwing on the detonation caps. This, at least, had the advantage of not holding up the other girls on the table, but the trouble was that it kept the whole table consistently down on its quota. Ruby calculated that up until the penultimate station on the table, they were actually well above quota, so it was a doubly bitter pill to swallow.

For Ruby, who was busily trying to establish herself as an effective and efficient supervisor, this was all far from ideal, but she wasn't sure how to resolve things.

She liked Dot and had no wish to make trouble for her, but neither could she let things continue as they were. At first, she was tempted to ask Miss Mason or even Leah for advice, but on balance she decided not to. No, if she was going to be a credible supervisor, she needed to sort this out on her own – not run bleating to management at the first sign of trouble. Ruby had been very careful not to throw her weight around with Dot, but she'd wanted to be a supervisor and now she needed to start acting like one.

By the fifth day, Ruby knew she had to act.

Inviting Dot to a managerial meeting – or even a cup of tea in the canteen – might rub her up the wrong way, but then Ruby had an idea. Elspeth had invited Ruby for coffee and buns that very break-time as a thank you for visiting Bonnie. What if Ruby invited Dot along too? She was sure Elspeth wouldn't mind, and that way it would just be the three women who had started at the factory on the same day having a catch-up rather than anything more heavy-going. Hopefully she could get to the bottom of what was bothering Dot without making a big song and dance about it.

Dot agreed to meeting up with Elspeth readily enough, but in the same sort of absent-minded way that she had been drifting through her shifts. That was the first potential problem surmounted. And Elspeth, appearing out of the night shadows as soon as Ruby emerged from the detonation shed, seemed happy for Dot to tag along too.

Phew!

'It's all on me,' said Elspeth. 'I have it on good authority that not only are there jammy buns in the canteen tonight, but Chelsea buns as well! If we're quick, we can have our pick – or even one of each.'

The three young women started walking across the compound, but then Elspeth stopped.

'Silly me,' she said. 'We can't go into the same canteen, can we?'

It was true.

Elspeth worked on the main factory floor, in direct contact with TNT, and was therefore required to take her breaks in a separate canteen. Given that Ruby had spent some of the previous weekend actually *in* Elspeth's home, this felt a little like locking the door after the horse had bolted . . . but rules were rules.

'We could sit outside,' Ruby suggested. 'It's a lovely night.'

Elspeth nodded. 'Good plan,' she said. 'You two find a space on the grass and I'll bring it all out to you.'

Ruby and Dot made their way over to the grassy bank, Ruby almost tripping over something small and furry in the darkness. There was a yowl of protest and Ruby caught sight of a red collar. It was one of 'her' cats – Balthazar, from the brief glance she had caught. Ruby smiled to herself. Balthazar might be stalking off in high dudgeon, but the bright red collar around his neck meant that at least he would be safe the next time the lethal chamber made an appearance at the factory. She felt a glow of satisfaction as she spread her skirts and sat down on the cool grass.

She turned to Dot. 'So, how are you enjoying the detonation shed?' she asked as casually as she could. Perhaps she could make some headway on the problem before Elspeth got back.

Dot gave a little shrug. 'It's all right,' she said, drawing her shawl tightly around her shoulders. 'Better than purifying TNT anyway.'

'It's certainly a bit quieter,' Ruby said with a smile.

Dot didn't answer and the conversation seemed to be over. The silence persisted – taut and awkward – until Elspeth joined them, laden with a heavy tray.

'Here we are,' she said, placing the three mugs of cocoa and a plate of cakes carefully on to the grass and then flopping down beside the others. 'A veritable midnight feast.'

'Thank you,' said Ruby, picking up one of the steaming mugs. 'It's ever so kind of you.'

'It's nothing,' said Elspeth. 'I'm the one who should be thanking *you* for all your help with Bonnie. She's doing so well. Her leg is much better and she's walking around the kitchen like she owns the place again.'

How Elspeth had changed from the vain, foolish girl in their early days at the factory.

As if she had read Ruby's mind, Elspeth took a deep breath.

'I actually wanted to say sorry to you both,' she said, stumbling a little over her words. 'I were a right idiot when we first started here, weren't I? I'm embarrassed just to think about it now . . .'

Well.

That was a surprise.

'I think we all . . .' Ruby started.

Elspeth held up a hand. 'No, please let me finish,' she said. 'It's just that you were so clever at school, Ruby, and then you lived away from Silvertown for years and years – and of course I've never been anywhere or done anything except help out in me dad's bookmaking business. So when I saw you on that first day, I felt a bit useless by comparison, and for some reason that made me decide to act like a prize chump. I'm ever so sorry. And you, Dot – all the work you do with the suffragettes, making a real difference to people's lives. I just felt I couldn't compete. And of course, I didn't have anyone away fighting, so I didn't really understand what you was going through. But now I do, because married men are no longer exempt. Me father has just enlisted and is off to France.'

Oh goodness.

'I'm sorry, too,' said Ruby. 'I'm sorry to hear about your pa, for one thing. And I'm sorry I were rude and I didn't give you a chance right from the start. I ain't got no excuse for that – only that you were so pretty and so popular at school that I suppose I felt I couldn't compete with *you*. And as for you feeling useless . . . I've never met anyone less useless! Look at you still working with all those chemicals day after day and throwing yourself into the football like that. You've done marvellously. In fact, I think all three of us should be proud of ourselves.'

Elspeth smiled and took a big bite of bun. 'Hear, hear,' she said, spraying crumbs in a most unladylike fashion. 'Here's to us all.'

A bell sounded. It was time to report back on duty. Reluctantly, Elspeth hauled herself to her feet.

'Well, it was lovely to see you both,' she said. 'Let's do it again soon.'

'Yes, let's,' said Ruby.

She stared thoughtfully after Elspeth's retreating back.

Against the odds, it seemed that Elspeth had become a friend.

Dot was also standing up and Ruby gestured for her to sit down again.

'But we need to get back inside,' said Dot.

'I'll take the blame if we get in trouble,' said Ruby. 'I want to know what's troubling you and I won't let you go inside until you tell me.'

Ruby was half-joking, but Dot immediately looked mutinous.

'There's nothing troubling me,' she said.

'Come on, Dot. We're friends. Don't be like this with me.'

'Honestly, Ruby,' said Dot. 'It's nothing that concerns you.'

'The trouble is that whatever it is *does* concern me,' said Ruby, somewhat more harshly than she intended. 'Quite apart from the fact that you virtually ignored Elspeth tonight when she apologised to us both, you're taking much longer than I expected to get up to speed in the shed. What on earth's going on?'

'I'm going as fast I can,' Dot said defensively.

Ruby's irritation ratcheted up a gear. 'It ain't fast enough,' she said bluntly. 'Thanks to you, we're down on our numbers, and if it continues, we'll have to think about allocating you elsewhere.'

Ruby was crossing her fingers by her side as she spoke. She knew she didn't have the authority to move Dot to a different department – or even to threaten it. In fact, if they continued to miss their quotas, perhaps Mrs Mason would move *her* to a different department!

Then she noticed the colour had drained from Dot's face. 'Please don't do that,' she said.

'Why not?' said Ruby. 'Maybe this just ain't the right job for you and you'd be better off deployed elsewhere.'

Dot's eyes filled with tears. 'Because I've already left the main factory floor under a cloud,' she whispered.

Oh!

If Mrs Mason had chosen not to tell Ruby the reason Dot was moving departments, then it really wasn't for her to ask why. After all, she had also left the main factory floor under a cloud and she had been very grateful no one in the detonation shed had seemed to know anything about it.

But, then again, this was Dot and Dot was her friend.

'What happened?' she asked gently.

Dot looked down at her hands. 'I had a hairpin in my hair when I presented for duty,' she said quietly.

Ruby inhaled sharply and her hand went involuntarily to her heart. Taking anything metal on to the main factory floor, accidentally or not, was a heinous crime. It had been drummed into them all constantly and everyone knew the potential penalties. Dot was very lucky not to have been sacked on the spot or even arrested. The papers were full of women and girls who had been imprisoned for less.

Ruby exhaled a ragged breath. 'I dread to think what Mr Briggs said about *that*,' she said with a little smile.

Dot gave her a weak grin in return. 'I think the only thing that saved me were that the policewoman who were checking me over found it before I actually got on to the factory floor,' she said. 'And luckily, *she* told personnel rather than Mr Briggs. I'm sure Mr Briggs would have made much more of a fuss.'

'I'm sure he would,' said Ruby. 'To be honest, I'm surprised personnel took it so lightly.'

'Oh, Mrs Clark didn't take it lightly,' said Dot with feeling. 'She gave me a right good dressing-down, let me tell you – and she deducted money from me pay, to boot. She told me she were moving me to a department where I'd be less of a danger to meself and to others, and that if I put another foot wrong, I'd be out on me backside.'

Ruby sighed. 'Then what I don't understand, Dot, is why you haven't been pulling your weight in the detonation shed. You've been given a second chance, and from what I can tell, you're doing all you can to throw it away. It's almost like you don't want to work here no more.'

'I do want to work here. I want to do me bit like everyone else.'

'Then what is it?'

For a long time, Dot didn't reply. Then she met Ruby's eyes and said, 'I haven't slept for the past couple of days. I'm so tired that I can't think straight no more.'

'Oh.' Ruby was confused. 'Well, I understand everything is beastly at the moment. You've got your sweetheart at the front and you work in a munitions factory where the enemy could try to bomb us all to smithereens at any moment, but . . .'

'It ain't that,' said Dot. 'Well, not just that anyway. A few days ago, our home came under attack and we've no idea if it will happen again. You've no idea what it's like.'

Ruby's heart sank. 'Under attack from what?' she asked, although she had a fairly good idea what the answer was going to be.

'Boys outside armed with bricks,' said Dot. 'Probably

the same boys who attacked Willow a few weeks ago and who broke Muller's window. Anyway, they broke Muller's window again and this time they lobbed bricks at our windows upstairs as well. I keep thinking they won't stop until we're all killed.'

Ruby exhaled. 'How dreadful,' she said.

She swallowed down hard on the rage suddenly coursing through her body.

Damn Charlie and his friends.

That really was a step too far.

'But why are they attacking *you*?' she mused out loud. 'I thought they were going after Muller's because it's owned by Germans. Not that that's acceptable either, of course, but either way, you and your family should be safe.'

'I expect they think they *are* going after the Germans,' said Dot. 'They're certainly only throwing bricks at the windows above Muller's. But you've seen our flat, Ruby. It runs above *both* shops. I thought I were safe in my room until a brick came through my bedroom window. Ma says if it had landed six inches from where it did, I'd have been killed.'

'Lordy,' breathed Ruby. 'Thank goodness you wasn't hurt.'

Dot screwed up her face. 'I was hurt,' she said.

She pulled up the sleeve of her overalls and then her shirt sleeve below and Ruby couldn't help but gasp. There was an ugly six-inch-long gash along Dot's forearm, barely healing over, and bruises in shades from purple to yellow.

'Goodness, Dot,' said Ruby. 'No wonder your work is slow. And no wonder you're finding it hard to sleep.'

Dot's eyes filled with tears again. 'It's one thing the enemy attacking you,' she said. 'They don't care who they hurt. But when it's your neighbours – the people you've grown up alongside – well, that's ten times worse. I feel like everyone hates us.'

Ruby put her hand over Dot's. 'No one hates you,' she said. 'Of course we don't. You've just got caught up in something that's nothing to do with you. Have you told anyone here what's going on? Why you're so tired that you almost took a hairpin on to the factory floor and the fact that you've got an injury to your arm that's stopping you from working properly.'

Dot shook her head. 'No one,' she said quietly.

'But why not?' cried Ruby. 'We could have tried to help you.'

And she could have had it out with Charlie once and for all.

Dot took a deep breath. 'Because it's not as simple as that,' she said. 'Me family owns the whole building and we rent the second shop to the Mullers.'

Ruby shrugged. 'That's not your fault,' she said. 'I expect when your folks rented the shop out, no one gave two hoots that it was to Germans.'

'They didn't,' said Dot. 'None of that mattered before the war.'

'So can't you just get rid of them?' said Ruby. 'They shouldn't be running a business now, anyway, should they, not if they're German? I thought the Alien Restriction Act – or whatever it's called – put a stop to all that.'

Dot sighed. 'I ain't told anyone this, so you must swear not to tell, but it's more complicated than that,' she said.

'Mr Muller is my aunt's husband. They're not just tenants. They're *family*.'

Ruby paused, trying to work it all out. 'So, your aunt married a German man?' she clarified.

'Yes,' said Dot. 'Hermann Muller. He's been here for years – probably more years than we've been alive – and in many ways he's more English than the rest of us. He's interned on the Isle of Man at the moment with me cousin Gus, but me aunt is British so they've not confiscated the business and she's continued to run it. The violence were terrible last year after the *Lusitania* were sunk, of course, but then it all calmed down. But recently we've had the Zeppelin raid and then the sinking of the *Queen Mary* and then Lord Kitchener being drowned, and each time something like that happens, it starts up again.'

'So what will happen now?' asked Ruby.

Dot shrugged. 'I don't know,' she said. 'Me ma is trying to persuade me aunt to leave London – to close the business and move near other relatives in Gloucester. And that would be all well and good, to be honest, but the most beastly thing of all is that me parents are talking about shutting up shop and doing the same. And even though I'm petrified to go to sleep at the moment, I couldn't bear that. I simply couldn't. Me pa's been a baker his whole life and he's built Fisher's up from scratch. It wouldn't be fair. And what happens if Johnny comes back home and I ain't here? Besides, I like working here. I like feeling that I'm doing me bit and I'm really excited about the animal hospital and getting involved with the education side of things and . . .'

'Hush,' interrupted Ruby. 'Don't get yourself all worked

up – it never did anyone any good. Now, my job as your manager – sorry, but there it is – is to look out for *you*, not your ma or pa or your aunt. So I'm going to have a chat with one of the Welfare Officers about you. I won't mention that your aunt is married to a German if that's what you're worried about, nor that your family own the shop that is being attacked – although I'm sure they wouldn't bat an eyelid about either. But I *will* mention that you can't sleep for fear of bricks coming through your window and that you have already been injured by one. Whilst I do that, I suggest you take yourself along to the factory surgery and get your arm properly cleaned up. Does all that make sense?'

'It does,' said Dot. 'I feel ever so much better for having told someone. Thank you, Ruby. Or should I say Miss Archer?'

Ruby smothered a smile. 'Ruby is fine out here,' she said.

'Either way, you're a pal,' said Dot. 'And, I might add, a very good manager too. I just dread the next time there's a clear, moonless night and the Germans send over more Zeps. What then?'

'Then we're all in danger,' Ruby said stoutly. 'And until then, we'll just have to keep soldiering on. What else can we do?'

28

What a night!

Sorting Dot out had taken ages and Ruby had barely got back to the detonation shed before the end of her shift – but at least she had made some progress. Sarah, the Welfare Officer, had been sympathetic to Dot's plight and had suggested Dot move to the workers' accommodation until things settled down at home. Dot, her arm freshly cleaned and bandaged, had happily agreed. She had been granted a couple of days' leave and would report back on duty at the beginning of the next week. It perhaps wasn't a perfect solution, but it was definitely a step in the right direction.

Ruby was exhausted as she made her way home through the quiet streets of Silvertown, but she was also strangely content. Dawn was breaking to the east and fingers of light were making their way down the road. The war continued to cast its hideous shadow over them all, of course, but who could have imagined all that would have happened to her in the few short months she had been home? She was supervising a table in the munitions factory. She was planning to open an animal hospital in a matter of weeks, and she had managed to get initial funding, some volunteers and equipment, *and* a place it could call home. And on top of all this, she had met a lovely man who, fingers crossed, was on the way to becoming her sweetheart.

In many ways, life was grand.

If it wasn't for her damn brother . . .

Back at home, Ma was already at the laundry and Charlie was still in bed. Ruby ran up the stairs two at a time and barged into his room without knocking. The first thing that struck her was Harry's possessions – a jacket on the back of the door, some clothes neatly folded on top of the cupboard, his model train still in pride of place on the shelves – and she found herself suddenly swallowing a lump in her throat.

'Wake up,' she said without preamble, prodding Charlie's feet over the eiderdown.

Charlie shuffled to a seated position, rubbing the sleep out of his eyes. 'What's going on?' he mumbled. 'Zeppelins?'

'No,' said Ruby shortly. 'Listen. I will say this once and once only. The brick you or Joe or another of your friends threw through the window at the top of the street hit my friend whilst she was sleeping in her bedroom.'

Charlie's mouth gaped open. 'We only targeted the shop and the storeroom above it,' he said. 'We don't want to hurt no one.'

'That's as maybe,' said Ruby, feeling strangely dispassionate at Charlie's admission of guilt. 'But a few inches in another direction and me friend would have been killed. If that had happened, you would most likely have been hanged. She's English. No one would think you were being clever or brave. They would think you were a murderer. It would bring shame on Ma as well as breaking her heart. Is that what you want?'

'No-no,' stammered Charlie. 'Of course not.'

'I repeat, Charlie – the rooms above Muller's belong to the Fishers who are *not German*,' Ruby continued. 'If there are any more attacks, I will personally go to the police and say that you have just admitted to being involved as well as taking part in animal cruelty. Don't make me have to do that.'

There.

Done!

Without waiting for Charlie's reply, Ruby swept out of the room and down to the kitchen. She grunted a greeting to Aunt Maggie who was stirring porridge on the range. Then she went out into the backyard to say hello to Mac. The little dog, as usual, showered Ruby with big wet kisses, his body wriggling with delight at their reunion, before the two of them headed back inside. As usual, Ruby sat at the table and Mac settled himself on the rug next to Tess and Steel. Aunt Maggie pushed a steaming bowl of porridge in front of her and she gave another grunt – this time of thanks – and tucked in. It was a well-oiled routine with minimal need – or desire – for conversation by either party. Ruby was thinking only of eating her food as quickly as possible so that she could browse veterinary supply catalogues and send off a few order forms before she went to sleep . . .

And then the front doorbell jangled.

Aunt Maggie wiped her hands on her pinny, patted down her hair and, with a little sigh, padded off to answer it. Seconds later, she was back.

'Someone at the front door for you,' she said. 'A young man,' she added archly.

'Oh.'

Ruby stood up in confusion.

Whoever could that be?

It was probably someone from work with a message about a changed shift or a last-minute meeting of the Cat Committee. Or maybe it was someone with a poorly animal who had discovered her address and needed her help. Jack was a possibility, of course – and Ruby's heart lurched with excitement at the thought of seeing him again – but as he didn't know precisely where she lived, that was unlikely. Perhaps it was the odious Mr Smith who had seen the error of his ways and was ready to jump on board with the animal hospital. He would apologise profusely for his previous rudeness and practically beg to be given a role now that Ruby's idea was fast becoming a reality . . .

Grinning to herself at the absurdity of that thought, Ruby walked down the passage to the front door, Mac at her feet. With a jolt of pleasure, she saw that it *was* Jack and that he looked just as handsome as ever with his strong jaw and his dancing dimples and . . .

'Hello,' she said. 'I didn't know you knew where I lived. Oh, get *down*, Mac,' she added, as the dog jumped up at Jack with a throaty whine and gave him an enthusiastic slobber. 'Sorry, he don't usually do that . . .'

Jack held up a hand. 'It *is* you,' he said, almost to himself.

Ruby stared at him, confused. 'Of course it's me, silly,' she said. 'That's why you're here, ain't it? Unless you're here to see me brother Charlie!'

What on earth was Jack talking about?

And why did he sound so strange?

His tone had been angry.

Almost accusatory.

It just didn't make any sense at all.

But then Jack looked slowly from Ruby to Mac and then back to Ruby again.

'That's Mick,' he said, pointing at Mac. 'That's me dog.'

For a long moment, neither Ruby nor Jack said a word.

Ruby found that she *couldn't* speak. Her mind had gone totally blank, devoid of thought or emotion, as she tried to absorb the impact of what Jack had said. And then Mac jumped up at Jack again and, without warning, everything sped up; words and phrases and questions and confusion and guilt and panic and . . .

'He can't be your dog,' said Ruby, yanking Mac down with more force than was strictly necessary. She grabbed hold of the first, rather random thought that crystallised in her mind. 'Not unless your ma is called Agnes Driscoll and you've got a sister called Maude.'

There.

That solved it!

'Me ma *is* Agnes Driscoll,' said Jack calmly, scratching Mac behind the ears. 'And I *have* got a sister called Maude.'

'No, she ain't!' said Ruby, in rising panic. 'And no, you haven't. You told me your name were Jack Kennedy!'

'It *is* Jack Kennedy,' said Jack.

'Then . . .'

'Bert Driscoll is me ma's second husband and Maude and Alfie's father,' said Jack. 'Bill Kennedy were me dad. But that don't matter now.'

Ruby's legs went weak beneath her and she sagged on

to the front step. Mac transferred his attentions from Jack and started licking her face, tail wagging furiously. Tears stinging her eyes, Ruby buried her face into his springy fur.

Oh, Mac.

How could this possibly be happening?

Jack was still talking. 'Me ma told me Mick were dead,' he said. 'I had no idea she'd *sold* him until Daisy up the street told me she'd seen him with you. That she'd lent you a pram to take him up to Nellie's and that you were calling him Mac. Then I asked Maude and she told me Mick's face had been burnt and that he'd gone deaf and that a short time later a girl who fits your description came to the house and, after that, she never saw Mick again. Imagine how that made me feel? Me own mother getting rid of me own dog because he can't hear no more. And here's me, discharged from the army for the very same thing. You couldn't make it up. But never mind all that now. The point is that this is my dog. There's no two ways about it, Ruby. Mick belongs to me and I want him back.'

'Never,' said Ruby, scrambling to her feet and squaring up to Jack. 'Your ma never told me Mac belonged to you. She said he didn't get on with Rex and that she needed the money. She sold him to me, Jack, and he's mine now. I paid ten shillings for him!'

'Ten shillings!' Jack made a dismissive gesture with his hand. 'It don't matter what you paid. He weren't for sale. Anyway, we both know that he's priceless. Come on, Ruby; I accept you bought him in good faith but you've got to return him now. I'll pay you back that ten shillings just as soon as I can.'

'No,' shouted Ruby, taking hold of Mac by the scruff of his neck. '*No!* Even if I wanted to, I wouldn't. He hated it there. Rex were violent to him and your ma kept him tied up on the street. And she poured petrol into his ears when he got the canker!'

'I know,' said Jack. 'But I'm home now and I promise I will take good care of him. Come on, Ruby. Please give him to me. You can see that he recognises me and that he wants to come home.'

'He doesn't,' yelled Ruby. 'And this is his home, and all.'

She tightened her grip on Mac's neck and, without looking at Jack, dragged Mac back inside and slammed the front door in his face.

Ruby was almost hysterical as she tried to pull Mac into the kitchen. Jack was hammering furiously on the door, Mac was barking loudly and resisting Ruby every step of the way, and here was Aunt Maggie standing in the kitchen doorway and barring Ruby's way.

'What is all this?' Aunt Maggie demanded over the din.

'Aunt Maggie, lock the back gate and the scullery door too in case Jack tries to come round through the alleyway,' Ruby gabbled, vaguely aware she probably wasn't making much sense. '*Quickly* now. There's no time to lose.'

'Don't take that tone with me, young lady,' said Aunt Maggie, over more thunderous knocking and barking. 'And I'll do no such thing until you tell me what on earth is going on.'

Damn Aunt Maggie.

Damn her!

'What's going on here?' said Charlie, appearing halfway

down the stairs, still in his pyjamas and his hair all tousled.

'Jack – that man out there – thinks Mac's his dog and wants him back,' panted Ruby, still trying to pull a resistant Mac into the kitchen.

'Yes, I gathered that from the way you two were shouting at each other and waking up the whole street,' said Aunt Maggie sourly. 'Charlie, go back upstairs and get dressed. There ain't nothing to look at here. And empty your chamber pot before you step in it!'

'No. Don't open the back door,' said Ruby. 'Jack might get in.'

'Stop being so ridiculous, girl,' snapped Aunt Maggie. 'The poor chap's still banging on the front door, so unless he can fly, he won't suddenly appear in the backyard. More to the point, I take it that Mac *is* his dog?'

'*Were* his dog, Aunt Maggie!' hissed Ruby, dropping to her knees and wrapping her arms around Mac. '*Were!* He ain't any more. Mac lives here now and he's moving out over me dead body.'

'Oh, for heaven's sake,' said Aunt Maggie. 'Stop being so dramatic! Ain't this meant to be the chap you're stepping out with? Open the door and *talk* to him. Sort this out between the two of you.'

'No,' said Ruby, trying to process the fact that Aunt Maggie knew exactly who Jack was. 'I can't bear this. I *can't.*'

There was another flurry of knocking and then Jack's exasperated voice. 'Come on, Ruby. You can't hide in there forever. Open the bleeding door.'

'No,' whispered Ruby, almost to herself. 'No.'

Aunt Maggie shook her head in frustration. She grabbed hold of Mac who, caught unawares, allowed himself to be wrestled into the kitchen. Then she beckoned to Ruby. 'Come in here,' she said. 'I'll talk to him. Try and get you some breathing space, at least.'

'No,' said Ruby. 'Don't. He'll burst in . . .'

But Aunt Maggie had gone. Ruby shut the kitchen door behind her, sank down on to the hearth rug beside Mac and gave in to a storm of weeping.

Mac had been with her since the start and she loved him with all her heart. It was because of him that the animal hospital had become an idea and very nearly a reality.

She couldn't lose him.

A couple of minutes later, Aunt Maggie was back.

'Well, that went much better than expected,' she said grudgingly. 'A most reasonable young man, I must say. He's gone for now, to give you a chance to sort yourself out, but you'll have to do the right thing eventually.'

'The right thing is keeping Mac here,' said Ruby hotly. 'He belongs with me now.'

Aunt Maggie shook her head. 'He don't, I'm afraid,' she said, not unkindly. 'He's Jack's dog and Jack has promised to make sure he's well cared for. You'll have to give him back.'

Impotent rage propelled Ruby to her feet. 'Why do you *never* take my side?' she demanded, squaring up to her aunt.

'Excuse me, young lady! I don't know how you dare stand there and say that. In case you've not noticed, I've just gone and spoken to your young man after you threw a tantrum and refused.'

'But you're saying I have to give Mac back,' said Ruby.

'Because it's the right thing to do.'

'It *ain't*,' Ruby exploded, thoroughly riled. 'Why do you never stick up for me? *Ever?* Things would be much easier if you weren't here, always moaning and groaning and sticking your tuppence-worth in where it ain't wanted. In fact, now I come to think of it, why *are* you here, lording it over us all and sleeping in the parlour? This ain't your family and it would be much better all round if *you* just did the right thing and slung your hook.'

There was a short, charged silence and Ruby immediately knew that she had gone too far. Aunt Maggie took a step forward and, for a second, it looked like she might slap Ruby. But then she took a deep breath and clasped her hands in front of her.

'Have you *seen* your ma recently?' she said, her tone icy cold.

Ruby blinked in surprise.

What had that got to do with anything?

'Of course I've seen Ma recently,' she said. 'I saw her last night for starters and . . .'

'No, but I mean *really* seen her,' Aunt Maggie interrupted. 'Really looked at her, talked to her, asked her how she's doing . . . ?'

Ruby swallowed and the first hint of unease lodged beneath her breastbone. To tell the truth, she hadn't done any of those things. Her mother was just . . . there, like the range or the sink in the scullery. Essential in that the household would fall apart without them, but you really didn't notice them so long as they were doing what they were designed to do. And now she came to think about it, she really hadn't paid much attention to Ma. She had been so wrapped up in the munitions factory and the animal hospital and everything else that was going on in her life that her family had somewhat gone by the wayside.

'Is Ma all right?' she asked in a small voice.

'Of course she ain't all right.'

'Is she . . . sick?'

Oh, please don't let Ma be sick . . .

'I don't think she's sick as such,' said Aunt Maggie. 'But she's lost a lot of weight recently, even allowing for the food shortages, so I can't be sure. The truth is, though, your ma ain't been all right since the day your dad died. Losing his income and suddenly having to work all hours at the laundry to keep body and soul together with no time to properly mourn him. And now her older son has joined up and he's off to the front at any time so she's petrified for him, to boot. And her younger son is off at all hours, goodness knows where. Of course she ain't all right, child. She'll never be the same again. And, in response to your question, that's why I'm here. I've rented me house out in Whitechapel so that I can help with the bills here. And I'm shopping and cooking and cleaning and generally trying to keep the home fires burning whilst your ma is working every hour she can in that godforsaken laundry to look after you all.'

Aunt Maggie paused for breath and looked at Ruby, obviously waiting for a response. But Ruby was so surprised – so stunned – that she simply didn't know what to say.

'So then you arrive home out of the blue after five years in service,' Aunt Maggie continued. 'I've never seen your mother so happy. Another woman – her *daughter* – around the house ready to do her bit and to help take the strain off us all. Another income – a big one at that – which might allow her to stop work. Someone who might be able to reach out to Charlie. But it ain't worked out quite like that, has it? You're here in body – some of the time – but your mind's somewhere else *all* the time; away with the fairies and with every sick animal in Silvertown. You join committees galore, you take a second job at the market, you have pie-in-the sky ideas about opening an animal hospital and you fill the house with strays and other people's animals. And yet you give your ma next to nothing in housekeeping and you do absolutely sweet Fanny Adams to help around the house. I can't remember when you last did the washing-up or spent time with your brother – let alone volunteered to help with the laundry or to bring in the coal.'

Ruby finally found her tongue. 'But Ma never asked . . .' she started.

'Your ma's soft where you're concerned,' interrupted Aunt Maggie. 'I don't know how many times I've told her to tell you to get off your backside and show an interest in family matters or to contribute more to the household – but, either way, she shouldn't have to. You're a grown woman and you should *know* to do your bit. After all, charity begins at home!'

That was enough.

'Well, it works both ways,' Ruby said angrily. 'When have you ever shown the slightest interest in *my* matters? The things I'm doing are important – they're *needed* – and yet you've never asked a single question, let alone volunteered to lend a hand. You just snipe and snarl and put me down any chance you get – and you know that's true.'

Aunt Maggie shook her head. 'No – let me tell *you* what's true,' she said. 'A dozen people have told me and your ma that you've been hanging around with that young man. You've been seen in the street and in the park and even in Fisher's together – just down the road, for goodness' sake! – and yet you've never once bothered to tell us yourself, let alone bring him home and introduce him to us in a civilised fashion.'

'Times have changed, Aunt Maggie,' said Ruby rudely. 'Gentlemen don't need to come to the house and leave their calling cards no more.'

'That's as maybe,' said Aunt Maggie. 'But an introduction would have been courteous. How do you think it makes your ma feel with her daughter running around Silvertown on the make?'

Charlie appeared at the doorway, looking stunned.

'Blimey,' he said, looking from sister to aunt. 'You on the make, sis? And yet you think it's all right to accuse me of things left, right and centre?' Nervously, he grabbed his sandwiches from the kitchen table and then bent down and patted Mac, kissing him on the top of his head.

And then he was gone.

Ruby, about to reply to her aunt in the strongest possible terms, suddenly found she was exhausted and all out of fight.

'I don't want to talk to you no more,' she said quietly. 'I ain't on the make – I never have been. And now I'm going to take Mac upstairs and try and get some sleep. Some of us *work* for a living, you know.'

'You ain't finished your porridge,' said Aunt Maggie.

Ruby didn't bother to answer.

She just clicked her fingers for Mac and left the room without looking back.

Darn Aunt Maggie.

Darn Jack.

Darn it all.

Sleep eluded Ruby.

She lay on the bed with her arm around Mac, crying gentle tears into his lovely, springy fur. Impossible, *unbearable* as it seemed, she knew she had to steel herself to say goodbye. Deep down, she'd known that from the moment Jack had turned up and laid claim to Mac – or at least from the moment she had seen Mac's genuine joy at their reunion. That was the point when Ruby had realised it was all over. And the worst thing was that she couldn't even blame Jack. Not really. She could – and did – blame his mother, but Jack himself had been as innocent and ignorant in all this as she was. Nonetheless, as Ruby lay there quietly sobbing, one thought kept going round and round her head. If Jack was falling in love with her the way she'd thought she was falling in love with him, surely he would have let her keep Mac.

Surely he would have done that for her.

By lunchtime, Ruby was all cried out.

It would never be a good time to let Mac go – it would never not be the hardest thing she had ever had to do – but she had to be brave. After all, she knew Mac wouldn't suffer – he clearly adored Jack – so at least she didn't have to worry about that. It would only be her heart that was breaking.

Oh, Ruby.
Stop it!
Don't be so sentimental.

She sat up and kissed Mac on top of his head.

'Don't forget about me completely, old fellow,' she said. 'But be happy. Be happy with Jack.'

Even if she couldn't be.

Downstairs, Ma was back from work and peeling turnips at the kitchen table with Aunt Maggie. She stood up as Ruby came into the room.

'Maggie told me, love,' she said, her face flooded with sympathy.

Ruby nodded. 'I'm going to take him round – home – to Victory Lane before I change me mind,' she said, hardly believing that she was saying the words.

'Would you like me to take him for you?'

'No, thank you. I should do it. Except, do you think I should wait until Charlie comes home from school so that he has a chance to say goodbye?'

Ma shook her head. 'He'll understand, poppet,' she said.

'I think he already said his goodbyes,' added Aunt Maggie, reaching out and patting Ruby on the arm.

Ruby gave her aunt a grateful glance. She hadn't even begun to process their blazing row but she did know that she had been very rude and that Aunt Maggie had made some valid points.

She would think about all of that later . . .

'Let Maggie and I say our goodbyes and then best get it over with,' Ma was saying.

The two women bent over the dog, talking softly and,

when they straightened up, Ruby saw their eyes were shining with tears.

The walk to Victory Lane seemed, at once, to take forever and no time at all.

To a casual observer, Ruby would have looked calm – her head held high, her pace steady – but inside she was in turmoil. Her mind was swirling with dozens of thoughts and memories; the first time she had walked down Victory Lane on the way to the factory and seen Mac tied to the lamppost; her daily visits, the sharing of treats; persuading Mrs Driscoll to part with him; Mac getting hurt protecting the house on Sanctuary Lane and his slow recovery. Oh, so much had happened. It felt like she had both known Mac forever and that he had only been hers for five minutes.

And here was Mrs Driscoll's – *Jack's* – house.

Suddenly feeling lightheaded, Ruby knocked on the door.

Please let it be Mrs Driscoll who answers.

Please don't let it be Jack.

It was Jack.

'I've come to return Mac,' Ruby said stiffly.

She would not – *could* not – call him Mick.

Jack's face was unreadable. 'Thank you,' he said. 'I were hoping you'd do the right thing.'

He took a step towards her – and it looked as though he was intending to hug her – but Ruby backed away.

'I must be going,' she said.

She bent and patted Mac awkwardly – once, twice, three times. Mac, busy wriggling with delight over seeing Jack again, completely ignored her.

Silently, Ruby started to leave.

'See you Friday?' Jack called after her. 'I haven't forgotten your table in Totteridge.'

Ruby turned back. Jack, crouching down, was rubbing Mac's head, a huge beam on his face. 'I don't think so,' she said.

Jack's face clouded over. 'Another time?' he said. 'A walk with Mick, perhaps? I know he's going to miss you.'

'No,' said Ruby. '*No*.'

'What, then?'

'Nothing.'

'Oh, come on, Ruby. It don't have to end like this.'

'I think it does,' said Ruby. 'I know returning Mac were the right thing to do, but I don't ever want to see *you* again, Jack Kennedy.'

And she walked away without looking back.

29

Keep busy.

Keep *very* busy.

That was the most important thing to do, Ruby continually reminded herself over the next few days. She needed to keep so busy during her waking hours that there was simply no time to think about Mac – and then hopefully she would be so exhausted that sleep wouldn't elude her when she finally got into bed.

And, to be honest, there was no problem at all with keeping busy.

Plans for the animal hospital had gathered steam and taken on a momentum of their own now that there was less than a month until their planned opening date, and Ruby would have found it very difficult to step away even had she wanted to. Besides, it wasn't just her who had been swept up by the project. Her friends were now fully on board, working around the clock and full of vim and vigour and ever more creative ideas. Leah and Ruby spent hours poring over their lists, opening a bank account, and continuing to source the various items from near and far. It was exhausting, time-consuming work, but they did manage to visit the parents of the little girl who had lost Fluffy and, with their permission, to present her with Steel. Dot – a different woman now the attacks on her home had stopped – and Ruby were carefully drawing up diagnosis crib sheets and treatment protocols from the various pamphlets they had accrued, together with educational information for owners. And Elspeth – *Elspeth*! – had pulled together a knitting circle at the factory to produce the bandages and blankets they needed and, together with her mother, was even busy planning a fundraising Christmas bazaar.

It was marvellous the way the four of them worked so well together, but of course it could only go so far to mend Ruby's broken heart. She had loved Mac so much and she missed everything about him – but how could she bear to see him with someone else? She'd thought she was falling in love with Jack – but if he loved her in return, how could he possibly have done this to her?

It was going to take her a long, long time to get over them both.

'I think we should set a firm date for the opening,' said Leah, a couple of weeks later.

She and Ruby had just returned from transporting the very grand examination table they had splashed out on. They had driven back from North London in a motorised van they had hired especially for the occasion, left the table in the depot, returned the van and were now drinking tea in Ruby's kitchen.

Ruby smiled. 'I can't make no decisions at the moment,' she said. 'It's going to take me a while to recover from your driving!'

'Silly!' Leah gave her a friendly shove. 'But seriously, we're just about stocked up now. There's no reason not to plan our first clinic.'

'I know, I know,' Ruby said. 'It's only ten days until the concert, and it would be good to have a proper date set by then. I'm just worried it ain't the right time. Not with the news coming out of the Somme and everything.'

A few days previously, on the first of July, a major new offensive had started along the Somme in northern France. The nation had collectively held its breath (it was all anyone talked about at work), but early newspaper reports had been so positive, bordering on jubilant, that everyone had breathed a sigh of relief and gone back to talking about more trivial matters.

Since then, however, it was gradually becoming clear that the newspapers were wrong – and that thousands of British lives had been lost on the first day alone.

The only good news was that the most recent letter from Harry had still been posted from Buckinghamshire and there was no indication that he was about to be moved to Surrey, let alone to France, any time soon.

'Do you want to know what I think?' asked Aunt Maggie, who, hitherto, had been sitting quietly in the corner of the room.

'Of course,' said Ruby politely.

She was pretty sure she already knew what Aunt Maggie thought. Despite a new entente cordiale between the two, and Ruby's attempts to be more helpful around the house, she knew her aunt still disapproved of the whole hospital venture.

Aunt Maggie rattled her cup back into its saucer. 'I think you should go ahead with your plans,' she said firmly.

'Really?'

'Really,' said Aunt Maggie. 'You can't do nothing about

what's going on over in France, and awful as it is, what's going on out there don't make our problems at home disappear. The animals still need your help. Besides, throwing yourself body and soul into a project is the best way to take your mind off your worries; I found *that* out when me husband died. So go ahead with your hospital. Set a date for the opening and give it all you've got.'

There was a short pause when Aunt Maggie finished speaking and then Leah started clapping.

'Brava, Aunt Maggie,' she said. 'I couldn't agree more. There will never be a perfect time. What do you say, Ruby?'

Ruby paused. So much seemed to be stacked against the venture and yet it was something she believed in with all her heart.

'I say yes!' she said. 'Let's go full steam ahead, and if we hit problems, we'll take them in our stride. I'll start using up some of me holiday from the factory to give me a little more time. After all, the room at the depot is already filling up with things we've bought and there's no point in paying for it if it ain't being used.'

'None at all,' said Leah. 'So, when will the grand opening be?'

'What about two weeks after the concert?' said Ruby. 'The thirtieth of July? That gives us three weeks to get everything shipshape.'

'Perfect,' said Leah.

'Dot's helping me pull together a poster,' said Ruby. 'She's used to designing and printing stuff for the suffragettes, and she's being ever so helpful now she's back on duty.'

'Marvellous,' said Leah. 'Let's plaster them all around town. Put them up in the canteens at work too. Word will soon spread.'

'And what about a task party to start sorting out the depot?' said Ruby. 'I'd like to distemper the walls and give the floor a good clean before we start laying everything out.'

'Cleanliness is next to godliness,' Aunt Maggie interjected.

'Exactly,' said Ruby. 'If the place ain't spotless, why would anyone trust us with their animals?'

'Well, I'm in,' said Leah. 'I could even do it tomorrow if you like.'

'And I'd love to lend a hand, if you'll let me,' Aunt Maggie piped up. 'I used to be quite a dab hand with a roller back in the day.'

Wonders would never cease.

Against the odds, it was a very merry party that set out to the depot early the next morning, laden with hastily bought rollers, brushes and buckets of white distemper. To Ruby's amazement, Aunt Maggie turned out to be worth her weight in gold. Within a few minutes of arriving, she had managed to winkle out a stepladder half-hidden in a corner of the depot and then she was off, scampering up and down with distemper as though to the manner born. Leah set to work painting the lower walls of the room and Ruby – half-relieved and half-disappointed there was no sign of Jack and Mac – concentrated on carrying out an inventory of everything they had already bought. After a couple of hours, the place was beginning to look a great deal better.

And then Nellie arrived.

'Morning,' said Ruby cheerfully, going over to greet her.

Nellie gave an almost imperceptible nod of her head. 'Can I have a word?' she asked, beckoning Ruby into a quiet corner of the room.

'Of course.'

Ruby thought she knew why Nellie was looking so serious. They had put in a request to the landlord, asking if it would be possible to create a dedicated entrance to their room; after all, they could mop the floors as many times as they pleased, but the depot was a messy, mucky working area and it would be very difficult to keep it clean. But Nellie had already said she thought a positive response was unlikely as the landlord was tighter than an elastic band, so Ruby knew that she was probably on a hiding to nothing.

Sure enough, Nellie started shaking her head as soon as she and Ruby were alone. 'It's a no, I'm afraid,' she said. 'I'm sorry to be the bearer of bad news.'

'Oh.' Despite it all, Ruby felt a surge of disappointment. 'Not even if we pay for it ourselves? Never mind — it's not the end of the world. Everyone will just have to come in through the depot.'

'*No.*' Nellie laid an insistent hand on Ruby's arm. 'You don't understand. I mean the whole thing is off. You can't rent the room no more.'

The world ground to a halt in a clash of discordant chords.

'Whatever do you mean?' said Ruby, trying to process Nellie's words.

They made no sense.

'I'm ever so sorry,' said Nellie. 'I tried to change his mind, I really did.'

'*Whose* mind?'

What on earth was going on?

Then Ruby realised.

It was Jack, wasn't it?

It had to be Jack.

He had clearly decided it would be too awkward for the two of them to bump into each other on a regular basis and had worked out the perfect way to scupper her plan.

The absolute *rotter*.

Despite getting Mac back, he was still out to make her life a misery.

Nellie was still talking. 'Well, the landlord, of course,' she said. 'He said he don't want you in here no more.'

Oh!

Not Jack.

It would never have been him; he just wouldn't have had that sort of influence, let alone had it in him to be so mean.

Ruby leaned on her mop handle and tried to absorb this new information.

'But why?' she said. 'I've paid me deposit. He's taken me money. And look at all the stuff we've already bought. We're planning to open the hospital in a few weeks, for goodness' sake.'

Nellie gave an elaborate shrug. 'Buggered if I know,' she said. 'Something to do with the animals.'

'But there isn't a "no animal" rule,' said Ruby. 'Half the depot is made up of stables!'

'I think it were more the fact you're planning to treat animals here,' said Nellie.

It still made no sense.

'Why should the landlord care about that?' said Ruby. 'From what you've said, he don't care what goes on here as long as he gets his rent.'

Nellie puffed out her cheeks. 'All I know is he'd heard that you were planning to treat animals here and he said you ain't qualified to do so. He said you'd be "undermining the livelihood of genuine veterinary practitioners" or something like that.'

Ruby's brain seemed to be working very slowly to join up the dots . . . but things were beginning to fall into place.

'I don't think you ever told me the landlord's surname,' she said carefully.

Nellie shrugged her shoulders again. 'Maybe not,' she said. 'It's Smith.'

Lordy.

It was a very common name, but . . .

'Don't tell me,' Ruby said wearily. 'It's Mr Robert Smith, isn't it? The veterinary practitioner.'

Nellie looked confused. 'No, dear,' she said. 'It's his father. Sir *Emrys* Smith. He owns a lot of the property around here.'

No.

No!

Ruby leaned back against the wall and exhaled slowly. She could hardly make sense of what she was hearing, but it sounded like Robert Smith *had* stopped her plans in their tracks. He had gone bleating to his father and, as bad luck would have it, his father just happened to be a pre-eminent East End landlord.

Worse still, Robert Smith's father was Sir Emrys.

The Sir Emrys.

Had Sir Emrys made the link with the housemaid who had thrown scalding coffee into his lap all those months ago? Ruby had no way of knowing, and of course it didn't really matter. What mattered was that, one way or another, the Smith family had taken their revenge.

It wasn't just bad luck.

Ruby could see clearly – perhaps for the first time – that she was never, ever going to be able to win against these people.

And here were Leah and Aunt Maggie, hurrying over to see what was going on, Aunt Maggie brandishing her roller as though it was a dangerous weapon.

Ruby gave Leah a wan smile. 'I'm presuming you mentioned the Silvertown Animal Hospital to Robert Smith?' she said, trying to keep her voice as calm as possible.

Leah wouldn't have done anything deliberately to sabotage the venture – Ruby knew she wouldn't.

Leah pursed her lips. 'What's that got to do with anything?' she asked, looking from Ruby to Nellie in confusion.

'*Did* you?'

'I might have mentioned it,' Leah said defensively. 'Only in a positive way, though. I asked him for advice on what sort of table to get and on which implements might be most useful . . .'

'And I'm presuming you told him that we was planning to house it in this depot?' Ruby persisted.

'Yes – but that's hardly a secret, is it?' said Leah.

'Hopefully *everyone* will know where the hospital is before too long. Isn't that the whole point?'

'But Robert, Leah. *Robert*,' said Ruby hotly. 'You *heard* how he reacted when I told him about the idea. You was there!'

'I thought he would change his mind now it was actually happening,' said Leah. 'He's a decent chap, really, he is. I thought he might even get involved.'

Nellie gave one of her trademark wheezing laughs. 'Well, I'm not sure about "decent",' she said. 'But he's got involved, all right. He's only got Daddy – who happens to own most of Silvertown – to pull the plug on the whole thing.'

Leah's eyes swivelled to Ruby's for confirmation, her mouth a circle of shock. 'Surely not . . .'

'Oh, yes,' said Ruby bitterly. 'That's exactly what he's done.'

'But surely the other workers are up in arms about it?' said Aunt Maggie, speaking for the first time. 'After all, Ruby's a local girl – she were born just round the corner; she's one of their own. Surely, they won't let some la-di-la landlord from goodness knows where throw her out on her ear for some petty grudge? She's a good girl, our Ruby, and this just ain't fair!'

Despite everything, Ruby's heart swelled to hear Aunt Maggie defending her like this.

Whoever would have thought it?

And Aunt Maggie was right.

It *was* unfair.

'We should rally the workers,' Aunt Maggie was saying,

waving her roller around. 'Make placards, form a picket line . . . surely we can do *something*.'

But Nellie was shaking her head. 'Thing is that some of the other tenants weren't best pleased about the animal hospital being located here, either,' she said. 'Not me, mind – I were the one who suggested it to Ruby in the first place – but there's a feeling that what happens behind the scenes should stay behind the scenes, so to speak.'

'Whatever can you mean?' demanded Leah. 'That makes no sense at all.'

But Ruby knew exactly what Nellie meant.

She had seen the man boiling his oranges over the brazier and she understood exactly why he – and all the others attaching false bottoms to measuring containers or mixing bad apples in with good – wouldn't want potential customers wandering around the depot. Who would want to give away their trade secrets – especially when the trade secrets were somewhat dubious – to all and sundry?

It was just a wonder Ruby hadn't realised it at the time.

Leah touched her on the arm. 'You'll find other premises,' she said. 'And maybe you'll find something *better*.'

'I won't,' said Ruby flatly. 'No matter how much we make at the concert, the rents everywhere else are simply too high. And even if I could, I get the impression that no one would take us on. This were me only chance and now it's gone. It's hopeless. Quite hopeless. I can see that now.'

'Don't give up, girl,' said Aunt Maggie. 'Where there's a will, there's a way.'

'Yes, Ruby,' said Leah. 'Something else will turn up. I could contact . . .'

'No,' said Ruby firmly. '*No*. I don't want you stepping in

and trying to make everything all right, Leah. Promise me that you won't? After all, it ain't worked out very well in this instance, has it?'

Leah pursed her lips and looked like she was about to make a sharp retort. But in the event, she just sighed and turned to Nellie. 'I assume, at the very least, that Ruby's deposit will be repaid to her in full by the landlord?'

Nellie looked evasive. 'Of course,' she said. 'In the, er, fullness of time.'

'No,' said Leah sharply. 'Damn the fullness of time. If the landlord is no longer willing to rent Ruby this space, the money must be returned now. We'd also appreciate him reimbursing us for the money we've already spent on distemper and other materials.'

Nellie's evasive expression turned to one of panic. 'I'll see what I can do,' she said. 'I'll just need a little time.'

Ruby understood, as plain as day, that not all of her five pounds had gone to the landlord. It had greased Nellie's palms – and goodness knew whose else's on the way. Still, she couldn't hate Nellie. It was just the way that things worked in the East End. And she couldn't really resent Leah either. Leah had acted in good faith and could not possibly have predicted the repercussions of chatting to Robert.

No, there was no point in blaming or resenting anyone.

It was just a sad – and perhaps inevitable – combination of events.

But the irrefutable fact was that she had lost her premises.

Did that mean that her dream was over?

'By the way,' said Nellie, drawing Ruby to one side. 'I've

336

only recently worked out that Charlie Archer is your brother.'

'I'm sorry?' said Ruby, her heart sinking.

She had no idea what that had to do with anything, but she did know that it was extremely unlikely to be good news.

'Yes, little Charlie,' said Nellie. 'He's often down here, he is, ordering around his friend Joe who wouldn't say boo to a goose.'

'Really?' said Ruby, intrigued, despite everything. Apart from anything else, that wasn't at all how she had imagined Joe. 'What do they get up to here?'

And did she really want to know?

'Why, they've adopted the stray cats who live in the scrubland outside,' said Nellie, gesturing through the window. 'Look after them ever so well, they do. They built them a shelter to keep the foxes away when one of them had kittens, they bring them food and they've even got ointment out of me.'

'Are you sure?' said Ruby.

'What do you mean, am I sure?' said Nellie indignantly. 'I've seen it with me own eyes. I've even been invited outside to inspect their handiwork from time to time. I must say that when I discovered that Charlie were your brother, I had a little chuckle to meself. Peas in a pod you are, both of you loving animals like you do.'

For once, Ruby was struck dumb.

30

Over the next few days, Ruby and Leah were kept busy transporting everything they had already bought for the animal hospital out of the depot.

It couldn't all go back to Sanctuary Lane, of course – there was no room to swing a cat there – although Aunt Maggie and Ma had both offered their bedrooms to store any odds and sods. But it was humbling how people had rallied around to help. Dot and Mrs Fisher offered a large storeroom at the bakery to house some of the furniture. Elspeth and Mrs Carson could make room in their garden shed for the cages. Leah's landlady had given them the use of a lockable cupboard for the medicines. And Leah, for her part, had been extremely helpful, sourcing a man with a van to transport everything and waving away the cost.

Nonetheless, despite the sympathetic and supportive response, it was dispiriting work.

'I should probably just have returned everything I could to the various vendors and got a refund instead,' said Ruby gloomily after the last item had been deposited and they were walking back from Elspeth's. 'Goodness knows when any of those things will see the light of day again.'

'Cheer up, misery-guts,' said Leah. 'It's not over yet.'

'I'm frightened that it is,' said Ruby. 'We're back to square one. What's a hospital without a building? I know

I said that we would tackle any problem head on – and I really will try – but should we be raising money at Clara Williams' concert? I want to, but I wonder if it's right to do so?'

'We're not giving up on the concert,' said Leah firmly. 'We *can't* give up on the concert. It's all organised; Clara Williams is singing at the Adelphi next week and the Silvertown Animal Hospital is already emblazoned across the posters and the programmes. We've got no choice but to keep going.'

'I worry we're defrauding people,' said Ruby.

'We're not,' said Leah. 'You can still treat animals in their homes, so any medicines we buy with the money won't go to waste. And if we raise a lot of money, let's take it as a good omen that things will soon be on the up, shall we?'

Ruby gave her friend a watery grin.

'You're right,' she said. 'I can't give up just like that. At the very least, I owe it to the animals to keep going until the bitter end.'

And she also owed it to Charlie to let him know what she had discovered.

Ruby thought long and hard about when and where to have a proper chat with her brother. In the end, she decided to invite him along to the next Brunner Babes home game. It would be difficult because she would always now associate the football with Jack, but she just had a feeling that Charlie would enjoy the atmosphere and the match as much as she had done. Besides, surely it would be easier to talk and share confidences whilst looking ahead, rather than staring intently and rather embarrassingly into each other's eyes.

Charlie, for his part, was thoroughly confused by Ruby's invitation. At first, he refused to entertain the idea and openly wondered what the catch might be. But Ruby gently insisted. It was only when she assured him that not only was there no catch, but that the whole thing was her treat – from the ticket to the meat pies and roasted chestnuts, to say nothing of the toffee apples – that he finally relented and agreed to come along.

And he loved it!

He loved everything, from the cheering crowds to the marching band and the thrills and spills of the match itself, and Ruby revelled in his reaction. Gone was the intense and secretive young man of recent months, replaced by the fun-loving and enthusiastic lad she remembered from years gone by.

Ruby waited until the second half – when the Brunner Babes were not only two-one up, but Ruby had been personally greeted by star-of-the-show-Elspeth – before her opening gambit.

'I owe you an apology,' she said, during a quiet period in the match and when the action was all down the other end of the pitch.

She felt Charlie stiffen next to her.

'What for?' he asked suspiciously, without looking at her.

'Nellie down the market told me of all the sterling work you've done with the stray animals near the depot.'

There was a pause.

'I didn't know Nellie knew I were related to you,' said Charlie, almost accusingly.

'She didn't until recently,' said Ruby. 'And I don't know how she found out.'

'So?' asked Charlie.

'So I reckon that when I accused you of hurting Willow, I was doing you a big disservice.'

She turned to him and Charlie's gaze flickered to hers. 'I told you I would never hurt an animal, didn't I?' he said fervently. 'Joe wouldn't either. I couldn't believe you thought we had that in us.'

'I'm sorry,' said Ruby sincerely. 'It was just that me friend Dot thought that the same people who had thrown bricks through their window had also hurt their cat. I'm prepared to believe that she got that wrong and I feel really terrible that I accused you like that.'

'S'all right,' Charlie muttered.

Ruby took a deep breath. 'The brick-throwing, though . . .'

Charlie sighed. 'Here we go.'

'Hear me out,' said Ruby. 'To be honest, I really don't know what I feel about that in principle, but I do know that it's gone too far already. I don't want to see people hurt and I certainly don't want to see you two getting into trouble.'

'Someone's got to do something, though.'

'Yes, but not you, and not that,' said Ruby. 'To be honest, at first I assumed it were your friend Joe who were leading you off the straight and narrow, but something Nellie said made me think that you might be the ringleader and I want you to stop. Apart from anything, Joe's got enough going on in his life as it is.'

'But we can't just let the Germans get away with it,' said Charlie hotly.

341

'Oh Charlie. Mrs Muller with her balls of wool ain't "the Germans",' said Ruby. 'Look, we all hate the real Germans and we all want to get back at them, but that ain't the way to do things.'

'What, then?'

'I don't know,' said Ruby. 'I ain't got all the answers. But look after each other, I suppose. Look after the animals. Open an animal hospital. Anything. Just try to do good in the things we *can* control. Not more violence and destruction. Do you understand?'

'Yeah.'

There was silence as the home team successfully defended two corners.

'This is nice,' said Charlie quietly. 'You and me together, even if Harry can't be with us.'

'It is,' Ruby agreed. 'Hopefully he'll be able to join us one day soon. Look, why don't you bring Joe round for supper? I'm sure we'd all love to meet him.'

Charlie nodded. 'All right,' he said. 'I will.'

'And what about both of you helping with the animal hospital if I ever get the darned thing off the ground?' she added. 'You could be head of publicity if you like. Tell people about it at school, put posters up around town – that sort of thing. I'd even pay you.'

'Rather,' said Charlie enthusiastically.

'Anything else that would make this blasted war more bearable for you?' said Ruby.

Charlie gave her a sideways glance. 'Another toffee apple?' he asked with a grin.

As Elspeth sent the ball thundering into the goal in

front of them and the crowd duly went wild, Ruby felt a little glow of happiness.

Despite everything, maybe some things really were going to be all right after all.

The days leading up to the concert passed in a blur.

Buoyed up from her conversation with Charlie, Ruby threw herself into finding new premises for the hospital, pounding the streets until there were holes in her shoes. It was in vain. There were next to no vacant buildings anywhere in Silvertown and those that *were* empty were invariably far too expensive for Ruby to even consider. At the same time, she wrote letter after letter to anyone who might be willing to volunteer at the hospital. Again, this failed to bear fruit; the vets didn't bother to reply and the charities were sympathetic but had no plans – or no resources – to get involved in Silvertown.

It all seemed hopeless.

As before, the only plus side to being rushed off her feet was that there was less time to dwell on Mac. Ruby still missed him terribly, of course. Occasionally she admitted to herself that she missed Jack too and that maybe she had been hasty in saying that she never wanted to see him again. After all, she hardly knew the man – but she did know that he had made her heart beat that little bit faster every time she was with him – and surely that was what it was all about. Besides, he had seemed kind and funny and complicated and clever and he loved animals and . . .

And no!

She still couldn't bear to see Jack with Mac, day after day, week after week.

It would only serve to underline all that she had lost.

That ship had sailed.

And suddenly the big day was upon them.

Ruby woke full of excitement and trepidation.

There was, she reminded herself, no real reason to be nervous; she was not playing an active role in the evening's proceedings. Leah, as Clara Williams' goddaughter, might say a few words as introduction or to promote the hospital, but Ruby would just be enjoying the concert. As founder of the 'good cause' linked to the event, she had received a fairly generous allowance of tickets towards the back of the stalls, and Ma and Aunt Maggie had fairly jumped at the opportunity to join her. Ruby had also invited Dot and Mrs Fisher; the latter, especially, was a huge Clara Williams fan and Ruby wanted to thank them for storing the hospital chattels and for their help in producing the literature and posters – to say nothing of providing the Archer family with a steady supply of cakes and buns over the past few weeks. In a gesture of goodwill, she had also invited Nellie – who had politely declined the offer as 'not for the likes of me'. Leah would also be sitting with them, although her mother and father – to Leah's disgust – had opted to sit in the grander seats at the front of the dress circle.

The little party, dressed in their best clothes, made their way to the West End with plenty of time to spare and in a state of high excitement. Of course, Leah's best clothes and Ruby's best clothes were somewhat different, but

Ruby was wearing her newest navy skirt and crisp white blouse and felt that she looked appropriately smart, if hardly grand or glamorous. The centre of London – whilst perhaps less busy than it had been before the war – still assaulted all the senses. They emerged from the Tube station and stood stock-still at the kerb, petrified to cross the road. Motorised omnibuses, packed to the gills, did an improvised dance with automobiles, horse-drawn carriages and the odd hand-pulled cart. How any of them emerged unscathed was a complete mystery to Ruby.

And the *noise*.

Silvertown was part of London, but this cacophony was something else! The roar of engines punctuated by bangs and whistles and shouts and neighs. Newspaper vendors shouting out the latest war news, and the stamp of leather on stone from all the soldiers marching by on their way to an uncertain future. It was all Ruby could do not to put her hands over her ears and sing loudly as she had done when frightened by loud noises as a child.

And there, ahead of them, was the theatre, a swirling carousel of colours and lights. Outside, posters of Clara Williams, photographed at her most glamorous, were emblazoned with *In Aid of the Silvertown Animal Hospital*.

'Look at that!' said Ruby, clutching Leah's arm in excitement. 'It's . . . real.'

'It is!' squealed Leah, squeezing Ruby's hand. 'And it's all down to you. Come on, let's go inside and enjoy the build-up.'

Ma stopped outside the pub next to the theatre. 'I don't know about any of you, but I could do with a drink,' she said.

That was so unlike Ma that Ruby couldn't help but laugh. But Aunt Maggie was nodding.

'Me too,' she said. 'I've barely been inside a pub since me husband died, but I reckon I need a half of stout to keep me wits about me tonight. Come on, you're only young once!'

'You go ahead,' said Mrs Fisher to Ruby with a laugh. 'Dot and I will keep an eye on your mother and your aunt.'

And the four of them were gone, disappearing inside the Nell Gwynne with conspiratorial giggles.

Ruby turned to Leah.

'Let's go in,' she said. 'And if this works out, I know – I just *know* – that everything is going to be all right.'

The two women ascended the steps and went into the theatre.

On announcing their names, Leah was immediately swept off to meet her godmother backstage. There was no such invitation for Ruby – 'she's always as grumpy as anything before she performs' – so, slightly self-consciously, Ruby followed a babble of noisy chatter upstairs to the circle bar. Not sure what she was actually going to do there, she peeked her head nervously around the door.

The lavish red and gold room was packed to the gills.

Most of the gentlemen – bedecked in evening dress – were propped against the bar or standing, one hand behind their backs, in little groups. By contrast, the women, in all their colourful finery, were perched on ornate gilded chairs, squawking like so many exotic birds. Ruby watched with emotions flitting from amusement to terror. They were largely all there because of her.

Her!

Little Ruby Archer from a terraced house in Silvertown.

A mere few months ago, she had been serving people very like these; curtseying in her smart black and white maid's uniform and trying to avoid getting her backside pinched. Now all these people were gathered here because of a vision that *she* had had. Maybe, despite the horror of the war, things at home really were changing for the better.

It was almost unbelievable . . .

'Excuse me! Girl!' A woman clad in gold lamé and sitting close to the door, beckoned to her imperiously. Tentatively, Ruby came out from behind the door and went up to her. Maybe she wanted to find out more about the hospital. Maybe she even wanted to make an early donation.

'Don't *skulk*,' the woman scolded her. 'I hate it when the staff skulk. No one can see you there, girl.'

Oh, Lordy.

Ruby was stuck somewhere between amusement and embarrassment and not sure which way to turn. To be fair, her skirt and blouse combination *was* quite similar to what the staff were wearing and a mile away from the evening dress worn by just about everyone else but . . . still!

'Yes, Ma'am,' said Ruby. 'Sorry, Ma'am.'

The words were out before she could stop them. Force of habit, she supposed.

'My coffee is terribly strong,' the woman continued. 'Quite undrinkable, in fact. I need more milk.' And then, when Ruby hesitated, '*Quickly* now.'

Amusement slunk away and abject humiliation won the

day. Ruby felt her cheeks burn and her eyes prickled with tears.

It was no good.

No matter how she tried, no matter what she did, somewhere deep inside she would always be Ruby, the housemaid. There was simply no escaping it and she knew it went much deeper than what clothes she was wearing. Despite herself, Ruby found herself slinking behind the bar for a jug of milk and seconds later she was topping up the coffee.

But that would be that.

She would return the jug to the bar and then she would go and join Ma and the others for half a stout in the pub next door.

Thank goodness none of them had been in the bar to witness her humiliation . . .

'Ruby! It *is* you.' Reluctantly, Ruby turned her head towards the voice. Goodness! It was Mrs Henderson sitting with a group of other women. Amongst them was Lady Smith, wife of Sir Emrys . . . the man who had pulled the plug on the depot.

Goodness, the evening hadn't even started and it was already going from bad to worse.

'Hello, Mrs Henderson,' Ruby said weakly.

'Lovely to see you again, dear,' said Mrs Henderson, holding out her hand for Ruby's and squeezing it warmly. 'The last I heard you were off to the munitions factory. Didn't it work out? I did say I didn't think you were cut out for . . .'

'No, no. I'm still at the factory, Mrs Henderson,' Ruby interrupted. 'In fact, I'm . . .'

'No shame in having a second job to make ends meet, dear,' said Mrs Henderson. 'You couldn't get me another sherry, could you? There's such a fearsome crush at the bar and, as you can see, Mr Henderson is deep in conversation and quite inattentive to my needs.'

Say no.

Just say no, Ruby.

'Of course, Ma'am. Right away, Ma'am. Can I get anyone else another drink?'

Waiting, half-laughing and half-crying, for four assorted drinks to be prepared at the bar, Ruby let the snatches of nearby conversation wash over her . . .

'Always wanted to hear Clara Williams sing . . .'

'Such an intimate setting as well . . . a real treat . . .'

'Not at all sure about tonight's charity though . . . ?'

'Yes. We said the same. "The Silvertown Animal Hospital"! Surely raising money for the soldiers would be more appropriate, especially given the dreadful news coming out of the Somme. And where exactly is Silvertown, for goodness' sake?'

'Deepest darkest East End, I gather. Real Jack the Ripper territory.'

'Indeed. And do we want to encourage the poor to be keeping animals at a time like this?'

'Or at any time, to be honest? I'm not even sure they'd bother bringing them to a hospital.'

'Quite agree, old fellow. We'll skip the donation tonight . . .'

'Hear, hear. Another round?'

Ruby implored herself to say something. To say *anything*. But again, she found that she couldn't.

Mutely avoiding everyone's eyes, she put the drinks on

to a tray and carried them back to Mrs Henderson and her friends.

'Thank you, dear,' said Mrs Henderson. 'You know, your old job is still open to you, should you ever wish to return. Sir Emrys and Lady Smith might think differently, of course, but I always found you to be quite a good little housemaid, all things considered.'

'Ever so obliged, Ma'am,' said Ruby demurely. 'I'll bear it in mind.'

And she skedaddled.

It was too late to go and join Ma and the others in the pub down the street. It was too late to do anything, really, because the bell was already sounding for everyone to take their seats. And here was Leah, walking up the stairs, a little frown furrowing her brow.

'You look very flustered, Ruby,' she said.

'Oh, I'm fine, thanks.' No point in bothering Leah with the fact that she had *twice* been mistaken for one of the staff. It would be funny, given time. Lots of time. But not quite yet. 'You look very serious?'

Leah made a little face. 'I'm sure it's nothing,' she said. 'But I've just checked and the collection box in the entrance hall is almost empty.'

Ruby's heart sank. 'Oh dear,' she said. She knew, because Leah had told her, that the donations were all-important. They would make some money, of course, from the ticket sales, but – although Clara Williams was giving her time for expenses only – the venue was very expensive, to say nothing of the orchestra, printing the programmes and all the other costs that were involved in putting on a concert in the West End. The profit really wouldn't amount to very much. 'Is that unusual for this stage of the evening?' she clarified.

'A little,' conceded Leah. 'I know it's early, but I would have expected the box to start filling up by now.'

Ruby sighed. 'There were some chaps in the bar braying on about how poor people shouldn't be allowed to keep animals,' she said. 'I suppose that might be why people ain't donating.'

'Maybe,' said Leah gloomily. 'Although I can't believe that people would be that insufferably short-sighted. I've asked Aunt Clara to say a few words about the animal hospital before she starts singing and I'll remind everyone again at the interval. Let's keep everything crossed that between us we can turn things around.'

Ruby nodded, flattening herself against the side of the staircase as more well-dressed people streamed upstairs past her. Oh, she couldn't bear for this to go wrong as well as everything else.

That really would be the kiss of death to the whole venture.

And here was Ma with the rest of her party, coming in from the street together, thick as thieves. Mrs Fisher had even linked arms with Ma, and behind them, Dot and Aunt Maggie were having a good old giggle together. Ruby – Leah in tow – went down the stairs to join them and, as they approached, Mrs Fisher pinched Ruby's cheek gently.

'Cheer up, dear,' she said. 'It might never happen.'

Ruby forced a smile. She didn't like to tell Mrs Fisher that it was already in danger of happening. They all looked so expectant and excited about the evening ahead.

Ma clutched Ruby's arm. 'Iris – Mrs Fisher – has offered me a job serving behind the counter at the bakery,' she said, her eyes shining. 'Can you think of anything more wonderful?'

'I can't,' said Ruby, suddenly feeling much more cheerful. Darling Ma – how lovely for her – and how kind of Mrs Fisher.

If nothing else, that already made the evening a success.

'It's all going to be marvellous,' she said. 'Come on, let's find our seats.'

The auditorium was filling up, the room abuzz with expectation and the rustling of programmes.

Ruby and Leah slid into their places halfway down the stalls, and despite herself, Ruby felt the first stirrings of excitement. The twinkling lights, the orchestra warming up, the rich silks and satins and ermines of the assembled guests . . .

Whatever the outcome, there was no doubting that this was all just magnificent.

And then the lights dimmed, the orchestra struck up the opening bars to 'O Sole Mio' and the curtains drew back. There, with her flurry of frothy ruffles, her cascading Titian curls and her enormous cleavage, was Clara Williams herself. A smile to the audience and she was off, her exquisite voice soaring and tumbling, bringing the music alive. On one side of Ruby, Ma grasped her hand and held it tight; she glanced at her mother and saw that her eyes were already shiny with tears. This evening was almost worth it for that too.

Oh, this was all quite, quite marvellous.

The song finished to rapturous applause and Clara dimpled prettily as she curtseyed her thanks. Then she stepped up to the microphone.

Ruby took Leah's hand and held it tightly.

This was *it*.

Clara looked around the auditorium. 'Thank you so much for inviting me here this evening,' she said. 'The fact we're all sharing this marvellous occasion is down to my lovely goddaughter Leah Richardson. Firstly, a confession. I have many godchildren – *dozens* of godchildren – and, whilst they are all almost as special to me as my own children, I do sometimes slip up. And on this occasion, I'm ashamed to admit that I was out of the country and I forgot to suitably mark Leah's twenty-first birthday. Now this was a while ago; I will trip delicately over quite how long because Miss Richardson is, quite inexplicably, still unmarried. A gentle hint to any bachelors who might be here today.'

The audience roared with laughter; Leah's hand stiffened in Ruby's as both women continued to stare straight ahead, smiles fixed rigidly to their faces.

This was excruciating.

Clara Williams gave a throaty chuckle. 'Clearly I was anxious to make amends,' she continued. 'I asked Leah what belated gift might go some way to make up for my oversight and she very generously suggested a concert to raise funds for a local animal charity which I know is very dear to her heart. So here we all are. Please dig deeply for dear little fluffies in need. I know that they – and Leah – will be deeply appreciative of your generosity. And now, how about a song for all the brave soldiers at the front?

Please join me in singing "Pack Up Your Troubles in Your Old Kit Bag".'

As the orchestra struck up and the audience joined in lustily, Ruby and Leah turned to each other in horror.

'Dear little fluffies?' echoed Leah. 'That's not going to convince anyone to donate.'

'She didn't even *mention* the East End,' said Ruby. 'Local charity could mean Hampstead.'

'She did, however, manage to tell several hundred people that I'm well on my way to becoming an old maid,' said Leah.

She looked so woeful that Ruby firmly suppressed her smile. 'I think we can both agree that were a disaster,' she said.

'Yes,' said Leah. 'I've never heard anything more perfunctory. Clara couldn't have made it all sound more frivolous and pointless if she'd tried. I'm so sorry, Ruby.'

'It's not your fault.' Ruby hesitated for a moment and then she nudged Leah. 'I want to go up there and say something,' she added.

'What – now?'

'No, of course not now. But before the interval.'

'No, Ruby. Don't . . .'

'Please. I can't make things any worse than they are already, can I? And I've got to try.'

'Are you sure?'

'I am.' It was time to show a little backbone. 'It's my idea, so it's up to me to make or break it.'

Someone sitting behind them tapped Ruby on the shoulder.

'Shhh,' a voice hissed indignantly.

Ruby half-turned and muttered her apologies. The rousing singalong had finished and Clara had launched into a quiet, contemplative number. 'Please, Leah,' she whispered as she turned back around.

'Righto,' Leah said doubtfully. 'Just before the interval, then. I'll introduce you.'

After that, Ruby couldn't concentrate on the music. She was too busy trying to compose a speech in her mind. Sadly, that proved impossible too; her thoughts kept going round in circles and flitted away every time she tried to pin them down.

Oh, this was hopeless.

It only seemed seconds later that Leah was tapping her on the shoulder. 'I've just checked the programme and this is the last song before the interval,' she whispered. 'There are some stairs up to the stage just on the left there. We'll wait at the bottom and then go up as soon as Clara leaves the stage – if you're still sure you want to?'

Ruby nodded. She crept out of her seat and followed Leah down the side of the auditorium. It felt as if every eye was boring into her back, but when she turned around, no one was taking a blind bit of notice. Everyone was gazing, rapt, at the stage as Clara belted out her final number.

'Still sure?' said Leah as the song drew to a close to thunderous applause. Clara curtsied, waved to the audience and then the house curtains swished shut.

'Not sure at all,' said Ruby, suddenly feeling queasy. 'But I've got to try.'

Leah squeezed her shoulder and then the two of them

walked up the stairs and on to the stage and suddenly every eye really *was* on them.

This was petrifying . . .

But then, the curtains opened again and there was Clara ready to take another bow. She rallied gamely on seeing Leah and Ruby standing there, kissed Leah firmly on the cheek and then stood back as the curtains closed again.

This was *excruciating*.

Leah stepped forward. 'Good evening,' she said and then stopped as a stagehand rushed out with a microphone. Ruby crossed her fingers that this wouldn't stop Leah in her tracks, but Leah was still smiling confidently. 'I'm Clara's goddaughter,' she continued, when the stagehand had disappeared. 'By now, you will all know that I am over twenty-one and that I am quite unmarriageable!'

There was a ripple of laughter which quickly grew in volume and Ruby glanced at Leah in admiration.

Who knew she had such a penchant for public speaking?

'I'm working at a munitions factory in the East End of London for the duration,' Leah continued. 'And there I've had the great fortune to meet and befriend Ruby Archer, who is one of the supervisors in the detonation shop. Vital war work, I am sure you will agree.'

There was a smattering of light applause, but Ruby distinctly noticed one or two of the men glance at their pocket watches. Anxious to get to the bar, no doubt.

'Miss Archer is the founder of the Silvertown Animal Hospital,' Leah continued. 'Now, I could wax lyrical about its virtues and what it will offer the people – and animals – of the East End, but Miss Archer will do a much better job than me. Over to you, Ruby.'

The applause this time was decidedly more lukewarm, and a couple of men melted discreetly towards the door. Ruby stepped forward, said 'good evening' in little more than a squeak and her mind went blank just as the microphone gave a long squeal of feedback.

Come on, girl.

You can do this.

Just think of Mac and Tess and Steel and speak from the heart.

Carefully not looking at anyone in particular, Ruby opened her mouth and let the words find themselves.

'I had a dog named Mac,' she started. 'He were the most wonderful, loyal dog, with the waggiest tale and the shaggiest coat and the most beautiful brown eyes you've ever seen. I don't even really know what type of dog he were, but believe me – he were the best. He could look fierce when he needed to look fierce – and round where I live, you really need to look fierce sometimes because there's always someone ready to steal the coal from the bunker or the clothes from the line – but he were really the most lovable friend you could imagine. Me and me family loved him to bits.'

She stopped and drew breath.

No one was leaving for the bar any more.

'There was another thing about Mac,' Ruby continued. 'Half his face had been burned away because his previous owner had poured petrol into his ear and set it on fire to try and get rid of his canker.'

There were audible gasps around the room. Ruby ignored them and pressed on.

'This weren't because his previous owner was a bad person,' she said. 'And she certainly didn't want to hurt

Mac. She wanted to keep him safe and well, because Mac belonged to her son who were away fighting in France. Like all of you, she loved her son and wanted to see him happily reunited with his dog. But unlike all of you, she couldn't afford to pay for a vet to look at Mac. It weren't that she chose to spend that money on sherry or cigars or going to concerts and all the things we are enjoying this evening. To pay for a vet – even if she could find a vet who were willing to treat Mac – she and her children wouldn't have been able to eat. That's how expensive vets are to people in the East End. That's why they sometimes have to take matters into their own hands and try remedies they hope will work and sometimes – often – do not. In this case, the soldier's dog went deaf and was no use as a guard dog no more. The woman couldn't afford to keep him and so when her son was invalided out of the war, his lovely dog weren't there to greet him. She told him he had died.'

The auditorium was silent.

You could have heard a pin drop.

'That's why we're setting up the Silvertown Animal Hospital,' Ruby concluded. 'It won't be free – people will pay what they can afford. But it will give local people access to medical care for their much-loved and much-needed animals so that hopefully what happened to Mac need never happen again. I hope you might like to donate to the hospital this evening, but either way I really hope you enjoy the concert. Thank you.'

Thank goodness that was over.

As Ruby exhaled a long, ragged breath, she became aware for the first time of the applause. Warm and loud, it was going on for far longer than she had expected. A couple of people were even standing up, clapping vigorously, and – no – it wasn't Ma and the rest of her party, but people she had never set eyes on before. Then someone shouted 'brava' and a couple more joined in for good measure and, really, it was all quite marvellous. Ruby almost expected someone to throw her a rose. Cheeks burning, she gave a silly sort of half-bow and then scuttled from the stage, cheeks aflame and Leah in tow.

'That was magnificent,' said Leah, touching Ruby on the shoulder as they left the auditorium. '*You* were magnificent.'

'I don't know where that came from,' said Ruby, giddy with the excitement.

'From the heart, that's where,' said Leah. 'Come on, the donations are bound to come flooding in now and I expect people would like to give them to you in person.'

Cock-a-hoop, the two women entered the bar.

Smiling faces turned towards them and there was even a little smattering of applause. Ruby fancied that no one was going to ask her to fetch them a sherry or more milk for their coffee this time around.

And there were Ma and Aunt Maggie and the rest of them on the far side of the room, beaming proudly. Suddenly Ruby wanted nothing more than to be with her mother and to be wrapped in her bosomy embrace . . .

'Ruby, dear!' said a loud voice obviously intended to carry. It was Mrs Henderson, reaching out and clutching Ruby's arm. 'I always said you were cut out to be more than a housemaid. Didn't I, dear?' she added to her husband.

Mr Henderson just grunted – as well he might – and wandered off towards the bar.

Undeterred, Mrs Henderson intensified her grip on Ruby's arm. 'I want to make a donation,' she fairly shouted. 'Maybe even some sort of endowment to help all those poor animals. And where's Mac now? I have to know. Whatever happened to dear little Mac and that brave soldier.'

Ruby was completely thrown.

She was deciding how best to reply when there was a little commotion on the other side of the room. A loud squeak . . . a chair clattering to the ground. Ruby turned round to see Sir Emrys staggering to his feet, bright red in the face. For a moment, she wondered if he was unwell and having some sort of turn, but then she realised he was very angry and had stood up with such force that the chair had fallen over.

Goodness!

'I've never heard so much nonsense in my whole life,' he shouted. 'Put your cheque book away, Fanny; save your money. Believe you me, this so-called hospital is a complete sham!'

It was fair to say that Sir Emrys had everyone's attention. The bar was suddenly completely silent, every face craning in his direction. Then Leah said, 'I say . . .' just as Aunt Maggie shouted, 'What are you talking about?'

Sir Emrys put up his hand. 'No. I've stayed quiet thus far, but I won't any longer. I've come across this "hospital" before. My son put me on to them and I'm very glad he did, because they're a bunch of quacks. And that's being polite about it. Let me make it perfectly clear that they aren't employing qualified veterinary practitioners – just any old Tom, Dick or Harry who fancies having a go. That's true, isn't it?' he added, turning towards Ruby and jabbing a fat finger in her general direction. 'Isn't it?' he insisted when Ruby didn't – *couldn't* – immediately answer.

'Yes,' admitted Ruby. 'But believe me, the medicines that the vets prescribe . . .'

'Why should we believe anything you say?' Sir Emrys interrupted rudely. 'What's to say *you* won't be pouring petrol into the ears of the poor dogs who are unfortunate enough to cross your path?'

'How dare you suggest such a thing?' spluttered Leah. 'That's shameful.'

'How dare *I*?' echoed Sir Emrys. 'I think you'll find what's *shameful* is you taking work from bona fide veterinary practitioners. Men like my son who have trained for years to earn their stripes. You are blatantly undermining my son's livelihood. I've had enough and I am not standing by to watch it happen. It's a dangerous precedent and I hope all you good people here will join me in having nothing to do with this venture.'

'You can't stop them!' Ma shouted stoutly. 'You and your type, always meddling where you're not wanted and trying to stop good, honest people doing things for themselves!'

Darling Ma and her loyalty.

But Ruby had a horrible feeling that things were about to get a whole lot worse.

Sure enough, a nasty smirk had taken residence on Sir Emrys' face. 'Can't stop them, my good lady?' he said silkily. 'I think you'll find I already have. It came to my attention they were attempting to rent a premises I happen to own. I put a stop to that pretty quickly, I can tell you, and I have it on good authority that they haven't managed to secure anywhere else. So this "hospital" that is demanding your hard-earned cash doesn't even have a building, and as there isn't a reputable landlord in the East End who will rent them space, I'm sure it will stay that way. It's a sham, ladies and gentlemen. Nothing more than a sham.'

There was a stunned silence.

Ruby didn't want to go down without a fight, but what was there to say? Sir Emrys had twisted everything. He had made it all sound simultaneously naïve and grubby – but the stark fact was that nothing he had said was fundamentally untrue. No one was going to donate anything after *that* tirade. At best, Ruby now looked well-intentioned but incompetent; at worst she appeared a complete charlatan.

It was pointless trying to think up a dignified response.

The whole thing was dead in the water.

Then a voice piped up from behind her.

A woman's voice from somewhere over towards Ma.

'Well, I can't speak for all the rest, but I don't know about not having a premises,' she said calmly. 'There's a soon-to-be empty building right in the heart of Silvertown which is owned by me family and we would be proud – *honoured* – to have the Silvertown Animal Hospital base themselves there.'

Ruby gasped, hand to heart.

It was Mrs Fisher.

Even if she didn't mean it, it was a lovely gesture. It allowed Ruby to retain some dignity hot on the heels of such a terrible public humiliation.

'It's true, Ruby, dear,' said Mrs Fisher. 'I ain't just saying it. Muller's Haberdashery will soon be vacant and it's yours if you want it. As you know, it's right at the top of Sanctuary Lane – just off the high street – so it couldn't be in a better location. And I think you'll find it has all the space you need.'

'But the Mullers . . . ?' Ruby asked.

'Mrs Muller has decided to retire to the West Country for a bit of peace and quiet,' said Mrs Fisher carefully. 'I hope very much you will feel that the building is right for your hospital.'

Oh.

Oh!

Despite everything, Ruby felt terrible for all that had happened to the Mullers and wished that her gain wasn't at the expense of their loss. But then again, this was wartime and life wasn't fair. Besides, Mrs Muller was old – at least fifty – and the West Country sounded like a lovely place to retire. And far worse things happened at sea.

'It's perfect,' she said, as a smattering of applause broke out. 'Thank you so much.'

'It's just East Enders looking after East Enders,' said Mrs Fisher with a sly look at Sir Emrys. 'Just as it should be and just as your animal hospital will be doing. And don't you be worrying about the rent or the costs, neither. We'll be able to match whatever you was going to pay at the depot.'

Oh, this was all marvellous.

Quite *marvellous*.

'This is all well and good,' Sir Emrys interrupted dismissively. 'But it doesn't get away from the fact you aren't employing trained veterinary practitioners.'

Finally – *finally* – Ruby found her tongue. 'I ain't putting vets down at all,' she said. 'And we'd love to have them on board – but the fact is that they ain't showing any interest. The important thing is that formulations used by vets are also available to us common folk. Apart from some dangerous drugs, there ain't no general medicines' legislation at all . . .'

'That isn't the point,' Sir Emrys interrupted furiously.

'It's true though,' came a male voice from over by the door. The crowd shifted to see who was talking and a man stepped forward. To Ruby's amazement, it was Robert.

Robert!

Ruby hadn't even realised he was there that evening.

'Pipe down, Robert,' said Sir Emrys testily and heads swung back towards him.

'I'm afraid I won't, Father,' said Robert pleasantly, as heads swung back. This was beginning to resemble the spectators at a tennis match. 'Not this time . . .'

Sir Emrys went puce. 'I'm trying to protect your livelihood, lad,' he shouted.

'I know you are and I'm grateful for your loyalty and support,' said Robert. 'But, in this case, I'm afraid it's misplaced. The Silvertown Animal Hospital will not be threatening my livelihood. Moreover, I should let you know my intention to volunteer my services there. That is, of course, if Miss Archer is happy to have me on board.'

Ruby gasped. That might be game, set and match to Robert Smith, but he had certainly changed his tune. After all, he had been responsible for Ruby losing her place at the depot in the first place and he'd been thoroughly rude and dismissive when she'd mentioned her idea all those weeks ago.

It didn't make any sense at all.

And then the bell sounded to announce the second half of the concert. With all the commotion, Ruby had almost forgotten there was to *be* a second half or even where she was at all.

Still, the show must go on.

She clapped her hands together. 'Ladies and gentlemen,' she said. 'Act Two is about to start. I hope you enjoy the show.'

With a bit of shepherding and cajoling, nearly everyone filed out of the bar. Sir Emrys plonked his glass down so heavily on the bar that it was in danger of shattering but duly stomped off back to the auditorium. Leah went off deep in conversation with a woman who looked so like her that it had to be her mother. And, after checking that Ruby was all right and patting her repeatedly on the back, even Ma hurried out to watch the second half of the concert. Only two people remained.

The first was Mrs Henderson.

'I've never liked Sir Emrys,' she said conspiratorially. 'What happened to you, that night you poured coffee over him, has happened to us all on numerous occasions. If your animal hospital is a success, I shall take it as a great victory against him and his type. I'll give you a hundred pounds now, dear, and there will be more to follow.'

'Thank you,' said Ruby, totally overwhelmed. 'That's ever so kind of you.'

'I'll pop a cheque into the donations box,' said Mrs Henderson. 'And I'd love to visit the hospital when you're up and running.'

'You'll always be very welcome,' said Ruby, realising that she meant it.

Mrs Henderson was a queer old stick – very much of her age and class – but underneath it, she wasn't bad at all.

The other person who had waited behind – loitering discreetly some distance away – was Robert Smith. As soon as Mrs Henderson had tottered off back to the concert, he came forward wreathed in somewhat sheepish smiles.

'You must be somewhat confused about my volte-face?' he said, leaning on the back of a gilded chair.

Ruby had never heard the expression before, but she could guess its meaning.

'I'll say,' she replied flatly.

She really wasn't inclined to make things easy for him.

'Look, I *was* annoyed about the hospital and I did mention it to my father in less than complimentary terms,' said Robert. 'But I hadn't meant for him to start throwing his weight around and I certainly hadn't meant for you to lose your premises. I really am most sincerely sorry.'

Oh.

That was very gracious.

Ruby felt herself immediately soften towards him.

'I accept your apology,' she said demurely. 'Besides, I

don't think I'm your father's favourite person anyway for reasons that have nothing to do with you.'

Robert gave a bark of laughter. 'I only heard about the incident with the coffee pot this evening,' he said. 'Ouch! I'm afraid that must really have sealed your fate.'

'I wonder if your father had made the connection before,' said Ruby.

'I don't think so,' said Robert. 'He never mentioned it to me. But he obviously recognised you tonight and I think that explains – although certainly doesn't excuse – his outburst.'

'Oh, I understand his outburst all right,' said Ruby. 'What I *don't* understand is your – what words did you use? – *volte-face.*'

Robert made a little rueful face and Ruby could have sworn that he was blushing. 'Leah brought me to my senses,' he said. 'She pointed out that as over ninety per cent of my caseload is horses belonging to the upper classes, you aren't exactly going to poach my customers.'

'But *I* told you all that too,' said Ruby. 'Why wouldn't you take it from me?'

She knew exactly why, of course.

Because she was from the East End, a working-class girl, of little consequence . . .

But Robert really was blushing this time. 'Between you and me, I think I was showing off that evening,' he said. 'I was throwing my weight around and trying to impress Leah. Fat lot of good that did me, though,' he added ruefully. 'The old girl's not talking to me after I blabbed to my father.'

So that *was* where the land lay. Robert Smith *was* sweet on Leah. A matter of weeks ago, Ruby would have been horrified at the thought of him stepping out with her best friend, but now she was quite inclined to change her mind.

'If you meant what you said about helping out at the hospital from time to time, I'm sure she would change her mind,' she said with a little smile.

'That's not why I'm doing it – or at least not the only reason – but I really meant it,' he said. 'I'd like to help out on a regular basis if you will have me. Your speech earlier on really drummed home that the veterinary profession has overlooked dogs as working-class companion animals for far too long.'

'Yes, I really think they have . . .'

Ruby broke off as an older woman and a young man she vaguely recognised – but couldn't place – bustled into the room.

'Mrs Enid Coleman and my son James,' the woman said. 'We met when you came to the Royal Veterinary College.'

The penny dropped. 'Ah, yes,' said Ruby.

Mrs Coleman was the very helpful receptionist and James was the young chap who had been hauled in for a carpeting by the insufferable Mr Cotter. Ruby hadn't realised at the time that the two were mother and son.

'I saw "The Silvertown Animal Hospital" on the posters for the concert and I knew immediately that it would be down to you,' Mrs Coleman said enthusiastically. 'And I told James about it and he suggested that we came along this evening. We'd like to volunteer. Both of us.'

Robert clapped the young man on the back. 'Good for you, James,' he said. 'Miss Archer, it's up to you, of course, but I'd say getting student vets involved would be a fabulous way forward.'

'Of course,' said Ruby. 'Thank you both so much. You don't know how much this means to me. And now, should we all go back and enjoy the rest of the concert?'

Everyone nodded and Robert offered Ruby his arm. He escorted her out of the bar to the top of the staircase and there they all parted ways. Ruby scampered downstairs to her seat in the stalls and the others headed off to theirs in the circle. As Ruby eased herself into her seat, Leah turned to her with a quizzical look.

'All right?' she asked.

'Oh, yes,' Ruby whispered back. 'Everything is more than all right. In fact, tonight has been like a fairy tale. Premises, money and staff . . . all three are finally in place!'

What a night!

If only Jack had been there to share it with her.

31

And suddenly everything really *was* happening all at once.

The old Muller's haberdashery really was a perfect base for the animal hospital and Mrs Fisher had been as good as her word in matching the rent Ruby had been due to pay at the depot. As well as the shop itself, which would serve as the reception and the waiting room, there were a series of offices and storerooms both immediately behind it and off the courtyard at the back which would be perfect as examination rooms and – in due course – operating rooms. There was running water and, best of all, there was electricity. Ruby could hardly believe her luck and finally admitted to herself that, if truth be told, the depot had never been what she'd had in mind. Not really. It had been off the beaten track with absolutely no passing traffic, her stall wasn't very secure and the whole place had been dirty and run-down. Leah, of course, had seen that right from the beginning, but Ruby had been blind to the facts because she'd thought that she had no other choices.

Although the new building was perfect, there was still plenty to be done. Aunt Maggie and Charlie took the lead with the cleaning and the distempering whilst Ruby set to retrieving all the furniture and goods they had deposited around Silvertown, thanking her lucky stars that the biggest and bulkiest items were just next door at Fisher's. To

Ruby's delight, Robert offered to drive her over to Elspeth's to pick up the cages, and Ruby, inviting Charlie along for the ride, felt ever so grand travelling in a motor-car for the first time in her life. Of course, with three of them in the car, there hadn't been enough room for all the cages – so Robert had had to make a separate trip back – but he hadn't seemed to mind at all.

How things had changed since the first time Ruby had met him!

Meanwhile, Leah was busy ordering all the last-minute items that Robert suggested any self-respecting clinic should own and Ruby then took the lead in arranging everything in the various rooms according to his specifications. The two examination rooms both had marvellous state-of-the-art examination tables with overhead electric lights – fancy! – and were equipped with everything from stethoscopes to tweezers. The reception area had floor-to-ceiling shelves – formerly housing wool – now neatly stacked with a wide variety of cages, tonics, ointments and medicines. Ma – who had handed in her notice at the laundry with immediate effect – and Mrs Fisher popped in when they could, often with cakes or buns to restore flagging energy levels. Dot helped Ruby design a poster announcing the grand opening, and then Charlie and Joe went around town putting them up wherever they were permitted (and sometimes where they weren't).

As the days ticked by, Ruby became aware of anticipation and excitement growing in the community. Several times a day, heads would poke round the door asking if it was really true that they would be able to bring their animals to be treated for free. Wasn't it wonderful, people would say, when they were told that it was. Fancy, a free hospital for animals, right in the heart of Silvertown – that would really put them all on the map. And wasn't it perfect that the hospital was on a road called Sanctuary Lane – didn't that just make it seem as if the whole thing was meant to be? Others pointed out that it was somehow fitting that the place where the treacherous Germans had been trading was now as British – and as fiercely East End – as it was possible to be? That was a turn-up for the books and no mistaking; there would certainly be no more violence or bricks through the window any more.

Ruby, not blind to the fact that this was exactly what Mrs Fisher would be counting on, had just nodded, and smiled and agreed that it was all quite marvellous. Because it *was* quite marvellous. It was just sad that Mrs Muller had had to lose her livelihood in this manner in order for the building to become free.

More importantly, what if no one came?

What if the naysayers were right?

What if, despite the people who had poked their heads around the door, others weren't inclined to bring their animals along for this reason or that?

Ruby put that thought firmly from her mind.

All she could do was continue with the preparations, continue plastering posters around Silvertown and continue keeping her fingers crossed.

And as for Jack . . .

As the days went by, Ruby had started to miss him more and more. She thought of him every time she shut her eyes at the end of a long and tiring shift, and he was the first thing on her mind when she opened them again in the morning. She daydreamed about him at work as she tallied up the detonators and trained up new recruits, and she tried to push him from her thoughts as she arranged all the spare pills and ointments neatly in one of the store-rooms. And the more she thought about him, the more she realised how much she had been in the wrong. Mac had been Jack's dog in the first place and Jack had been more than entitled to demand his return; Ruby would probably have done the same thing had the tables been reversed. It had been ridiculous of her – not to say childish – to try and punish him by saying she never wanted to see him again and then to abruptly cut off all contact. It was laughable, too, because probably the only person she had ended up hurting was herself. When this was all over and the hospital was open, she would go round to Jack's house and apologise to him for her rude-ness and her stubborn-headedness. He would, no doubt, want nothing more to do with her, but it would be the right thing to do.

In the meantime, and, as she had told Dot not so long ago, there was nothing for it but to keep soldiering on.

Like all the days that week, the morning of the grand opening of the Silvertown Animal Hospital dawned clear. The war had changed a lot of things, but at least the world was still turning round and summer days could still be long and bright and sunny. And everything at the hospital was ready; Ruby and the other girls had all taken a few more days' holiday from the munitions factory to make absolutely sure of *that*.

Ruby and the rest of the team were all present and

correct by eight o'clock, getting the last few things ship-shape and Bristol fashion. Ruby looked round at them all with affection: Aunt Maggie sweeping the floors, Leah arranging the reception chairs and Dot laying out the educational literature, Charlie and Joe – small and dark, with an earnest manner, and touchingly eager to help – giving the windows a last-minute polish before they headed off to school, and Robert, bustling in with his smart mahogany case and lending a much-needed air of professionalism to the proceedings. A few short months ago – or even weeks ago – who would have thought that this motley band would have come together in common cause and with her at the centre of it all? It was almost unbelievable. How far she had come since she had left service in Hampstead and how lucky she had turned out to be. She sat down behind the reception desk, tidying her already tidy piles of registers and forms, and found that she suddenly had tears in her eyes. Today was wonderful, of course, but if it hadn't been for the kittens in the river all those years ago and for Jess, Fluffy, Sir Marmaduke and Mr Darcy at the factory, none of this would ever have happened. And that, of course, made her think of Harry and how he had shared her beating for getting wet and muddy way back when – and, oh, how she wished he could be here today too.

She would never forget any of them, and she would never forget that she was doing this in their names.

'Penny for them,' said a voice Ruby recognised.

She glanced up.

Yes, it was Nellie!

'What are you doing here?' Ruby asked, delighted.

'I'm here to help,' said Nellie simply. 'If you'll have me, that is. Anything you want me to do, I'll do it. Make the tea, sweep the floor . . .'

'I think we'd be wasting your skills and knowledge on *that*,' said Ruby with a smile.

This was getting better and better.

'Whatever you say,' said Nellie. 'You're the boss!'

'If you could help me assess the animals as they come in, that will free up Leah to help Robert,' said Ruby. '*If* the animals come in,' she clarified, nerves gnawing at her stomach again.

'*When* they come in,' said Nellie with a laugh. 'They're queuing down the street already.'

'Are they?'

Ruby leapt to her feet in excitement. She had been so busy poring over her paperwork that she hadn't looked outside for hours. She bounded to the door, stuck her head outside and . . .

Wow!

A raggedy queue stretched almost as far as Ruby could see all the way down Sanctuary Lane. There were young children with cats, an old man leading a donkey, dogs and rabbits and, goodness me, was that really a parrot? Ruby stood there for a moment, hand on heart, taking it all in, and then she headed back inside, the sound of a dog barking insistently echoing in her ears.

'Now I'm frightened for a whole host of other reasons,' she said to Nellie with a laugh. 'What if I don't know what to do?'

'No need to be,' said Nellie. 'You've got it all worked out and you know exactly what to do. There's another reason I'm here, by the way,' she added. 'I seem to remember that I owe you a fiver. And an apology.'

Ruby smiled. 'Thank you,' she said. 'If you'd like to pop it in the donation box which is screwed to the shelf over there, I'd be very grateful.'

Nellie bustled off and Ruby headed back to the consultation rooms to tell Robert and Leah about Nellie's arrival and the change in plans. As she was about to head back out again, she heard the shop door opening again. Honestly, it was like Piccadilly Circus around here. She was blooming well going to lock that door until they were officially open.

Then she heard a voice saying, 'What the bleeding hell is going on here, then?'

She recognised that voice, too.

It belonged to Harry!

Her lovely, brave, big brother Harry, looking wonderfully dashing in his soldier's uniform.

With a little squeal, Ruby rushed across the room and flung herself into his arms. 'Harry! What on earth are you doing here?' she said, half-laughing and half-crying. 'Does Ma know you're here?'

'I ain't been home yet,' said Harry. 'I were walking from the station and I saw the queue and then the posters outside and then I realised this were the place you'd talked about in your letters. Bloody hell, Sis. I thought it would just be you on a stool in the backyard. This is a proper hospital.'

'I know!' said Ruby. 'I can hardly believe it. Oh, it's so lovely to see you. Ma's just next door – and I think Aunt Maggie's popped round there too to borrow some string – so there's no need to go home.'

'Next door? Oh, yes – Ma works at Fisher's now, don't she?'

'She does. Go and surprise her. It will make her year!'

Harry grinned and Ruby watched him leave the shop, holding the door open for someone who was coming in.

A hundred emotions rooted Ruby to the spot.

It was Jack.

What was he doing here, today of all days?

There were a thousand and one things she had to do and she needed to have her wits fully about her . . .

Ruby turned urgently to Leah who had just come in from one of the back rooms.

'Can you just tell him I'm not here,' she said. '*Please.*'

'He's already seen you, silly,' said Leah, with a laugh.

Suddenly a furry cannonball shot over towards Ruby.

Mac.

Mac with his dear, scarred face and his shaggy coat and his tail that was wagging so hard his whole body was wiggling along with it.

Oh, Mac.

Ruby crouched down and Mac ran straight up to her and started licking her hands, her face, her neck. Ruby gave herself up to the moment. Clasping her arms around the little dog, she nuzzled her face into his neck, breathing in the familiar doggy smell, hearing the little whines of pleasure.

Oh *Mac*.

Another thought struck her.

Was something wrong?

Had Jack brought Mac along to be treated?

Her heart started thumping even faster.

Please let nothing be wrong. Please don't let Mac be hurt or ill.

Because, no matter how much Ruby might hate being without him, she would never, *ever* wish any ill on him.

And here was Jack, coming over to join them.

'Is Mac all right?' she asked, pulling back to look up at him. 'Have you brought him here because he's ill?'

'No, he's not,' answered Jack. 'In fact, he's very much *not* all right.'

Oh, no.

'What's wrong?' Ruby looked back towards the consulting room, about to call for Robert. No matter that there was a queue of fifty outside, Mac was more important.

'His heart,' said Jack.

'His *heart*?' Ruby echoed.

Mac's heartbeat sounded strong and steady enough against her ear, but . . .

'He's heartsick,' Jack said. 'I were walking past just now – couldn't resist taking a look at the place – and Mac saw you come outside for a moment. And he just went mad, barking for all he was worth and practically pulling me in here.'

'Aw, Mac. Thank you, my friend,' said Ruby, kissing him again.

'He misses you,' said Jack. 'He misses you to pieces.'

Ruby pulled away and looked at Jack. 'I miss him too,' she said neutrally. 'You know that. You *knew* I would.'

'I don't think I did,' said Jack. 'I think I were so lost in me own hot-headed belief that I were in the right, that I didn't realise it were more complicated than that. I think he wants to go home.'

Ruby gawped at him, the words not really sinking in. Then she shook her head firmly.

She wouldn't go down this road.

She wouldn't get her hopes up only to have them dashed again.

'No,' she said. 'No. That wouldn't be fair on anyone. On Maude for starters.'

'Maude is starry-eyed over a new kitten which is hers alone,' said Jack. 'She will be fine.'

'And it ain't fair on you, either,' said Ruby. 'You *love* Mac.'

'I do,' said Jack quietly. 'But I were away a long time and, despite what I might want, things have a habit of changing. Rex has got his feet under the table at home, and even though he just needed a firm hand, I think Mac ain't as happy as he could be.'

'Maybe we could share him?' Ruby suggested quietly.

'Maybe,' Jack replied. 'Maybe in time we can. But I want to put right the wrong I've done and so, for now, he's all yours. You own him. No ifs, no buts. Just yours.'

Mac had gone all blurry.

It took Ruby a while to realise it was because her eyes were blinded by tears.

'I'd say that Mac isn't somebody you own,' she said softly. 'He owns himself. I'd say he's just someone you have to love. Like all the animals.'

Mac was coming home.

He was coming home!

'Mac ain't the only one who's missed you to pieces,' said Jack softly.

Suddenly Ruby's heart felt full to bursting. She looked

at Jack's dear, handsome face and the last of her anger and resentment simply melted away.

'Rex miss me an' all?' she asked, with a grin.

And then, when Jack suddenly looked uncertain, she knew that this was no time for playing games.

'I've missed you, too, you daft ha'porth,' she said, standing up and punching him gently on the arm.

Jack smiled, and the relief on his face told Ruby all she needed to know.

Jack gestured around the room. 'Room for another one?' he asked, rolling up his sleeves.

'Always,' said Ruby.

And Jack leaned forward and kissed her gently on the mouth.

Acknowledgements

I am so lucky to have many wonderful people – and animals! – in my life who have helped *Wartime on Sanctuary Lane* see the light of day.

Firstly, enormous thanks to my 'old' agent Caroline Sheldon – wise, calm, an absolute legend – for helping me to develop this idea, and to my 'new' agent Safae El-Ouahabi – advocate, therapist, and co-conspirator – for picking up the reins so enthusiastically. To Madeleine Woodfield and all the team at Penguin Michael Joseph including Hattie Evans, Bea McIntyre, and Sarah Bance; thank you for buying this series on a partial and for all your help in making the story better. Let's have lunch soon!

I'm in debt to all those individuals who kindly took the time to share their extensive knowledge with me. In particular, I would like to thank my lovely ninety-six-year-old uncle, Patrick Skilling ('UP') – who started training to be a vet shortly after the war – for allowing me to extensively pick his brains! UP also introduced me to his best friend, Bruce Vivash Jones, who graduated from the Royal Veterinary College in 1951 and who, for the past twenty years, has been studying and writing on the history of veterinary medicine. He was even awarded an honorary DVetMed degree by the RVC in 2019 for his services. I am exceedingly grateful to Bruce for patiently answering – and sometimes researching – my many and varied questions by email. He even invited me and UP to his wonderful home in Gloucestershire to browse his extensive library and for a slap-up lunch! Needless to add, any mistakes, inaccuracies and opinions expressed or implied are mine alone.

I've said it before, and I'll say it again, but writing really can be a lonely old business. Thank goodness for lovely chums who are always there to support, encourage and to pour the drinks. Huge thanks to Kim Bennett and Susanna Scott for my first pre-orders, to the Nanas: Frances Brindle, Marilyn Groves, Sarah Edgehill, Kate O'Sullivan, Kate G Smith, Kate Sheehan Finn, Anne Woodward, Gemma Allen, Christine Koch and Mim Landor – to the Sister Scribes: Susanna Bavin, Kitty Wilson, Jane Cable, and Cass Grafton – and to The Saga Sisters: Vicki Beeby, Susanna Bavin (again!), Rosie Hendry, Lesley Eames, Johanna Bell, and Helen Yendall. Mine's a limoncello!

Enormous thanks to those – already busy – authors who read early copies of WOSL and gave such lovely quotes: Susanna Bavin, Vicki Beeby, Louise Fein, Victoria Darke and Gillian Harvey.

A big shout-out to the DB clan – lovely Mum; Ingrid, David, Iain, Alexander, and Anna Hamilton; Tonia, Richard, Matthew, and Laura Lovell and, of course, UP. COYB!!

A massive huge thank you to you, the reader, for choosing *Wartime on Sanctuary Lane*. I hope you enjoyed it and, if so, that you'll consider reviewing it far and wide.

Finally, thank you to my husband, John, to our fabulous children, Tom, and Charlotte, and to our two fluffy moggies, Oscar and Ozzie, who know they rule the roost. You're the best. xx

Want to find out what Ruby and her
friends get up to next?

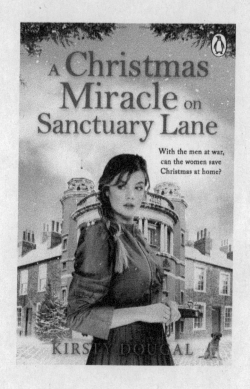

Keep reading for an extract ...

WHICH BOOK WILL YOU READ NEXT?

A Christmas Miracle on Sanctuary Lane

KIRSTY DOUGAL

Prologue

December 1916

Boom!

The sound came from nothing . . . turning the world upside down.

A second later, the lights went out. Where once had been a little group of people chatting around the oil heater at the Sanctuary Lane Animal Hospital, there was now just inky blackness.

Ruby was hurled from her chair. There was the shattering of glass, the rumble of collapsing masonry, and then something hard landed – crack! – across one of her legs.

Ruby lay there in shock and disorientation and tried to control her raggedy breathing.

What on earth was happening?

What had happened to the others?

And would they all get out of there alive?

I

October 1916

'Is this the Sanctuary Lane Animal Hospital, Miss?'

Ruby smiled at the girl with the dirty face and the patch-work dress who had poked her head around the door from the street. 'Yes,' she said. That wasn't the name written on the posters plastered in all their windows, but that hardly mattered. 'Yes, it is.'

'And is it really all free, Miss?'

Ruby's smile widened. It didn't matter how big the writing on the posters or how many flyers they handed out informing people about the Silvertown Animal Hospital, people still continually wanted to be reassured that they wouldn't have to pay an extortionate amount to have their sick or injured animals treated there. Ruby must have fielded half a dozen such queries already – and the hospital had only been open for an hour that damp autumn morning. She supposed she shouldn't really be surprised; the young girl probably couldn't read. Everyone around here had grown up knowing that vets were prohibitively expensive and supremely uninterested in the likes of them – so the very idea of the hospital simply seemed too good to be true.

Ruby nodded at the dirty-faced girl and said, 'Oh, yes. Quite free. We do ask for a donation from those who can afford it, but if you can't, we won't charge a penny.'

The girl's face split into a gap-toothed grin. 'Thank you ever so much, Miss,' she said. 'Me friend said it were free but I didn't quite dare believe it. I'll go and get Teddy now and join the queue.'

She turned on her heel and, with a little wave, was off at a run, disappearing around the corner and on to the high street. Ruby shut the door behind her, wondering idly whether Teddy was a dog, cat or a rabbit, and what ailed him or her.

No doubt she would find out soon enough.

Before she returned to her duties, Ruby stood with her back to the door, surveying the little scene in front of her. The morning clinic was in full swing and there were already a dozen or so owners and their assorted sick or injured animals sitting in the reception area waiting to be seen. Nellie was going from one to the next with her clipboard and pen, assessing which animals needed to be properly examined and which could be simply dealt with then and there.

'So, what's wrong with your fella, then?' she was asking a tall, gangly youth with a miserable-looking mongrel almost as spindly as he was. She took hold of the dog's face and peered into its mouth. 'Looks like you both need a good tonic,' she added. 'I've got just the thing for your boy, but can I recommend a pint of stout at the Queen's Head for you?'

To his credit, the youth grinned as a little titter went around the room. Lovely Nellie — straight-talking and blunt she might be, but she always dispensed a potent mix of wit, warmth and wisdom as she did her rounds. Nellie must have been sixty if she was a day, but she was full of energy and good humour – even if Ruby had noticed she was a little slower than she had been and her arthritic fingers were beginning to give her gyp. Silvertown born and bred, Nellie ran the dogfood barrow up at the market and Ruby strongly believed that what Nellie didn't know about animals probably wasn't worth knowing.

'I'm almost certain your boy ain't got distemper,' Nellie was saying. 'But I wouldn't mind bouncing it off someone round the back to make sure.'

'I'll take him,' offered Ruby. 'I think Robert's free; I saw the lady with the ginger cat leave just now.'

Hopefully it wasn't distemper. Ruby didn't have much experience of the virus, but she knew that once it hit a community, it could run amok and be difficult to get on top of. If they did have a case, she wanted to be the first to hear about it. She took the clipboard from Nellie, checked the names and then smiled reassuringly at the youth. 'Would you bring Dexter and come with me, Mr Andrews?'

Ruby led the way to the back of the reception room and into a narrow corridor. A few months ago, this had been a haberdashery, but the plethora of storage rooms behind the shopfront now served very well as two consulting rooms, a recovery room and a variety of storerooms. Robert Smith, their qualified veterinary practitioner, had taken the larger room with its window looking over the back courtyard, and the other was used mainly by Jack Kennedy, who might not have any formal qualifications – and who might be presently eking out a living running dunnage from the docks – but who had worked with dogs and horses at the front and who had such a way with animals that he had already thoroughly impressed Robert Smith.

Jack Kennedy, of course, also just happened to be Ruby's sweetheart.

Goodness, that sounded good.

It *felt* good, too.

Jack and Ruby had been stepping out for a few months now; in fact, Jack had first kissed Ruby the day the Silvertown Animal Hospital had opened, and the two had been going strong ever since. To be honest, it had passed in a blur because all of them had been run quite ragged managing the weekly animal hospital clinics on top of their proper jobs. But it really had been the most wonderful blur and Jack was part of the family now. The animal hospital was quite the family affair as well: Ma worked in the bakery next door and popped in with tea and buns on a regular basis, and Aunt Maggie volunteered at the clinic too. Even Ruby's brother Charlie popped in after school from time to time, and to Ruby's relief, they all got on like a house on fire. In fact, Jack and Aunt Maggie were in the second consultation room at that very moment; Ruby could see Jack bent over the table examining a fractious terrier whilst Aunt Maggie was doing her best to keep the poor animal still.

Ruby knocked on the door of Robert's consultation room and ushered Mr Andrews and Dexter inside. Robert and Leah Richardson were standing perfectly properly on either side of the consultation table – both, as ever, professional to a fault. But Ruby fancied that Leah's cheeks were a little too flushed for the chilly day, and Robert's eyes were far too twinkly for ten o'clock on a busy Friday morning. Neither Leah nor Robert had confirmed that the two of them were stepping out together, but something was definitely afoot . . .

'Hello, M'Leah,' said Ruby.

'Ruby!' cried Leah, in mock frustration. 'When are you going to stop calling me that?'

'I'm trying,' said Ruby. 'It's *hard*.'

Ruby and Leah both worked at the government munitions factory down by the river. Although the two young women were fast friends out of work, Leah was a manager from a well-to-do family and was by far the senior on duty. Ruby had become so used to calling her 'Miss' that it was proving very difficult to break the habit, although sometimes at work she had the opposite problem and Leah's name came out as L'Miss.

'Who have we got here then?' said Robert, turning away from his paperwork with a professional smile on his thin, clever face.

Robert was a trained veterinary practitioner and getting him on board with the hospital had been a real coup. Despite being less than wholly enthusiastic when Ruby had first mooted her idea, he had turned out to be a complete stalwart, turning up to volunteer at most of the weekly clinics with grace and good humour – and there were naturally many times when his five years' training and experience simply couldn't be beaten. In this case, it only took a couple of minutes before Dexter was pronounced clear of distemper and was prescribed aspirin and a tonic instead.

A very relieved Mr Andrews was just preparing to lead Dexter away when a loud commotion in reception made them all jump. Shouts, screams and – thank goodness – the odd cackle of laughter as well. As one, Ruby, Leah and Robert ran down the corridor, with Jack and Aunt Maggie joining them on the way . . .

'What on earth's going on?' asked Ruby, looking around in confusion.

The young girl with the dirty dress and the patchwork pinafore was back, standing in the middle of the room looking anxious and distressed. Everyone was staring intently at the top of the shelving unit behind the reception desk. When the shop had been a haberdashery, the shelf would, no doubt, have been stuffed full of wool in some of the less popular hues. Now, however, it was totally empty . . . save for a small, light-brown monkey staring back at them all and clutching something furry to his chest.

Teddy was a monkey.

A very cheeky monkey at that!

'What's he holding?' Ruby muttered to Nellie, praying that it wasn't someone's precious pet mouse or hamster.

Nellie gave a discreet little cough. 'I believe it's Mr Arnott's toupee,' she said, gesturing to a bald, red-faced man sitting over by the door.

Ruby found herself fighting an overwhelming desire to giggle.

'I'm ever so sorry, Mr Arnott,' she said, as seriously as she could. She turned to the young girl. 'Can't you call him down?' she added gently.

The little girl shook her head, looking close to tears. 'I've tried to,' she said. 'He don't always take much notice of me and me pa's working at the market today.'

Now Ruby recognised the girl. She was Mabel, the organ-grinder's daughter.

'Don't worry,' said Robert kindly. 'I'll go up and encourage him down. There doesn't seem to be much wrong with the little blighter's climbing ability, anyway.'

There was a movable ladder attached to the shelves and Robert pulled it around until it was directly under where Teddy had taken refuge. He climbed a few rungs and stretched out his arm for the little monkey.

Too slow!

Quick as a flash, Teddy had reached out for *him*. The toupee was discarded, tumbling forlornly to the floor, as Teddy grabbed the stethoscope around Robert's neck. As Robert cried out in annoyance, Teddy swung himself casually around the shelves and over towards the front window.

Nellie clutched Ruby's arm, and Ruby could see that the old woman was nearly doubled up in silent laughter which made Ruby's desire to giggle even stronger.

'I'll grab him,' said Jack, setting off in hot pursuit.

And then Ma appeared through the front door laden with her mid-morning tray of cakes. Without warning, Teddy dropped the stethoscope and launched himself through the air, landing smack bang on Ma's left shoulder. Ma shrieked but managed to keep the tray of cakes admirably level.

'What do I do now?' she yelled.

'Don't worry, I'm coming,' said Jack.

He was fast closing in on Teddy but . . .

Wham!

A cream bun caught him squarely on the cheek.

Whack!

A Chelsea bun hit Robert right in the middle of his forehead.

Smash!

Poor Mr Arnott had no sooner picked up his discarded toupee and carefully replaced it on his head than a jammy bun landed on top of it and duly exploded.

Ruby looked around at the little scene – at all her wonderful friends and co-conspirators – and collapsed into laughter.

Whatever she might have expected – and no matter that they were all exhausted to the bone – working at the Silvertown Animal Hospital certainly wasn't dull.

He just wanted a decent book to read ...

Not too much to ask, is it? It was in 1935 when Allen Lane, Managing Director of Bodley Head Publishers, stood on a platform at Exeter railway station looking for something good to read on his journey back to London. His choice was limited to popular magazines and poor-quality paperbacks – the same choice faced every day by the vast majority of readers, few of whom could afford hardbacks. Lane's disappointment and subsequent anger at the range of books generally available led him to found a company – and change the world.

'We believed in the existence in this country of a vast reading public for intelligent books at a low price, and staked everything on it'
Sir Allen Lane, 1902–1970, founder of Penguin Books

The quality paperback had arrived – and not just in bookshops. Lane was adamant that his Penguins should appear in chain stores and tobacconists, and should cost no more than a packet of cigarettes.

Reading habits (and cigarette prices) have changed since 1935, but Penguin still believes in publishing the best books for everybody to enjoy. We still believe that good design costs no more than bad design, and we still believe that quality books published passionately and responsibly make the world a better place.

So wherever you see the little bird – whether it's on a piece of prize-winning literary fiction or a celebrity autobiography, political tour de force or historical masterpiece, a serial-killer thriller, reference book, world classic or a piece of pure escapism – you can bet that it represents the very best that the genre has to offer.

Whatever you like to read – trust Penguin.